BETWEEN EXTREMITIES

Between Extremities

a novel

Jacqueline D'Acré

Autumn
Books

Excerpt from "Vacillation" reprinted with the permission of Simon & Schuster from THE COLLECTED WORKS OF W. B. YEATS, Volume I: THE POEMS, Revised and edited by Richard J. Finneran. Copyright 1933 by MacMillan Publishing Company; copyright renewed @1961 by Bertha Georgie Yeats.

Excerpt from "The Song of Wandering Aengus" reprinted with the permission of Simon & Schuster from THE COLLECTED WORKS OF W. B. YEATS, Volume I: THE POEMS, Revised and edited by Richard J. Finneran (New York: MacMillan, 1989).

Excerpts from "Vacillation" and "The Song of Wandering Aengus" are reprinted with the permission of A.P. Watt, Ltd. on behalf of Michael Yeats.

Permission to quote from the poetry of Matthew Arnold has been granted by Mrs. Jacqueline Duncan, England.

Excerpts on pages 33, 34, 35, 36, 37, 38, 39, 40, 41 are from ELEMENTAL TAROT (pages 14, 16, 21, 23, 42, 62, 75, 94, and 104) by Caroline Smith and John Astrop. Copyright © 1988 by Caroline Smith and John Astrop. Used with permission from Cynthia Parzych Publishing Inc., New York.

Permission to quote from *The Mystic Path to Cosmic Power* granted by Virgil Howard.

The selected excerpts from the book *Alcoholics Anonymous* are reprinted with permission of Alcoholics Anonymous World Services, Inc. Permission to reprint this material does not mean that A.A. is in any way affiliated with this program. A.A. is a program of recovery from alcoholism <u>only</u> – use of this material in any other non-A.A. context does not imply otherwise.

Excerpts from *24 Hours A Day* by Anonymous, revised edition, copyright © 1975 by Hazelden Foundation. Reprinted by permission of Hazelden Foundation, Center City, MN.

First Edition

Designed by Stephanie Stephens
Author Photograph by Kerri McCaffety

D'Acré, Jacqueline.
    Between Extremities: A novel / by Jacqueline D'Acré
    1st ed.
    p. cm.
    ISBN: 0-9653145-2-9

    1. Women artists—Fiction.   I. Title

PS3554.A23B48 1997   813'.54
                                    QBI97-41203

To Nelson

$\mathcal{A}$ c k n o w l e d g m e n t s

Thanks to Diana Christensen – who saved my life. And to those who kept me going: Ellen Lynn Lee, Jan Simon, Kim Potvin, Sandy Miller, Karen Sears, Karen Atherton, Carmen Davis, Gail Page, Annette Powell, Regis Scott, all in New Orleans and Sherry Aalto in Thunder Bay. And thank you, Diane King, Jim Biermann DVM, Linda Biermann, Keith Cooper DVM, Craig Klimczak DVM, Frank Potvin, Marcel Rivera, Patrick Graham, Daryl Allen, John Joly and especially Arthur Christensen and Malcom Fugler.

My children, Douglas Cooper, Catherine Lehmberg, Tripp Funk who believed I could write a book.

I thank my parents, June Montgomery Cryderman and John R. "Jack" Cryderman, my special thanks to my uncle, Bill Montgomery. My siblings, Jane Ely, John Tracy Cryderman, Jennifer Cryderman, Della Cryderman Godin, Roy Cryderman and Joel Cryderman. You gave me a rich, funny, tumultuous environment without which I would never have become a writer.

Winter C.R. Neil at Pontalba Press, my editor. Thanks for your patience, insight, and praise.

There is no such Methodist church on St. Charles Avenue, and neither, to my knowledge, does such an A.A. club exist in Covington. These are sheer invention, as are all the A.A. meetings. Some places, like Que Sera, has been renamed, other places I made up, but many sites are real. No one in this book is real. I made everyone up, and it's been a joy experiencing their antics.

And to *Azeem, my stallion, who taught me that love is boundless. Your majestic spirit moves with me, your stallion neigh will ring through all the years of my life.

Jacqueline D'Acré,
Green Street, New Orleans, 1997

$$P \quad a \quad r \quad t \qquad O \quad n \quad e$$

LOST CAUSES

…Middle Age
Home of lost causes…
– *Matthew Arnold*

O N E

The sound of breaking glass woke Brit. There was pain at her temples. Below her loft bedroom she heard curses, felt the thud of bare feet on her kitchen floor, and smelled gin. Had Scott broken her last bottle of Bombay fumbling for a picker-upper?

"Shit!" yelled Scott.

Happy Birthday, Brit, she thought. Now Scott had probably stepped on the broken glass, cut his foot, and his careless blood was staining her unsealed wood floor. *Happy Fiftieth Birthday, Brit.* Now thirty-seven-year old Scott would call his "Older Woman" to make it better.

"Brit!" She was psychic.

She took her arms from under the covers to find the top sheet wrapped around her neck. She pulled at it, wondering why it was clammy…night sweats or wild sex? Had there been wild sex? She couldn't remember.

"Britannia!"

A pitiful cry. Thud, thud. *Hopping on one foot?* She scrabbled at the red sheet, then grabbed and jerked. If she didn't get to him soon he'd cut his other foot. The sheet tightened around her throat. Shaky with hangover, she clawed at it, scratching her face. Now she *and* Scott were bleeding. The sheet gave, her neck was free. She sat up, then had to steady herself against a feeling of nausea, yet as her feet touched the sheepskin rug on the floor she felt a wave of lust from last night. The sheets were clammy from sex, not menopause.

"Britann-i-aaa! I am bleeding to death!"

Naked on the edge of the bed, she looked into a cheval mirror. The pine log walls, the black lacquer bedstead, the red sheets, starkly showed a sallow-white woman. Her untidy black hair with its gray temple strands looked more bag lady than porn queen. But it did hide most of her face. Five folds of flesh started under her breasts and loped down to her graying pubic hair. Where had those rolls come from? She looked at her legs. Still long. Still lean, but the flesh of her upper thigh hung, her inner thigh was loose. Was she starting to look, to be, her real age? She heaved herself up and the five lopes uncoiled, but her belly kept a pouty sag from diaphragm to pubic bone. It was emphasized by small lightning strikes of purplish flesh zigging out from her hipbones, stretch marks from carrying Anastasia. She stepped away from the mirror. Too much of a hangover, on this birthday, a half-century old.

Clothes were exploded all over the room. She couldn't find her robe and she didn't want to parade her suddenly old body in front of Scott's still fairly young one, so she grabbed the damp sheet, wrapped it around her sarong-style, and headed for the stairs.

"Coming!" she called.

"That's what you said last night, ten times!"

She laughed, though it hurt her head, and descended to her living room, red sheet trailing. Covered, she felt a small resurgence of her power as a sensuous woman. Wasn't this pungent sheet evidence of that? She turned and there was Scott. Gorgeous Scott—naked, one hand on a kitchen counter, right foot in his left. His turquoise eyes implored.

She wanted to sketch him just like this. A fat chunk of charcoal, one thick-thin sinuous line, and she'd have him.

The gin bottle was intact on the counter. He'd broken only a glass, but his blood had stained her floor. She went around the center counter, snatched up a stool, pressed it beneath his buttocks.

"Sit."

He sat. From a drawer she took a towel, then lay on his back dangling it before him.

"Here. Staunch the flow."

He took it, wrapped his foot. Reluctantly she slid her hands from his back, tightened the sheet around her and, imagining she was wafting, wafted from the room.

"Going for first aid."

"Not the stuff that hurts!"

"No. Iodine hurts. I'll use hydrogen peroxide, okay?" Silence. "Scottie?" No return banter. A Scottie mood-swing. *Please don't sulk, Scottie, not on my birthday.* She slammed the door to the medicine cabinet and returned with tweezers, gauze, and hydrogen peroxide.

"Shall I?"

In answer he thrust his foot at her, then withdrew it.

"Brit-baby. Fix me some gin. And maybe a line. Ease the pain." A half-grin.

Feeling uncomfortably maternal, she regarded him. Would she feel this way if she was thirty-four? But didn't even young women minister to men? Do women take an aghast look at their age and adjust their behavior, upwards to older, whether they feel their age or not, when it came to caretaking men? A flash, her mother Viola, cutting her long hair at forty. She'd aged ten years shortening her hair.

"No cocaine, Scott. You know I won't allow it." Even so, she knew he ran out to his car to snort. "But gin? I guess so. And maybe Nurse Brit will have some too. After all it is my birth–"

"Your birthday! Oh, Baby, Baby! Happy Birthday! Hey–hey–we gotta celebrate!"

"First we fix your foot." She knelt, sheet billowing around her. Unwrapping the towel she probed with tweezers.

"Yeow!"

More blood than cut.

"Hold still! I'm sorry, Scottie. I've got to see if there's glass in there."

She peered at his sole. Would she have to use her reading glasses in front of him? Christ! But the light was good, she could see. She looked up, smiling.

"Lucky you. I can't find any splinters."

Towel under his foot, she doused it with hydrogen peroxide. It fizzled and she yearned for champagne. Again she looked up into Scott's eyes, the exact turquoise of the Gulf of Mexico at Pensacola. He looked down fondly, one side of his mouth crooked up in a half-smile, face tanned, blond-streaked hair mussed. An out-of-shape lifeguard.

He thought about Britannia's birthday…how amazingly young she looked. Even though they'd fucked their brains out all night, and both had raging hangovers, her skin had this surreal quality. In this morning light she looked like a girl. He wanted to photograph her just like this, long hair messed up, that red sheet spread out like the robe of some…*power* goddess. He studied her long white arms, fingers. Artist's fingers, that did such artistic things to his body. And her eyes, like now, looking up half-grinning, almost making fun of him. He automatically checked the light, decided it was good, ethereal on her white-white face. The red was a good contrast. Her black eyelashes and eyebrows stood out, but what the hell color were her eyes? He was not poetic. But he was a professional photographer…he saw poetic things he couldn't put into words. The color of her eyes, familiar, nagged at him. What? What? The color of the lilacs his mother grew in their South Dakota backyard.

His Nikon was in the car. Damn! If he could take her picture now, like this, no makeup–he was sure he'd convince to lose all this "I'm too old" bullshit.

She was still kneeling before him. "Band-Aid?"

"Nah. Gin."

She rose, poured gin and V8 into Old Fashioned glasses.

He saluted her, "Happy birthday, Britannia," and swallowed half the drink. "After work, we'll really celebrate. I promise." He took another sip, staring at her. "You know, you look about twenty-five years old." He was detached, serious.

Britannia restrained herself from a knee-jerk simper, "I do!?" and said, her voice a dull monotone, "But Scott. Today. I am. Fifty. Years old." Her eyes met his and she felt her blood drain away, soaked up by the red sheet.

"I know. And I'm pretty amazed. I'll be honest, Brit. Sometimes you look twenty-five, maybe even younger. You move easily, like a teenager. Other times you look thirty, forty, even fifty. Depends on the light, whether you've got a hangover, lots of variables, but even when you look 'half a century' you look it in an alive kind of way. Few young women have that. Hell. Few women have that." He was solemn. "That's what I love about you, Brit."

Even though he was saying things she yearned to hear, still a great hollow fear pushed up from the basin of her pelvis, as if spawned by her ovaries. She hadn't menstruated in three months. She hadn't told a soul, she felt such shame. Now the void ballooned, pressing hard against her diaphragm, flattening her lungs so it was impossible to breathe. But she held Scottie's gaze, forced a shallow breath and said, "Thank you, Scottie. What a nice thing to say. You're on call today?"

Scottie slapped his bare knee. "Jesus, Britannia. Don't brush me off!" He continued in a falsetto imitation. "'Thanks, Scottie, what a nice-nice thang to say'–annnnnnd–'You're on call today?' as deftly, my lady, you change the subject."

Now she understood her fear. His television cameraman's day was filled with beautiful women–younger than she. She couldn't bear to lose his body, not the very minute she crossed the great divide from Middle-Aged-Forties to Genuinely-Old-Fifties. Oh God. Soon she'd be eligible for the Senior Discount at Shoney's. Could she sit in a booth with thirty-seven-year old him and say, "Senior Burger, hold the fries?"

She rose, raised her drink to her mouth, but the gin's juniper smell sickened her, the V8 smelled like rotted vegetables. She set it on the counter and trying for a smile said, "Wherever did you learn such big words as 'deft?'"

He hopped over. "I'll show you deft," and he peeled off the sheet and nuzzled her into his arms. Britannia almost swooned as their bare skins met. Was there any feeling greater than this, one soft-skinned human touching another?

He breathed through the hair covering her ear, "I just want to be with you as long as you'll let me, Brit."

She yearned to believe him.

A horse whinnied outside. Scott groaned. "Now I'm jealous. You've got that old horse for company, and you won't let me move in."

"When you grow up, I might," she whispered, reluctantly taking her skin from his skin. "I'd better go feed him. It's the thrill of his geriatric life."

"Won't old Jimmy do it?"

Old Jimmy, a handyman and friend, had been with Brit since she bought her farm twelve years back.

"I suppose. He'll be here soon enough."

"Let him feed Mokhtar. It's your birthday, Britannia." He kissed her, hard.

She tried to smile. "I suppose if you've got to work...any idea where you'll be today?" Digging, and hating herself for it. In particular, she was scared of the new weekend reporter, a woman with pouty lips, husky voice, body by Nautilus. Young. How could Scott resist such a woman? How could such a woman resist him? Perhaps she, Britannia Rhodes, ought to do something about her belly, the sagging thigh-skin, the hint of wattling under her chin...maybe, during this epochal year, she should consider some personal caretaking. She'd been coasting on her good genes for a long time. Perhaps all this alcohol wasn't so good...and the smoking? The horse whinnied. Scott gave her a fierce hug, rotated her, and gave her a gentle swat on the behind.

"Sounds like old Jimmy's late. Maybe you better go feed that horse so I can get to work."

He watched as she gathered the sheet around her and again yearned for his Nikon. She had the long white body of…a…a…woodland nymph, something like that. His cock stirred.

Brit floated out of sight through her living room. On the verandah, a black dog rose, stretching and staring up at her accusingly.

My God! Wilton! In her drunken lust she'd forgotten him. She bent, took his head in her hands and the dog went into his forgiving love-dance, yipping, licking her face.

The porch was cold even though it was a sunny February day. Brit stepped into white rubber shrimper's boots and, unconcerned about wearing a sheet, trudged to the stable.

After her second husband Art Scarpelli died she had searched the hilly lands north of New Orleans, and in Washington Parish found what she wanted: twenty acres, cheap, surrounded by thick woods with a fifteen-acre clearing up the center. Three oaks stood on a small rise near the back of the property, marking a natural house site. A trio of pecan trees–she'd imagined roasted pecans, pecan pies, pralines–stood some distance away, staking out a natural place for a pool, a garden. From the oaks the land abruptly rolled down, then up to a plateau. She'd dammed the swale…now ducks swam on a pond. A weeping willow planted by her daughter Anastasia drooped romantically over the water.

The plateau was pasture and a place to ride Mokhtar, her horse. The bordering woods of live and water oak, pine, magnolia, dogwood, and hickory were a gorgeous but solid wall against the world and gave the isolation she wanted as an artist and as a widowed, single mother. And so she could run around in a sheet.

She built a big log house with matching stable and escaped New Orleans' wolves. She'd been safe until she married Grant Griffin…but that was over, forgotten.

Britannia Rhodes had created a paradise on earth. So why, with Scottie, her studio, her animals, did she feel old, leached of talent and…lonely?

Wilton snatched at her sheet as she strode into the chilly stable. The cement aisle was littered with hay, pine shavings, stray balls of manure. She must get after Jimmy, getting careless. Why wasn't he here? Had she given him the day off? Sometimes when she drank she did things she forgot.

Mokhtar's head stuck out of his stall door, indignant. He neighed. Wilton, a Miniature Schnauzer with a Rottweiller attitude, barked at him. The horse gave Brit and the dog a disgusted look and withdrew his head. Bantie chickens scattered as she pushed open the feed room door. She was feeding her creatures when she heard Scott.

"Bri-tan-nia!"

She ducked out of the barn and saw him by his car. He hollered, "Babe, gotta hit it." Boots flopping, sheet clutched, she ran up the hill, right into him. He took a step back when she landed against his body.

"Whoa, Babe, hey!" Arms around her, he leaned back looking at her. At five-ten, Brit was eye to eye. "Hey, I'll be back tonight. Then we can celebrate."

She fed her long arms around his neck. "Scottie. You don't suppose–since today's Thursday–you could wangle tomorrow off? Maybe...go to the coast?"

With a serious look he touched the scratch on her face. "Britannia, you gotta take better care of yourself. I care, y'know."

Her eyes warmed. "Scottie." She smooched his lips. "Thank you."

He grinned. "And don't worry. I'll ask Glen if I can take off tomorrow. I'll call you. Pack nothing. I like you nekkid, gal." He ground his hips into hers. Laughing, she bumped back.

"Swell, Hunk." She wanted to bite him. She could not get enough of him.

They kissed lightly, her belly tingling. *I am a dirty old woman,* she thought. "Now, Scott, ace videographer, get out of here before I eat you alllllllll up."

He moaned. "That's my line." But he stepped away. "Babe, I am gone."

He opened the door of his white Camero, slumped inside, and backed down her driveway splattering rocks. She watched, worried a chicken might be crossing the road.

T W O

On the afternoon before Britannia's birthday, her former stepson Saunders Griffin had arrived home from school and squeezed through the door to his room. He was supposed to clean the room–now. He dumped his schoolbooks on the floor, tried to kick them under his bed. When they failed to go he flopped down on all fours. There was no more room under his bed. He saw Mardi Gras throw cups, beads, unspooled cassette tapes, dirty socks, old sneakers, dirty T-shirts, bowls crusted with food, empty Doritos bags, balled-up bikini panties caught at Mardi Gras parades, video cassettes, Budweiser and Dr. Pepper cans, and raddled pages from *Penthouse, Playboy, Hustler.* A page of *Hustler* distracted him. Gently he smoothed it out. It contained three excellently photographed, laser color-separated, meticulously printed close-ups of vulvas. *Hustler* was definitely his fav. No bullshit there, they cut right to the crotch. The pussies looked so real he could almost smell them.

Maybe a little cleaning up in here…then…

Saunders picked up some clothes and walked on his knees to his dresser. He reached up and shoved the top drawer shut. Well–almost. Three socks and a T-shirt dangled, trapped in the mouth of the drawer. He jerked at the bottom drawer. It jammed.

"Son of a bitch." He jiggled the drawer. "You piece of shit!" He slammed his hand against the drawer. Saunders, "Griff" to his buds, was five eight–still growing, he insisted–and built broad. He was unusually muscular for a fifteen-year-old, and not from working out either. He was genetically programmed through his mother's family to grow the physique of a short Saturday-Night wrestler. As he jerked and cursed the entire oak dresser wobbled. He put a hand up to hold it. He was a strong boy.

The drawer opened after a knock sounded at his door. He scooped up *Hustler*, thrust it deep between his jeaned thighs under his crotch. Just thinking what was on the page made his penis twitch. He assumed a bashful look.

"Come in."

Rita, his father's housekeeper, poked her thin face around his door. "Heard a racket. What you up to?" She looked into wide, light gray eyes.

"Nothing, Rita. I'm just trying to clean up my room and this darn ol' drawer wouldn't open. But, see," he gestured, "it's open now."

Rita's purpled lips grinned. "Clean up your room? Why Saunders, honey, you just holler when you finish. I'll come in here an vacuum for you!"

Rita had orders from Grant, Saunders' father, not to clean up Saunders' room unless it was first cleared of the larger hunks of trash. Rita agreed with Grant. Yet over and over the trio played out the same home video in the living room of the Griffin's New Orleans condo.

Punch Play.

Enter Rita.

"Mr. Grant, I can't get his door open. Somethin's behind it. Somethin big!"

Wearily Grant lowers his newspaper and peers up at her over his bifocals. The only woman ever to see him wearing them is Rita. Otherwise he wears contacts, which he hates. He sighs, runs his hand over his tan-free bald head–ah! to leave off that damn hairpiece!–and scratches his monkish ruff of hair.

"Okay, Rita. Get Saunders out here." Rita dissolves.

Furtively Grant glances back at his paper. He wants to read *The Far Side*. Two old guys in safari suits with binoculars and cameras are parting tall veldt grass-es–Rita materializes before him. He glances up at her then back at the paper...two old guys...Saunders slouches in. Grant lowers the paper.

"Saunders. Rita can't get into your room. Have you let trash pile up again, block your door? How do you expect her to get in to clean?"

Saunders fights the urge to smirk. Creases in his forehead smooth out, his gray eyes widen, the downturned corners of his lips straighten. Grant is pleased, he believes he has his son's attention. Rita, the martyr, is gratified. Now his daddy's gonna give him whatfor.

Other than changing his expression, Saunders doesn't speak. Silence, Saunders' weapon, grows. The refrigerator rumbles, unloads ice cubes. Rita shifts the heavy cross she feels across her shoulders.

"Well? Saunders? Answer me."

Saunders dares a tiny shrug. His eyes grow larger, luminous.

Is he on the brink of tears? Or about to explode in rage? Grant can't tell. He decides it must be tears. This kid had it rough growing up. Grant experiences a quick flash...blood, Margie's dangling white arm, a little boy curled up beside her, thumb in his mouth...his tone is soothing.

"Well. You can't expect Rita to deal with a mess like that, son. It's not fair."

Rita sniffs. Her shoulders straighten slightly.

Grant lays his paper on his lap. He removes his bifocals, recalling with pride his optometrist's words: his far vision is enhanced, almost 20/20, and his night vision is better now than a teenager's. A few things improved with age.

"Okay son. I want you in there now. Clean up that room." His head turns.

"Rita. When he gets all that trash out you go in and just vacuum. Saunders is a big strong boy. And, Saunders, if you want clean socks, make sure all your laundry is out of your room. Do you hear me?"

Saunders eyes are enormous, bulging. Almost colorless. He doesn't nod. He stares.

Grant replaces his bifocals, shakes his newspaper, glances down, sees the two fat *Far Side* guys, behind them a huge buffalo with horns like a handlebar mustache...he glances back up....

"Got that, Saunders?"

Father and son stare at each other out of near-identical eyes, Grant's a more decided, darker gray. Other than that they don't look like father and son.

Saunders has his mother's auburn hair and skin dead-white as Crisco. Grant's remaining hair is gray-speckled brown, with dark teak skin. Saunders short, thick, Grant, long, six-four, with great lanks of leg. Sometimes their physical contrast makes Grant feel uneasy, guilty.

Finally, Saunders dips his chin a millimeter. Grant accepts it as acquiescence and nods firmly at his son. He glances at Rita, now chin up, proud. He nods at her. Maid, boy, turn and exit, Rita briskly, Saunders in a lolling slouch. Grant looks back down at *The Far Side*. The guys are oblivious to the enraged buffalo behind them—snorts spout from its nose. One guy, camera to eye, is saying: "Henry! It's those incessant little snuffy-huffy noises you're making. You'll scare the game!" Grant guffaws.

Stop. Rewind. In three days, hit Play.

Since Saunders rarely cleaned his room unless he wanted something, like tickets to a rock concert, it became part of unwritten family law that Rita seldom ventured there. Grant and Rita thought they were punishing Saunders for his untidiness, but he had what he wanted, near-inviolable privacy. He could have been running crack out of his room, neither Rita nor his dad would have known. Saunders was bitterly pleased by this. He took time each day to snigger at how easily he managed these totally dumb adults.

Grant believed by letting his son get away with his untidy room—providing it didn't get too out of hand—Christ! You had to be able to open the damn door!—he was allowing a harmless expression of teen rebellion. Better an untidy room and heavy metal music than booze or dope. Grant believed he was engaged in some sophisticated parenting.

Back in his room, Rita watching through the jammed-open door, Saunders settled his rump onto his heels. He wondered where those *Hustler* crotches were. He kept his wide-eyed gaze on Rita as he picked up trash and schoolbooks.

"You pickin up this room real good now, Honey?" She was smiling. At some cost.

"Ah. Rita. I've got tons of homework. I'll finish cleaning up tonight after I do my homework. Besides, aren't you finished? Don't you want to go home?"

"Well…"

"Rita. Wrap it up. Go on home."

"You sure?"

"I'm positive."

"Okay then, Saunders honey. I'll vacuum first thing tomorrow morning.

Make sure you gets all them little bits and pieces. They clogs up the vacuum. You know your daddy's goin somewhere tonight. You okay till he gets home?"

"Rita! I'm fifteen! I can take care of myself."

"You sure? There's cookies in the pantry. I picked some up today. And your dinner's in the refrigerator. Microwave at…"

"Rita. Cut it out. I know how to mickey-wave. You get home. You're interfering with my homework now."

"Thought you was gonna clean up your room first."

"No. After the homework."

He widened his eyes and they acquired the whiteness of a Weimaraner's. She looked hard at him, a bit fearful, then let her suspicions die. She backed away, pulling the door closed behind her. He threw back his head, laughing soundlessly. Then he reached behind and punched up his stereo. Metallica screamed. His left hand found the page of *Hustler*. With his right, he unzipped his jeans.

T H R E E

When the rocks on the drive settled, Britannia drooped. Feeling her hangover and her birthday, she trudged back to the stable. Mokhtar stuck out his head and watched interestedly. He expected turnout.

Suddenly she twirled around, her sheet flaring, and she skipped into the barn, into Mokhtar's stall. She bridled him then ripped off the sheet, goose bumps shimmying over her. Kicking off her rubber boots, grabbing a hunk of mane, she hoisted herself onto the horse. She rode naked from the barn.

She hoped Jimmy had the day off.

F O U R

Saunders crammed clothes, CD's, *Hustlers,* tapes, Walkman, black hightops into his school backpack. The music crashed to an end. He turned off the machine, the tray slid out, he extracted the CD. He slid it into its plastic protector, stuffed it into the bag, and zipped it closed.

Flopping across his bed, he fumbled in the open drawer of the bedside table and found his leather-sheathed dagger. He laughed silently when his fingers brushed against the rough surface of the knife sharpener. Rita had been looking for it for weeks. All along he'd had it. He really had her going over this. Turn on his wide-eyed look…. "Gosh, Rita. I haven't seen it. You sure you didn't wrap it up with some fish guts and throw it out?" Rita backed away, fearful she'd thrown it out. Dumb nigger wench. He grabbed his black leather jacket from the top of his dresser and was about to sling it on when he looked down at the death's head on his T-shirt. Reluctantly he decided it might scare off rides if he decided to hitchhike to Brit's. He changed into a white one with a Gulf Shores Redneck Riviera logo.

Jacketed, he hefted the backpack and stalked from his room, combat boots half-laced, tops flopping. He had plenty of time. Dad spent every night in bars, often not home till past midnight, once with a drunken bimbo. An old bimbo. Dad just couldn't attract the young ones any more. Especially with that fucking phony rug he wore. Too bad, ol' Dad.

In the kitchen he found the Sam's double chocolate chip cookies and carefully made room for them in his backpack. He paused in the study, clicked the computer on and typed:

DAD...SPENDING NITE AT DAVE'S

He left the computer on, then patted his hip. His wallet was there with almost a hundred dollars, four blue condoms Snake had given him, the two joints he'd boosted off Jon. All set to run away from home. Brit was a pushover. Lonely old woman like her–she'd be glad of his company, especially with his stupid ex-step-sister away at college. Brit had money, too. And out in the country nobody could tell him what to do. Brit would let him–hell, she'd help him–get his driver's license and he could probably get her car or truck any time he wanted. Goddamn!–Brit would probably buy him a car! He clomped from the condo. He'd be ol' Brit's special present. It was real lucky he'd remembered her birthday....

F I V E

Brit rode up the swale, around the pond, up to the plateau, shivering in the February air. Only her buttocks and inner legs were warm against the horse's body. The paddock gate stood open. Her pubic bone grated painfully against the horse's spine, so she hunched her thighs up to bear more of her weight. Her buttocks were comfortable now on the fat tubes that ran down each side of the horse's spine. If he was any skinnier, riding naked and bareback would be impossibly painful. She checked her balance. Fine. Then leaning slightly back, she took handfuls of mane and clucked to her old gray stallion. He was game and took off as though from a starting gate. His mane blew across her breasts then flew up into her eyes and she was blinded. It didn't matter, she trusted him. Heat flowed up from his undulating body, warming her. His hooves pounded on the brown, dead grass and the movement tremored up through his body, synched up with hers. Britannia and Mokhtar–"The Chosen"– became one big palpating heartbeat thudding over the surface of the earth. Joyous, the horse snorted, dipping head and neck, lightly tossing her body. She rode effortlessly, and began to feel lighter than air, immortal.

Round, round they went, her black and silver hair streaming mane-like, her legs pale on the white body of the stallion. His silver tail shimmered, glinting in the pale sunlight as though flecked with mica. They were like coalesced moonlight braving the day. Her hangover, her fears, wisped away like vapors out the ends of her hair, his tail.

Thank God I can still ride.

Eventually her breathing became painful so she leaned further back, pointed her toes forward, and Mokhtar, also breathing hard, slowed to a jog. She threw back her head and yelled, "Happy Fiftieth Birthday, Britannia Rhodes Lange Scarpelli Griffin!"

Her voice echoed around the wall of forest.

"Happy birthday to youoooooooooo!"

She was gasping as she half-sang, half-screamed. Mokhtar halted. She drew in great breaths of air. Like bellows, the horse's sides moved her legs up and down. She fell forward on his neck. His mane was harsh silk against her breasts and belly. He arched his neck up against her body then turned his head. Her hand reached down to cup his muzzle and he licked her palm with his soft tongue.

The horse's eye was big, black, knowing. She gazed into it. *What did he know? What did he feel?* Then they both looked away, as if embarrassed at their intimacy. She sat up and stroked his sweated neck.

"I always wanted to do that, old man. Was it good for you, too?" Brit asked, and laughed at all the men, from Medieval times on down, who thought riding a horse was a sexual experience for a woman, as if the idea of a woman's sexual organs moving against anything created a sexual feeling in her. This thought was so persistent in men's minds they had forced women to ride side saddle. Protect that mons veneris, that hymen, for them alone, even though the woman's life was risked in the dangerous aside-seat.

They were so wrong. It was a power experience. Astride a half-ton of muscular, submissive animal was one of the rare times a woman felt in charge.

Today, she knew, about ten times as many women than men rode horses. No wonder. She slid off.

"Better walk, Mokh. We don't want to seize up."

The February sun had risen above the treetops and felt warmer on her flushed body. Cooling down, horse and woman strolled the fence line. When Mokhtar's breathing was normal and his wetted chest felt cool to her palm she slid his bridle off and flopped on the cold ground. It was like plunging into snow after a steambath. Good for a hangover. Beside her the horse dropped his head and searched the dead grass for spring sprouts.

She looked down at her belly. Still there, those unpleasant little rolls, trembling now as she shivered. She studied Mokhtar. He was nineteen, old for a horse. They'd been together for sixteen of those years. Was his back swaying? Yes, a bit. She saw age hollows above his eyes and tears sprang to her eyes. Was his lower lip growing pendulous, like her throat? The mealy folds on her belly, the droop of skin under her eyes, this was just the beginning. Her body was engaged in an inverse evolution. She'd grow smaller, withered, monkey-like. Her neck would sink into her shoulders, her jaw jut, her chest cave in like a Lucy—the three-foot tall, 350-million-year-old woman whose bones had been dug up in Ethiopia. Probably Lucy hadn't lived long enough to experience menopause—dreadful word—the final change now stretching before her like those arid lands where Lucy had lived.

Ugly little Lucy's bones were revered by the male anthropologist who'd found her. Yet Brit's new stage of life meant diminished attention from men. Was Scottie her last lover? Would loss of passion, memory, artist's skills, creep sullenly over her? Had loss already occurred? She hadn't had a fresh idea in two years and her agent in New York was clamoring for new work. She shuddered. Would Mokhtar's death and Scottie's inevitable desertion of her—for a younger woman, of course—mean she'd end up alone in her log fortress, hidden behind her private forest, a mad-artist crone?

She wept.

While she cried her artist's third eye detached from the weeping woman and swooped up and away. It saw a beautiful, long-limbed woman sitting naked by a white horse. They seemed sculpted of alabaster. The eye began to snap pictures. Click!…a master shot of the entire scene. The eye angled around, shot a medium closeup. At a distant forest sound the horse raised his head and stared, the woman looked up at the horse: Click! The eye swooped around and snapped again, from the back. Then it began clicking madly: the woman's sad face, her dimpled, striated belly, the horse's sagging testicles, her buttocks flattened on the dead grass.

Lost in pain, Britannia was unaware this was happening.

S I X

The morning of Brit's birthday, Grant Griffin rode his condo's elevator to the ground floor. He had another hangover and his briefcase, the contents of which he hadn't bothered to look at, felt heavy. He patted his toupee–never felt right–and blinked as his eyes teared under contacts. The optometrist had said some couldn't adjust to them. But he looked like a monk in his bifocals! The elevator landed. He strode out into the foyer with his stern "I am an attorney" look. To do this he furrowed his brow, which caused his hairpiece to shift. His free hand skittered up to make sure the damn thing wasn't going to pop off.

Pulling himself up to his full height, he pushed open the glass door. Crisp February air hit him in the face. He was living such a decadent lifestyle, its freshness gave him a twinge of guilt. He forbid himself to breathe deeply. He ignored the splendor of Audubon Park and its loudly chirping birds. He wanted to clap his hands over his ears.

He reached the grassy median where the streetcars run on St. Charles Avenue. One clanged around the bend from Carrollton, screeched to a stop, and he climbed on and found a seat. A few other suited Central Business District types sat stiffly amongst African-American maids heading for housework in the Garden District. The maids chattered as happily as the birds sang. The professionals stared silently at the passing avenue. As the streetcar trundled and clanked along the neutral ground, the spine of St. Charles Avenue, Grant saw that every maintenance box and city trash can bore a graffiti word, "Kaos," spray-painted in fuzzed, dripping black. Idly, Grant wondered, *rock band or prophesy?*

Rocking along past *Gone With The Wind* mansions, under arching boughs of live oaks, past dusty camellia bushes, Grant thanked God Saunders had gone to Dave's last night. He'd been so drunk…he'd staggered in with that–woman! He'd had no idea she was a prostitute. They'd danced to *Hey Jude*…and when she'd asked him to clear up their business first, he'd been too embarrassed to let on he hadn't known all along. He'd peeled off fifty bucks then fucked her–right in his living room–fast as he could. Show her he could still get it up, even drunk as he was. Probably she thought he couldn't. Drunk as he was. Probably she thought she'd collect her fifty bucks for nothing. But tootsie–surprise, surprise–the

Granite Man can always get it up. Brit had called him "Grant, the Granite Man." He took a deep breath. His forehead was sweating, his head under the toupee itched. His sweat smelled like bourbon. The thought of the day ahead was torture.

What if Saunders had been home? His hand shook and he clutched the chrome rail of the seat before him. What if Saunders had caught them? What kind of an example…?

Had he worn a condom? *Oh my God.* He couldn't remember. This drunken fucking around had to stop. If the booze didn't kill him, AIDS would. What was he anyway? Some kind of middle-aged crazy?

He had to admit. Being single sucked. But so did the alternative.

S E V E N

Brit freeze-dried on her plateau of dead winter grass. Mokh had wandered off, so she unkinked her cold, naked body and, walking stiffly, made for the house. As she came in the front door she remembered the sheet pooled on the barn aisle, boots tossed near it, and laughed. A puzzle for old Jimmy whenever he materialized. *Oh well, let him wonder. It's my birthday, I can do anything I want just for today.* She went up to her loft bedroom and pulled on a black velvet robe, tossed across a wicker armchair. *Why couldn't I find it earlier?* she wondered. She pulled open both of the narrow French doors that led to her bathroom and, climbing the steps to her enormous black tub, turned on the hot full force. She dumped in the last of the bathsalts, a gift from her best friend Lee.

While the tub filled she leaned over the sink creaming her face. She had to look in the mirror. Lines on the brow. Two small lines at the corners of the eyes. Engraved smile grooves. Tiny lines feeding into her lips. Facelift time? Could she afford one? Did she want one? Could she stand the shame of having had one? Aren't artists supposed to age naturally, like Georgia O'Keefe, proud of her New Mexico weathering? Also, gray hairs grew too abundantly from her temples. Women failed to look distinguished graying at the temples. Or was that just more cultural brainwash? Well, she could afford a box of L'Oréal. The mirror had fogged, the air steamy and pungent with the scent of roses. She tested the water, added slightly more cold, stirred with a long-handled bath brush, then lowered herself into the near-scalding water. Frissons scurried over her body as it contacted the water. *Oooh.* She shuddered, waited till her body adjusted.

Lifting one streaming leg, she squirted it with shaving cream. Just as she raised a disposable razor, her phone rang. Four rings then her voice, "Brit Rhodes. Leave a message, if you wish." Viola's voice, "Hi, Sweetie. This is just your mother calling to wish you happy birthday, dear." Sigh. "I'll never forget giving birth to you...what a night I had. Call me back when you can. Have a happy, happy, happy day, Darling." Click. The phone rang again. Brit lowered her creamed leg. Another voice, this time it was Annie, old Jimmy's wife.

A sob. "Brit?" Weeping. "Brit. A bad thing has happened. Don't look for Jimmy today." Sob. "Or any other day." Click.

My God. What's happened to Jimmy? Water cascading, Brit leaped from the tub and wrapped herself in a black towel. She skidded to the phone at her bedside table and rapidly punched out Jimmy's number.

"'Lo?"

"Annie." Brit's hand clutched the receiver hard.

"Brit...Jimmy's dead!"

"Oh my God–Annie–what happened?"

"Oh, Brit. He went down to feed the chickens like he always does before breakfast. When his eggs got cold I went lookin' for him. An..." She was weeping. Brit waited, her throat tightening. "...and I found him. Dead. Laid out on the ground. But he got those chickens fed and he gathered up all those eggs. Of course, all of those eggs was broken, spattered every which way, all over him, all over the yard–"

"Oh, Annie. I am so sorry, Annie. Do you need anything? I'll come over–"

"No. No thank you, Brit. Whole family's here." And indeed they were. Brit now heard the babble of Annie and Jimmy's huge family in the background. They'd had ten children, which had multiplied, which had multiplied, and they were the great-great grandparents of one little boy.

"I want to help you Annie."

"Well, the–the funeral's Monday. Wake's over here."

"I'll be there. But is there anything you need right now?" She meant money, Annie knew it.

"No...but thank you. Jimmy took out a burial policy a long time ago and there's his school pension, so I'm fine." The decibel level from the background rose and one voice, male, rose above the others. Annie murmured something away from the receiver, then her voice came back to Brit. "Uh, Brit? You need help today? Leroy's off work. Says he can come over."

"Oh, Annie. You tell Leroy thanks but he needs to stay home, take care of you, mourn his father."

"Okay, Brit. Thanks." And again Annie began to weep. Brit swallowed.

"Annie. I want you to know how very sorry I am. Jimmy was a wonderful, wonderful man. I will miss him very much."

"Thanks, Brit. I got to go now."

"Goodbye, Annie."

She hung up slowly, staring at nothing. Jimmy! Poor old Jimmy! How old was he anyhow? He'd seemed so spry and strong–he was what–sixty-nine? Seventy? She'd ask Annie. She started to cry. She'd seen and talked to Jimmy nearly every day for the past twelve years. He was gone. No warning. Vanished–his sense of humor, his relentless insistence about "doing things right" his love–nay–his adoration–for Mokhtar. So Mokhtar had lost a friend too. Wilton padded up the stairs as if telepathically drawn to her need. A white cat appeared and leaped into her lap.

The cat was silvery white and puffy-coated like a Persian but with a pointed "regular cat" face. It had searching green eyes. She'd named her "Godwin" after Gail Godwin...she'd been reading her novel, *Father Melancholy's Daughter*, when she got the kitten from the SPCA. The name soon shortened to "God," but she felt uneasy calling a cat God so, to herself, she spelled it "godd," and laughed to friends that her kitten was the e.e. cummings of cats.

Britannia also liked to say, "godd is with me," and it wasn't entirely irreverent. Each time, her mystical side would muse...*Is God with me*?

Wilton put his paws on her knees and looked up at his weeping mistress, tail hesitantly wagging. Brit parted her hair and pulled him up into her lap alongside godd and wept harder.

"Oh Wil, oh godd, we've lost a best, dear friend. We've lost Jimmy." Her shoulders shook as she cried.

After a time the phone rang. Without thinking she picked it up and hoarsely said hello.

"Britannia. Whatever is the matter? Have you come down with a cold on your birthday?"

It was Viola.

"Oh, Mother...I just talked to Annie. My dear old Jimmy just died." She kept crying.

"Oh my dear, that's awful and on your birthday too. Oh my dear. I know you'll miss him." Pause. "Do you want me to call back later when you're feeling better?"

"No. It's okay. I'm getting calmer. Just let me change phones."

She wanted a drink. She set the receiver down beside its base, placed Wilton on the floor, and ran downstairs. She grabbed the cordless phone from the coffee table and held it to her ear.

"I'm here." Noise on the line. The receiver to her ear, she sprinted upstairs and replaced the receiver on the other set. "Now, Mother, that's better."

"Yes. Well, I was just wondering if you've received your present or not. If it doesn't fit–"

Brit went back downstairs, walked to the old walnut buffet she used as a bar. She picked up a glass, went into the kitchen. "No Mom, it hasn't come yet. Probably be in the mailbox today."

"No. I'm getting modern. I sent it by the United Parcel Service. You know. You see those ugly brown trucks everywhere." Viola lived in Cincinnati, where Brit had been born. Brit opened the freezer and twisted an ice tray. Cubes popped out onto the floor. She swooped down and her towel fell off.

"Brit. Are you there? What's that sound?" Brit let the towel lay but gathered up the ice, threw three speckled with Wilton or godd hair into the sink, and tossed the cleanest into her glass.

"I'm here. I'm getting ice."

"Ice? What for? You're not drinking this early in the day?" Brit retrieved her towel, and dragging it, started from the kitchen.

"Yes, Mother. I am going to have a drink this early in the day. A dear friend has just died and"–she started to cry again–"and it's my damned fiftieth birthday!" She was aware that it was soon to be her mother's seventy-fifth birthday, so she couldn't wail too much about her own advancing age.

Brit made her way to the buffet. She opened a door, rummaged amongst liqueurs, bourbon, scotch, rum, vodka, till she found brandy. She poured four fingers over her ice and took a sip. Made a face. Took another sip.

"Oh my dear. Try not to be so sad." Viola tinkled a little laugh. "After all, *you know* I'm seventy-four! And...I've still got my figure! Among other things..." The emphasis on "you know" was to remind Brit she was never to reveal Viola's age. Not that Brit blamed Viola, a gorgeous woman who'd always looked a decade younger that her actual age. After the hair-cutting fiasco at forty, she'd immediately let her hair grow back to shoulder-length, even though all her other lady friends were wondering how soon they could begin tinting their hair blue.

And, as Brit was also finding out, why date oneself? Why give people the opportunity to pigeonhole you in an age group when you didn't feel any different at
fifty than you did at twenty? If you admitted your age, especially if you were a
woman, people instantly started treating you like a doddering old goose. This
was dangerous, because you might succumb to such treatment. Expect less of
yourself.

Brit couldn't resist mouthing, "And I've still got my figure!" Doing so linked
her with her sisters Elizabeth and Victoria. Viola had trilled "And I've still got my
figure!" probably, Brit and her sisters had calculated, since she was twenty-nine.

Pause. "Have you heard from Anastasia, dear? She's doing well at that college,
isn't she? She always did love animals." Brit clenched her teeth. LSU was a fine
school, but Viola acted like it was a junior college in the boonies. Perhaps to
Viola the entire Deep South was the boonies.

"Yes, Mother. The homesickness lasted only a week. Every now and then I get
frantic phone calls. You know how changeable her moods are. How sensitive she
is. But she calms right down."

"Yes. I know. You two always were too close. Well. Don't be too hard on her,
dear. With her condition–"

"Let's not start underestimating Asia again, Mother." Brit tossed back some
brandy. "She's an A student after all."

"I suppose you know best," Viola lied.

"Mother. If she's happier cozying up to a cougar or an orangutan than some
heartless young stud perhaps, 'In This Day and Age'"–a favorite expression of
Viola's–"we should be grateful. She could just retreat into her shell and never
come out. You know that!" Brit then thought, *Let her grow up her own way,
Mother. Let her fall down and hurt herself then learn to pick herself up and carry on,
Mother. How else does anyone learn?*

There was a long silence on the line and Brit thought, *there's a lot of space
between us, we communicate only through a satellite far from planet Earth.*

She sipped brandy, trying not to let the ice make a giveaway clink.

"How're Elizabeth and Victoria?" Her sisters' names reflected Viola's
anglophilia. Every two years Viola wangled a trip to Great Britain. She'd examined every stone in every castle in the entire British Isles. Nunan, her husband
and Brit's stepfather, researched pubs.

"Fine. Elizabeth called last night in tears. George has been philandering again.
I don't see why she continues to endure that man! He's an inveterate letch! All she

gets from him is grief."

*And a huge house on a golf course in the outskirts of Chicago. And a Mercedes, shopping and theater trips to New York, winters in the Caribbean...*but Brit said, "When she gets fed up she'll cut him loose."

"But it's not like she doesn't have the goods on him, Britannia! She could sue for divorce. Take him to the cleaners!"

"Maybe she loves him, Mother."

"Love!" A snort. "Love is for fools! I'm glad you seem to have learned that, Britannia. But—are you still seeing that Scottie person? That young man?"

"So far."

Enormous, forbearing sigh. "Well. I guess if he helps you let off steam. I suppose it's your artistic nature. You should have been a man, Britannia."

"Thanks a lot, Mom."

"Now don't get sarcastic. It's true. You've always acted like a man. Very headstrong. You never listened to me!" Silence. Another Viola sigh. "Men!"

So you want me to be like them? Brit laughed to herself at her mother's contradictions. Contradictions that had been confusing while she was growing up but were now a mere annoyance. And Viola—how skilled she was at manipulating the other species, mankind. How kind men were to Viola! Nunan was possibly the happiest man alive without the faintest idea that his wife manipulated him like NASA putting a space station in orbit. Her reward was a faithful, wealthy husband. Viola just couldn't understand why her daughters refused to emulate her...why did they persist in believing a woman could be honest with a man?

"He's very young, Brit. Now Grant—"

"Mother. Grant was younger than me, too. Chronologically, anyway."

"Oh, but Britannia! A world of difference. And only four years. Grant was so mature!"

Grant is an attorney, Scottie a news videographer. Viola saw every man in her daughter's life as a potential mate, as women were incomplete without legal male companions and providers, creatures weighed on Viola's Man Evaluation Scale: Occupation "Attorney" scoring a ten and Occupation "Cameraman" a zero. Everyone knew photographers were flaky. Viola also airily overlooked that Britannia had come to love living by herself, most of the time. Brit let her mouth flood with chilled brandy. Slowly she swallowed and speaking, allowed a taint of sarcasm.

"Certainly, Mother. Grant was so mature." Pause. "Every forty-year-old man just has to have his very own twenty-year-old girl, doesn't he? What about that,

Mother?"

The women stood listening to each other breathe. Viola spoke, "Well…he never actually got her into bed, did he?"

"Beside the point. He wanted to." Then she said, "Look. I was in the tub. I'm naked in my living room."

"Oh! And all those windows you have! Okay, Dear. Watch for that big brown UPS truck. They said they'd deliver even though you live so far out in the country. I love you!"

"I love you too, Mom. Bye."

Brit hung up and black towel dragging, ice cubes rattling, re-ascended her stairs. She slid into tepid bathwater.

E I G H T

Saunders pushed a pillow from his face. Eyes slitted, he checked the clock radio on his bedside table at the Lakeshore Motel in Mandeville. 1:30 p.m. He groped for the remote bolted to the bedside table, turned on the TV, clicked till he found MTV, then turned up the volume.

Too bad this joint didn't have room service. But he could easily hoof it to the Burger King down the road. Probably Super Dome hadn't yet tumbled his son was gone.

The 6:00 p.m. Greyhound had taken him across the lake to Mandeville the evening before. He'd managed to buy a six-pack, enjoying the beer all the way across Lake Pontchartrain. Now he had to figure the easiest but most dramatic way to Brit's estate way the hell out in Washington parish. Did cabs exist on the primitive Northshore?

N I N E

Grant slouched in his tobacco-colored leather chair. His immense mahogany desk separated him from two green leather chairs. The office was decorated in New Orleans' Attorney Traditional, mahogany, leather, oriental carpets. The wall opposite Grant was old brick, a coveted touch, and a benefit of the renovated building on Lee Circle. The remaining walls were dark wood with brass wall sconces. The far end had a large window through which he saw the statue of General Robert E. Lee stonily facing north. Before the window two green leather wing chairs faced a tobacco leather sofa. A glass-topped table with a square of pink granite as its base separated them. The table held a Waterford crystal ashtray and a pale peach orchid in bloom.

His desk was scattered with files, crumpled pink message slips, and three scribbled-on legal pads. There was a wavy line around the edge of the desktop where the janitorial service had carefully wiped. Beyond the line, in the heavy litter, the mahogany didn't shine.

Sometimes he wished he could just trash the damn toupee, live life bald. But his pink, shiny pate conjured images of monks or sexually inadequate old men, and he was neither…yet.

Work held more promise. Three of his cases didn't have adequate assets to send a Grant Griffin into battle over the assets they wished to contest. Then fat old Mrs. Wiffins had called again.

His secretary Opal smirked when she gave him the message. Not only did Mrs. Wiffins seem to have a crush on him, but Alf, her diminutive husband, had kidnapped Pucci, their Shih-Tzu, one more time. Mrs. Wiffins would be distraught. She would desire comforting. Alf's lawyer would be laughing when Grant called him one more time to insist Alf return Pucci to Mrs. Wiffins. Her first name was Juliette, nickname, "Spiffy," but Grant rigorously maintained the formal address, despite Mrs. Wiffins' pleadings to please call her "Spiffy." Imagine! "Spiffy Wiffins."

Good thing the assets were abundant, this one was going to court, but he'd be a laughingstock. A custody case over a dog. Oh, there were precedents, but that the Marvin Mitchell of New Orleans–that hotshot divorce attorney Grant Griffin–should go to trial over a dog!

Sighing, Grant punched his intercom button, got Opal. "Get me Jim LeBoeuf, Alf Wiffins' attorney."

Opal sniggered. "Certainly, Mr. Griffin."

"Opal. Cut the sniggering. The dog is very important to Mrs. Wiffins and Mrs. Wiffins is one of our most important clients."

"Yes, Mr. Griffin," she sniggered. As soon as Opal, a six-one African American with a face for *Vogue,* a body for a swimsuit calendar, and a mind that was crunching through law school nights, spoke, Grant realized Wiffins and Griffin rhymed. He groaned. *The headlines!* All three local news channels would pounce on this one.

GRIFFIN DEFENDS WIFFINS IN CUSTODY BATTLE
OVER PAMPERED POOCH PUCCI

A high wind would take his toupee as he was interviewed live by three channels on the courthouse steps. The only relief in the whole mess was that the sit-com *Alf* was no longer on the air. Little, furious, Alf Wiffins could actually be said, with his huge nose, to slightly resemble a certain television star, an alien puppet.

He had to get this one settled out of court.

Grant leaned back in his executive armchair petting his toupee, checking its position. Waiting, he gazed at his collection of Britannia Rhodes prints mount-ed on the brick wall, set apart from his framed law degree from Tulane and the pictures of himself shaking hands with mayors and governors. They were from her *Wildflowers of Louisiana* series. He had four, numbered and signed by the artist, his former wife. The delicate orange-pink of a swamp azalea. Vined Cherokee roses artfully strangling a baby magnolia. Black-eyed Susans–better than those million dollar *Sunflowers,* said Grant when she painted them. A lush passion flower growing in a ditch, the murky ditchwater alive with the fetal-pink shapes of Louisiana crawfish. Brit's work had subtle levels.

Grant's eyes regained focus on the passion flower. Passion. The one thing Brit had been very good at…their marriage hadn't broken up because of a lack of pas-sion. Now, four years later, he couldn't get a solid fix on why, exactly, they had broken up. Was it something he'd done? Back then he knew she'd been impossi-ble. Married to her art. Idly he wondered how ol' Brit was doing these days. His phone rang, he hit the speaker button, heard Opal's clear Aretha Franklin voice.

"Mrs. Wiffins, line three."

"Thank you, Opal."

He punched the blinking button and heard Mrs. Wiffins' sobbing. For the fifth–or was it the sixth?–time he launched a mollification of sad, fiftyish, rich Mrs. Wiffins whose passion, it seemed, had dwindled to one little pooch.

T E N

Brit sat at her vanity, a piece of furniture not seen since Forties' movies. It had triple mirrors, a mirrored top, drawers down each side of a kneehole. Brit had gotten it at a not-quite-antique shop on Magazine Street in New Orleans. She loved it. More comfortable than trying to put on makeup in a steamy bathroom. Naked on the matching bench, image tripled, she worked to cover her hangover and fifty years of an artist's life. The pouches under her eyes were more pronounced than usual, yet with her face on, staring at herself in triplicate, she decided she wasn't too bad. Viola's genes. Didn't know about her dad. Viola had learned, ten years back, that Blair Egbert Rhodes died, derelict, at a Salvation Army hospice in Portland, Oregon.

She was finishing blow-drying her hair when she heard a scream, and music? *Shake it up baby...Twist and shout...*Outside? Now Wilton barking, high pitched. Brit's headache spiked.

She dropped the blower, shimmied a robe on. *What now?*

Clutching the neckline which plunged almost to her nipples–Scottie loved it–she flew down the stairs, black velvet rippling around her. The front doorbell rang, music pulsed, Wilton barked. Brit tiptoed through her living room to the foyer. A beveled glass door was bracketed by two windows overgrown with ivy. As she peered through the glass the door flew open. The dog's barks neared the shatter stage, music vibrated into the house–Brit glimpsed a white van–and she scrambled back as a muscled young man jerked toward her, pelvis thrusting. He wore a gold lamé bikini, codpiece so big it must be stuffed. Stretching his arms, he grinned lasciviously while The Beatles screamed "Shake it up, Baby... " Brit, smiling nervously, moved down the hall, around the corner and into the living room, the body driving her back. *One of Damien's outrageous gifts?* Flowers with mylar balloons splayed behind him. He looked like a Mardi Gras float.

Brit stopped, the music stopped, the man dropped to a knee and sang *Happy Birthday.* Voice almost as good as his body. The fan of flowers and balloons sank to the floor behind him.

Brit reddened, not a normal blush, but one of those damn full-body heat waves, with perspiration on her chest, forehead, upper lip. A makeup wrecker. She prayed Muscles would think it was an overwhelmed blush, not a hot flash–the humiliation of looking menopausal in front of a twenty-something man! Stiff, she waited, sweat trickling between her breasts. He finished on a high note, surged to his feet and bowed as though taking a curtain call. Brit clapped politely as heat ebbed from her body.

"Britannia, Happy Birthday, Girl!" Lee, her very best friend in the "whole entire world" jumped from behind the balloons. Brit shrieked like a coed, Lee shrieked back. They hugged.

"Lee, I should've known, only you'd be this crazy." Brit leaned back, arms still around her friend.

Lee looked at Brit, who tried not to flinch from the inspection of her thirty-year-old friend.

"Don't look fifty to me, Girl," she whispered.

Brit kissed her. "Thanks, Lee."

They'd met at Ruby's Roadhouse, a Mandeville saloon-jazz joint where Lee bartended. Brit had been a solitary drinker on a slow night and when she found Lee was a writer, "struggling to be a bartender," they made plans to get together. That was several years ago. Lee was small, bones of a cheetah, skin the color of a cheetah's, between the spots. She hooked her bobbed black "honky hair" behind her ears, and grinned at the young man. She had her Masters in History with emphasis on the evolution of European Monarchies. "Why not?" she'd said when they'd first met over coffee. "I'm about one-fourth African and three-fourths honky, girl. Just explorin' my roots."

The cheetah impression was so strong Brit had painted her portrait, Lee's face emerging from a cheetah's body, stalking marble corridors. Brit named it "The Takeover." Her nose, Lee's despair, was big, jutting from her face with a dangerous Semitic hook. She said when her novel got published she was gonna buy a nose-job. Brit said that would ruin her look. On slow days they squabbled about Lee's nose.

"Harry, thanks a whole bunch. You were fuckin' A fabulous!"

She turned back to Brit. "Can't he shake that thang?" Back to Harry. "Now look at my friend here. Doesn't she look cool? You'd never guess she's sixty today, would you?"

Harry's GQ jaw moved down. "No, Ma'am, never would!"

"Dammit, Lee." Brit laughed. Taking her arms from Lee she turned to the young man.

"Can't believe a word she says, Harry. There she goes, flattering her old, old friend again. Actually, I'm seventy-five. It's wonderful what a great preservative brandy is." Harry stared as the women laughed. Then Brit asked, "Is that all he does—dance? Sing?"

Harry's eyes went from woman to woman. Brit extended her long artist's hand, and pointed at the codpiece.

"Is that part of my birthday present, Lee?"

Harry blushed.

"No, Brit, he's just your birthday card." Brit threw her head back and howled. "Thanks, Harry. Great job," continued Lee.

Harry's aplomb came back. Grinning, he bowed from the room.

Lee walked to the balloons and lifted a shopping bag from behind them.

"Get comfy, girl, your birthday's just begun."

ELEVEN

Saunders strolled from Burger King. His problem was he had four hours before showing up at Brit's. He wanted to arrive after dark and he wished it would rain so he could appear cold, hungry, wet—a pathetic waif on her doorstep. Unfortunately there wasn't much to do on a weekday February afternoon in Mandeville. He'd seen plenty of Lake Pontchartrain on the bus. It made waves. Hands shoved in his back pockets, he frowned up at the blue sky, picturesque white clouds. Too pretty, no sign of rain. Maybe they'd let him stay in his room longer. He sauntered down the shoulder of Highway 90 back to the lobby. The clerk, not bad, but old—probably in her twenties—spoke when he entered.

"Mr. Griffin! Want your backpack?"

He liked "Mr. Griffin." With a sneer he thought, *that'd make Super Dome wild.*

"No. I was wondering…my stepmother won't be home till later. I called from Burger King. She asked me to take a cab to her place this evening. Can I get one around here?"

"Of course. When do you need it?"

"That's another problem. Not till about six or seven o'clock. I don't suppose I could wait in my room? Even though I've checked out?"

The girl regarded him. Housekeeping had already made up his room and Hilda'd said it was left in good condition: One teenager that hadn't trashed the place. And he was such a cute guy—fab eyes! Usually she wasn't attracted to red-headed men, too many freckles, no eyebrows. But this guy had no freckles and he did have dark auburn eyebrows. Too bad he wasn't older—eighteen was a bit young for her, although she was only twenty-three herself. Unblinking, he stood before her, eyes so wide she wondered why they didn't water. Her eyes slid down his body. What the hell. Business was slow. Mr. Haines wouldn't know the difference. She reached under the counter for a key and extended to him. He reached out, their fingers touched, she felt a tingle. This kid was pretty mature for eighteen.

Saunders wondered just how busy this bitch was this afternoon. Maybe…? He allowed his index finger to brush once across her palm as they stood, arms over the counter, hands covering the key. Then Jane Stachs, her name pinned on the upgrade of her left breast, relinquished it.

"Okay, now, Mr. Griff—"

"Saunders. You're Jane?"

He still hadn't blinked. She felt a blush coming. *Yes, Tarzan, me Jane. The shoulders on this kid.*

"Yes, well. Saunders. You can use this room. It's not your old room. Just don't mess anything up, you know? You can watch cable, okay? But you'll have to be out by six. That's when my shift ends."

"Six. Sure Jane. Fantastic." He started to leave, stopped and turned back, gray eyes silver. "Thanks, Jane." He pushed open the glass door and left.

Jane was amazed. Her knees were trembling. *That kid packed a charge. Give him a couple of years and*–her eyes lighted on his backpack, huddled at her feet. He'd need it. Maybe she'd take it to his room. Check on him.

T W E L V E
"Mrs. Wiffins–"

"Spiffy. Do please call me Spiffy, Grant. Even Hartwell calls me Spiffy, Grant."

Hartwell was the senior partner in Grant's small but prestigious, he reminded himself, law firm. Whitfield, Whitfield, Galliano & Griffin.

"If Hartwell can call me Spiffy, Grant, why not you? After all, this divorce thing has been dragging on for two years. I feel antique being called 'Mrs. Wiffins,' it's as bad as 'ma'am!'" She sighed. "Alf is just impossible." She began noisy crying.

Grant waited, as always. He felt a little sorry for Mrs. Wiffins, oh hell–Spiffy! Alf was making her life all kinds of hell and he doubted the man cared one whimper for the dog. What Grant hadn't figured out…were Alf's shenanigans to protect his financial pile? Or was there still a tender feeling for Spiffy?

Alf had been foolishly middle-aged crazy. It had hit him at sixty-three, way too old for such nonsense, thought Grant. Because of that though, his client had Alphonso X. Wiffins by the balls. Spiffy'd caught him with those same appendages in the mouth of a young woman, Alf sprawled, skinny legs akimbo on the burgundy leather chesterfield in his baronial office in Kenner. Grant could just imagine…! Not thinking, he chuckled.

"Grant," said Mrs. Wiffins, "are you laughing at me? You must try and understand how much I care about Pucci."

"Oh no, not at all, Mrs.–Spiffy. Opal just put something on my desk, that's all. Please go on."

"I'm finished."

"So this note from Alf says if you want Pucci back you're to meet him at the what? A motel?"

Motels on Airline Highway featured waterbeds, XXX movies, and the added convenience of your choice of rock stars right outside the door, in case the movies didn't provide sufficient satisfaction. The area was populated with skinny whores who fed on "rocks," crack cocaine, which some wag had extrapolated to "rock stars." Maybe Alf was plotting to have Spiffy taken out in this neighborhood? Her plump body, her dog's in a dumpster? Alf was "connected."

Or...? A wicked thought came into Grant's mind. He felt so hampered by the damn hairpiece, like a hot sticky hand pressing down on his brain, the contacts in his eyes like horse's blinkers, and actually, his whole damn constricted life. Why not venture forth just this once?

"Spiffy...of course, as your attorney I must as advise you not, under any circumstances, to do anything that ridiculous note says."

Grant leaned back cradling the receiver and laced his fingers together, palms down, knuckles opposing. He turned his hands over. His laced fingers stuck up. He stared. Spiffy was chirping in his ear. His hands were playing the childhood game of–

Here's the church and...

Here's the steeple,

Open the doors and...

There's the people.

His fingers waggled. Then hastily–*God, if Opal walked in*–he tore them apart and steepled them, but this time, fingers pointing up reverently. A lawyerly gesture.

There were snuffles on the line. Grant cleared his throat.

"Spiffy...as a friend, I'd like to ask something."

Her breathing quickened, she was almost panting–he felt aroused. He moved the receiver a centimeter from his ear.

"It's this, Spiffy. You and Alf seem to have a tremendous amount of emotion to expend toward each other."

He paused. The breathing–more intense?

"This emotion, on the surface, seems to be in the hateful category. Still...it's an impressive amount of emotion. Are you with me, Spiffy?"

More breathing, a gasp, the silence of held breath.

"And, despite the despicableness of Alf's action two years ago–and it was genuinely despicable, Spiffy–I find it interesting that Alf dropped that hot little petunia instantly. Are you with me, Spiffy?"

Silence. *Had she hyperventilated, passed out? God.* Hartwell better not hear a word of this. Besides this lucrative divorce, the Juliette "Spiffy" Wiffins Trust was important to the firm. *Speak to me, Spiffy. One little pant. So I know you're alive at the end of this line.*

He had to continue. "In fact, Spiffy–please correct me if I'm wrong–Alf immediately bought a condo in the very building where I have my condo. There are a great many condos in that building, Spiffy, but I pass by him occasionally, in the foyer, the elevator, at the rooftop pool and so on, and, Spiffy, never once have I seen him in the company of another female, bimbo or otherwise. It looks to me as though Alf's straightened himself out. Now, could it be that these…volcanoes of hate you and Alf spew at each other, well–" his voice picked up speed "–as you know the opposite of love is indifference. Not hate–"

"Grant Griffin. Are you trying to tell me that that big-nosed, big-eared pipsqueak doesn't hate me? That all this Pucci-napping is a twisted kind of love?" She sounded full of hate. Hate-full.

"Yes. Possibly. Something to consider."

Big, big sigh. Then crying. *Oh God. She'd go straight to Hartwell.* "Spiffy…" he began.

"Oh, Grant," she wailed, "I've wondered the same thing, too! But how can we be sure? Maybe it really is hate–and the reason he wants me to go to that triple-X waterbed motel is not for–you know…but…you know…to have me taken care of?" Her voice climbed, Southern, a statement made into a question. She finished in a whisper, "Alf knows people."

Grant had long suspected.

"Ah. Yes. I have some awareness…Spiffy, that possibility did–fleetingly, I assure you–cross my mind." Sobs. "But Spiffy…maybe he wants, may I say, to rub on you, not…rub you out?" The sobs stopped.

"How can we be sure?" No more Southern-Belle vacillation.

Her second reference to "we." He didn't like that. He ran his finger around the edge of his starched collar, releasing the smell of Irish Spring blended with last night's bourbon reincarnated as sweat. His hand strayed up. Itchy scalp. Carefully he scratched his toupee. Wasn't working. His head itched furiously. But he sensed Spiffy was coming around, so he gritted his teeth against the itch. And suddenly, decisively, he lowered his hand from his head, swung his chair around to face his desk, straightened his shoulders.

"Spiffy, we are going to go down to Airline Highway. We are going to *recon-*

noiter that motel. Bring the note. If we see anything suspicious, we'll drive away. If, however, all looks benign, perhaps you could take a chance and knock on the door? I'll stand by, of course, make sure…"

Big breath. Grant slid his middle drawer open and groped for a Cert. He thumbnailed two out, popped them in his mouth. He sucked, waited. Another big breath. *Please, Spiffy Wiffins, don't hyperventilate.*

"Grant. I'll do it. Let's do it! One way or another," her high voice dropped an octave, "we'll settle this thing. Once and for all."

"Good girl, Spiffy!" Grant slapped his hand down in elation. It landed on his Mark Cross pen, which hurt. Nevertheless he felt his blood quicken over this adventure.

"The note says what time?"

"2:00 p.m. Today."

"Gotcha. Spiffy, I will pick you up at your home at 1:00 p.m. That'll give us plenty of time to–case the joint."

"I'll be ready." Still the lowered tone.

"Great. And, uh, Spiffy? Just in case this could be positive, wear something–you know–"

"Sexy? Grant Griffin, I have just the thing."

"Good going, Spiffy! See you at one. Bye now." He heard an anxious little breath then the receiver clicked in his ear. Hanging up he felt pleased with himself. He buzzed.

"Opal? I'm going to be out of the office from one till…three this afternoon. Reshuffle my appointments, will you?" Was Opal sniggering? But she answered "Yes, sir," her normal sarcastic self. He raised his finger from the intercom button and reaching up, tore his toupee from his scalp and scratched wildly, with both hands.

THIRTEEN

Britannia and Lee sprawled on a huge soft leather sofa, oyster-colored, U-shaped, open ends pointed at a stone fireplace. Their heads were reflected in a mirror on the mantel. French doors on either side of the fireplace let in a lemony spill of light. Scarlet and black silk cushions were scattered around them. A glass and brass coffee table before them held empty Lean Cuisine trays and two champagne flutes. Bubbles idled up the sides of the glasses and broke silently at the surface. Crumpled tissues in primary colors, ribbons, gold and silver foils were strewn about the sofa, the table, the shining pine floor. Wilton curled, asleep on royal blue tissue, a gold bow loose on his neck. A flame speared up from a pecan log in the fireplace. The room smelled of winter sun, pecan smoke, the distinctive freshness of new clothes.

UPS had brought Viola's gift, a navy suit with Chanel cream piping, navy and cream spectator pumps, silk scarf, gold chain belt, navy hose and a cream pillbox hat drenched in a froth of navy net. An entire coordinated outfit. An outfit through which Viola telegraphed her message: Quit wearing those bohemian caftans! As Brit opened each gift her dismay grew. She sighed over the beautiful suit she'd probably never wear. Would her mother never get tired of trying to recast her in a conventional shape? Brit was in the dregs of her hangover and sorrow over Jimmy's death, so she had no energy for her usual adolescent rage at her mother. She could almost laugh. And, who knows? Maybe someday she'd wear it. Looked almost bridal–the second marriage sort. She liked the hat. Viola had been shrewd. It was so tempting in its theatricality it nearly seduced Britannia into wearing everything. Now the hat perched on Brit's head, netting flared like the wings of an exotic bird.

UPS had brought more than Viola's gift. When she opened the gold-wrapped box from Damien, her New York agent, she thought he must be in cahoots with Viola. She supposed since he'd taken care of her career for twenty years he had the right to make these sledgehammer suggestions. The box had a plane ticket to New York, a long weekend at the Pierre, theatre tickets, his invitation to dinner. Wherever she wanted. This she interpreted as, "get your ass up here *toute suite* so I can kick it."

There was a gift from Halima Orestes, the gallery owner in New Orleans who'd introduced her *Wildflower* series in the deep south, artsy copper-wood jewelry, silk caftans from Elizabeth and Victoria and, eeriest of all, a dozen long-stemmed roses from the Trust. Al's Trust, now her and Asia's Trust. Al's will instructed the Whitney Bank of New Orleans to send roses to her every year on her birthday. Roses from a dead man. She gave them to Lee.

Britannia held a cigarette between her fingers, palm of that hand under her chin. Smoke rose, just missing her eye. She frowned through granny glasses at Tarot cards on the sofa. Lee, crosslegged, faced her and read from a small book called *Elemental Tarot.*

Lee's gift. She laid the cards out so expertly Brit guessed she'd practiced some. Brit had objected to a reading.

"For fun, Brit. It's your birthday. Who knows what'll come up?"

"Yes. Who knows?"

"I know we don't believe in this stuff–but maybe we can have some fun with it."

You can have fun with it, thought Brit, but said, "Actually I love the cards. The art is great, sort of quasi-primitive-stylized, with a *soupçon* of Egyptian tomb art–"

"You're trying to say you dig 'em."

Brit continued, touching one, "The exotic names of these ancient forgotten gods, the provocative quotations illuminating each card–"

"Gimme that, smarty." Lee snatched the card from under her hand. "Quit evading. I'm gonna tell your fortune."

Brit fell back on a scarlet cushion. "I hope it's fortuitous…"

"We are the creators of our own reality."

"That's what I'm afraid of. What I do today may rise up and wallop me ten years from now. Therefore, what I did ten years ago may be lurking in the undergrowth to wallop me today." Brit lit another cigarette, inhaled. "Hit it, Lee, I want to hear some good stuff."

"Okay. You've got a lot of number five cards here, Brit." She thumbed through the book. "Five means 'Security and complacency challenged by unexpected change from an outside source.'"

"Five? Make that Five-O, honey, and do I feel challenged."

Lee looked at Brit, pursed her lips. "You're good at change, Brit."

"Good! Hell!" She gestured, ash flying off her cigarette. "I've got The Change, the fucking menopausal one, terrorizing my body, now I've got this other change, this fucking, horrible, old birthday!" She threw the cigarette in an ashtray and began to cry. Lee stared, book in her lap.

"I hate it, Lee, I absolutely despise it." Raising her head she flung her arms in the air, "I ask you, as you sit there in the complacency of your thirtieth year…" face wet, hat askew, she jumped from the couch, "…is there life for a post-menopausal woman in the United States of America today? The answer is–NO! Dammit, NO!" She stomped and shrieked around the room. "No, no, no, NO!" she yelled. Wil barked shrilly, hopping at the skirts of her robe.

"Fifty-year-old women are supposed to be dead! Never before in the history of mankind have so many women lived so long! Men don't know what to do with us!" She stopped. "As far as I can figure we have two options, both pathetic."

She held up a finger, "One, and this is what I'm supposed to do because I'm an artist—let it go, the face, the bod, the sex life, and become an old crone. I call that Crone-ism." Raising a second finger, "Two. Become a Tom Wolfe Social X-ray—remember? *Bonfire of the Vanities?* Starve to anorexic thinness, stretch our faces to line-less masks by obsessive visits to cosmetic surgeons, erase all erotic feeling in our nipples from boob lifts, and still be condemned to watch husbands of twenty-five years take trophies: Trophy Wives, women whose birth-dates match our wedding date, and so, we are abandoned."

Lee, small voiced, said, "Brit. You don't have a husband."

"I know!"

"And you left your husband—"

"I know. I speak for the Women of America, not merely for myself." She stared off at nothing. Her hand moved to her lower abdomen, long fingers splayed across the black velvet, that hid her belly. Holding herself, she felt a shifting, as though foundation stones were moving within.

"Lee," she was calmer now, "There is nothing in between! I have researched this, I read Germaine Greer's *The Change.* Are you old enough to know Germaine? A bee-you-tiful woman—one of our leading liberated ladies—pardon!—women. Men used to gnash their teeth and moan: 'What a waste!' They thought Women's Libbers had given up fucking. Her picture's on the back of this newest book. Depressing. Germaine has chosen Crone-ism, is opposed to hormone replacement therapy. But if my hot flashes don't disappear quick, I may try it. And I will be damned if I want to become a Crone-Hag or a Social X-ray!" She collapsed on the sofa. "So, Lee, what do I do?"

"You'll figure something."

Lee waited. Brit lit a cigarette, staring again at nothing. Lee saw she avoided looking at herself in the mirror.

"Now, Rhodes, shall I read your cards, or pack them up and leave you to wallow in misery?"

"Sorry, Sweetie."

"No, you're entitled, Rhodes. You're right. It sucks."

"Oh! That feels better. Now, how about you read my fortune?"

Lee smiled, then leaned across, hugged her, "You know I love you."

"I love you too."

Lee straightened the cards. "At the beginning, you have The Fool."

"Great."

"Be calm, Rhodes. Let's see what it says." Lee ducked her head to read, her silk hair falling forward. She raised her head. "Maybe it is you."

"Terrific. A Fool." Despair in her voice. *Having an affair with a drinking-doping younger man...only a fool...*

"It says, 'I know I want to do something but I don't know what it is.'" Lee raised her eyebrows. "Any bells ringing, Britannia?"

"Yeah. Big Ben."

Lee laughed. "There's more. 'On a tiny island, a carefree youth leans against a great tree. The island symbolizes individuality, safety, and isolation.'" Lee made a sweeping gesture. "Brit's island–this farm, her safety, her isolation."

"I get it. Continue."

'The tree is life and knowledge. The trunk is the same color as the boy; they are one entity.' You are that boy, Brit. 'The boy gazes up into the rich foliage of the tree whose fruits are symbols of the five elements. The branches indicate the infinite choice of opportunities and directions. In the surrounding sea, there are similar islands, each supporting a tree...' Then it says, 'I am the unlearned and they can learn from me.'"

"In other words," laughed Brit, "I don't know shit–yet, I know it all?"

"Something like that." Lee looked up, black eyes plaintive. "I've never done this before, Brit."

Britannia smoked, looked at the fire. "You're doing fine. What's next?" She pulled off her glasses. "Damn. My fire's going out. Literally." She leaped up, a graceful arc of black velvet, grabbed the poker. Prodding aside the mesh curtains she poked the log. It tumbled, a flame wavered up and, like incense, woodsmoke drifted into the room. She hefted another log, laid it across the half-burned one, slapped her hands to dust off ashes. Then she took giant steps over the dog, the gifts, back to the sofa.

"What else you got, Girl?"

"I got–this." Lee picked up a card, Brit stuck her glasses back on her nose and looked at it.

"A Virgin? Me?"

"I don't think it's necessarily referring to your sex life, Brit."

"Oh. So what does it say?"

"Wait a minute. Take a look at the art here. This could be you. You on this farm of yours."

Beyond the French doors darkening clouds ate up the weak February light.

The perimeter forest grew blacker.

On the card Lee pointed out the sights. "Here's your forest, with a full moon behind it and that's you, nude, asleep on your plateau, forest surrounding you."

Brit thought of this morning. In all these years on her farm she'd never ridden naked, but many nights she'd sat out on her verandah naked, drinking wine, watching the moonrise. Smoking, listening to frog songs.

A rose dangled from the virgin's hand, a drop of blood dripped from a finger. *Some pain coming,* Brit wondered? *And what was the significance of the furled fan beneath the woman?* She pushed the card back at Lee. "What does it mean, Lee?"

"'A pale, naked young girl dreams in a moonlit forest.'"

"Young? Not me. Not after today."

"Brit. You're young, younger than a lot of the twenty-year-olds I work with–your mind is young. Do you want me to read these cards or should we pause for a whine session?"

"Sorry. I'll hush."

"Okay–her flowing hair is 'the symbol of the release of unconscious emotions.' And 'ten great trees protect and shelter her.' Ten. Ten–that's significant, I think. Let's see what ten means." Lee riffled through the pages. "Here it is. Oh God. Don't get depressed."

"Don't keep me hanging."

Lee took a deep breath. "Okay. Ten. 'The passing of perfection.'"

"You can say that again." Brit stubbed out her cigarette, lit another. Her hand shook.

"Go on."

"Okay. 'Collapse and disintegration–'" Lee's eyes widened, her voice rose, "'–lead…to a completely new beginning.'"

"I need one. But do I have to collapse and disintegrate to get it?"

"Wait! The next card is One of Water. One is 'the start or birth of something.' And, 'Excitement at the birth of new feelings. Love awakening. A great release of emotional energy after a period of control.' Feel better?"

"Sure. I am about to become a foolish virgin again, I lay around naked in my forest, everything's going to collapse, but I'll have a new beginning. That got it?" She smiled. "But I don't see how in the hell I can become a virgin again."

"Oh, you can! Anyone who goes six weeks without sex automatically reverts to virgin status."

Brit flung her head back and laughed uproariously. "I love it! I love it! With

Scottie around, however, I don't see how anything like that's going to happen. Unless—"

She looked away. *Unless pouty-lips at the TV station gets her false fingernails into him.* She hated feeling jealous. She looked back at Lee.

"You, Lee, must be pure as driven snow. How long's it been?"

"Seven months…since I broke up with Richard. I am pure. And sometimes I feel driven." They laughed. Then Lee sighed.

Britannia reached and squeezed her hand. She'd helped Lee through the breakup of her eight-year affair with Richard. When Lee began calling him "Dick" Brit knew her friend was over it.

Brit took her hand back as Lee spoke. "Don't panic, but a little warning here from this One of Water. Beware of…gullibility, one-sided love.'"

"Oh shit. Scottie doesn't love me! How could he? I'm a fifty-year-old woman! No one loves a fifty-year-old woman…not in America anyway."

Lee's hand to Brit's knee. "Brit. Quit. No one would ever suspect you're fifty!"

"That's the problem. If I looked fifty no one would love me. If I don't look fifty, yet I am, and I tell a potential lover my age, he won't love me."

Her head down, she started to cry. "And that's awful, you see? To you I look forty, okay, fine, I'm a teeny bit flattered. But what happens when I'm sixty? Do I then face the horror of looking fifty? When I'm sixty? And on and on. When the fuck does it end?"

She blotted her face with tissue. "You're only thirty, Lee, you look twenty-five—"

"I see what you mean…we can never be…what we are…"

"Yes." The tissue was blue.

"Brit. Your face is blue," Lee pointed out. Brit looked at the tissue in her hand, balled it up, tossed it across the room. "Matches my feelings." Wilton woke, retrieved the tissue, dropped it back in her lap. She laughed, patting him. "Thanks, chum."

She sat shredding damp tissue. "Okay…tell me about the fan," and she pointed at the Virgin card.

"Ah! That is not a fan. That is the '…leaves of a book as yet unread…' You've got lots more living to do." She looked at Brit and smiled. "Your face really is blue."

"So? Queen Bodicea painted her face blue then led the Picts to war against the Romans. She did it before Mel Gibson, too. What do these other cards mean?"

"I knew that—I told you about the blue queen, remember? Britannia, this can't be rushed, these cards have many-layered meanings. The Virgin card also says, 'I am shame and I am boldness/I am shameless and I am ashamed.'"

"My attitude with Scottie, exactly. I don't know if I can take anymore of this. Lee, I feel uneasy—"

Stones grating against one another, like the crusts of continents grinding.

"Okay," said Lee, "hang in, I'll condense. Here's a male person. This guy is sitting on the 'plume of Maat' signifying 'truth and justice.' Gotta be Grant. He's a lawyer."

"Yeah, Honey, Grant's a lawyer, which has nothing to do with truth and justice."

They laughed. Brit continued. "Besides, I haven't thought about Grant in four years. All I know, he's out there trying to inject his ejaculate into young women in the belief this will magically restore his youth."

"Grant's successful."

"With work, yes."

"But with younger women?"

"I don't know for sure. I've heard gossip, that's all. Sugarplum."

"Sugarplum? Gawd! You can't believe her."

"She knows people in New Orleans. Sometimes she gets it right."

"When? In the fleeting moment when the valium and the wine happen to wear off at the exact same time?"

"Sugarplum *is* difficult."

"Difficult? Are you getting senile? She's a using-taking bitch! Brit, she's always trying to rip you off! Did she ever pay you for those prints of yours she's got hanging on her wall? Did she ever pay you for breeding your stallion to her mares?"

"Well, Mokh enjoys it…"

"Doesn't matter! If she bred to an outside stallion, it'd cost her thousands! You're not rich…Al's trust doesn't even cover expenses now that Asia's in college. You need that money, Brit. You need to start sticking up for yourself. Don't let her mow you down! Now, back to Grant."

"Let's quit talking about Grant, okay? Between you and Mother—" Lee looked at her sharply.

"Viola's talking about Grant?"

"Yes. She mentioned him today. I can't imagine why. She hasn't said his name in months."

"Viola has depths, Brit. Don't discount her just because she's your slightly controlling mom. And there's more about this guy who might be Grant. He's 'helpful to those he believes have talent and ability.'"

"Not Grant." She squashed out another cigarette. "He was jealous of my art, and the time I put into it."

"Listen, it says, 'Negatively, may dominate or crush unwittingly those he helps.'"

"That's Grant. Especially the unwitting part. Grant, for all his smarts—and there is some kind of mind beneath that thick dome of his—is probably the most oblivious trampler of emotions I've ever met. I'll give you an example. Grant looks at every woman, any age, any size, that crosses his path. Once I saw him scrutinizing a middle-aged woman, little bit dumpy, you know? For a change, instead of getting angry, I asked him: 'Grant. What do you see in that woman that's sexy?' And he said, never taking his eyes off her, 'If you look really hard you can always find one good part.'" She drained her champagne flute, then examined the bottle. It was empty, so she upended it in the bucket. "Grant's gone, Lee, he'll never enter my life again."

"One question. Why were you with him?"

"At first I didn't see this—tick of his—and oddly, he was a faithful husband. But it was my body that loved him, Lee, my fickle, fickle body. It sees him, it thinks about him, there's a click, and my motor's running."

"Still?"

"I don't want to find out." She tapped the cards. "Read on. Find something good in this mess."

"Okay. Now this card must be Anastasia. Has she called yet?"

"Not yet. I'm giving her another hour, then I'll call her."

"'An adolescent girl stands naked, in an attitude of partial concealment.' Definitely Asia. 'Wings on her head signify imagination, speed of thought, flights of fancy.'"

"It kind of fits."

"'Drops of water and blood show initiation and the awakening of sexuality.' Does she date?"

"As far as I know—not. Asia, being so odd—I don't know if she can handle 'awakening sexuality.' She's getting so beautiful, it's scary. I worry about…seduction. Even—rape. She trusts. She has no mechanism for filtering out bullshit."

"Sometimes we don't either. Besides, you talk as if she was some sort of mental case, Brit. Good God. She went through depression for a while, she's a little shy and introverted. That's all."

"I know, I know. But I worry." She tapped the cards. "Anything else?"

"Yes. 'Emotionally naive and vulnerable. Negatively, lonely and/or exploited.' Is she lonely at LSU?"

"Don't think so. Loves zoology. But in middle school, I found out she'd been picked on, teased. Not one of her teachers told me, not till she was leaving the school. They did nothing to stop it. How can people–teachers!–stand by and watch a little girl suffer? What kind of a lesson is that to the teasers? And Saunders never said a word. He went to the same school–he had to know kids were doing this." Brit lit a cigarette.

Lee studied the cards. "Here's an interesting one. 'A powerful shaman...is the instrument of communication between spiritual heaven and material earth.' Brit. You're the Shaman! You've got it all–the mind, the talent, the sensitivity, the trust fund!–this is you. 'He–She–is above the swirling black clouds and able to see clearly what is hidden from others.' Your future, Brit. You'll be able to see clearly. It also says, 'I am alone in the universe; no one else can share this experience. For a brief moment, I can see everything clearly and my life is changed.' Wow."

"When is this great ability going to come to me?"

Lee waved her hand. "Sometime in the future."

Brit pointed at the cards. "All this is going to happen, all these people, me, the virgin in the forest dripping blood, my naive daughter, the heartless young man, the truth and justice guy, all this terrifying change, then suddenly I'll be able to see clearly. Is that it?"

"Yes. I think that about gets it. But wait...there's one more."

Brit covered her blue face with her hands. "Oh no."

"Stop it now. This one is really terrific. You will achieve victory! You have a 'fighting spirit' and there are 'waving flags and banners.' Brit, your next show is going to be a great success. Feel better?"

"Nope. I don't want to think about my work. I haven't had a fresh idea in two years."

Lee pulled a mock pout. "You don't like my birthday present?"

"Oh, Sweetie," Brit leaned forward and hugged her friend. "I love it. The art on the cards is beautiful." She leaned away. "I've been...off...the past few weeks." She plucked the hat from her head, ran a hand through her hair. "I don't know—have you ever had a gnawing feeling, a foreboding?"

Lee nodded as the phone rang, muffled. They searched through cushions. Lee found it and said hello.

Grinning. "Oh hi, Scottie. Sure. Right here." She handed it to Brit.

"Hi." Brit fell silent. While she murmured "uh-huh," Lee slid a card with a young man on it and the words, "Black seeds lie dormant," back into the deck. Brit talking, "Okay. I'm sorry too. Bye, Scottie." She dropped the phone, face rigid.

"Brit, honey, what is it?"

She shook her blue-streaked face.

"C'mon, Rhodes, what's wrong?"

"Scottie has to go to Biloxi to shoot some stupid thing about gambling—with that new anchorwoman. Tonight. They will be staying overnight. The two of them."

"So? Scottie cares about you. He's not going to have sex with her, for God's sake. You're imagining stuff that will never happen. Quit!"

"I've seen how she looks at him. Predatory. Licking her poufy, collagen-injected lips. Scottie won't be able to resist. He'll feel bad, and he may even want to come back to me, but I can't have an affair on those terms, Lee. I really can't. What a hell of a birthday!"

"Hey, Brit! You're writing this script! This stuff has not happened!"

Their conversation was interrupted by a harsh voice as a black and white Great Dane padded into the room, "HEY! Y'ALL!" Pink tongue flapping, it clambered over the sofa back and licked Brit's face. Wil whined, godd rose from red tissue hissing and streaked from the room. Lee rolled her eyes.

"Mime, Mime! Down girl," Brit was saying as Sugarplum Lewis walked into the room.

"MIME! GET DOWN!" Sugarplum continued her roar. Mime crouched on the sofa, head on Brit's lap, tail wagging. Wil's excitement grew. He focused on the wagging tail, loving Mime.

"WELL. GUESS I'VE MISSED THE PARTY!" Lee was raising her hands to cover her ears when Brit shook her head. Lee lowered her hands, crossed her arms.

"CHAMPAGNE ALL GONE?"

Brit started to rise but Lee motioned her down. "I'll get it."

Sugarplum was red-haired, four foot eleven, but she swaggered into the room like John Wayne. She wore tight white jeans with a matching jacket open over a pink tank top. It showed generous breasts with obvious nipples.

Sugarplum was fifty-two years old. She looked a hard forty.

She leaned over the sofa back and kissed Brit. She'd been thrilled to have her hysterectomy, wore hormone replacement patches, worked hard to keep herself young-looking and hated sex. Her forgiving, kindly husband traveled a lot.

"Happy Birthday, Honey," she whispered. "Brought yah something," and handed Brit two marijuana cigarettes tied with a pink bow. "How come you got a BLUE FACE?"

"She's Queen Bodicea," said Lee.

"OH. Mardi Gras costume." Sugarplum looked around at the gifts. "Looks like you CLEANED up, Sweetie. NICE suit. Chanel or KNOCK-OFF?"

"Knock-off. Mother's gift."

"STILL. Real NICE."

"How's your mares?"

Sugarplum was organizing herself on the sofa between Brit and Lee. She moved Brit's ashtray, took one of the gift marijuana cigarettes from Brit and lit it. After a deep drag she handed it to Brit, teeth clenched in a smoke-holding smile. Lee leaned back–she refused to smoke marijuana with Sugarplum.

"Mares are great. Happy Birthday, Girl," on the exhale. "Real PREGNANT-looking, Nadia's so BIG I'm SCARED it's TWINS. Come SEE 'em–after all, Mokhtar's the DADDY."

"Planning to give Brit a check today, Sugarplum?" asked Lee, her tone vinegar.

Sugarplum's head whipped around. "CHECK? For WHAT?"

"You've got three pregnant mares. Appears to me you owe her about three thousand dollars."

"I THINK NOT, LEE! Brit wouldn't DREAM of charging MONEY for such a thing! Mokhtar will be IMMORTALIZED by these foals. Besides, LEE, Britannia and I go BACK MANY years–THIS arrangement was BASED on LOVE, not MONEY!"

"The stallion has to eat, twice a day, Sugarplum. Costs Brit money. You'll be getting three valuable colts–"

"COLTS!? I sure as HELL don't want colts! Only FILLIES."

Brit had begun to grin. "Lee, Sugarplum can't stand the male sex whether it's got two legs or four."

Sugarplum gave Brit a hurt look. "NOW that's JUST NOT TRUE, Brit."

Brit touched her knee. "Kidding."

Sugarplum instructed. "A colt is a young MALE horse, Lee. A FOAL is either gender, and a FILLY–I LOVE my GIRLS–is a young FEMALE horse."

"Thank you, Sugarplum. From now on I'll watch what I say around you."

Sugarplum's black eyes lashed across Lee as she stood. "Gotta go, Britannia, FEEDING TIME. Just wanted to POP IN and LET you KNOW I haven't FORGOTTEN YOU." She bent to exchange air kisses. "Any SKETCHES lyin' AROUND?"

"No, Shug, wish there were, but I haven't had an idea in months."

Lee rolled her eyes. Sugarplum raided Brit's studio, taking sketches because she thought they might be valuable some day. It aggravated Lee.

"BYEE, Brit, you look FABULOUS for FIFTY–ain't so BAD is it, sweetie? Just NEVER tell ANYONE how OLD you are. DON'T give the ASSHOLES ANYTHING to JUDGE you BY!" She was around the corner, the front door was opening, Mime leaped over the sofa. "Come SEE the GIRLS, HEAR?"

The door slammed.

"How can you stand her?"

"We go way back, old horse show buddies. She's an unhappy woman, Lee."

"I'm changing the subject. I have an idea about dinner."

FOURTEEN

Jane Stachs held Saunders' backpack. She knocked on the door of Room 129.

A chain rattled. The door opened a few inches, Saunders peered around it. A guileless grin and her knees went all melty.

"Jane. Come in."

"Hi. I brought your backpack."

"Great." He disappeared and the door gaped wider. She saw Madonna grabbing her breasts and writhing on TV, sound respectfully low. She stepped in, happy he liked MTV too.

The curtains were drawn tight over the window and no bedside lamp was on, so except for the light from the television set, the room was dark. She blinked. Suddenly Saunders stood before her. All he seemed to be wearing was an oversized black T-shirt printed with three contorted deaths heads. His legs were bare, muscular, covered with red hair.

God! Is that an erection poking out the front of his T-shirt?

She felt nervous. Before she could react, his arm encircled her waist and she was pulled against him. The backpack fell from her hand. She could feel his penis press on her thigh. *My God, he is strong for a short guy!* He kissed her and his tongue, thick and hard, stabbed into her mouth. He was panting. He half dragged her over to the bed and as he pushed her down she cried, "No!"

His mouth came down on hers again, so engulfing she gagged. It was impossible to make a sound. She grabbed handfuls of T-shirt on his backside, trying to pull him off. His hand scrabbled at her skirt, shoved it up. *He is naked under the T-shirt,* she thought wildly. He ripped open the crotch of her pantyhose, penis jabbing painfully against her pubic bone, again and again until it found her vagina. He forced himself in. It hurt, her vagina was dry, and she wondered as she began to cry, *Doesn't it hurt him, too?*

But after a few short, painful shoves he collapsed on top of her. She felt a flood of shame. She shoved against his chest.

"Let me up! I want to go!" she sobbed. He rolled off her, then put a hand on her bra.

"Don't rush off. I can get it up again in a minute."

She jumped up pulling her skirt down, trembling, yelling, "You little creep! Have you ever heard of AIDS? Do you know what a condom is?"

He eyed her lazily, eyes silver, irises black pinpoints.

"Sure I know. I don't have AIDS."

"How old are you anyway?" Her crying subsided. She figured only a raw kid would have that short a fuse.

A smirk came on his face. "How old do you think I am?"

Oh, shit. Game playing.

"I think you lied when you checked in. I don't think you're anywhere near eighteen."

He stared at her, eyes blank. *Christ,* she thought, *only lizards could go so long without blinking.* She folded her arms across her chest.

"I'm not going to play kiddie games with you, you little fuck–but I'll tell you what, bud, you fuck like a twelve-year-old."

He came at her, and his fist caught her on the temple, hard. She fell. Then he was down on the floor stroking her back and, almost tenderly, helping her to her feet.

"Hey, Jane, I'm sorry."

She was dizzy. He was pulling her back to the bed. But she resisted and he let go. Then he stepped back and flopped onto the bed, green light from the TV rippling over him, T-shirt rucked up, penis moving like a drowsy snake. She took a wobbly step toward the door.

"Hey. Jane. Stick around." His hand moved down to his penis.

She took another step and he uncoiled from the bed and grabbed her arm. She wrenched it away and raised her face to him, tears coming.

"What you just did is rape."

His eyes widened, but his expression didn't change. She smelled old french fries on his breath. Eyes dull as neglected pewter, he stared down at her.

"You wanna talk 'rape,' Jane? Try this one on. I'm not eighteen. I'm fifteen."

Jane's hand flew to her mouth. *Could statutory rape go the other way?* She slumped against the door. He bore down on her. Behind her back, her hand felt for the knob.

"How old are you, Jane? Twenty-four? Twenty-five?"

"Twenty-three." Her voice was a hoarse croak.

"Close enough. If there's gonna be any talk of rape around here, Jane," he jabbed a thick index finger at her then into the skulls on his chest, "then you are guilty of statutory rape—of me. See Jane, my dad's a lawyer. I know all about this stuff." He moved closer. She pressed against the door. He turned his broad hand, index finger still extended and poked her left breast.

"Got—that—Jane?" Stab. Stab. Stab. She nodded, bearing the pain. Her hand was on the doorknob now. Moving sideways, she opened the door and he retreated from the light she let in, almost dissolving in the gloom of his room. MTV squealed behind him, light strobing behind his body. As she backed out she saw a gleam of teeth, a smile? Then he raised a hand and like a child opened and closed his fingers over his palm, bye bye. As she slammed the door she heard him.

"Bye-bye, Janey. Thanks for stopping by with my backpack."

She stumbled away, his greasiness oozing between her legs. With a sob she realized she'd have to work the next two hours with the crotch ripped out of her pantyhose.

FIFTEEN

Grant pulled up in front of the Wiffins' Upperline home at one. He'd had to hustle. He'd taken the streetcar to the condo for his car, skipping lunch, and hangovers made him ravenous. But this caper shouldn't take long. He was stepping out of the car to walk to the front door when Juliette Wiffins stepped onto her columned entryway. He almost whistled, seeing how she'd gotten her nickname. From here she didn't look fat or in her fifties.

Petite, provocative, she paused on the brick landing, dwarfed yet empowered by her soaring white columns. Her vast, costly yard spread out from her to Grant's feet, a giant carpet. *The real estate alone was worth about a mil, and*, Grant thought, *underutilized. She needed a bolder gardener for sure–clumps of azaleas and overgrown ligustrum? C'mon.* Looking closer, he saw the lawn needed thatching.

Her gold hair was like a helmet. She wore a full-length fur, dark and rich–had to be sable. Her legs gleamed in silken hose and her tiny feet were mounted on stiletto-heeled sling-backs. As she teetered toward him he caught the dazzle of diamonds at her ears, throat, wrist. He smelled the leading edge of her *Joy.* She was ready to take her man. Or–Grant thought with a queasy shudder–to be taken out by her man.

He moved to greet her, help her along the brick walk. She accepted his hand and with tiny, firm clicks marched to the car. Bending double, Grant opened the door of his red Corvette.

"I must say, Spiffy, you're looking quite terrific."

"Why thank you, Grant. I do hope so." Her voice was low, her usual squeak vanished. She stepped down from the curb, smiled dazzlingly, and rotating her hips, lowered them into the car. The sable splayed open. Grant gasped. The hose ended at mid-thigh and, from there to a round pink belly, Spiffy was nude. He saw curly blonde hair glinting under her belly.

"Mrs. Wiffins–Spiffy–my God! What have you got on under that coat?"

She seated herself, pulled the coat back around her, and smiled up at him.

"Stockings."

"That's all?"

"Yes. It's Alf's favorite outfit on me."

"I–I bet it is, Spiffy." Grant's throat was dry, his collar squeezed his neck, and, as he closed the door, he thought of a third horrendous possibility: What if Alf caught him driving a near-naked Mrs. Wiffins? Alf would get everything, Spiffy nothing, his career would be ruined. *Oh my God–what had he gotten into?* Shaken, he stood. *Breathe, Grant, breathe.*

He squared his shoulders and marched around to his side of the car. Just as he reached for his door handle he was nearly sideswiped by a black kid on a bike. He had to press his body against the car. His heart pounded. The kid laughed, riding on, no hands. Grant called out, too late, "Hey, watch where you're going!" The kid's lighthearted "Sorry, Man" trailed behind him.

Grant jerked his door open, muttering that no one was safe on the streets while also wondering if he, also, should watch where he was going. *Existentially speaking, where was he going? And, would he be a sorry man?*

He wedged himself into the 'Vette, wondering again about this damn car. It didn't seem engineered for a six-foot four-inch human.

Women, well some anyway, purred when they got a load of it.

His sexy red machine came to life.

"This is some car you've got, Grant," Spiffy purred.

"Thanks." He was ducking his head to see out of the rearview, waiting for a rattly yardman's truck to pass, praying the guy wouldn't dent the 'Vette. The truck got past. He pulled out and headed for St. Charles, figuring the quickest route to Airline Highway. Spiffy was saying, "–but don't you find it's a little uncomfortable for a man of your height?"

"Just getting in and out–" he glanced companionably down at her, and his eyes widened. Her sable had fallen open to reveal one pink-nippled breast.

"Spiffy, please cover yourself!"

Glancing down, she saw her exposed breast and casually drew the sable around her. She smiled pertly up at an aghast Grant.

"Sorry, Grant. I forgot what I was wearing–or rather–not wearing." She giggled.

Then, calm as squash, "Could you please turn on the air conditioning? I don't want my makeup to melt."

"Yes. Certainly. Of course, Spiffy."

Makeup melt! Good grief–he could melt! *A flash of blonde pussy–another of tit–what did she think he was–A Man of Steel?* Then he smiled to himself. *No. He was A Man of Granite, or so Brit said.* He turned on the air conditioning and warily looked at Spiffy. The sable was up to her chin. He breathed in relief, his hand casually frittering up to his toupee. It seemed firmly seated, he'd reapplied it in his private bathroom at the office after his scratching session. Even his contacts felt almost comfortable.

He guessed the only way to get to Airline was to go up St. Charles, right onto Carrollton, (left would put him in the Mississippi River) proceed to the intersection of Tulane, then take a left where Tulane became Airline. It confused tourists, this name change. Of course, the only tourists seeking Airline, Grant thought, would be looking for Adult Book Stores, or more...

They drove in silence. Was Spiffy planning her encounter with Alf? But now

Grant was having flashbacks of Mrs. Wiffins' surprising private parts. Flash–ten-drils of blond hair peeking from beneath the too-generous tummy–his mind shifted to it–an even greater surprise than the blonde pubic hairs. The belly looked nuzzly soft, pink, smooth. He wasn't adjusted to washboard abs, he hadn't yet worked up the desire to lay his head on a washboard. *Had Spiffy had children?* Yes. Two married daughters, no factor in the divorce dispute. Somehow she'd managed those pregnancies with any scaring–flash–a breast glowing in his mind, rosebud nipple…in his office all he'd seen was a short, fat, expensively dressed older woman, maybe noticed her pretty calves, ankles–not that he was contemplating a dalliance with her–*good God, the fallout!* What really surprised him was that at her age she had intimate body parts that held allure. This con-firmed his theory: Every woman no matter how old, thin, fat–you name it–had at least one good part–even if it was only an ear.

Probably her upper thighs had cellulite, her butt sagged, but nevertheless a man could still have a very nice time with that tummy, those hot-pink nipples…

Alf was a fool.

Grant changed lanes in front of Five Happiness restaurant…a place he and Brit'd enjoyed…hadn't been there in years. He began to wonder what other trea-sures, shall we say, mature women hid under tailored exteriors; he wasn't scoring so hot with the young honeys. He shuddered, remembering the young hooker. What about Mrs. Wallace in the law library? She had long legs. That brunette waitress at the Bonne Chance? She had great hips. Brit used to have one hell of a body…

Why, all of a sudden, four years after that raging divorce, was she popping into his mind? Probably, because as much as he'd screwed around pre-Brit and aprés-Brit–he'd never had sex of that caliber. *Cut it out Grant, everyone knows older women can't get wet.*

He stopped where Tulane became Airline. Traffic raced across the intersection. Spiffy was sunk into her sable. Had her bravado ebbed? He tapped his fingers on the steering wheel. It was freezing in the car, but he better not touch the A/C. Light took forever. At one time the intersection before him, old Highway 90, had been the way into New Orleans, and the motels he'd soon encounter on Airline were places where mom and dad and the kids could stay, reasonably, during their New Orleans vacation. Now hookers prowled a strip of XXX peep shows, adult bookstores. Former family motels advertised waterbeds and porno movies.

This strip summed up his life. He shuddered. Family life in the country with

Brit, Saunders, Anastasia, had transmogrified to nightly drunks, screwing around…he was starring in his own dirty movie. Last night's booze still oozed from his pores. His stomach tightened–had he finally contracted AIDS?

Not a good father, either.

Even with frigid air blasting his face, his forehead was stippled with sweat. He'd have to make some changes. By God–after he (hopefully) reunited Spiffy and Alf–tonight, this very night, he'd start. Go straight home. Shower all this sour booze away, take Saunders to dinner, a movie. Really talk with the boy. Really–for a change–listen.

And no booze.

The light changed. On the ramp to Airline, Spiffy squeaked, so he glanced down at her. She'd burrowed so low only her eyes looked out. Fear. It had to be–she had a lot to be afraid of. Then suddenly his fear came back. *Jesus Christ! His big mouth! How in hell had he gotten into this?* But he reached over, carefully petted a fur knee, and spoke dolorously.

"Hang in there, Spiffy. We're almost to the home stretch. You look sensational."

"Peep."

He tooled past motels that had attracted all those families years ago. The Old London Lodge, the Travel Inn, The Sleepy Hollow Motel. Then he passed their destination, The Texas Motel. Spiffy was mute beside him. On he went until, finally, he saw a turnaround. He put on his blinker and eased over. Traffic this time of day was light so, sooner than he wanted, he made the turn. The clock on the dash read 1:40, which left twenty minutes for surveillance. He pulled into the right lane, slowed to twenty and checked the parking lots of each motel–The Trade Winds, The Sugar Bowl Motor Court, The Candlelight Inn, The Deep South Motel. He slowed to ten. The Texas Motel had its vacancy sign on. He looked around. Everything seemed quiet. A quick scan of rooftops revealed no glints of rifle barrels. Then he saw the rump of a white car sprouting TV, car-phone, CB, and radio antennas. Alf's limo, parked deep in the heart of The Texas Motel parking lot. It jutted past the purple pickup next to it. Big Earl lounged against the trunk, a toothpick in his mouth.

"There's Earl!" Spiffy cried, grabbing his arm. "Grant, it's going to be all right! Alf's in a room with Earl on the lookout. Earl's so sweet. He wouldn't harm a mosquito."

Grant wasn't so sure. He'd always wondered why Alf needed a former Saint–a defensive tackle–as a chauffeur. The few times he'd encountered Earl he'd thought Earl had…undertones. Earl knew Grant's red 'Vette. Then Earl straightened and his left hand emerged from his sportcoat holding a…? Cell phone. Jawing the toothpick aside, he raised it to his lips. Was he talking to Alf in the room? Wasn't that a bit much? Alf was so melodramatic.

The 'Vette smoozed past The Texas and Grant's palms sweated on the steering wheel. He found another turnaround at the base of the overpass, and again drove past the sleazy motels, trying to think. He could find a pay phone, call The Texas Motel, ask for Alphonso Wiffins, and see what happened. Or, drop Spiffy at The Texas Motel, and gun the 'Vette the hell out of there. That was attractive. Three, he could be a man, drive Spiffy up beside the limo, get out, say "Hi, Earl," hand the lady out, escort her to whatever door Alf hid behind, have a calm reasonable discussion with the little guy, observe the possible happy reunion of Spiffy/Pucci/Alf, and depart. He decided Three was the most lawyerly. Also the only option A Man of Granite–to expand Brit's label beyond its original erotic meaning–could chose. He rode back to Texas.

"Okay now, Spiffy, get ready. I am going to calmly drive up behind Earl, help you out–for God's sake keep that coat closed–ask Earl where Alf is, then you and I will walk to the correct door and knock. Got it?"

She squeaked.

He took it she assented. And…there's The Texas Motel. His stomach flipped. He signaled a right, then nosed into the lot. His stomach flopped. Earl unlounged his vastness from the haunch of the limo to wide-legged attention. His upper arms were so beefy his hands couldn't touch his sides. Slowly Earl laid the phone among the antennas. Flexing gigantic shoulders, his hands curled into fists the size of boxing gloves. Grant forced a dry-lipped smile and nudged Spiffy. "Smile!" he hissed between clenched teeth.

She obliged.

He pulled up at an angle to Earl and gave a cheery wave. Was Earl glowering? He moved the steering wheel up, swung his door open and ducked his head to his knees, the only way he could jackknife himself out of the car. Immediately his head was clamped in hot polyester. He couldn't breath. Earl had his head in the vise of his arm. Clawing at the suffocating beef he felt his hairpiece move. Then his body was unpleated from the car–shoulders, waist, hips–ouch! A knee banged on the steering wheel–knees to ankles, shit!–and his feet were dragged from the car. His knees hit the pavement with a crack. His long body, accordioned into partial-fetal, was lugged across the smelly parking lot, ruining the knees of his

Armani. Asphalt, then a yellow line, passed before his eyes, not, thank God, his life. He felt the terrible scuffing the toes of his Gucci's were taking. Spiffy was squeaking wildly from the 'Vette. Earl hauled him upright, flung him against the limo. Grant slumped against the car and slid till his rump hit pavement. Gasping for air, he sat, knees up to his chin and felt for his hairpiece. Awry. Hands shaking, he tried to swivel it into place. *Damn*–there went one of his contacts!

Basso profundo, from above. "Up. Assume the position!"

Position? Blearily, he looked up at the polyester mountain.

"Position?" He had an idea it wasn't something sexy.

Earl boomed. "The position, man! Up against the motherfuckin' car!"

That position.

"Earl" cried Grant, "don't move for a minute, please! I lost a contact." Silence. Earl's legs looked like the pillars under the new St. Charles on-ramp.

"You lost a contact?"

"Yes."

"Freeze right there. I'll take a look." Size fourteen snakeskin cowboy boots rose on tiptoe, the huge knees bent, Earl's torso dropped, two fingers contacted asphalt. The entire edifice that was Earl was on two fingers–as though once more in the lineup, Saints vs. Falcons. Gently he brushed his free hand over the asphalt. Grunting, he painstakingly covered the ground between Grant and the open door of the 'Vette.

"Got it!"

The huge knees unbent, the huge body rose up past Grant's line of vision. His contact lens came in sight, glinting on the tip of a finger the size of Dorignac's Cajun sausage. Grant plucked up the lens.

"Thanks, Earl."

He spit on it, leaned forward, popped the lens in. His eye teared violently.

"Up against the car, motherfucker!"

Oh shit. On trembling legs, Grant stood, turned, and slapped his palms against the trunk. *Goddamn, the metal was hot!*

"Part 'em."

Shuffling, he moved his legs astraddle. Spiffy's squeaks had reached a higher pitch and suddenly they merged with shrill woofs. *Pucci? Had she smelled her mistress, Spiffy's Joy reaching out for her?* Briskly Earl patted Grant down. Grant heard a motel door bang open. More woofs, and the hurried scritch of tiny toenails. He looked under his armpit and saw a white and black mop skittle across the lot.

A boom from behind–"I say you could move?" Earl shoved his shoulder and Grant quickly stared back down at the trunk. Then, "Pucci ! Oh Pucci! My sweet little Pucci! Mama is so happy to see her little poochie-woochie."

Then, "Goddammit, Earl, let go of Mr. Griffin! Spiffy! Release that dog!"

Grant pushed up from the car and carefully turned around. *Caution was essential, and dignity must be regained.* He straightened his shoulders, adjusted his tie, shot his cuffs and, head up, slowly advanced upon petite, big-nosed Alf. *No sudden moves here,* thought Grant as he raised his right hand to the "shake" position. Alf looked up at him, looked at his hand, then past him. Grant saw Alf's eyes widen, Alf's eyebrows shoot up, and his mouth make a giant "O."

In trepidation Grant turned, saw Mrs. Wiffins, and swiftly turned away. But he'd seen enough–she held the sable open–he knew what Alf gaped at. He glanced at Earl, who was studying cloud formations.

Just as Alf was regaining the power of speech–or at least, the power of sound–gargling came from the "O"–Spiffy snapped her sable closed and, like a model down a runway, moved toward Alf, her slung-back stilettos going snick, snick, snick, with each deliberate, voluptuous step.

Grant swiveled his eyes from Alf to Big Earl. Earl watched non-existent traffic. Was Alf going to embrace Spiffy or strangle her? Mesmerized, Grant watched her progress, with only the smallest tingle in his groin, her walk hip-swayingly seductive.

Alf's nose had turned boiled-crawfish red. Was it lust? Or murderous rage?

"Alf," said Spiffy, in the husky seductive tone she'd used when Grant picked her up. Had Alf's knees sagged?

"Alphonso." Snick…snick…snick. She stopped before him, sable undulating.

Grant watched her back: lush fur shimmering in the sunlight, diamonds glittering at her wrists, sun bouncing off her blonde head. She and Alf were eyeball to eyeball, and the fur parted one more time. Alf's pupils moved down, pulled by enormous gravity. Suddenly, a high quaver, "Oh. Oh. Oh. Juliette. My Juliette!" Grant winced. He could bet what was coming.

"Alfie, oh, Alfie, Alfie, Alfie–my Romeo." Grant winced. *You would think a Newcomb grad could do better.* But Alf's skinny arm snaked around her furred waist and whisked her from sight. In the doorway, Alf glared at Grant, then Earl, then slammed the motel door shut. Neither Grant nor Earl moved. A second later, the door banged open and Alf scooped up Pucci. He glared, fierce.

"Griffin!"

"Sir!"

"I want you to tear up them goddamned divorce papers, hear?"

"Yes, sir!" Grant nodded, thinking, *I will need Spiffy's signature, but that can wait.*

He looked at Earl, hulked apologetically beside him.

"Mr. Griffin...sorry about that 'up against car' shit..."

Graciously, Grant raised a hand. "No problemo, Earl. Thank you for finding my contact."

Earl ducked his bowling ball head. "No problemo, Mr. Griffin."

Their gaze went to the motel door. They heard grating repetitive music–a porn flick soundtrack? Then, "Peep! Squeak! Giggle..."

Grant couldn't resist. "All's well that ends well, Earl."

Earl nodded solemnly. "That's very pretty, Mr. Griffin."

"Thank you, Earl."

Grant spun around and in three strides regained his Corvette. He ignited it, gave Earl a regal wave, and turning onto Airline, floored it. Eight powerful cylinders roared in his eardrums.

Goddamn. He was starving.

SIXTEEN

Solemnly Britannia and Lee handed Sugarplum's gift back and forth. They sucked, held their breath, expelled pungent clouds. Wilton lay between them, head on Brit's lap, worried eyes following the passing of the toke. The wine and the marijuana had caught up with Brit. She'd spent the past hour crying about what Scottie might do with the anchorwoman. Now she lay limp on cushions. Lee kept saying "You don't *know* Scottie is going to succumb to seduction. There are some positives in your Tarot reading." Then Brit blew out a fog of smoke and giggled.

"Feel like an art student again. This stuff's wonderful. See? Sugarplum's not all bad."

Holding her smoke, Lee spoke out the side of her mouth. "Two piddling little marijuana cigarettes for your birthday gift, girl?" Tiny puffs came out between words. "After all you've done for her?" She exhaled the last of the smoke, noisily. "Hell. She should've brought you a bale!"

Britannia smiled with Zen calm, smoked and handed the toke back to her friend.

After taking a hit Lee rummaged in her backpack.

"Tah Dah!" She brandished an envelope, then gave it to Brit. Brit tore it open, took out a card and read, "'Dinner for two at Dakota!' Oh Lee, as they say, you shouldn't have!"

Lee grinned. They bussed.

"Thank you, Sweetie. This is just fabulous."

"Tonight's lobster night."

"You're right! But what are you going to wear? Those jeans and that Saints' sweat shirt won't cut it at Dakota."

"Well...I kinda wondered if I could borrow one of your floaty things...you know...maybe some jewelry?" She pawed through her backpack and held up a gold shoe. "I brought this, and these." Ivory panty hose dangled.

"Goody. We can play dress-up." Brit stood, stretching. "Also, I'm going to count to ten and if Asia doesn't call instantly I'm calling her."

Under a pillow, the phone rang. Lee dug it out and handed it to Brit.

"Hello? Asia!" She covered the receiver and whispered, "We have ESP. She's singing 'Happy Birthday.'" Brit listened, nodding her head, her eyes getting wet. Lee felt a familiar anxious tension in her belly...it happened whenever anything about Asia came up. Asia, a smaller, paler version of Britannia, was a conundrum. Doctors had never diagnosed her, but there had been some form of emotional disorder.

Brit blinked, nodded. "Thanks, Hon. That was great. How are you?" She listened intently to Asia's too-soft voice.

"I'm fine, mom. I aced Latin."

"Great!"

"I mailed you a gift. Did it arrive?"

"Not yet, I'll look forward to it." She thought of Jimmy's death. Better not say anything till Asia came home on her next visit.

"Lee's here. She's taking me for dinner at Dakota, and before that she brought me a man as a birthday card."

A small groan. "Mother. You don't need any help finding men. Tell Lee to return him and get her money back." Brit began to laugh, but Asia continued deadpan, "I wish I was there. I love Dakota. Are you going to check out our cows?"

"Wouldn't miss it, Sweetheart. I'll enjoy them for you."

An acrylic of two Holstein cows, head to head, one with her pink tongue

swishing from her mouth, hung in the restaurant. When Asia was small she'd
called them Mother and Daughter cows.

"I wish you'd buy that picture Mom, and send it to me. Sure would perk up
this dorm."

"Honey, you know I've tried. The artist won't sell. You've got a couple of
Rhodes prints."

"Yes, they're great, but why don't you do something with animals? Cows are
hot right now, aren't they? I see Holstein everywhere."

"So I'd better avoid cows."

"Ah, but, if *you* did cows they'd be unlike anyone else's cows—your beeves
would have subtle depths, existential, mystical auras—"

Britannia laughed in huge, relieved delight. Asia was okay.

"Quit, unruly child! I promise when you come home for Easter we'll hit
Dakota on lobster night and adore the beeves together."

"Excellent. How's Mokh, Wil, godd?"

"Good. They miss you. And the ducks, geese and chickens are fine, too."

"I miss them too. How's old Jimmy?"

Brit choked. "Fine."

A sigh. "I gotta ask. How's Scottie?"

"Don't ask. Instead, how about you? Dating?"

"No. I do have coffee with a gang though, and the male of the species is there."
There was a pause. "Mom. You get so…prickly whenever Scottie's name comes
up. It's okay, you know. I like him."

"Good. Your coffee-klatches sound like fun."

"What you really mean is, they sound safe. Right?"

"Well, yeah—still, I'd like to see you date some nice men." Brit felt her anxiety
that something she'd done had caused Asia's shyness around men. What—? Losing
her father so young? Couldn't trust a man not to abandon her?

"I'm building up to it."

"That's great, Honey. Well, if you're okay, I guess I'd better get ready for my
big night out."

"Happy Birthday, Mother. I love you."

"I love you too, Asia."

"Bye."

"Bye." Brit thumbed the phone off.

"How is she?"

"She sounds great." Both women's shoulders fell to a normal position. Brit clapped her hands. "Wanna play dress-up?"

Lee stood. "Okay, girl." And she sashayed off snapping her fingers, humming *Puttin' on the Ritz.*

S E V E N T E E N

Back in his office Grant worked through a message stack. The minor high he'd experienced from the Spiffy adventure had evaporated. When he could drop by a bar, have just one martini, he'd feel better. A quavering voice inside said, *Grant, honey? Where is your resolve from this morning?* He also dreaded the father-son encounter he'd vowed to have this evening. He just never knew what to say to Saunders. The kid could be so deadpan. Half the time–hell! most of the time–he couldn't figure where the kid was coming from. What did he care about, other than music that sounded like the thunks and roars of a dumpster pickup, singers like wild animals squalling?

He was pretty sure the kid wasn't on drugs, and, as far as he could tell he hadn't begun dating yet. Saunders never mentioned girls. A while back, Grant had had some scary moments, worrying the kid might be gay. Then Saunders had shown an attentive, healthy response to heterosexual sex scenes in rented movies, so he couldn't be that. At times he seemed to–to seethe with resentments. Certainly, some seething was appropriate for his age, but as much as Saunders seemed to contain?

Grant still worried about the early years with Margie, Saunder's mother. Margie, tiny hour-glass figured Margie. Red-headed, blue-blooded Margie, Queen of Comus, the most exclusive of Mardi Gras Krewes. How he'd loved her, and how grateful he'd been that she'd loved him back, the son of Mississippi dirt farmers. He'd brushed off nervous, too-eager smiles from her family, been oblivious to their excessive gratitude to him on the wedding day. So tiny, yet so regal she could have strode the corridors of Versailles. Classic white redhead's skin. Rich auburn hair, falling in coils and ringlets over her pale forehead, spilling over her shoulders, cascading to her waist. Soft and fluttery as bird's wings it fell all over his arms when he hugged her. Soft, too, against his naked skin. Her damask-white body, veins blue and luminous on her coral-tipped, snow-cone breasts. The startling flame at her crotch...and all of her, always framed with that glory of hair. Her eyes, beneath the slanting auburn brows, ringed with thick auburn lashes, were translucent blue, except when the sickness came on her, then they'd shutter and seal dark as jet. Yet when she was well, which she was for four years until Saunders came, they'd laughed and played at house like kids, cooking together, drinking then spilling wine over each other. Her laugh–a joyous gutsy peal that eviscerated him each time he remembered it. Even that glorious laugh had changed, gone strange, acquired an echo when no echo could be there….No one had told him of her schizophrenia. It had come out again while she was pregnant with Saunders. Had his son been harmed, even in the womb? No!

He'd been busy then, working to make partner. Margie had seemed normal…most of the time…had other things happened between her and the infant Saunders with far-reaching effects? *Get honest here, Grant,* said a stern inner voice. *Things did happen between Margie and Saunders. Awful things–too terrible to think about. But all before his third birthday, so young, surely Saunders had no memory of them? Even so, could that stuff have traumatized him?*

Grant remembered a session with Saunders' therapist: "Everything impacts, Mr. Griffin. Children are impacted in the womb–the first eight months of life–" He resisted a quick strobe of memory– blood on the blue bedroom carpet, the iron smell of it, Margie's small arm dangling from the bed, baby Saunders clinging to his unconscious mother, thumb in his mouth, eyes clamped shut. He was surely too young to remember that, wasn't he? But, who knew? Saunders wasn't telling. Not his father. Not even the therapist he'd been seeing since he was what–four? Grant winced. Another flash of Saunders, just before he'd married Brit, still in the Lowerline Street house where they'd lived as a family. Margie was gone to the White Oaks facility. He'd heard eerie whining from the backyard. He ran out through the kitchen, the screen door thwacking behind him. Saunders and the neighbor's puppy–at first he'd thought the puppy was covered in blood–then he saw Saunders' toys, a truck, a front-end loader, splotchily sprayed a dripping red. Saunders was spray painting the puppy. He dashed down the steps, grabbed Saunders and hoisted him high, the puppy mewling. It stared up at him, eyes spray-painted red. *God. It was horrible.* He'd taken the puppy to the vet, Saunders to his pediatrician. When he told the pediatrician what had happened, the doctor had said some scary things. First, that this behavior showed an incipient personality disorder, second, with a mother who herself was schizophrenic and whose family for generations had had schizophrenia, it was a distinct possibility, genetically, that Saunders might have it as well. Get him into therapy, pronto. Grant had. He'd thought that would take care of everything. And Saunders had had Rita to care for him, up till he married Brit. Rita was kind, loving, reliable. Even though Grant had to work late many nights, he knew Rita gave his boy good care. He knew it! And the therapist always told him when he called to check on his son's progress, "It's slow, but we're making headway."

Had he done enough? A stark stab of terror went through him. *Had he failed his son in some terrible, irreparable way?*

He opened his drawer for a Certs and saw a pink booklet titled, *Meetings for Alcoholics Anonymous.* He'd gotten it and a blue-covered book called *Alcoholics Anonymous* months ago at an A.A. office on Tulane. *Not really an original title,* he'd thought, but glancing through it, he saw it was a sort of textbook for those who drink too much. Parts made sense. For a couple of years he'd carried around a growing fear he might be...an alcoholic. But–how could he be? Alcoholics hung out around Camp Street and the Hummingbird Grill in clothes that matched the wrinkled brown bags of *Thunderbird* or *Ripple* they clutched. These were people so addicted to alcohol their entire lives revolved around getting it. His life didn't revolve around it–but he sure as hell wanted that martini. Had some of those sad sacks once had jobs, families, lives–was he addicted?

No!

But perhaps there was an interim phase where a person wasn't addicted–yet. But real addiction, enslavement to alcohol, was on its way? A terrifying thought–he remembered Jack Lemon and Lee Remick in *Days of Wine and Roses,* a movie about alcoholism. Jack–or was it Lee–scrabbling through flower pots, in the dirt, for a hidden bottle. *No pride whatsoever. Christ!*

He'd seen it when he was in his early teens. He'd sat in the chilled theater thinking, *I will never let this happen to me.*

These meetings could maybe help him learn how to drink...sensibly. There was a meeting tonight at a church on St. Charles, not far from his condo. Nice neighborhood. Surely they wouldn't let Camp Street bums into a place like that. The winos gave him a sleazy feeling. He closed the booklet, replaced it in the drawer, and forgot to get a Certs.

EIGHTEEN

Saunders left the Lakeshore Motel and hitched to the mall at Covington's I-12 exit on 190. Remnants of pine and magnolia woods backed the mishmash of stores and service stations. Sitting in the window at Burger King he ate two Whoppers. Clouds were rolling in. *He might get lucky. Rain by nightfall.*

NINETEEN

As Britannia and Lee were led to the smoking section of Dakota, Brit again vowed she'd quit smoking, if only to sit in the non-smoking section. Deep teal walls, good paintings by local artists, palms, heavy white tablecloths. She disliked the chintz curtains, dark-green oilcloth tablecloths, and mediocre prints in the smoking section. Crossing the lobby she was hailed by three people sitting in the gorgeous other-world of non-smokers. One of them was Dierdra, but Brit pantomimed helplessness, following Lee and the maitre d'. Dierdra! When was her fiftieth birthday? She was too tired for Dierdra's solicitousness and to see Dierdra's mouth permanently stretched by surgery into a smile. In cultures where smiling meant aggressive intent, Dierdra would have been long dead. Poor Dierdra! Her affair with cosmetic surgery began when she was in her thirties, coinciding with her husband's affairs with his secretaries.

She was too tired for this, but she couldn't let Lee down, she must have saved for weeks. The women settled into a windowed corner with an unpleasant view of Highway 190, caftan's floating into place around them.

Lee had picked one in ivory silk. Brit had loaded her arms with gold bangles and had given her giant gold hoops for her ears. When Lee had gelled her hair straight back she looked like a tough Arab princess. "God," cried Brit, "you're wasting your time here, Lee. You oughta be in Noo York City–*Vogue* needs you."

Lee batted at her, "Quit, now. Not with this honker."

"You quit. It's more elegant than Barbra Streisand's–and look where her proboscis got her."

Lee's hand on her nose, mumbling, "Proboscis, proboscis…"

"Sounds like a witch's chant, 'Proboscis, hibiscus–'"

"Get the fuck off my face!"

"You'll learn to love it. It will be your trademark."

"Yeah, yeah, yeah, so what you gonna wear?"

"Yeah. What should an old woman wear?"

"Quit now, hear? I'm tired of your whining all day long. You're getting me exhausted!"

Brit stopped on the threshold of her closet. She slumped. "God. I have been awful, haven't I. I'm so sorry, Lee–"

"No, I'm your friend…and you put up with me crying about Dick for eight weeks. Get dressed, let's have fun. At least we can still enjoy eating."

Brit went into her closet and came out in a jade caftan, bronze sandals with many skinny straps on her feet. She put her fists on her hips.

"Look at my tits, Lee, too low-slung? I don't feel like wearing a bra if I don't have to."

Lee looked at Brit's chest. Faintly she saw Brit's nipples.

"No. They're fine. You think guys measure? No! They see nipple, they're thrilled."

Brit spritzed them both with *Magie Noire* and they glided down to the living room. She pawed through her gifts till she found Halima's jewelry.

"You clean up pretty good for an old woman, Rhodes."

"Thanks, Robinet, let's hit Dakota."

Brit paused at the foyer closet, grabbed an ankle-length mink, and handed Lee a cream angora sweater-coat.

In the black Jaguar, they roared down Highway 450 to Covington.

As Brit shook out her napkin she realized she recognized no one. Everyone she knew had quit smoking. Another battle.

Out the window she saw a teenager in front of Burger King. A cab pulled up, the kid climbed in, dragging a backpack. For a moment, she thought there was something familiar about him and she stared after the departing taillights heading north. With a spatter, rain hit the window. She turned back to Lee, who was engrossed in the menu.

"Here's the rain, Lee."

"Um hum. I think I'll have the mesquite grilled lobster."

"Me too. But first why don't we have some of those yummy little puffy things with crawfish in them? And I need a Bloody Mary. A *vodka* Bloody Mary. Can't stand gin anymore. Lee?"

Lee looked uncomfortable. Brit reached across the table and squeezed her friend's hand.

"You get dinner, sweetie, I'll get the booze." Lee started to protest.

"No arguments. I don't want to feel guilty about every sip of wine I take. I want us to take forever with this meal, get a little sloshed, forget about *everything*."

A waiter appeared and Brit looked up. "We'll want separate checks—drinks and wine on one, food on the other."

The waiter looked startled. Lee giggled.

"Uh...yes ma'am. Ready to order?"

"Yes. Those crawfish fritter things to begin, but Bloody Marys first, please."

Lee's hand went up. "None for me."

The women smoked in silence. The Bloody Mary came, then the fritters.

Brit removed the celery and took a long drink. She ate a fritter, raised her eyes, met Lee's.

Even in this subdued lighting Lee saw the red veins in Brit's eyes. No wonder. For months Brit and Scottie had been partying like college students. And Lee had never seen her as erratic as she'd been today–of course, losing Jimmy–but all the drinking–was payback time about here?

"Lee, I've got to make some changes."

Lee watched. *Got to tread carefully. Got to be her idea.*

A pause between them and, as if the sound had been turned up, they heard Mozart on muzak, the clink of silver, a sudden laugh stifled, and a coalesced murmur of conversation that seemed to float in midair. A layer above that held the scents of baking bread, charcoal, and mesquite fire. A layer of cigarette smoke topped everything.

Lee fought to keep hope from her face.

"I looked at my body this morning, Lee. Time is Beginning to Tell. I can't keep on like this...boozing it up every weekend with Scottie." She sighed. "Of course, that affair is probably ending as we speak, so other than a broken heart, I may have nothing to worry about there." She ran a hand through her hair. "I've got to start taking better care of myself." She poked the Bloody Mary with a long white finger. "And maybe...I'm drinking too much."

Lee nodded gravely. "I laughed when you spoke to the waiter, 'cause when most people want separate checks they want everything divided–not booze on one, food the other."

"That was just to help you out, Lee. The alcohol is the most expensive part."

"Was it?"

Britannia turned her head away.

"Or was it because it gave you the freedom to drink as much as you want without having to worry about my budget?"

Brit looked back at her, chin tucked, lilac eyes slanting up through her thick eyelashes. "That would be pretty awful if it were true."

Lee did a mock cringe saying, "Okay. Sorry."

Then Brit glared, not really angry. Lee smiled and asked, "Want to order the lobsters now?"

"Absolutely. That weed gave me super munchies."

Lee hailed the waiter, gave their order. Brit asked for a wine list. They ate fritters.

Lee swallowed the last one. "Better than an orgasm."

Brit grinned at her. "Almost."

"Well," said Lee, affecting primness. "I would hardly know. Since I've definitely regained my virgin status. It's been six times six weeks for me. There's just one problem with this re-virginized thing."

"What?"

"You can't let a man within two feet of you or you go up in flames."

Brit laughed. "Self-immolate?"

"Yeah. Turn hot all over."

"Maybe its early-onset menopause."

"I wish."

"You don't wish. It's awful."

"No more period for the rest of my life? I can dig it."

"But these so-called hot flashes are dreadful, really, Lee."

"Two weeks of PMS every month is no picnic, Rhodes. So I'll have a few hot flashes. I'll get some hormones, fix that right up and never have PMS or all that leaking of blood, ever again."

Brit's hands grasped the edge of the table. She stared at Lee. "I never thought of it that way. Never having a period. Never having to worry about spots on the back of a skirt–someone's sofa….Never having to wait till it's over to have sex–not that that ever stopped Scott or Grant–Lee! It means I'll never, ever, again have to worry about birth control! Funny. Until this moment I saw the whole menopause thing as a loss."

"Sweetheart. That's because you're buying into all that 'nubile' bullshit men think they want. Nubile, which most men think of as young and sexy also means *fertile*. I bet not a single one of them ever considered the advantages of a sexual relationship with a woman who never whined about PMS, like I do." She changed her voice to high nasal, "'I can't have sex tonight, or tomorrow, or the next day, or the next. I've got PMS.' And is it fun sharing a bed with someone who's bleeding? And someone whose 'nubile' biological clock is ticking like the timer on a homemade bomb, saying 'get pregnant quick?' He doesn't want pregnant, he wants nubile sex."

"Lee, you are definitely onto something."

Lee's hand went up, "And most younger women don't enjoy sex all that much. Remember, a woman hits her sexual stride between thirty and thirty-five. I'm just on the edge of mine. Before that, I'd as soon have a candy bar as an orgasm. Both were the same fun. It was only recently that the voltage upped, that last month with Dick." She leaned forward, urgent. "Do you still really enjoy sex?"

"Oh, my dear, vastly."

Lee pounded a fist on the table, once, hard. "I suspected it. I knew it! Damn!" She looked away, thinking intensely. Brit loved to watch Lee have insights, make her unusual connections. Lee whipped her head around to Brit, hair flying. "Men don't know what they're missing with older women, the fools. The way I see it, menopause is freedom. I envy you. Have your periods quit yet?"

"They're sporadic. Some months nothing, then a little spotting, then a real period. This started six months ago. I felt such relief when I had a real period. Maybe I've been brainwashed about nubile and fertile, like the guys. It might be nice not to worry about tampons falling out of my purse, feeling embarrassed when the checker at Winn-Dixie is a guy. I need to think about this." She reached across and squeezed her friend's hand. "Thanks, Lee. Now, if I recall, we were discussing what being re-virginized is like for you." She leaned forward, grinning wickedly, but Lee continued, pensively.

"It's just that now, suddenly, I get hot for a real, live guy. Otherwise re-virginization is great. Without Richard, that big dumb dick, to distract me, I'm almost finished my book."

"And when you're a best-selling novelist you'll be able to pick any stud you want."

"Yep. And stud's the right word. I'll just say: 'Do me, honey—do me good. Do this. Yes! Do that! Uh-huh! Bit more of that. Harder. No—no—no—no-you're not allowed to come just yet! Very good, Stud.' Then byeee. 'This girl's got to write another best-seller.'"

Brit leaned back, running both hands through her hair. A waiter came and handed her a wine list. She glanced at it, ordered a Pouilly-Foussé.

"You know something, Lee? As long as I live I don't think I'll ever figure out men."

"I'll drink to that."

"And you can, as soon as the wine gets here." Brit paused. "You know, Lee, Professor Lange, my first husband, was a sex-crazed rogue. Why did he bother to marry me? He could have any girl on campus. Including me. And he did. Even after we were married. Of course, when he came out with the *Hands* series, I should have known. That was my idea! The son of a bitch." She slammed her fist on the table, silverware jumped. "I told you about the professor's hand job on me, didn't I?"

Lee's chin was cupped in her hand. The room was darker now, windows black, candlelight flickering in her dark eyes. "Tell me."

"Well. I had this idea in my senior year to sculpt hands, old hands, young hands, wimpy male hands, soft, ineffectual female hands, baby's hands, callused hands."

"Sounds great to me."

"I took photos of hands, I did sketches of hands, and I'd decided through my sketches which ones I would sculpt. I'd work in different mediums: papier maché, marble, bronze, fiberglass, clay–the medium part of the message, you know?"

"Wonderful."

"He did it."

"Did what?"

"My husband did it. He photocopied my sketches, and secretly sculpted my hands!"

"The low-down, no-good, *nasty* son of a bitch."

"Thank you, Lee."

A waiter appeared, a wine bottle. Britannia glanced up. "Just pour, please."

While he worked the cork from the bottle the women's eyes cruised him. A handsome young jock. Working his way through college? Brit saw Lee licking her lips. Brit giggled and kicked her under the table. Lee's eyes jumped to hers. Solemnly Brit picked up a glass of ice water, extended it to Lee. "Here, Chick. You look like you could use a cold drink. Or shall I pour it over you?"

The waiter glanced at Brit in alarm. She batted her eyelashes.

"Private joke."

He smiled, uncomprehending, and poured a taste in her glass. Britannia sipped. "Wonderful."

Silently the waiter poured for both of them. Lee disappeared behind her napkin, convulsed with silent laughter. The waiter left. Lee threw down her napkin, let the laugh surface. Her face and sleek black hair glowed.

"You're a wild woman. You know that? What'll that guy think?"

"Absolutely nothing. He hadn't a clue." She raised an eyebrow. "You want him? He can be had. Just give him the eye next time he passes by. Bet you can plan a self-immolation for tonight."

"Quit. I'm enjoying my celibacy."

"Sure you are, Honey."

"Really, Brit. I am. The Joy of No Sex."

"Maybe you need to turn thirty-five." The lobster came and they ate seriously for some minutes. The wine waiter returned and Lee turned her exquisite face full up to him.

"Thank you." Giving it a lot.

The waiter gave her a real smile.

"You're very welcome, miss." He left.

"See," said Brit, "nuthin' to it."

"Yeah. Sure. And I could get AIDS."

"There is that. But what did God make condoms for?"

Lee waved a hand, dismissive. She pulled lobster meat from a claw, took a huge bite. She chewed. "This is suc–u–lent."

"Yes. A wonderful birthday gift, Lee."

Lee patted her mouth with her napkin. "Wanna hear a joke?"

"Sure."

"Why did God give men different faces?"

"I give up."

"So women can tell them apart."

Brit took a minute then laughed, "Kinda like, all dicks are alike, right?"

"Yeah. And they're all dicks."

"Oooh. So…you do still feel a need to trash men."

The waiter began refilling their goblets. As he poured Lee's he asked, "Haven't I seen you somewhere before?"

Brit began nudging Lee's leg under the table.

"Ever go to Ruby's Roadhouse?" Lee moved her leg away.

"Yeah. Great music."

"I work there."

"You don't say!"

She straightened her body, face cold, and put her hand out to stop his pouring. She spoke formally, "That'll be all. Thank you."

Chastened, the waiter withdrew, and Lee leaned across to Brit.

"A child. I don't fuck children."

"He is young. Early twenties."

"I want 'em at least twenty-five. By then they may have learned something."

"Back to this man thing."

"Back? When did we depart?"

Brit shook out a cigarette, lit it. "Maybe I'll never learn. But I can't believe that all men are egocentric megalomaniacs who see women as a slightly better way to jerk off. Where are the wonderful men? They've got to be out there somewhere."

"What about Art. Wasn't he wonderful?"

"He was. He gave me space. He was a fabulous father to Asia. And, Art loved my art. But he was lousy in the sack. Mild, quick, grateful. But I was younger then and I hadn't hit my full sexual stride. Only dimly did I surmise it could be better than it was." She stared up at the layer of smoke in the room. "Not until Grant–" Lee studied her friend's smooth profile. *Now she's mentioning Grant.* She started to speak, but Brit turned back with a musing smile, and a hefty slug of wine.

"Dessert?" she asked Lee.

Lee grinned. "I'm handling that."

"Oh no. Not the singing waitpersons."

"Just you never mind. Finish your thought."

"Okay. What I want in a man, I guess, doesn't exist. I want an Art–who can make love like a Grant."

Lee waggled a finger at her. "You've said his name twice now girl, not me. But, I find this significant–Scottie's not as good as Grant?"

Brit shivered. "Oh. Scottie's good, he's very good. But I always have a low level awareness–a sort of static buzz–that I'm older." A busboy came to clear the table.

Brit flicked a glance at him. "Can you please tell our waiter we need him? I'd like coffee and a Grand Marnier."

"Coffee for me, too. But Brit. Hear yourself. This age difference thing is all in your mind. I bet Scottie isn't hearing your static buzz, he's thinking–"

Brit tilted her head. "I don't know." She slapped at Lee. "Quit thinking dick all the time. Although, Grant's dick weighed against Scottie's dick…" Hands palm up, as if weighing. A wicked smile. "Speaking of dicks–how was Dick's?'

Deadpan Lee answered, "Dick had a big dick."

"And how was Dick?'"

"Great. Except, he wouldn't go down on me."

Brit eyed her, shocked. "Then how could he be great? You went down?"

"All the time. I've told you before. I love to suck dick."

Brit shook her head. "Sweetie. Take a lesson. No man's great unless they love going down on you…that's the climactic climax."

"I never cared if I had an orgasm–"

"Oh my God! And I thought a young thang like you was a real liberated woman! Now you'll say 'just being close was good enough–'"

"It was."

"Did you ever have an orgasm with this guy?"

"Sometimes. Little bitty ones. Afterward, when I went home, I took care of myself."

"My poor dear. That is so sad–and that's not how it's done. But maybe you're right, your engine isn't mature enough yet. Come to think of it, I really didn't get with it till I got with Grant. Then I went crazy. I thought it was all because of him–not because my sexuality had changed. Sweetie, you are going to love being thirty-five." She began lighting a cigarette when she looked over Lee's shoulder. Her eyes widened. "Oh no, Lee."

A phalanx marched to their table. The point man carried a tiny cake, a single candle lit. Behind, four waitresses held mylar balloons. Raggedly singing "Happy Birthday," they gathered round the table, Lee joining. Brit laughed and blushed, which became a hot flash. *Of course,* she thought sarcastically. *Good thing it's dark in here.* The song trailed off and other diners, craned around in their seats, clapped. The waiter set the cake before her.

"Can I make a wish?"

"Of course, silly."

Brit smiled at the servers and at Lee.

"I've got one." She blew. The candle flickered, reflamed, then died. Everyone clapped. Her wish was, *God help me.*

Lee thanked them. "Can you bring us two coffees and one Grand Marnier?"

"Certainly miss." The waiter cut the cake in half. "This is our double suicide chocolate cake with rum and white and dark chocolate swirled through it."

Brit took a bite, rolled her eyes. "I'm going to swoon. This is so good it's dangerous. Great choice, Lee."

"So glad you like it, dahling."

"I do! Thank you."

"But you didn't finish about the differences between Scottie and Grant."

"I thought I did. Okay. Well. Scottie is terrific. Great staying power. No hangups about kissing any part of a woman's body."

"But…" Lee stopped as the waiter served their coffee and brandy.

"Yeah, 'but.'" She picked up the brandy, sniffed, and sipped. "The 'but' is intangible. It might just be my age hang-up. I can tell you this though. Dick was not man enough for you, honey. In the sack or out of it."

Lee set down her fork. "Define your perfect man."

She sighed. "My perfect man. My soul mate. Okay. Humor, grace, strength. Loves music. Loves to dance. Loves the country and animals. Loves to fuck. And especially, loves a scatterbrained, long-haired, long-toothed artist, but…" She lit a cigarette. "… I'm past my prime. If such a paragon exists, he'll want a younger woman."

"That's a contradiction, Brit. If such a paragon exists and he's your soul mate, chronological age is meaningless. Because he will, as they say, love you for being uniquely you. And you could not be what you are today without having lived your whole fifty years. You weren't this you twenty years ago!" She leaned in, whispering, "Besides, no one in this room would believe for one second that you have just celebrated your fiftieth birthday! No one! Forty, maybe."

"But dahling, this is what fifty looks like! To paraphrase Gloria Steinham."

"Exactly. We've all been brainwashed to think forty, fifty, sixty, seventy, et cetera, et cetera–all the way to shriveled residence at a nursing home–has a particular look. We've been taught that we can simply look at someone and guess their age! We've been trained in these stereotypes. And I think we make ourselves look like we 'should' look at these ages. We pre-age ourselves! Didn't you tell me Viola cut her hair when she became forty, aging herself ten years? You are no stereotype, Brit. I want you to quit all this age stuff. You are a beautiful, glamorous woman. Men can't take their eyes off you. So stop it–or I'll beat you up."

Brit was looking down, flicking her lighter off and on. "Since it's let-it-all-hang-out night–I have another…terrible, scary confession to make."

"What is it?"

"I'm afraid I've really caught menopause."

Was Brit drunk, Lee wondered? *They'd already talked about this.* But patiently she answered, "It's not a disease, baby."

"I suppose, but I've got it, not you, no matter what you say about PMS. Old overnight. Osteoporosis. Wrinkles. Serious ridge-like wrinkles–as opposed to mere lines. More gray hair, a vagina dried out like the husk of a katydid or as the articles all say, 'drying and thinning of the vaginal walls'…Katy-did, katy-did–past tense, you notice." Tears ran down her cheeks. "I'll never be able to fuck properly again. 'Wait a sec, darling, while I squirt myself with my special old woman's lubricant!' They advertise that shit on TV now!"

"Brit, honey, stop. Are you dried out now?"

"No." Small, pouty voice.

"Look at Viola. She's beautiful. She doesn't look much older than you right now and Nunan's crazy about her."

"Mother?! She probably doesn't allow sex. And Nunan's soused most of the time."

"Well, can you at least talk to her? Obviously she's survived menopause. I'm sure she can help you. Kind of the next big Mother-Daughter talk: Like the pre-menstrual Mother-Daughter talk, the Birds and Bees Mother-Daughter talk, the Great Trilogy of Mother-Daughter Talks."

Brit dabbed her eyes with her napkin. She had a faint smile.

"Okay. Maybe I'll call her tomorrow."

"Good. Stop panicking, woman. And when she 'splains things, call me up and 'splain 'em to me. Now drink up your brandy like a good girl, and I'll call for the check."

TWENTY

In the thunderstorm, Brit drove peering through a rain-lashed windshield. In the backseat balloons bobbed like grotesque heads, glinting in each dagger of lightning. The women, sated, talked out, were tense about the storm. If this kept up, the road home would flood. Halfway there, Brit looked at Lee.

"Spend the night at my place. It's going to be miserable driving all the way back to Abita Springs."

"Thanks, but no. I really like sleeping in my own little bed. I'll be fine."

Soon they turned into Britannia's drive, she pulled up close to Lee's battered Ford Escort, an older model than her daughter Anastasia's. They hugged.

"Thanks, Lee, for a superb birthday. I'll never forget this day."

"Hey. I loved it. Plus–as they say–you're worth it."

"Now scoot and take care. Call me when you make it home."

"Shall do."

Rain pelted Lee as she darted to her car. Brit waited until she heard the engine catch. She tooted, Lee tooted, Brit pulled up the circular brick drive to her front door. To avoid the rain she slid over the seat out the passenger side–the balloons could spend the night in the car. Oddly, Wilton was barking from inside the house. He knew her car and never barked when she came home. Dashing up the steps she wished she'd left the outside light on and, as she reached for the doorknob, a shape rose up on her left. She yelped as lightning snapped.

A voice, soft, said, "Brit? Maw? Didn't mean to scare you. It's me. Saunders."

Lightning cracked again, silhouetting a twisted-limbed tree and the dripping boy. She couldn't see his face, only a pearlescent glow.

"My God, Saunders–you scared me! You're soaked! Why are you here?"

"A long story."

From a leak in the overhang drops hit Brit's right temple cold as melting icicles. She stared at his wan face. "Well then. Come in and tell me."

When she opened the unlocked door Wilton raced out snarling and grabbed the boy's pantleg.

"*Wil*–cut it out. This is our boy."

She reached down for the little dog but he hung on. Saunders hadn't moved. He stared at the dog, Brit.

"Wilton! Let go!" Brit stooped and pulled the dog off Saunders. In her arms Wil growled. "Hush!" said Brit. "Come on, Saunders, in…he'll learn to love you."

She led the way into her home.

P a r t T w o

FORSAKEN BELIEFS

...Middle Age
Home of lost causes and forsaken beliefs...
– *Matthew Arnold*

ONE

New Orleans has more bars than any city in America. Driving home, temptation clawed at Grant from bistros, dives, taverns, fern bars, sidewalks, and patios. People and happy hour music spilled onto St. Charles Avenue from crowds at Que Sera, and from the seersuckered upwardly mobiles that lolled under the columns of The Columns Hotel.

He could smell glacial gin in a perfect martini. Like a long, thin waterfall in the Andes, he felt it slide down his hot, dry throat, and pool serenely in his stomach. Then, in seconds, relief pumping through his body. He sighed deeply as he braked for a fat, red-faced white woman pushing a purple K&B shopping cart across the Napoleon Street intersection.

An oily, plump, gray-green olive roiled around in his mind like a hamster in a plastic ball.

The magical martini grew in his mind as he continued to weave the 'Vette through late-afternoon traffic on The Avenue till he fancied a beach-ball sized olive glistening in icy Tanqueray. Even though he drove with the air conditioning on full, the late-winter sun veiled by new clouds, he arrived at the condo sweating. A giant green ball loomed before him. Striding into the foyer, he decided a cold shower would fix him. He and the ballooning olive squeezed into the elevator. Hands shaking grotesquely, he tore his tie off. He couldn't wait to get into his condo to tear off the hairpiece, pop out the contacts. Shower. Pull on old sweats. Then he'd be fine. But the olive seemed to be growing, growing–it was flattening him against the back wall of the swiftly ascending elevator. His legs weakened, he couldn't breath, he was sagging **down the wall**, he thought he heard

Margie's distant laughter. The elevator doors swooshed open, the giant olive popped out the door. He was wet with sweat on the elevator floor. Trembling, pushing his attaché before him, he began to crawl from the elevator. He did not give a flying fuck who was in the hallway. Breathing shallowly, he got his shoulders out when the elevator doors slammed into his waist. He felt like crying. He moved a leg forward. Steel grooves of the door tracks bit into his knee. The doors slammed against his hips. Slowly he crawled, the doors banging open and closed against him, until he was free.

Still on all fours, he turned his head from side to side to see who—or what—was in the hallway. The plush beige carpet with the mauve stripe was empty. He caught a whiff of urine, but then he'd seen Mr. Whippler's Pomeranian lift a leg at the chrome ashtray by the elevator.

No one—thank God—was in the hallway and no hallucination—thank God—of a giant olive was in the hallway. His breathing was better, and the Great Martini Longing subsided slightly. He got to his feet and walked off in a caricature of his confident, lawyerly self. As he fumbled for his keys, he thought, *I can relax, read the paper, have a little talk with Saunders…and this hallucination of a giant martini will never return.*

He stuck his key in the door but it swung open before he could turn the knob. Rita was revealed, wringing her hands.

"Oh, Mr. Grant. I'm so glad you're here. Come see what I just read on your computer!"

He dropped the briefcase, and followed her to the office and read, DAD…SPENDING NITE AT DAVE'S, noting Saunders had correctly used the possessive in 'Dave's.'

"Why all the flap, Rita? He spent the night at Dave's."

Rita looked at him gravely. "That's not all, Mr. Grant." Slowly she slid a hand into her apron pocket and withdrew a sandwich baggie containing some smeary creamy lumps beside…a collapsed balloon? A tiny aborted embryo? She spoke in a solemn voice.

"I found this—under the sofa."

Grant peered closer then jerked back. Horror and relief washed over him. A used condom that had leaked its contents into the baggie! *I did use a condom.* He resisted the urge to sink to his knees right there in the hallway in front of Rita and actually pray. *Thank you, God I…do…not…have…AIDS!*

Sternly Rita pointed at the baggie. "Mr. Grant. It's used."

"Yes. I see that…very good, Rita. Flush it and we'll go into the living room and sort this out." He wanted that martini.

"Yes, Mr. Grant. And that boy should have been home two hours ago!"

Grant headed for the living room, calling back over his shoulder, "And bring me a big glass of orange juice." But the sound of the toilet drowned him out, so he made an about-turn and headed for the kitchen. He was incredibly thirsty. He jerked open the refrigerator, grabbed a half-gallon carton of orange juice. *What the hell.* He lifted the carton, tilted his head, and poured the cold juice down his throat.

"Mr. Grant! If Saunders could see you now, all those times I give him what-for! I'm always tellin him, 'Get a glass. Don't drink out of the carton.'"

Grant couldn't stop. Throat convulsing, he drank and drank, draining the carton. He set it on the counter, turned to her. He'd drunk so fast his eyes were tearing. Again. Blinking, he removed his cufflinks and said briskly. "Right, Rita. Won't happen again. Now. I am going to my room to change. Do we have Dave's number?"

She nodded. "I'll get it."

"Fine. Meet you in the living room in ten."

Rita, he thought, as he stood under a lukewarm shower—all that cold shower stuff sounded good in books, but the reality was a little too much to take—*was prone to exaggeration, flying off the handle and experiencing unnecessary alarms.* Even so, he hurried. He turned off the taps and toweling hastily walked into his bedroom, jerked open a drawer and rummaged around until he found the faded royal blue sweats that Brit had given him years back. Not bothering with under-wear he pulled them on. He noticed his hands shook. Of all days for Saunders to dawdle getting home from school, he would pick today to pull a stunt like this, the very day Grant came straight home for a father-son evening.

Dave answered the phone, startled to hear Saunder's Dad. Before he could scramble to cover for Saunders (whom Dave knew was not at school that day) Grant had him confessing Saunders had not spent the night with him. Grant hung up—he wasn't an attorney for nothing! Dave said goodbye into an empty phone, relieved Mr. Griffin, with his deep important voice, hadn't found out Saunders had skipped school.

"Hum," said Grant, scratching his bare head. He adjusted his reading glasses on the bridge of his nose. "Rita, maybe you're right. Perhaps we do have some-thing to worry about. Do you have the phone numbers of his other friends?"

"Sure do."

"Well hand 'em over. I'd better call them all till we track him down–or he shows up."

Grant was beginning to experience a hollow feeling on top of his day-long hangover. Fretful needles of anxiety skittered over him. *Damn that kid.*

By the third call Grant learned his son had not been in school. No one had any idea where he was. His stomach began an odd lurching movement.

"Okay, Rita. Room search. See if anything significant is missing."

They stood and marched down the hall. In Saunders' room Grant took one look at the disarray and yelled, "I thought he was cleaning up this mess last night!"

"Me too," said Rita. "I come in here this mornin to vacuum and he ain't touched nuthin."

"Obviously he lied. This is terrible! Where do we start?"

Rita marched over to the dresser and began opening drawers. Grant stood in the middle of the room, hands on hips. He wanted a drink. He swiveled around, shaking his head. *Those posters. What's with kids these days...they're into death's heads?* He'd had The Bomb in the hands of The Evil Empire to worry about. Now The Bomb wasn't such a big deal. Neither was The Evil Empire. *Where does this nihilistic death-fixation stuff come from? In my day, besides The Bomb, it was good old fashioned pussy-fixation. That commercial was right,* he thought smugly, *we used up all the fun.*

Rita finished looking through Saunders' dresser drawers and said she couldn't tell if anything was missing. She was opening the top drawer of his bedside table when she gave a shrill cry. Grant's heart leapt to his throat.

"Good God, Rita, what is it?"

Rita was waving a wand. Or, a miniature sword?

"My knife sharpener," she cried, "I bin goin crazy lookin for this! Scared I'd throwed it out by accident! He had it all along! An he knew I was goin outta my mind lookin for this thing!"

"Well. I'm happy you found your knife sharpener, Rita. Find any knives?"

She bent and pawed through the drawer. She turned back to Grant.

"Nope. Just my sharpener." Grant breathed in relief.

Rita slammed the drawer shut, fell to her knees. For a second Grant wondered if she was going to pray–but she scrabbled under Saunders' bed, pulling out heaps of trash, while Grant pondered: *Why would Saunders disappear? With a knife. Did he have a knife? The sharpener suggested he did.* He was about to sneak out of the room for a quick slug of gin when Rita let go another shriek.

"What?" Grant felt breathless.

She jumped to her feet making "eeoouuw" sounds.

"What is it, Woman?"

All of this could be handled so much better if he just had a cold martini in his hand.

Rita was hopping around and waggling her hands at something she'd excavated from beneath Saunders' bed.

Grant bent over and began pointing.

"This?" A Dr. Pepper can.

"That."

She eeoouuw'd and shook her head. He pointed at a soup bowl of gray fur. A bad smell came from it. But that wasn't it. He nodded at a paper plate with green lichen-shaped mold forms. "Those?" More denial. Grant wrinkled his nose. The whole room had a bad smell.

He picked up a crumpled page from a glossy magazine.

"This."

"That's it. Oh...an I touched it!"

Grant smoothed the page and cried, "Holy shit! Sorry, Rita."

Furtively he looked again. Smooth bulging buttocks, gaping vulvas, pneumatic breasts, spread legs, more gaping vulvas. For sure the kid wasn't gay and he looked at more than skulls. He just couldn't pin these hot little numbers on his wall.

"Rita, Rita. It's okay. I admit, this is pretty hard-core stuff. But at least we haven't found any marijuana, or worse." Rita did not seem mollified and Grant decided to add a bonus to her next check.

The rest of the search, all of which was conducted by Rita, uncovered more trash, more glossy porn pages, more clothes in disarray, more decayed food. All Rita was able to divine was that his combat boots, his black hightops, and his backpack were missing. The schoolbooks remained on the floor where Rita had seen them last night. She mourned that he'd misled her about cleaning up his room. They trailed back to the living room and fell into the sofa. Grant sighed.

"Well Rita, looks like our boy's run away from home. Damn!"

Ain't my boy, thought Rita. *That spoiled brat is your boy.* To think he'd looked her *right in her eye* every time she asked him if he'd seen the knife sharpener.

Never blinked. Not once. *Something weird about that kid.* She'd felt it all along. *Now, Mr. Grant was okay. Just another big dumb honky man. But Saunders, he was different. Strange different.*

"Well, Rita, you've been wonderful. I guess you better get on home to your family."

Rita rose from the sofa. "They can take care of themselves. You sure you all right? Dinner's on a plate in the refrigerator. Just put it in the microwave for two-three-O."

"Two minutes and thirty seconds?"

"Uh-huh." She started towards the hall closet. "You get somethin to eat now, hear?" She had opened the closet, extracted her coat. "An don worry about that boy. He'll turn up." *Like a rotten boomerang, swing on back and knock his daddy and whoever else right in the haid.*

"Thanks, Rita. I'll be fine. I'll figure something out." He wanted her gone so he could grab a drink. Now he really needed one.

"You find him, you call me." She was at the door, pulling on her coat. "Hear?" She buttoned her coat. "Anytime. No matter how late. I'll be worryin." *About you. Not that rotten kid.*

"Thanks, Rita. I sure will." He stood, walked over to the door, and opened it for her. "Thanks again, Rita, you've been wonderful." He closed the door and returned to his deep sofa.

He stared at the Plexiglas phone, the kind where all the high-tech works showed. Who to call next? *I better have a drink while I think about this. Should I call the police?* A drink would relax him, help him focus. *No. The police won't pay any attention until twenty-four–or was it seventy two?–hours, although–if he left last night...is there any gin left?* He picked up the phone. He knew some people down at headquarters. He punched out a number.

After he left a description of Saunders with a bored female officer: 5'8", well-built, fifteen but maybe looks older, dark auburn hair, gray eyes, dressed like a teenager, (i.e.: jeans too big, T-shirt too big, unlaced combat boots or black high-tops, black leather jacket) carrying a black backpack, no, definitely not on drugs...he lay back on the sofa. He actually felt too drained to walk across the room to the ebony entertainment center where, next to his stereo and his television set, was his bar. Behind it he'd installed a glass and rattan dining room set...rarely used, family dinners never seemed to happen. To his left, a sliding glass door opened onto a balcony overlooking Audubon park, The Avenue to the left, Mississippi river on the right. His favorite thing about this condo were the nights he'd lie in bed, hearing lions roaring in the zoo and the lowing of foghorns on the river. He became a Great White Hunter on the Serengeti, or a character in a Joseph Conrad sea novel, easing through shrouds of fog into sinister, exotic ports.

Opposite the glass doors was a fireplace in black and gray stone which sprawled over most of the wall. Grant's own design, installed at his expense. He'd collected bromeliads and niched them into the stone and they plumed green, orange, pink from the rock. Four of Brit's watercolors from her *Wetlands Fauna* series—raccoon, nutria, beaver, red fox—hung to the right of the fireplace. He'd had them framed in weathered cypress. They worked well, Grant thought, on the charcoal gray wall, so after the divorce he'd left them up. Besides, they were gaining in value. Beneath the teak coffee table was an old zebra-skin hide he'd found in a pawn shop three years back for which he'd had to apologize many times to his animal-rights acquaintances. ("But this zebra died years before the term 'animal rights' was dreamed up," he'd protest, to no avail.) Maroon paisley silk swagged across the top of the glass doors and pooled extravagantly on the floor. This was flanked by Victorian palms. His sofa was white cotton, vivid with emerald and maroon cushions. (He'd suffered over the sofa. With it, Saunders definitely couldn't have a dog. Finally, having worked up a three-martini courage, he'd asked Saunders what kind of a dog he'd like to get. Saunders had shrugged and said he'd rather have a stereo for his room. Grant ordered the white sofa the next day. Yet not without a tinge of regret…he rather hankered for a dog himself.)

Grant enjoyed taking care of plants and he loved the faint, earthy smell they added to the place. He'd often thought he'd like to grow orchids when he retired. Have to sell this condo to do that, though. Move to a place with a yard. Memories of Brit's forest enclave drifted into his mind. The crushed rock road that wound through pines and oaks alive with birdsong, how slow you had to go because Brit's "Duck Crossing" sign was truth.

They'd talked about naturalizing wild azaleas through her forest. *Had she gotten around to it?*

Fowl often wandered up from the pond and roosted in the drive. He remembered honking and then having to get out of the car and shoo birds from his path, geese honking at him. At this point he'd have reached the clearing and to his left would be the split-rail pasture enclosing the horse Mokhtar, which looked white to him, but Brit said it wasn't the done thing, white horses were actually gray horses and one must always call them that. Back then he'd thought, *There's that useless, expensive horse,* Brit gone every weekend to some horse show. She wanted him to go, *but—hell, what did a divorce attorney have to say to a crowd of horse people? Why couldn't the woman have golfed for Chrissakes?* But then came a favorite part. The small log stable, fieldstone planters beside the stable doors. Hibiscus and petunias spilling from the planters. He remembered Sunday mornings in front of the those doors, sipping chicory coffee, thick and dark like velvet, listening to his wife coo to the horse, inhaling the perfume of the flowers, the sweet hay in the loft, the pine shavings in the stall, even the surprisingly not too unpleasant tang of manure.

The dip in the land ahead suddenly flattened to become the pond, the drive curved around it, and the land rose still higher to the log house. The front yard was a tangle of greenery, seemingly planted haphazardly but actually carefully planned by both he and Brit. Brit's "lucky carp," standing on its tail, had become her fountain and water burbled from its open mouth. She'd bought it on their trip to San Francisco. This time of year Grant figured everything would mostly have died back but old Jimmy had probably planted pansies and snapdragons. Broad, shallow brick steps led to the front door of beveled glass and the fieldstone columns beside the steps were thickly lashed with wisteria vine. In April it would cover the entrance with mauve blooms like grape clusters. From a Creole wraparound verandah the house rose huge, multi-faceted, odd-shaped sheets of glass and stone breaking up the shiny surface of the logs. Grant mentally walked to the backyard. He and Brit, with the help of old Jimmy, had laid out octagonal, square, triangular, and rectangular raised beds and developed the herb garden, the rose garden, and the vegetable garden, scattered marigolds and moss roses growing amongst peppers, tomatoes, eggplant, and okra. Cucumber, cantaloupe, and watermelon vines coiled over railway ties onto grass walkways between the beds. Pink and lavender cosmos, dusty blue ageratum, yellow and scarlet dahlias and pink, tangerine, scarlet and white zinnias dazzled as though in a Cezanne—all summer long. All of it enclosed by a stone wall. He used to wander through this garden under rose arbors, past stone benches, then open the gate on the north wall, stroll out to the swimming pool. There he and Brit had created their subtropical garden of palms, banana trees, elephant ears, passion flowers, bougainvillaea, mandevillia, white, crimson, yellow, blue hibiscus, with scarlet trumpet vine clambering over the small poolhouse. Cardinals, bluejays, mockingbirds, and finches battled for nesting sites. Hummingbirds fluttered in on late afternoons. Always there was a rich earthy smell, the fragrance of herbs and flowers. He sighed hugely in remembrance. Of course, Brit had had much of the garden blocked out before he'd married her, but he'd helped make it reality. His hands itched–they missed so much the feel of the moist black compost. The only thing that damn horse was good for–manure for the compost heap.

The phone rang. Grant picked up the receiver. A raspy wheeze filled his ear.

"Fitz? That you?"

"Hey, Grant." Wheeze. "What's that boy a' yours up to?"

Grant pictured Detective Roberto Fitzhugh, dark as his Mexican mother, fey as his Irish father, only five-five, but wide as he was tall, his clothes always stretched so tightly over his body it looked as though he'd gained weight since putting them on that morning. Grant had wondered, did his wife help him pull those shirts across his vast chest, grunting with the effort, crying "Suck it in, Fitz, suck it in!" as she buttoned each button? Fitz clutching furniture, like a Southern Belle clutches a bedpost, while her maid tightens the laces of her corset? These same clothes were permanently impregnated with the smell of cooking grease. Fitz loved oyster, shrimp, catfish po-boys and ate them even for breakfast. Grant could almost smell him over the phone. His breath was also odiferous from chain-smoking cigars. But within the huge skull Fitz had a quick, rueful brain.

"You tell me, Fitz. He left a note on the computer saying he was spending the night at a friend's. He did not. He wasn't in school today. His backpack, some clothes are missing."

"He's run away from home."

"Seems like it. I haven't heard a word from him."

Wheeze. "You check with his friends?"

"Yes. All that Rita and I know of."

"Any relatives he might run to?"

"Not around here. Well...he has grandparents in Bay St. Louis. But he can't stand them. And you know my folks live in Tylertown."

"Might be worth a call, Grant. Both places. Anything else? What about his mother? Would he try and see her?"

Grant sighed and felt sorry he hadn't gotten himself that martini. His skin crawled, and he heard his grandmother say: "You got the heebie-jeebies, boy."

"Fitz. His mother terrifies him. I haven't taken him to visit her in two or three years. She's batty. You know that. And what's he going to do with himself at a mental home?"

Wheeze and sigh. "Yeah. That's really sad, Grant. Still. Might not hurt to call out there. With kids, you never know. She has her lucid moments, don't she?"

"Oh sure. Once in a while. But even Saunders' therapist said he shouldn't see her until he works through his problems with her."

"His therapist. You call him?"

"Her. No. Should I?"

Wheeze. Slurp. Fitz was drinking something. "C'mon, Grant. You're a fairly sharp guy. Gotta cover all the bases." Icecubes rattled.

"Well–I–"

"Yeah. I know. You're real upset about the kid."

But Grant realized with guilty clarity he wasn't that upset about Saunders. He was more upset about not having a martini. Maybe Saunders' departure hadn't sunk in yet. He kept thinking any moment Saunders would slouch through the door.

Fitz was still wheezing into the phone. "Making all those calls will help. Give you something tangible to do. Meanwhile I'll check around here. See if anyone's noticed a kid of his description hitchhiking or anything. Money. How much money'd he have? Enough to catch a plane?"

"Oh, he wouldn't have that much."

"Check your credit cards. Any missing?"

"Uh…wallet's in my bedroom. I'll check it out."

"Let me know if any're missing. Okay, Grant. You get busy. Keep in touch." Wheeze. Click.

Compulsively Grant wiped sweaty hands over his hairless head. He stared unseeing at his soothing living room. Finally he stood and marched to his bar. He jerked down the small door that became a shelf and clanked the bottles around, searching for his Tanqueray. Rum, bourbon, Creme de Menthe–*Christ, everything!–but his gin. Did I finish it last night during my caper with the hooker? Hadn't I been drinking bourbon? Christ! He really was losing his grip. This close to getting AIDS, not enough forethought to keep the bar properly stocked, now my son has run away from home! Son-of-a-bitch! What next?* He slammed the bar door shut. He'd fantasized for so long about that giant martini nothing else appealed to him. He went back to the sofa, shakily relinquished his body to it, pulled the phone toward him and stabbed out Saunders' maternal grandparents' number in Bay St. Louis.

By seven-thirty he'd had long stressful conversations with both sets of grand-parents, his sister in St. Louis, the mental home inhabited by Margie, and had re-called every one of Saunders' friends. In most cases he'd gotten their parents. No one had heard anything. Margie, he was told, was lucid, but he didn't want to risk telling her their son had disappeared. He'd checked his wallet, still had all his credit cards. He'd called Fitz back but he wasn't in so he left a message. He sat defeated, captive to his comfortable sofa. Then he remembered opening his desk drawer earlier, searching for a Certs. The little book...

Grant sat, knees wide, his hands dangling. They shook. *Of course your hands would shake if your son disappeared. Wouldn't they?* He wiped them on the old blue sweats and looked up to see rain spitting on his glass doors. That, and nightfall, deepened his anxiety. Fighting the voluptuous grip of the sofa he rose and walked to his bedroom where he stripped off the sweats and pulled on a pair of gray-green Dockers and a dark gray golf shirt. He stuck his bare feet into a pair of Topsiders. From his closet he took a lined gray windbreaker. There was nothing to cover his bare—*literally*, he thought in disgust—head.

Riding down in the elevator he still wasn't sure where he'd end up...Audubon Tavern...or...? At the door he hesitated. *Helluva night.* Thunder cracked in his left ear, so loud that side of his brain felt stunned. *Couldn't hurt to drive by the place.* Moments later the 'Vette insinuated itself onto The Avenue, rain hitting it like peas shot by angry aborigines. Too quickly it reached the Methodist church. He ducked his head and through the dribbled-wet passenger window saw the side street was jammed with cars. *Well, I tried. No one could expect me to walk any dis-tance in this weather...parking close is impossible.* But now he had to make the turn to get some idiot off his ass...*there's one small spot the 'Vette might squeeze into.* It fit. He turned off the ignition, slipped the keys in his pocket. Rain gobbed on his windshield. He turned the rearview mirror toward himself and by the light of a nearby street lamp stared at his reflection. No one had seen him minus hairpiece in years. He had some fear that maybe, just maybe, someone from his career life would be there and recognize him. *The shame of it—going to a meeting of Alcoholics Anonymous! Hartwell would have a fit if he found out that one of his partners was an alcoholic.* Of course, he wasn't *positive* he was an alcoholic—he was just going to this meeting as a kind of...*photo* safari...if what he saw and heard appealed, next time he might pack his rifle—so to speak. He saw the eyes, forehead, and shiny dome of a man wearing big, comfortable, rather old-fashioned horn-rimmed glasses. He barely recognized himself. *Who in the hell is that guy, any-*

way? Then he chuckled. No one would recognize him like this. Being himself was the perfect disguise.

Cold rain bounced off his scalp as he dashed to a lighted side entrance of the church. The door opened for him as he reached it, held wide by a rotund man with pink bunchy cheeks, gold-rimmed glasses, and wispy gray hair. "Hello! Hello!" the man boomed in a voice too big for his body. "Welcome! Welcome!"

Who was this obnoxious jerk who grabbed his hand? But if he hadn't, Grant might have bolted.

He beamed up at Grant. "Come in, come in! Glad to see you in this weather! New?"

Grant's mouth went dry. He stared nervously down at the guy. Santa Claus without the beard and the red suit. *I have not been a good boy, Santa.* Santa pointed down a hallway.

"First door on your right. Small crowd tonight. Guess the wet's keeping them in. Or–let's hope it's the rain, not the bottle, eh?" And he laughed–like Santa.

Grant was appalled. *This crazed person was* laughing *about* drinking! He'd like to take this fruitcake for a drive past Lafayette Park, show him all the brown-bagging bums, show him drinking was no laughing matter!

Ruffled, he walked down the hall, pushed open the door. It was a Sunday School room. A long formica-topped conference table took up the length of the room. The walls had blackboards, bookshelves, and a few cardboard boxes overflowing with religious brochures. At the far end of the room about eight men and two women stood around a coffee maker, Styrofoam cups in hand, chatting as though at a cocktail party. A large sign was thumbtacked over the coffee machine, "One Day At a Time." Another sign to his left said, "Let Go, Let *God.*" *God,* he thought, *I hope this isn't too religious.* Two pull-down posters like window shades were titled, "The Twelve Steps," and "The Twelve Traditions." One man saw him and detached himself from the group. He strode up, hand out.

"Hi," he said, "I'm Gary. New here?"

Grant took his hand. "Yes. Grant Griff–" The man held up his free hand, grinning.

"No last names here, Grant. This is Alcoholics *Anonymous.*"

"I'm not–really sure–if I'm even...an alcoholic..."

"Of course. You just want to sit in and see what we're all about, right?"

How did he know? "Yeah."

"Well, Grant, come on and get a cup of coffee, find yourself a seat. The meeting's about to begin. And if you have any questions after the meeting, don't hesitate to ask me."

"Thanks…"

"Gary."

"Gary. Coffee sounds–good." *It sounded like shit.* He hated to admit it–he couldn't admit it–not around these goody-goodies–but what surged up in his mind was the crystalline picture of the perfect double martini. It rotated, fat olive lolling around the stemmed glass, beads of condensation glistening on the sides of the glass–the glass was tipping, tipping, coming to his mouth, the olive growing, growing–he almost screamed out loud.

His life had become a B-movie.

"Grant? We're ready to begin, care to grab a seat?" Santa herded him to the table and pulled out a chair for him. He moved to sit down and cracked his knee against a lip hidden under the tabletop so hard it brought tears to his eyes. *Shit!* he cursed inwardly, then eased himself all the way down into the chair, furtively massaging his knee. Everyone had brought cups of coffee to the table. A few had that book *Alcoholics Anonymous.* He was sorry he hadn't gotten a coffee.

A woman at the head of the table spoke briskly.

"Welcome to the Closed Thursday Night Discussion Meeting of Alcoholics Anonymous at Christopher Methodist Church. I'm Suzanne and I'm an alcoholic."

Grant stared. She said it so matter-of-factly. He wanted to say, "Funny, you don't look like an alcoholic…" but everyone shouted, "Hey Suzanne," then lowered their heads as she continued, "We'll have a moment of meditation followed by the Serenity prayer."

Then, her voice, softly, "God grant–"

His name! What the hell–? But people were murmuring all around him and he began to catch some of the words.

"…serenity murmur things I murmur change, courage murmur, murmur, murmur…"

Suzanne said, "Now Gary will read the preamble."

"Hi, I'm Gary and I'm an alcoholic."

"Hello, Gary." A chorus.

Good grief–they all said it again. He stifled an urge to laugh. He felt as though he'd stumbled onto a Saturday Night Live skit parodying an A.A. meeting. Behind his hand he sniggered, a dry, stifled sound like he heard from Opal.

Someone else was reading aloud, droning on and on. He couldn't pay attention. He tried to wet his dry lips, but failed. He should have gotten coffee. *What am I doing here?* He looked up in panic and met the eyes of the man directly across the table from him. A shock. *My God–it was–Hartwell! Jesus Christ–Hartwell, head of Whitfield, Whitfield, Galliano & Griffin. His boss had caught him at this meeting of weaklings who couldn't hold their liquor!* Wild, he looked around. There was no gracious escape. As if from a great distance he heard Suzanne's voice, "...Twelve Promises."

He lowered his head, dared a glance at Hartwell. *Was he recognized? Minus the rug, in horn rims, not contacts...maybe not...?* Hartwell looked back at him, his face as serious as if he stood before the Supreme Court. Then he gave a half nod–not of recognition, but of encouragement. Then the stern, third generation leader of Whitfield, Whitfield, Galliano & Griffin, said, "I'm Hartwell and I'm an alcoholic."

Voices cried, "Hello, Hartwell."

Numb, he tried to hear what Hartwell was reading, afraid he might be quizzed later but heard only parts of sentences..."new freedom...not forget the past...painstaking..." It made no sense.

Suzanne asked if anyone was here for their very first meeting.

Grant felt his elbow juggled, looked to his left, and saw Santa grinning up at him. His mouth was so awfully dry, so all he did was nod at Suzanne, who smiled brilliantly and said, "Could you identify yourself, first name only?"

"Agh." A strangled sound. "I'm Grant."

"Hello, Grant. Welcome, Grant." The chorus again, this time saying his name. *So loud!* He felt stupid.

T W O

Next to Suzanne a man named Sheldon was talking.

"...so, Grant, as a newcomer, you're the most important person in the room tonight. In keeping with A.A. tradition, my topic will be the first step, 'We admitted we were powerless over alcohol and that our lives had become unmanageable.'"

Grant adjusted his horn rims with a shaky hand and settled lower in the metal chair. He tried to pay attention to this guy, *who was what–thirty-five? Fresh-faced, big hammy arms. Must work out, but his diction advertised college.* The guy was looking right at him. Grant wished he'd pick on someone else. He didn't feel important and he didn't want to be–perhaps for the first time in his life. He just wanted this awful engulfing fear and craving to be gone. He dropped his eyes to the fake woodgrain table. Sheldon was still talking.

"My first A.A. meeting was at Bridge House." Grant's head jerked up. "I went there mainly to bum cigarettes and get a meal. They said if I hung around for a meeting I'd get both. So, I hung around. I was homeless, addicted to booze, crack cocaine. A drunk. A junkie. My address that week was under the Claiborne Avenue ramp. Under the bridge. Guess I've got a thing about bridges." People laughed. Grant was shocked, laughing about someone admitting they lived under a bridge? He knew that neighborhood. He always drove as fast as he could past it. He'd seen dirty shambling men under that ramp–*what if one of them had been this guy?*

"...had my first drink which I snuck from my Dad's bar, at ten. Marijuana at eleven. Harder drugs after that. My first rock, I was twenty-five. Thirty-six now. After that first meeting, where not one word sunk in, my life was saved. I was on the bridge, not under it, although I didn't know it at the time. A man named Charles came up and began to talk to me. I smoked his cigarettes, tried to listen. Maybe heard every third word. Among other things he said I stunk. I hadn't noticed. I'd been living on the street for three years–my family had written me off, I'd written me off. I stole, cheated, lied, begged, connived to get the booze I needed to fill the gaps when I couldn't afford a rock. I weighed one hundred-thirty pounds. My family had written me off, I'd written me off. I was dying." Sheldon took a sip of his coffee. "Now I am alive." He looked right into Grant's eyes. Grant wanted to tear his eyes away but that would be obvious, his evasion. It was, he saw, terrifying to look someone right in the eyes. He realized he often avoided doing this. Sheldon was talking to him.

"...Grant, I learned I have a disease called alcoholism. I wasn't *bad*–I was *sick*. That brought me to the first step." Sheldon looked at the window shade over the coffee urn. "I 'admitted I was powerless over the disease of alcoholism.' I will always be powerless over alcohol and crack cocaine and my life was not just un-manageable, it wasn't. The living dead had it better than me."

Grant was grateful Sheldon now addressed the group. He lowered his eyes to his lap, vowing never to raise them until this ordeal was over.

"...Charles arranged a week of detox for me, then got me into Bridge House, a halfway house for recovering bums like me. I lived there for a year and a half, staying clean and sober one day at a time. Now, thanks to my Higher Power, whom I choose to call God, I'm an RN. I work at Charity hospital. I have a wonderful wife, a two-year-old son, and my family not only speaks to me, they're happy to." He nodded, big hands flat on the table. "Thanks for letting me share. I open the floor to volunteers." People called out, "Thanks for sharing, Sheldon."

Hands shot up. Grant drifted, words in his mind. *This stuff didn't apply to him. He'd never been homeless, never lived under a bridge…the guy cleaned up amazingly though. You'd never guess he'd been a drunk junkie.*

People talked, one by one. Grant felt as though he was moving in and out of consciousness. Grant noticed each "sharer" began with, "Hello, I'm Bob," or Ted or Alice, followed by the chilling words, "I'm an alcoholic." *How could they say that? Out loud? In front of all these people?*

Meaningless words, thoughts, impressions, sifted through him. A long silence, and he peeked up. *Shit. Everyone looking at him. He was supposed to talk?* Heat came in his face. He cleared his throat.

"Uh–hello. I'm–Grant." Mouth open he waited as they cried in unison.

"Hay-ay, Grant."

"And–I don't know if I'm an alcoholic."

A man's voice, "You're in the right place."

"I–don't know what to say." He croaked, "I'm a lawyer." That got him a laugh. But suddenly his eyes teared. *God. How humiliating. Was he going to weep in front of all these strangers?* He found his voice and forced down the tears, "My son–my son, ran away from home last night. I don't know where he is." He had to gaze at a far wall, stare hard, to stop from crying. He swallowed. "I really wanted a drink tonight. Not just any drink. I wanted a icy double martini with Tanqueray gin." Murmurs. Acknowledgment, encouragement.

"And. I've been screwing around–I'm divorced. Twice divorced. Last night–I did a very stupid thing that could have gotten me–AIDS."

Warm murmurs.

"My son lives with me." He felt tears surge up, nearly uncontrollable. *I haven't cried since I was eight years old, for Chrissake!* His throat spasmed. He couldn't speak.

Gently Santa laid a hand on his arm. "Grant. You're among friends. Everyone of us has been where you are right now. And what's said here stays here."

But Grant had lowered his head, shaking it. A long silence. His throat was locked, shut tight. *Wouldn't someone rescue him?* "I–I…" The quiet continued. They were stranding him here in this awful island of–weeping, wanting to weep?

Anger surged up in him. *The callous sons of bitches.* But the anger took care of the tears. He raised his head. "I–just thought maybe I could come here. Learn how to control my drinking. That's all."

Smiles, knowing. One laugh cut short. Some woman.

Then he heard someone calmly speak. "Grant. Thank you for coming tonight and for sharing your pain. We pray for your son's safe return. And yes, if you keep hanging around here you'll learn a lot about drinking. So welcome. Keep coming back."

Suzanne's crisp voice.

"We use the chip system at this meeting." She held up a green plastic disc about the size of a quarter. Beaming at Grant, she continued.

"Anyone have twenty-four hours sober or–a desire to stop drinking?"

Santa nudging his arm whispering, "Go on now, get you a chip." Alarmed, Grant looked at Hartwell who gave him a half-nod. Clumsily, scraping the chair over the floor, he got to his feet. Everyone clapped. They continued to clap as he walked, unsteady, to Suzanne. He put his hand out to receive the chip but Suzanne flung herself at him and hugged. He was surprised when his arms snapped around her, holding tight for a moment. Relief. The clapping grew louder. She stepped back, put the chip in his hand. It read, "One day at a time." As he went back to his seat he heard her saying: "Anyone got one month? Three months? Six…nine? A year or multiples of years?" No one else went up. Grant sat back down. Aware of the lip, he didn't bang his knee.

"Close in the usual fashion." Chairs scraped, people stood, Grant with them, head bowed, hands took his hands, and with a terrible ache in his throat, he listened to the Lord's prayer.

He let himself into his dark condo. Flicking on a light he called, "Son? You home yet?"

Silence.

He walked down the hall and opened the door to Saunders' bedroom. Only that funky smell and the chaos–he closed the door. In his bedroom, not bothering to turn on the light, he fell face down on the bed. *Strange people! Peculiar rituals they had, like some arcane tribe…*"Hello, Grant, welcome." The chorus of acknowledgment of The One Who was To Share. People didn't talk, they "shared." Weird and wimpy, Saunders would say. And imagine, Hartwell an alcoholic! He'd never have guessed. He'd thought Hartwell was being trendy when he ordered Perrier with a twist. This was a new Hartwell–a vulnerable, kinder

Hartwell.

Hartwell, Gary, Santa, and Suzanne stayed on after the meeting broke up. They'd talked to him, and gradually the ache in his throat diminished. The men gave him phone numbers, insisting if he felt like taking a drink, or just wanted to talk, call them. Anytime. Day or night. Hartwell was especially insistent. They all were recovering alcoholics. He still wasn't convinced that he, himself, really was an alcoholic–more like, he just had a little drinking problem, but–couldn't hurt. It couldn't hurt. He felt so hurt.

Hartwell did seem newly impressed with him.

The living room phone rang twice. His recorded voice: "Griffin residence. Please leave a message." Huge wheeze. Fitz. He started to rise from the bed.

Fitz was saying "–nothing yet, Grant. No news, good news. I'll keep on it. You got my number."

He fell back on the bed. He'd never felt so helpless in his life. Not even when Margie finally, completely, stepped over some invisible line and…vanished into herself. Tears came in his eyes. The ethereal Margaret Evelyn Decroix, daughter of the Kings of Carnival. Perhaps there was an irony there, not just in New Orleans' exaltation of its Mardi Gras royalty, but the bizarre insanity of the carnival season…*Had Saunders' birth triggered her insanity?* The doctors weren't sure. Perhaps the hormonal change had shifted some delicate chemical balance within her, sent her spiraling away from reality. Not even when his marriage to Brit dissolved…over what? Why had he and Brit gotten divorced? He couldn't remember. Meeting Brit, what an impact she'd packed. So alive, so vital, so healthy! Such a cleansing change from furtive little Margie. He knew she'd never become insane. Yet–something about Brit's white skin, her fine bones–even though she was model-tall–held glimmers of that fragility he'd found so appealing in Margie…He sighed, bunched the pillow up under his head, and stared at the dark ceiling. He heard a lion roaring from Audubon Zoo–argh, argh, argh, *what was he trying to say?* He felt pity for the lion, trapped, not free to roam the savannahs of Kenya…Until now, the most wretched time of his life was seeing Margie loaded onto the gurney, the gurney trundling over their flagstone walk under blooming mimosas–blossoms the color of her lips, her nipples…*God.* He pressed his face into his pillow. Now this. Margie gone, Brit gone, Saunders gone. *Why does my life always turn to shit?*

God help me.

T H R E E

Damn! thought Brit. Grant's machine. You'd think the man would have enough con-
cern for his son to stay by his telephone–tonight of all nights! But he probably hadn't
even figured out his son was missing–probably out playing the swinging single. Beep!
She began to speak.

"Grant. This is Britannia. Saunders is at my place. We need to talk. My number hasn't changed. I'll be up another hour. It's going on eleven now. Please call
as soon as you can. Thank you."

She hung up thinking, *some birthday.*

F O U R

Argh, argh, argh, cried the lion.

Pity, fear, loss, bittersweet love mingling in him, he tried to summon some
sense of a "Higher Power" as he drifted toward sleep. Then he was dream-
ing…and…miraculously…wondrously…clearly he heard Brit's voice speaking to
him.

F I V E

Brit hung up, turned to Saunders. She hadn't been able to get him to sit down. Poor
kid…dazed, sodden, forlorn, in need of mothering and fathering.

"Saunders, honey. You heard. Your Dad isn't home. You can't stand there dripping. You'll catch something–hitchhiking in this terrible storm! Look, Sweetie,
why don't I fix up your old bed for you while you take a nice hot bath?"

The child turned such huge sad eyes on her she thought she might start weeping for him. A gush of maternal love surged through her, she wanted to hold and
reassure him. But a boy-man of fifteen might hate that. Now, fury. Grant was not
going to get away with this. She must convince him to let Saunders stay with her
until they worked out a better relationship. She wanted to do this. Why? Was it
because of those awful flashes surging over her body with the same intensity as
her earlier surge of maternal caring? Screaming that her biological clock had
ticked its last tock? Was this one more chance at mothering? Was this why so
many women went bananas over grandchildren?

Perhaps Saunders, so obviously needy, was her finest birthday gift. Suddenly
she felt blessed–she could do this–help him. She felt fierce, strong. Animal mother defending threatened young. She wasn't a grandmother–yet–she was a mother!

Asia'd be thrilled her brother was back. She adored him in her solemn, intense way. Spring break on the farm would be the most fun in years, Asia and Saunders around, even if they were too old to hunt Easter Eggs....

Still standing, Saunders gazed around the room in a disoriented fashion. *No wonder!*

"Saunders. Take a bath in my Jacuzzi. I'll turn it on for you. While you're bathing I'll fix you something to eat. Omelet okay?"

He turned his pewter eyes on her, skin so pallid, auburn hair startling, and nodded. The child was so physically and emotionally exhausted, she was certain, he could barely speak. Despite her long day, despite the drinks, even the marijuana, she felt charged with new energy. Silk caftan susserating, she flowed upstairs to her bathroom.

Saunders was pleased. Old Brit had not chastised him...she'd blamed his father. As he looked around the familiar living room, he saw he'd forgotten how cool it was. The huge room soared two stories to a raftered log ceiling. A great bronze chandelier hung in the center, flanked by ceiling fans. Behind him a smooth white wall, artwork floor to ceiling. Dominating was an oil Brit had painted as a student, big as a whole piece of plywood. A herd of horses galloped over a desert. When he was a little kid living here he'd lie on the floor and gaze up at that picture. White, reddish, black, gray, brownish horses reared and plunged: a mass of manes, tails, big startled eyes. Behind them, the reason for their fear–a sandstorm. The sun, a sullen orange ball, glowed through a murk of dun mounding into a sick-yellow sky. In the distance, barely suggested, a cluster of palms. He knew if those horses could just get to that oasis before the sandstorm hit, they'd survive. As a little boy he'd wondered at the terror of the horses–the way Brit had painted them they looked real–and although he'd never say it out loud, he scoffed that a dumb animal could feel fear.

His stupid stepsister used to urge them to gallop faster, faster, to get to safety. Of course, the sandstorm eternally threatened, the oasis eternally beckoned, the horses never got to safety. Brit always kind of laughed about the picture. He knew her dumb fag agent Damien made fun of it when he visited, saying, "Thank God, Brit, you got that equine art thing out of your system so you could settle down and do some real art!" Though Brit was slightly embarrassed by it, she stubbornly kept it hung as the centerpiece of her living room. But the agent would go on and say–Saunders guessed he didn't want Brit to get too upset–"I have to say, Britannia dahling, you managed to capture something there. It has the look of an Old Masters, it could pass for one of Rosa Parks' great equine works!" Brit winking and waggling her eyebrows at Saunders and Asia behind the guy's back. Their private joke. That spacey Asia always had to pipe up: "But, Mr. Damien, it's my favorite picture of Mom's." Everyone smiling indulgently at the space cadet, that fairy petting her on the head and she'd start naming all the horses while everyone listened like she was Einstein or something. Terminally cute.

When no one was around, Brit often sat with him and Asia and they'd look up at the picture. She'd tell stories about the horses. He and Asia often fought over names. She picked wimpy names like "Ashley" or "Emily" while he wanted to give them good names like "Rocket-Blaster" or "Ninja." One guy, Saunders knew, some rich oil guy, once offered Brit a hundred thousand dollars for the picture but she said no thanks, she wanted to keep her Youthful Folly, whatever that meant. Saunders looked at the picture again: *a hundred grand–just hanging there. Too bad. Too big to hock.*

Below the horse picture hung a variety of others, some of Brit's work–the animals and crabs and weeds stuff, then a few interesting nudes, women and men–some Brit's, some other artists. The floor was shiny wood with oriental carpets here and there. The end walls were natural log–that big old walnut thing at one end–still here with all the booze in it. Every other wall was filled with pictures, too–*Super Dome's walls all plants, hers all pictures, go figure.* The U-shaped sofa in front of the fireplace was new. He liked it–better than that white thing the Dome was always fussing about. Presents scattered everywhere, flowers with helium balloons on the hearth. "Happy Birthday" said the balloons wavering in unseen currents. *He'd hit it right.* Funny he remembered her birthday but always forgot Dome's. She still had the two wing chairs covered in birds. Brit had made those birds herself. He remembered her stitching away like a madwoman night after night. Cruel, she called it, shaking out the fabric for Anastasia and Saunders to have a look. This is cruel embroidery. He couldn't see anything cruel about it. The birds looked pretty happy. Nothing was killing them or anything. No cats in the picture she'd stitched on the cloth.

The place had a real rich feel to it. Here and there she had mirrored pedestals–with more statues on them, *pardon me,* "sculptures." *Bet those suckers were worth a bundle.* The green velvet draperies over the French doors were open, he saw small stabs of lightning from the departing storm. The north wall also had The Door, which he and Anastasia were forbidden ever to open without permission. He shuddered. He hated limits. He hated The Door. Led to Brit's studio. Oh, she let them in sometimes. It smelled good–turpentine, paints, linseed oil, stuff like that. Its walls also went the whole way up to the roof with two sky-lights–for the light, said Brit. The outside walls floor-to-ceiling glass. Big trees outside the windows. And flowers. She'd painted his picture and Asia's when they were little and these hung in their bedrooms' across the mezzanine from Brit's humongous bedroom, where his dad and Brit had slept. He'd often heard weird sounds come from that bedroom, even though the whole of the living room was between the bedrooms, sounds he now understood. *Boy, wouldn't old Brit be surprised to find out now he knew all about fucking, too.* He'd never let on. The bitch was really buying his orphan-Annie act. She came downstairs now. Took him by the shoulders, pushed him up the stairs.

Brit was just slightly taller than him, still.

"I hope you've brought some PJ's in that backpack of yours, Saunders."

"Uh, no, I forgot." PJ's! Did she think he was still a little kid? He slept raw now.

"But I did bring some underwear, another T-shirt."

"Good. That'll have to do until your father can bring some clothes out for you."

Was she going to let him stay?

"Okay."

They stood in her bedroom. *Jeez what a mess. She better not say anything about his room, if it got in a mess.*

"You get into that warm tub. I'll bring your backpack up and leave it by my bed so you can change. There's an old terry robe of mine in the bathroom you can wear over your T-shirt and underwear." She rotated his shoulders toward her.

"Cheddar or Swiss?"

"What?"

"For your omelet. Do you want Cheddar or Swiss cheese?"

"Oh. Cheddar."

"Fine. It'll be ready when you get down." She smiled at him. "Saunders. I'm sorry you've been having a tough time. You're welcome to stay as long as you want."

Yes!

Standing over her stove, she suddenly felt extremely anxious that the omelet would fall apart as she eased one half up–*damn!*–it broke. *Oh hell.* She flipped the broken side over, gave the pan a good shake. *This will have to do.* It had been some day.

As she laid out a plate, napkin, cutlery, an inner voice piped up: *Think about this one very carefully, Brit, taking on this boy—are you biting off too much? Oh shut up. He's a little weird. Hush! Just scared, that's all. I'll talk to Grant, get to the bottom of this. If it's in his best interest—well then, he stays. Grant will probably love it.* Total freedom to be an asshole.

Okay-ay.

Saunders' shadow fell across the table and she whirled and smiled at him. He had such limpid, innocent eyes. Wet, his hair was the color of dried blood, like the splotch on her pine floor left by Scottie. His skin was so pale she wondered if he was anemic. He stood, helpless, so she sat him down at her oak breakfast table and watched while he wolfed the omelet, and drank two glasses of milk. She'd have to buy or make cookies. She sipped ice water. *So quiet! Worn out from his dreadful day.* Wilton still wouldn't go to the boy and kept crowding onto her bare feet, toenails scratching her ankles as he restlessly changed positions. Finally, she pushed at him, speaking firmly. Drooping, the dog walked a few feet away and plopped down with a mournful sigh. She looked at Saunders.

"Your dad hasn't called."

Saunders stared back at her while he took a bite of English muffin, chewed, swallowed.

"Um, he might not be home yet."

Poor kid. Damn Grant! Out every night. Besides the confusion from all his hormonal changes, the child was lonely—and with Margie as a mother—had he stood a chance?

Yes! If Britannia Rhodes had anything to say about it.

"If he doesn't return my call tonight I'll catch him in the morning. Finished?"

Saunders nodded, she got up, picked up his plate.

"Your old room is ready for you so maybe you better hit the sack, kiddo. We can tackle everything tomorrow after a good night's sleep."

"Thanks…Brit."

Brit, she noted. *In the past he'd called her "Ma."* He stood. The kitchen window was black, the rain a patter. Thunder rumbled far away sounding almost friendly. Good sleeping weather.

She stepped toward him.

"Could you use a hug?" and was surprised how quickly he stepped into her open arms. She was a little alarmed at how solid—manly—his body felt. She bussed him on his fresh smelling, smooth boy's cheek, then stepped back.

"Off to bed, Saunders. Sweet dreams."

He grinned at her, wide–the first smile she'd gotten all evening. Then he was gone. Exhausted, she rinsed dishes, stuck them in the dishwasher. She turned off lights as she passed through the great living room and, hand on the banister, pulled herself up to bed. She would make herself change the bed. *Clean sheets, muuum.* To flute-like rain sounds, thunder thrumbling like a bass fiddle, she lay flat on her back in bed, silence settling round her, sheets smelling of her home-made potpourri. godd moved softly over the down comforter to her, Wil snuggled into the crook of her arm. She caught a whiff of damp dog and whispered, "Wil, you smell like a dog. But never mind, tomorrow I'll bathe you, put the comforter in the wash."

Her mind drifted, trying to make sense of the day. Sleep edging up.

Fifty...good God....

Ring! She groaned, fumbled the receiver to her ear, hearing another distant ringing sound. Took a moment to figure what it was...voice on the other end saying, "Hello? Brit? Hello?"

The other ringing was Mokhtar, neighing. *She'd forgotten all about him! Damn!* No Jimmy to put him in his stall, the horse had been outside in the storm.

"Hello," she managed.

"Brit! Just woke up–heard your voice–Saunders–is he all right?"

Grant. She struggled up to a sitting position, dumping Wil off the bed.

"Oh, Grant. I was just falling asleep. He's here. He's fine." She pulled the sheet over her bare breasts.

"I can be there in an hour."

"No, please. I'm so tired. I've put Saunders to bed in his old room. The poor kid's beat, Grant. Apparently he hitchhiked all the way out here."

She heard the offensive edge to her voice and braced.

"My God. Is he–is he all right, Britannia?" He spoke softly. *Where was the anger,* she wondered, *why isn't he screaming like old times?* The deep voice continued, subdued like the thunder.

"You sure he's all right? I've been very concerned here, looking for him. I called everyone, but I never thought he'd go out to your place."

Thanks a lot Grant. I was his mother for seven years.

"He's fine now. I got him to bathe, eat, then to bed. Look, Grant, I'm very tired. I've had a long day. Could we handle this in the morning?"

"Well. Are you sure he's okay?" *This paternal concern was a bit late.*

"Yes, Grant, he's fine. Morning will be better. Besides, Mokhtar is yelling his head off and I've got to get out of bed and put him up. I forgot to feed him." She winced, now he'd say "that damn horse." But no.

"What. Old Jimmy slacking off?"

"You could say that, Grant. Old Jimmy died today." That was below the belt but she couldn't resist.

Ouch, thought Grant. "Oh, Brit, I'm sorry. Jeez. I'm really sorry. I liked Jimmy. He was a special person." Her hand was clenched on the receiver. *Now he'll start yelling "that useless horse."*

Instead, "Can't Mokhtar wait till tomorrow? You sound beat."

She was beginning to feel annoyed, cross-examined. "I am. But he can't wait. I left him outside and all this rain isn't good for his arthritis."

"Well, then, Saunders can help you." Grant was strangely solicitous.

"He's sound asleep. I can manage." *What do you really want here, Grant?*

"Oh. Well. How about if I get there by eight?"

"Eleven would be better. As I said, it's been a long day."

"Okay, Brit. Be careful outside." *This concern couldn't be genuine, or maybe Saunders' running away had shaken him. But so much his actual character was changed?*

"So, then, I'll see you around ten?"

"If you insist. Bye." She hung up. Wilton gazed at her, wondering when he could get back in bed.

"C'mon, Wil, let's go take care of Mokhtar."

Downstairs she remembered she'd left her boots in the barn. She pulled on old sneakers, a poncho. Mokhtar was waiting at the gate, trembling with cold. She opened the gate and the horse trotted stiffly across meadow and driveway to his barn, into his stall. She ran after him, cold wet grass slapping her bare ankles. Hastily she dished up his grain, threw him hay, refilled his water bucket, then while he ate, toweled his shaking body. She slid a blanket onto him, buckled it, petted his neck, and streaked to the house.

Back in bed, a pungent Wil beside her, she tried to remember exactly what Grant looked like...but before she could quite get his face in focus...something else...something about Saunders, an elusive image...something she should remember...*getting into a car?*...she was drifting, drifting...so mellow...tired... so much had happened...bad things...good things...the clean sheets felt so fresh against her damp cold naked body...when a sensation of inrushing coalesced in her brain–an electronic zap. Sizzle in her head–like that nasty crackle when a television set is turned off abruptly. It hurt in the disorienting way an electric shock hurts. The sensation repeated–Zap! She held her breath, very still. *Was something wrong with her brain?* It felt like a giant thumb was clicking the OFF-ON button on a remote control, playing with the electronic energy that kept her system operating. Like a TV set, she felt a brief flare in her picture tube, feeble protest against the killing, then, swift fade to a white dot, the dot vanishing, then rapidly the sensation dissolved on trailers of electronic fizzles, her mind the mute drab olive of a blank screen. She lay, blanked out for eternal nanoseconds.

Turned over. Squeezed the sides of her head between her palms, her damp hair feeling greasy. Held her head pressed together, her hands like bookends.

What the hell was that?

This had happened before. She remembered when. Twice, after smoking just the tiniest bit of marijuana. *Like today. One very mild joint–well, two.* She pushed her face into a pillow, as if trying to smother herself.

A reaction to the dope deep inside, her brain shorting out. *No!*

Did this mean–no more marijuana? That rare, small pleasure?

Did she have to give it up? Besides smoking, alcohol, sex, her relationship with Scottie?

Frightened, thinking brain tumors...brain cancer...she burrowed under the covers and waited to see if God was going to zap her again. Her heart picked up speed, strange electronic fizzles in her brain...zizzle...zizzle...ziz...ziz....

Maybe she was dying.

Ziz. Off.

She waited to see if she had a mind left.

Slowly turned over–autonomic nervous system still functioning. Opened her eyes. Saw stars. Real stars, through the skylight above her bed.

Maybe He was just trying to change her channel, not turn her off completely.

From *Playboy* to–*TLC?*

The Learning Channel.

TLC. Tender Loving Care.

She relaxed. Her wandering left hand brushed the fur of her cat. She stopped her fingers, moved them into the warm softness. godd purring...purrs vibrated into her fingertips, through her wrist, along her arm, made a U-turn at her shoulder and poured down into her quieting heart...vibrations of benign energy seemed to emanate from godd's purrs. All the feelings of fear, irritability, anxiety, fled.

Her brain felt normal again. Yet, a teeny part of her mind continued to wonder even as she drifted off in almost perfect peace...*exactly how much would she be required to give up?*

S I X

Lee crouched over her computer. An overflowing ashtray and an insulated hot-pink mug sat near her mouse. It held half a pot of chicory coffee. Her favorite and the cheapest. Black, two pink Sweet Things. Couldn't afford Equal.

The spare bedroom in her two-bedroom trailer was her studio. A hollow-core door on two filing cabinets was her desk. The door butted to the wall and across that wall, resting on the door-desk, were her *Roget's*, a six-inch thick *Webster's New Universal Unabridged Dictionary*, four editions of *Writer's Market*, an untidy stack of *Publishers Weekly, Writer's Digest, Cosmopolitan, New Woman* and *Redbook*. She'd bought those to research their short stories and articles. One *Redbook* contained a short story she'd written. They'd paid her two thousand dollars and while the money was needed, the recognition of her writing ability was desperately needed. It made her a real writer. Published.

After the breakup with Richard she'd put aside her struggles with her first novel and now worked on an article she hoped to market to *Cosmopolitan: Is There Life Without A Man?* She was trying to make it witty, pungent, short. She wasn't sure if *Cosmo* would go for it since everything in the magazine was engineered toward *How to Get a Man* but she thought if her subtitle was, *Survival Between Men,* it might sell.

The other walls of her studio were lined with homemade bookshelves sagging under the weight of many books.

She was stuck. The article sounded too hostile. *Damn!* Anyone who thought inspired writing gushed was wrong.

Her computer said 8:04 a.m. Okay to call Brit, even though she'd be no help on this article. Brit, despite three awful marriages, still hadn't learned to hate men. Lee was doing a hard-sell of her current position: they're only good for fucking, but since even sport-sex might uncork a dangerous softening of attitude, women best stay away from them entirely.

She reached for the phone, punched out Brit's number.

SEVEN

In bed Brit was still trying to bring some order to the confusions of the day before. Saunders hadn't stirred. *Didn't teenagers need twice as much sleep as adults? Let him lie.*

Her brain wallowed against her unyielding skull like half-set jello. This was not entirely the result of the big zap from the universe, she didn't think. Hangovers often felt this way.

She had risen, knotted a robe around her, and had gone downstairs to make coffee. She sprinkled a big mug with cinnamon, a blue package of Equal. Now it was in her hands resting on the comforter.

After a few sips she brought up Jimmy's death and found herself in angry, frustrated weeping. Did God really have such a black–pun intended–sense of humor to take Jimmy on her birthday? And the worst possible one. Pretty selfish on her part, she knew, to think about her birthday and his death, juxtaposed. Yet in some weird way maybe it was a message from Jimmy. He was so patient, so funny. She always felt calmer around him. Had all his years as a school teacher developed these skills? Whenever she'd worried he was "overqualified" he'd gently remind her that she'd given him his dream retirement job. One day, when a redneck hayman refused to unload a hundred bales for him–these racist fools had to accept Jimmy–what if she were in New York? The animals would starve!–she'd stormed out hollering, "How dare you insult my–Estate Manager!" Peripherally, she saw Jimmy's eyes roll up, his lips twitch with suppressed laughter. Then, as if he might have an itch on his nose, he brushed the back of his finger against it rapidly in old gesture signifying snob. She calmed down, held back her laughter, told the man to work with Jimmy or take his hay and shove it. The guy cowered, practically pulling his forelock. Jimmy completed the transaction with the diction and manner of a skinny James Earl Jones. Ironically they had the same initials, except Jimmy's middle name was "Earnest." From then on she always introduced him as "Mr. James Earnest Jones, Estate Manager." It became one of their best inside jokes–her twenty acres and log house would barely make the grade as a farm, never mind estate.

She'd never had to worry about her animals, her garden, when work meant seventy-two hour stretches of painting or flying to New York, not with Jimmy in her life.

Now he was gone, Asia too, except for vacations. Everyone gone, everything changed–Saunders was back. Still, she wept again.

How much longer do I have? she wondered. *Thirty years? Twenty? Ten? I could die...anytime.*

An acid inner voice said, *So could anyone, idiot.*

With that she stopped crying and, just as she was about to try and make herself feel happy, she realized she was scared.

She didn't have the energy for this fear. If she felt it, she'd have to do something about it. *So please, not today.* Today she wanted to be mindless, emotionless. She'd deal with it tomorrow.

She clicked on her TV and Willard Scott came on the screen. Today he was bald. She liked Willard, his down-to-earthiness, the casual way he used his toupee, like a hat. She forgot her fear. Grant had some of that expansiveness, she thought, when he forgot to be haughty, a hauteur that was fake. Grant had grown up on the outskirts of Tylertown, Mississippi. Redneck dirt-farming family. Although, not to forget, Grant had been a scholarship law student at Tulane. He'd hauled himself up a long, long way.

Now Willard was interviewing a man who raised giant bullfrogs.

Then Hallmark Cards opened. Four people a hundred. One lady in Wichita was 109. Brit leaned. *Could she walk? Talk? Think? Didn't look bad...awful Polaroid...*Willard saying "...this beautiful lady does needlepoint every day..."

Needlepoint! An artist! And I'm whining about fifty. She fell back on her pillows. Thoughts, feelings, meandered through her but she was too hungover to work for epiphanies. She let impressions fall through her like streamers from a departing cruise ship.

During a life insurance commercial she considered rising. Creatures needed feeding. She needed to clean up. After all. That attorney about town, that swinging single, Grrrrr-ant Griffin was on his way.

God help me.

When she and Asia used to come to Grant's to get Saunders for trips to the zoo, movies, or the aquarium a few years back, Grant had been absent or lurking in his gray-shadowed living room. No change from the last year of their marriage. Lurking in shadows. Absent. She always ignored him—her focus was on the child. Then Saunders became a teenager. Metal music, hanging out. Monosyllabic responses to her questions, indifferent to her suggestions for outings. She told herself this was a normal phase for him. One day he'd come back...hadn't they loved each other?

Now he had! She felt the smug warmth of redemption.

An interview, Denzel Washington. Attractive man. A sexual tingle then a hot flash, confusing itself with her faint arousal. It whooshed from forehead to feet and she was slick with sweat in the cold room. Throwing the covers off she looked down. Sweat all over her. Ugly mottled red on chest and stomach. *God! Like an orgasm.*

Wilton began to lick her belly. She pushed him away. The fan whipped around drying her and she was chilly again. She pulled the covers back.

She thought of Scottie. Out in restaurants, arm and arm in movie theater lines. Were people whispering, *Look at that old woman, young man?* She'd ask Lee. Then shuddered. Lee would tell her the truth.

She thought of her periods, now they were like…stutters…sometimes there were only a few brown-pink spots on the pad. *I want my period back! I don't want to be an old woman!* She had cried more than once, seated on the toilet, hunched over herself.

She fingered her upper lip. *Was she growing a mustache? Chin hairs? Would her vagina dry up and she'd never again be able to enjoy sex without a–lubricant?* "Hold it, darling, gotta get the K-Y…?"

Then–the belly. It pooched up the covers slightly. She looked at the TV. Katie Couric interviewing Cindy Crawford. Brit thought, *even you, Honey!* She felt a moment's mean satisfaction erased by another rush of heat. Her pores erupted. Panting, she threw off the covers. *It was almost like going into labor.* It was horrible to care about a body that was just going to disintegrate, like cut flowers wilting. So what should she care about?

Brit, old girl, see the gynecologist, maybe she can give you something for this. These flashes hit with no warning. *Awful. They couldn't be hidden.* At least with menstruation, and hyper-vigilance, no one had to know.

Why did both words begin with "men?" *'Cause it's the Greek for month, girl, and months are created by the moon–so it's moon-a-pause. Got nothing to do with "men." It's a woman's show, solely.*

Viola had never mentioned menopause, not the done thing. And Viola was gifted at denial. Once she'd heard her grandmother refer primly to The Change. That sounded better. Except "change" was one of the most frightening words in the English language and only women got to do it! And damn, was she changing!

She felt bushwhacked. She'd known nothing about this. When she'd gone through the first female change, child to woman, they'd taught it at school–movies with animated wombs, fallopian tubes, ovaries in artistic flow charts, a pink-faced phys-ed teacher explaining the anatomies of sexual organs to a class of embarrassed, riveted girls. Their concentration was intense as they intuited beyond all this clinical stuff there was some great secret that would help them get–boyfriends!

Then, she was learning about a new power. She'd make babies.

What did this second change mean? The end of fertility–creativity? She hadn't been creative in two years. Sure, crawfishes, in ditch waters like tubes of human flesh, hunkered down at the root of a passion flower blooming above the slime, were in a feeble way, revealing, seeing. They sold well. But she'd painted that series, when? Eight, ten years ago? Since then, she'd been coasting on print sales.

Damien was impatient. Despite their good relationship, its core was business. He'd drop her. That was where the serious money came from, that had paid Jimmy, bought her Jaguar, her Arabian horse, taken her and Asia to Paris, London, Montego Bay. Bought good champagne, oyster sofas and now, cosmetic surgery? But she couldn't afford any repairs–not on the farm, or herself. She needed a brilliant new show. She lay sweating for a time, not a hot-flash sweat, a blocked artist's sweat.

A lot to sweat about.

If Scottie had sex with that anchorwoman, who probably, at thirty was not a drying-up crone like herself, maybe she couldn't blame him. *Was she drying up?* She touched herself. *Damp.* And she'd seen Denzel two commercials back.

Forty had been easy. She'd mildly wondered why people made such a big deal of it. There were no significant changes to her face, body, energy, creativity.

Now she felt unbalanced. Life loomed rather than beckoned. The Big Five-O.

She was on a runaway train, lurching down narrow train corridors, hips banging side to side through hurtling cars that swayed dizzyingly. Dimly lit passageways, mute indifferent passengers. No conductor, engineer dead, frantic, jostled, scrabbling, she couldn't find the brake cord.

She pounded her fists against her knees.

I hate this.

So? Work on it. Handle it.

She cried for a few seconds, then her head came up.

I need books.

Get some. Gotta be lots on menopause and aging out there.

The phone rang, she grabbed it.

Lee. "How are you?"

"Better."

"Than what?"

Brit laughed. "I just flashed my degenerate lifestyle before my eyes and beat myself up. Now I think my head's in a better place."

"Oh. That kind of better. Well, I find I'm hating men this morning."

"Interesting. I found I was hating Brit this morning."

"Maybe we'd both better lighten up."

"Absolutely. I just have. Want to quit smoking with me?"

"Right now?"

"God, no. Not till I can get some patches."

"Sweetie, I can't afford patches."

"Sweetie, if you'll try and quit with me, I'll share my patches."

"I can't—"

"Lee—cut the 'poor but proud' stuff. Yes you can take patches from me. You'll be saving the rest of my life. My next fifty years. My last half-century. I've decided living to seventy-five doesn't give me enough time. So now my aim's locked onto a whole hundred years. Maybe I'll have Damien arrange a show for me exactly fifty years from now."

"Oooooo. I get it. Post-birthday blues. You bring to mind something I read the other day. Now I get to use more of Lee's trivia."

"I could stand some trivia right now."

"Ready?"

"Yup."

"What is the fastest growing demographic group in America today?"

"A riddle. Hum. Has to be something about Baby Boomers—of which group I am one."

"Wrong!" Triumphant. "The fastest growing demographic group in America is…people over a hundred!"

"No shit, Sherlock."

"None whatever. This fact from some impeccable source like *Reader's Digest* or *Newsweek* gleaned whilst waiting for the dentist.

"Lee, I just love how your mind reads my mind." Brit felt happy. "So. How's the novel coming?"

"The novel. It's not. Instead I'm trying to make money writing an article for *Cosmo*. And that got me thinking how much I hate men."

"I guess I'm going to have to let you work through the hate men thing on your own. You won't listen to Auntie Brit. Men are not that bad."

"I hate to be cruel, but have you heard from Scottie?"

"Ouch. No. Maybe I'm getting over him. Maybe he's not what I need in my life any more. Among other things, we both drink too much. I'd like to cut back on the booze."

"Excellent. Sounds like your beating up had some good effect."

"Yes. Speaking of men, guess who's coming to my house?"

"Gotta be a man. Damien's flying down? Is Damien a man?"

"Nope. And, nope. Hint: He's one of your favorites. Even though you don't know him, have never met him–"

"Goddammit, Brit! Grant! How'd you swing that, girl?"

"I didn't swing a thing. I plan merely to endure his presence, for the sake of another, more needy party."

"And whom might that party be?"

"Saunders."

"Saunders. That little shit?"

"Lee. I won't have you speaking of my stepson in that fashion. Just because you didn't hit it off with him that time we went to the zoo."

"He's a spoiled, surly, manipulative little brat, but if you want to love him, okay by me. And I guess now's the time. There was one card I palmed, you were getting so down from the reading. A young man. I remember one line from the card. 'Black seeds lie dormant.'"

"What hogwash. Well, the child is here."

"Child? Was Vlad The Impaler ever a child?"

"He had a very unhappy childhood."

"I bet old Vlad did too."

"Lee. You're not usually so intransigent!"

"Brit. There's just something about that kid…So. Saunders is at your house right now? I gotta have a cigarette." Brit waited, heard a lighter's click, then a long exhale. "Gol-darn. Good thing we haven't quit smoking yet, Rhodes, my nerves can't handle all this drama. Okay. Spill it."

"Here it comes, Robinet. After you dashed to your car last night and I dashed to my front door–there he was, on the porch, waiting for me."

"Wow. That would have scared the hell out of me."

"It did me, for a moment. I didn't know who it was. Poor kid. He'd hitchhiked all the way out here in that awful storm. He was sodden. I didn't get much out of him last night—"

"Can anyone? Ever?"

"Hold the sarcasm, Lee."

"Okay, okay."

"So I fed him, got him to bathe in the Jacuzzi, talked briefly to Grant. So the child is sleeping in his old bedroom and Grant will be here at ten."

"Well. Not boring."

"Not. So, how are you?"

"Oh, I'll be fine."

"I hate to sound like a male chauvinist but you maybe need to get laid, Robinet. Remind yourself what men are for."

Big sigh. "I think I agree. But I'm not calling Dick. That bastard would fuck me and drop me just like before."

"I didn't mean Dick, Honey. Anyone but Dick. Any dick but Dick's."

Laughter, a sigh. "At the moment no one is rapping at my door."

"I know. They will though. Beautiful woman like you? Better go. My prodigal son and faithful steed need care and feeding."

"Okay, Sweetie. Watch it with that kid. And the ex."

"I will call and report as soon as the interview is over."

"Do that. Bye."

"Bye."

E I G H T

When Britannia heard the crunch of tires up her drive she got nervous. When the doorbell rang, her palms were damp. *Is my hair all right? Should I have dressed in something other than black leggings and an oversized white shirt? Is the ankle bracelet silly? Why didn't wear a bra?* She whipped the front door open and she and Grant stared at one another. He held a red rose. *The naked woman on the card held a rose and a single drop of blood dripped from her finger.* Then she thought, *why, his eyes are tearing, he's really upset about Saunders.* Then almost laughed out loud at the ridiculous hairpiece he was wearing—*surely he could afford better?* Last she heard the divorce business was booming, even with no-fault.

Grant stared down at Britannia with mild surprise. *She didn't look...too bad. Must be the dim light in this dinky foyer.* Wilton came, greeted Grant with manic joy. Grant knelt.

"Hey, now, boy. Cute dog, Brit."

"Wilton. Stop bothering the man. Let's go in."

Grant looked up, blinking fast, "It's no bother, I miss having a dog, but I've got this white sofa–" he stood, closed the door behind him, and held out the rose. "For you."

"How nice."

She took it and darned if she didn't prick her finger. She turned and, despite herself, felt a bit of awe that he was still the tallest man she'd ever been with. He looked fairly good. Bags under his eyes, but she had them too. Wilton, damn him, was still all over the man.

In the living room each sat at the opposite ends of the sofa's U.

"Wil, quit now." She smiled sweetly at her ex-husband, laid the rose on the glass table between them, and folded her arms. The fire she'd lit earlier crackled and was the only antidote to the gray light from the windows. It looked like rain again. Grant sat upright. He smiled back–nervously?–hands squarely on his knees. His eyes watered. He blinked and looked around.

"So. Where's Saunders?"

"Asleep."

"Oh. I guess then, we can talk."

"Coffee? Bloody Mary?"

"Uh, coffee."

"Be right back."

When she got back with a tray Grant was standing, gazing up at the big horse picture.

"Still got it."

"Yep."

"One of my favorites."

"Don't say that to Damien."

They laughed.

Brit set the tray down. He was staring at her again, eyes narrowed, a little amazed–in this daylight she looked almost...beautiful. For someone her age, of course. He wondered how her body had held up. His eyes strayed to her breasts, nipples occasionally outlined under the white shirt. *Was she wearing a bra? Were they lower than four years ago? Had to be. She must be menopausal by now, dried up where it mattered most, tits drooping, belly sagging, cellulite all over her ass and thighs*–he suppressed a disgusted shudder. *Old woman. Not for him.*

Brit felt defenseless in this merciless daylight. He was seeing the bags, the wat-

tle, the gray at the temples. But she could stare too. He was still a good big hunk
of a man. Bit of a pot belly, haggard, no doubt from hangover and worry. She
stared at his pot belly, not seeing him evaluating her breasts. She looked back up
at his face.

"Why are you blinking?"

He blushed. "Oh. That." Blink, blink. "Contacts. Can't seem to get them
right. Fourth pair."

"Why don't you just wear glasses?"

"Well, you know–"

"Chicks don't make passes at men who wear glasses?"

"No, no–"

"I think you would look spectacular in horn-rimmed glasses."

"I would?"

"Yep. But if you want to be miserable in contacts, of course, I understand.
What happens if you lose one?"

He flashed on Big Earl at The Texas Motel and that meaty finger balancing
the tiny contact. He thought of Cinderella's glass slipper, shattering, becoming
useless. The ball was over. He reached into an inside pocket. Drawing out his
horn rims, he showed them to her.

"I have these. My eye doctor says my far vision is 20/20. I don't need glasses
except for reading."

"Me too. I have granny glasses. I love them. I feel like a hippie. And I see far
just fine, too. Why don't you take off that jacket? I'll pour coffee."

The fire was warm. He slipped out of his jacket while Brit poured him coffee.

"Still take it white and sweet?"

"Yes, please."

She served him and then poured herself some black. Wilton, turncoat, slept at
Grant's feet, but then godd came and curled up next to her.

Grant sipped, set his cup down. "Place looks good. Saw old Mokhtar outside.
He looks good."

"Getting old." *Aren't we all,* she thought.

"Yep." *Aren't we all,* he thought.

Was he looking at her in that critical way again? Now he was blinking.

"Grant. Please pop those contacts out. Your constant blinking is driving me
nuts."

"Oh. Sorry. Hope I don't do this with clients."

"I'm sure you don't." *I'm sure you do.*

He took them out, put them in a case then looked around, blinking once more.

"Better. Thanks, Britannia."

"So Grant, why did Saunders run away from home?"

"God, Brit. I don't know! He seemed fine. Never said a word."

Brit remembered Lee's words about Saunders: *Does he ever?*

"Well, Grant, he's always been difficult to draw out. I remember when we were all living together, I had a hard time getting him to talk about what he thought, what he felt. It was almost like he was divorced from his feelings in some deep-seated way."

"Margie, you know, all that…"

"Yes. But we can't continue to blame Margie for everything. I admit I feel guilty right now that I didn't do more for him when I was his stepmother."

Abruptly Grant leaned forward. "Oh no, Brit, you were wonderful with him. Wonderful! Far better than I. Actually, you were the only mother he ever really had…"

"I'm glad you said that Grant, because I would like to keep him out here with me. For a while."

"Oh no! That would be too much. Besides, he's got to learn—"

"What? What does he have to learn?"

"Why, that he can't just run away from things, situations he doesn't like."

"What doesn't he like?"

"I haven't a clue."

"Maybe if he stayed here I could find out."

Grant broke a sweat and his hairpiece began to itch. *Would Brit find out that he, Saunders' dad, was out every night? Seldom home for dinner? That he came in late, almost every night, drunk?* His ex-wife could not find this out.

"Well, I have been busy at the office a lot lately—working a lot of nights—"

"Working or womanizing?"

"Brit! What an idea!"

"What else is that hairpiece for?" Grant jerked his hand down, he'd been scratching. "Those contacts? And I couldn't miss the middle-aged-crazimobile you arrived in." She leaned forward. "How *do* you get those long legs into that little bitty thing?"

Grant adjusted the crease in his chalk-stripe pants then looked at her sternly.

"Perhaps we'd be wise to stay away from personal topics. Focus on Saunders."

Brit sat back. *Gotcha*, thought Grant.

The phone rang.

Brit said, "Excuse me," and picked it up.

"Hello," she sang then shot a look at Grant. Scott. She began to blush, or was it a hot flash? Abruptly she stood, the phone to her ear, and turned her back on Grant. It was a hot flash. She couldn't bear for Grant to see her red and sweating–he'd know. And he absolutely couldn't know she had a younger lover, he'd snatch Saunders away. She strolled into the kitchen, Grant watching, alert, curious.

"I can't talk now," she muttered.

"What's up, Babe? Got your other boyfriend over?"

"No other boyfriend, Scott. Something's coming down right now. I'll have to get back to you."

"Real sorry I missed your birthday."

"Why didn't you call earlier?"

"I…got back late. After the shoot, Sue and I–"

"Sue and you what?"

"Now, Brit, don't get all bent out of shape. It's not like–"

"You fucked her."

"Brit, baby, now–"

"Scottie. You did. Say it."

"Well, we had a few drinks and then–"

"You son of a bitch!" Her voice had risen. Had Grant heard?

"I have to go." And she clicked the phone off, Scottie saying "Brit, baby, don't–"

In the living room Grant looked at her quizzically. She would not enlighten him. Sitting back down she sipped lukewarm coffee. "Sorry, Grant. Where were we?"

"We were deciding to stay away from personal topics." *Ouch.*

"Right. Here's what I think. Grant, if you let Saunders stay for a while, maybe it'll help him sort things out. Also, perhaps, I can get him to talk about what's really bothering him."

"But he has school–"

"There's school here."

"Yes, but, changing now–the year's almost over–"

"Running away interferes with school attendance, don't you think? Maybe we can get him into St. Paul's. He might run away again if you take him back–somewhere not as safe as here. Also I'd like to get him in therapy. I'm going to start myself."

"He has a therapist. Had her for years."

"Hasn't done him much good, has she? Maybe a change is what he needs."

"I hear you, Brit, but–"

"But what? Why don't we try it for a month? If we don't see Saunders growing happier…well, then, we'll figure out something else. Take him weekends if you want. If he wants–"

Grant got up. Pacing the room he scratched his hairpiece. "I don't know what to do. I guess I feel pretty guilty I haven't been a good enough parent for him." *Grant Griffin feeling guilt and admitting it? The old Grant was never wrong.* She felt a twinge of pity for him.

"It's tough, Grant." The clock on the mantel was going for eleven. She had a crawly feeling, the hangover's edge. "Why don't I fix Bloody Marys for us, make lunch, wake Saunders, and get his input?"

"Lunch sounds good, but…pass on the drink."

"What, you've gone teetotal or something?" She had an unbalanced feeling again.

"Something like that."

She cocked her head at him. "What's going on, Grant? I've never seen you turn down a drink." *Please have a drink, Grant, so I can have one.*

He blushed, but kept his eyes on hers. "Don't pass this around, but I've joined A.A."

"A.A.? Why, to protect that crazimobile?"

"Not Triple A. *A.A.*" He whispered. "Alcoholics Anonymous."

She laughed. "You? A successful lawyer? You don't need that! That's for all those bums on skid row! Really, Grant!"

He spoke calmly. "You'd be surprised by the people at A.A.. Not a single bum."

"You're kidding! You mean you actually do that stuff, 'Hi, I'm Grant and I'm an alcoholic?'" She giggled.

"I know it's difficult to comprehend, Britannia, but yes, I'm…trying…to do this. I've only been to two meetings–one last night, another at seven this morning–and while I don't understand a lot of it, I respect it. I know it's currently fashionable to make fun of twelve-step programs. Often the ones making fun are the ones who might need it, too."

"Are you suggesting that I–"

"No, no, no, Brit. I'm referring to comedians on TV, constantly making fun of us. We can laugh too, you know. I've haven't laughed so hard in years as I did at this morning's A.A. meeting. There are some smart, funny guys at these meetings. Gals, too."

"So women go too." She was no longer laughing, still in the unbalanced feeling.

"Yes, they do."

"Do you think I'm…?"

"An alcoholic?" *Yep. Sure do, Brit.* "I'm learning only the individual, by themselves, can decide that, Brit."

He sounds so fucking pompous, she thought. *The old Grant.*

He leaned forward, his elbows on his knees, and clasped his hands. "It's helping me. And I've only just started. If you like, when you're in the city sometime, call me up and I'll take you to a meeting. See for yourself."

Was this a date? Go to an Alcoholics Anonymous meeting with him? Gee, how fun, Grant. Sit around with a bunch of self-righteous teetotalers?

There was a cough from above. They both looked up to see Saunders leaning over the railing. Each wondered how long he'd been up there, listening. Grant's face got pink.

"Hi, Dad."

"Saunders. Good morning! I'm so happy you're safe."

"Do I have to go back with you?"

"Not necessarily. Brit and I have been talking. She's going to make lunch. Come down and let's you and me talk about this."

Saunders, Brit's old robe on, slouched down the stairs and flopped onto the sofa in the belly of the U, far from each of them.

The phone rang. Britannia picked it up saying, "I'll take this in the kitchen, so you can talk." She left.

"So, Saunders, here you are."

"You pissed?"

"No, I'm not angry, Saunders, just confused and hurt."

"I had to get away."

"I can understand that son. I…haven't been the best father lately–"

"You're never around."

"I know that, Saunders, but–"

"I want to stay out here."

"I understand you are hurt and angry with me, Saunders, but I don't see how staying here–"

"At least Brit's home all the time."

"Yes. She works at home. However, as you know, my work–"

"I'll just run away again, Dad. You can't stop me." Super Dome was really squirming. He'd got him good and he had more. "You never took me for driving lessons. You promised. I'm the only kid who hasn't got a driver's license."

"Is this about driving?"

Saunders squirmed on the sofa then dropped his head. A long silence. They heard Brit banging pots and pans, murmuring on the phone. Grant stared at his son, his son stared down. They tried to make out what Brit was saying.

"Dammit, Scottie!" Banging a skillet onto the stovetop, Brit raged. "You admit you slept with the woman, yet you expect me–"

"I shouldn't have told you."

Brit flung open the refrigerator, stared into it. "I know you, Scottie." She jerked open the freezer. She had frozen shrimp creole somewhere…

"It's not like we're engaged or anything, Brit."

"We were having an affair! You and me. The two of us! How'd you like it if I casually called you up and said 'Hey, Sweetie, let's get together tonight, by the way I just boffed Grant?'"

"Your ex? You fucked him?"

She dug beneath bags of frozen vegetables from her garden, labeled in Jimmy's hand, and she felt like crying again. "No. Don't go stupid on me. I was speaking rhetorically."

"Is he out there?"

She pulled the shrimp toward her, a bag of corn slipped out and landed on her bare foot. "Ow! Damn, damn, damn!"

"What? What is it Brit?"

"Corn fell on my foot. Ow! I've got to go, Scottie. There's nothing to discuss. Hear this–we are through." She clicked the phone off, shut the refrigerator, limped to the microwave.

"Lunch in a minute guys," she called.

Grant was staring at his son's Adam's apple. Saunders head was thrown back on the sofa, mouth open. He seemed to be staring at the ceiling. A log rustled, fell. Grant thought Britannia had just said "Scottie." *Who the hell was that?*

Grant cleared his throat. "Son. I have something to say. I want you to know I'm turning over a new leaf." His son did not move. Grant felt encouraged.

In the loft bedroom he'd been listening to them the whole time. He restrained a chortle.

"I've stopped drinking."

Saunders chin slowly came down to a proper ninety degree angle. *I'm supposed to cheer or something?* He allowed his eyes to meet his father's.

"...I'm trying this organization, this special club and I think..."

Sure Super Dome, "I'm Grant and I'm an alcoholic"–how long's that gonna last, Big Bald One? He said nothing. He enjoyed this. *Let the old dude squirm.*

"... and I think this is really what I need. I won't be drinking. I will have to attend meetings every night–"

Saunders eyes widened. Grant's hands flapped the air.

"I know what you're thinking, son. I'll still be gone every night even though I won't be drinking,"

You think I care, Dad? I'm way past caring, Dad. He continued his unblinking stare.

"But these meetings take only an hour, then I'll be right home for you, they even have a club for kids, teenagers, I'd like you to try it–"

You're the alkie and I'm supposed to go to some weenie club? Get real, Dome.

Grant sighed. "Saunders. Please don't clam up on me. Please say something."

Saunders drew out his stare until The Dome's eyes averted, then he stared at his father's temple, where a vein stood out, vibrating. *Would he have a stroke?* He spoke.

"Sure. I want to stay with Brit."

Grant drew breath, held it. He was sweating. "Okay. Fair enough." He breathed again and ran a shaky hand over the hairpiece. "Okay. I can accept that. I under-stand. I haven't been there for you lately, I know, and if, well, staying out here with your ex-stepmother is what you want–well, she wants it too apparently–"

Britannia was in the doorway. "Come and get it."

Grant leaped up. "Let's go eat, son."

N I N E

Brit wanted to go over to Annie's that afternoon and she was surprised when Grant offered to go with her.

"Don't you have to go back to the office?"

"I took the day off. Besides, I knew Jimmy too. I'd like to see Annie."

Saunders hadn't wanted to come. He said he was still tired, so they sent him upstairs to nap. Brit changed into a dark brown caftan and dull brass jewelry, and they rode to Annie's.

Annie's house, on the outskirts of Covington, was all but obscured by the cars and trucks that filled her driveway. A group of men around a tailgate were passing a bottle. Brit wanted to join them, just a for a while, but Grant strode past, jaw set, so she scurried along with him.

Inside, it was hard to find Annie. The house was filled with people and food. After greeting and meeting a few dozen folks, black and white, Grant helped himself to ham, turkey, fried chicken, macaroni and cheese, and potato salad and got into conversation with one of Jimmy's beautiful daughters. Brit found Annie and sat next to her. Her eyes went up looking for Grant. She saw him. Frowned. From his alert posture, his smile, it almost looked like he was flirting with this exotic teenager–no. It had to be her imagination.

Annie was a small woman with smooth burnt-amber skin, but now her features stayed crumpled as she alternately laughed and cried. Now Annie was crying and Brit started to cry too and other women flung their arms around them and everyone shook, looking like a huddle in a football game. When they calmed, everyone giving little pats, the huddle broke up. But the women stayed close, ready to huddle, when the next need arose.

Brit gave Annie an envelope. Annie squeezed it and her eyes widened.

"Annie. I was going to give this to Jimmy for his birthday. Part of his pension."

"Pension?"

"The pension he earned with me. He and I discussed it. He didn't tell you?"

"Didn't say one word, Brit."

"Well, of course, I planned to give him a pension. He wanted it on his birthday, in March, and a month before Christmas, more like a bonus system than a pension. It's not much."

Annie felt the envelope again. "You sure you're not making this up?"

"Annie, it was planned." She was fibbing and Annie knew it.

"You're going to need every dime, Brit, that teenage boy staying with you."

Brit had told her about Saunders. Annie had babysat him and Anastasia. Brit put a hand over Annie's.

"No more discussion." Annie stared at her a moment then leaned over and kissed her cheek. "Thanks, Brit. You call me anytime you need me, hear?"

"I might really need you with that teenager around." They laughed. Brit leaned closer.

"How old was Jimmy, Annie? Seventy-five?"

"Brit, Jimmy was eight-five."

Brit, in awe, stared, then spoke. "He sure didn't look it or act it."

Annie smiled. "No, he sure didn't."

Grant appeared and Annie smiled up at him. Brit thought, *If Jimmy looked so good at eighty-five...* She froze. It was like Jimmy just sent her a message: *"You can look good, too, Brit." Thank you, Jimmy,* she prayed.

Annie was speaking. "Grant, I sure am glad to see you and Brit together."

"Oh, well, I just happened to be out, and when I heard–"

"That's okay. You take care of this pretty woman, you hear?"

"Annie–"

Brit cut in. "It's not what you think, Annie. We're not getting back together. He's just out to make arrangements about Saunders."

"Uh huh."

"Really, Annie..."

Annie patted Brit's knee. "Sure, Sugar. It's just for the sake of that boy, sure it is."

"Well, Grant," said Brit, with a plastic smile, "better go now."

It was dark. Grant had lingered, helping her feed, saying with Jimmy gone these chores would be good for Saunders. Brit agreed. They felt almost mellow, neither admitting wanting a drink. Saunders would stay through the end of the school year, Grant could come out any time, provided he called first, and he would begin helping financially immediately.

They strolled up from the barn toward the house which blazed with light, both fairly relaxed, with the animals and people fed. Brit had fixed a light dinner. Grant was having entire moments when a crazed inner voice was not nattering at him to have a drink.

Occasionally Brit bumped into Grant or he bumped her. Each time, they'd apologize, move away. The moon was rising over the plateau three-quarters full and Brit remembered the tarot card, the white virgin sleeping in the forest under the full moon, finger dripping blood, unread book before her. She couldn't tell Grant any of this–he'd think it was sillier than she did. Grant was talking.

"…you know, Brit, I have to tell you, you're looking pretty good for–"

"My age?"

"No, not that," he lied, "just–you're looking good."

Of course he meant "for her age!" She pushed down the anger and began talking about getting Saunders into school when Grant interrupted.

"Are you expecting someone?" A car was coming down her drive and they flinched as headlights swung into their eyes. It braked before them, a figure jumped out, car still running, halogen headlights trying to light up the world.

"Britannia?"

Scottie. She began to shake. Then quickly she put her hand on Grant's arm to keep him back. Grant, standing back, was deliberately attentive.

"What are you doing here, Scottie? I told you–" Brit cried.

"Brit, don't kick me out like this. That other meant nothing–"

"Scott, dammit, Saunders' father is here. I'm very busy–"

Scottie looked up and strode past her, hand outstretched. "Hello. You must be Grant Griffin. Scott Webster, pleased to meet you." *Was Scott crazy? Did he want to ruin everything for her?* She scurried to the men who were shaking hands. She saw Grant frowning.

Silence. If Scottie said anything, anything at all, Grant would have Saunders in his car and gone. The men's hands were still joined. She stepped beside them and put a hand on each of their arms.

"Scott's a friend of mine, Grant, he's a television news photographer," and she turned and looked hard into Scott's eyes. He'd been drinking, she could smell it. His eyes were pretty wild, too. Coked up. She pushed against their arms, they unclasped hands. "Scott, I didn't expect you. You have to go now. I'm sorry you had a long drive for nothing."

"I want an explanation, Brit."

Grant looked from one to the other, incredulous. At first he'd thought this guy had to be some model or other for something Brit was painting. But the guy was drunk and angry. If he didn't know better he'd think he was drunk and jealous.

"I owe you no explanations, Scott." Brit was angry. Grant peered at the guy. *How old was he anyhow? Thirtysomething? Was Brit banging some young guy, and he hadn't gotten to first base with a young chick?* Grant began to feel angry.

"Look, Britannia, I'd better get going. You sure you want Saunders out here?" And he stared at this guy, so Brit would get the message. Brit looked from one to the other. She could choke Scottie. He knew what he was doing. She hadn't served up instant forgiveness...now he wanted to wreck things.

She took hold of his eye with hers. "Scott. You are drunk. You have no business here. I told you that earlier. Mr. Griffin is an attorney. If you don't get into your car, leave right this second, I will have him draw up papers and have you–have you–"

"I believe you're talking about a restraining order, Britannia."

"Thank you, Grant. I'll get a restraining order–"

Scott began to back away, not before Brit saw his eyes tear. His hands flew out, fingers stretched, palms down, he made placating gestures as he backed to his car. "I don't want any trouble, Brit. I thought we could talk this out like adults."

"Adults? Scottie, you're drunk." She whirled to Grant. "Doesn't he seem drunk?" Back to Scott. "I have nothing to discuss with you, Scott. Get in your car. Go." Even though it was chilly, she felt hot all over. Forehead sweat. Hot flash. *Shit!*

Maybe Grant wouldn't see in the dark, but Scott's damn headlights were probably making the sweat beads sparkle like tree lights. Scott was still moving back when he stumbled.

Brit wished to evaporate, that men she'd loved might see menopause sprout on her brow.

"You heard the lady, Mr. Webster. She wants you to leave." Britannia sagged. She could almost hug Grant, he was on her side. Scottie caught himself without falling. Then he turned and slouched into his car. Flooring it, fishtailing, he backed out of the drive. The headlights bounced, then were gone. Silence whooshed back in.

"Thanks, Grant."

"Don't thank me. Who the hell is he anyway?"

He couldn't see her face. She seemed to be swaying toward him, so he reached down, caught her arms above the elbows, then let go. He peered down at her bowed head. "Brit. Who is he?" She swayed again and he caught her again. "You all right?"

"Yes. Very tired. The last two days...have been tumultuous."

Oh God, she wanted a drink. Brandy. Grant should go. She'd settle down, gather Wil and godd to her and sip brandy. Play Mozart. But Grant hadn't let go of her, his hands were firm on her upper arms.

"Who is he?"

She couldn't think of a lie. "We–he–"

"Are you saying that guy and you–?"

She raised her head. "Yes. We were lovers." Violently Grant turned from her. He slammed a fist into his palm. "Goddammit! Jesus Christ!"

She turned cold. Grant would take Saunders and she'd be alone again.

He turned back, hitching up his pants. "How old is he?"

"What's that got to do with anything?"

"I want to know. How old is that guy?"

She shrugged. She was fucked. "Thirty-seven."

Grant turned again, pounded a fist into his palm. Then back, arms akimbo. "How the fuck do you rate?"

"Rate?"

"How in the hell did you manage to get that young guy in the sack? Tell me! I would...really...like to know."

What? "Well, we met at the TV station, and one thing led to another–"

"You're fifty years old!"

What? He was angry I've had a younger lover? She sniffed. "I'm not completely over the hill, Grant."

"Must be that older woman thing." He stepped closer to her. "Was that it? This guy into the older woman mystique or something?"

"Possibly."

"Well. I'd like to know why there isn't an Older Man mystique."

Britannia laughed. "There is. Thousands of men across America are divorcing their wives and marrying younger women."

"Yeah. But not because the younger chicks have an Older Man mystique!"

"Why then, Grant?"

"I don't know."

"Sure you do. Older men have more money than younger men. How many young women do you see married to poor older men? Some women don't want to wait while a younger man 'makes it.' They want a sure thing. You have money. I don't see what the problem is. That crazimobile screams it. But maybe instead of that sinuous, phallic Corvette you should have picked a BMW. Maybe you're advertising your big cock, Grant, not your bank account." Now she was angry.

He tore off his toupee, held it out to her. "I did everything. I got this–" he

shook it, in his hand it looked like an infant opossum–"I got those damned contacts, I got that car, and I was nice. I was very, very nice."

"In your sexy Corvette. They knew what you wanted." She began yelling.
"That type of young woman will come across, Grant, but only for money backed
by commitment, a lavish wedding and a second family. Your second family. Their
first. They're aware of the ticking of their biological clocks and the flashing numbers on the big board at the stock exchange. Maybe you were too nice. Too solicitous, too tremblingly eager to do whatever they wanted if only they'd let you put
your big hands on their nonexistent bellies, their silicone breasts."

Her mind was in counterpoint with her words, crying out, had he actually
said, "You're fifty," as though she'd entered a living death? She wanted to slap
him, shake him, berate him, *"You fool! Except for the occasional hangover I don't
feel one minute over twenty! I can ride stallions bareback!"* She clamped her hands
over her belly, but kept her shoulders back.

He paced around her. "Jeez, Brit! You can sure be cruel!"

Me? An old woman like me? He continued to pace, self-absorbed, unaware of
her except as ears for his woe. His arms flailed like a swimmer seeking water.

"I don't know. I can't seem to do a goddamned thing right. Now my son runs
off." He paused and shouted at the rising moon. "What the fuck am I doing
wrong?" Even though she shook with cold and with wanting a brandy, Brit felt
stronger. He couldn't attract young women. Serve him right. When she and
Scottie began it wasn't like that. She hadn't been seeking a young man's penis as
if his young come was a magic injection to return her youth. Hell, she hadn't even
felt old until her birthday. They'd just both been attracted and the age thing,
while it bothered her, wasn't the reason they'd made love.

"Scottie and I had nothing to do with age, or the differences. It was lust. And
it was wild while it lasted."

"Sure you're not kidding yourself, Brit?" His voice was a bleat in the darkness.

Wearily she answered. "No. I'm not kidding myself. The age difference bothered me. Not Scott." She felt warmth on her calves, godd brushing against her.
She picked up the cat.

"I'm tired, Grant. I'm sorry you're not happy. I'm sorry you couldn't find a
young woman to make you happy." Hugging the cat she trudged to the house.
Grant caught up with her.

"The way you say that, the way it sounds…"

"It sounds what, Grant?"

"It sounds, well, it sounds as if I really am middle-aged crazy."

She walked, stroking the cat.

"Maybe we both are." Relaxed now. He wasn't going to take Saunders. "It's been such a long day. I'm tired."

"Yes. I'll go. I'll just duck in and say good night to Saunders." Yet on the verandah, he stopped her. "That Scottie guy's not going to be moving in here, is he?"

"No, Grant. I told you and I certainly told him, that thing's over. There are no others. I'm fed up with affairs right now. I want some calm. I want to try and get my life going again and I want to take care of Saunders. That's all."

His eyes were large and frightened under the yellow porch light. She almost felt sorry for him. She touched his arm. "I promise."

"I'd like to see Saunders over the weekend." He looked down. "And I'd like to see you. Just—to talk."

She was surprised to hear her mouth say, "Okay. Call tomorrow. Maybe you can come out on Sunday."

"I'll call."

TEN

Saunders was sprawled on his bed watching television. No cable—too primitive out here. He'd have to talk her into getting a dish—he needed his MTV. Otherwise, he felt satisfied. Super Dome caved in just like he expected and Britannia was doing this mother-flutter thing. He did not feel mothered. No matter. She felt like she was mothering. That's what counted. Next, a driver's license, he couldn't wait to peel around in that Jag, then, ix-nay on the chool-say. He laughed silently. Years back, Brit had taught him and her weird daughter, his so-called stepsister, pidgin language. Surprise to him that Asia, the Chink, actually thought pidge-talk was fun. He clicked through the five miserable channels.

Nothing. He could, however, go out to the barn, up in the loft, and smoke a joint. Tell "Maw" he needed some exercise.

ELEVEN

Grant was on The Causeway, the 24 mile bridge across Lake Pontchartrain linking Mandeville, Madisonville and Covington to Metairie and New Orleans. Usually he drove it fast, but tonight he was schmoozing along at 55. The moon hung in a black sky. City lights blinked in the distance, the lake was still, black and empty as the sky. Traffic was sparse. He came up on a horse trailer, traveling even slower. He saw the haunches of two horses looming above the trailer's back door. He thought of crazy old Brit and her horses…what did she see in them? One tail escaped the trailer and blew sideways, riffling silver like Mokhtar's. He felt a pang and his eyes filled…and he wasn't wearing his contacts. Britannia's place. His son and Brit cozy around her fireplace, dog and cat snuggled up to Brit, they're talking softly, Saunders telling secrets about Dad late every night…*and Rocky came in, stinking of gin*…Rocky Raccoon. The Beatles. He and Brit had loved that song. Did she still?

He couldn't bear to go back to his empty condo and he flashed on the loud voices, music, the smell, sound of gin gurgling over ice, a bar. *Have a drink Grant…And you won't be lonely any more…Was that another song?* If so, since when did he think in melodies?

Have a deep soul-searching conversation with the drunk on the next bar stool. This person, whom you've never seen before, and never will want to see again, will listen to you. Drunken intensity. And then you hear his voice and you will not listen, just as he didn't listen to you, he, like you, was just waiting for you to shut up, so he could have his turn. In a bar you could say anything, no one heard a word. If they did, it was dissolved in alcohol, vanished forever. So you never had to change anything about yourself. Just go to a bar the next night, tell some other drunk the same story.

And how come old Brit gets a young lover and he doesn't? *She's four years older than me, dammit!*

He needed an A.A. meeting or he was going to the first bar he saw. His mind began scanning possible bars in Metairie–a place no one would know him–didn't want to bump into anyone he knew. *Just one drink. Maybe two or three–?* He couldn't think of a single Metairie bar. He slowed for the end of the bridge. The car bumped off the bridge. *Just drive the fuck down Vets Boulevard and there'll be a bar on every corner.* He drove alongside the Lakeside Shopping Center and put his blinker on to turn right…he made the turn. Then a voice started nattering in his head. *Serenity…courage…change…Higher Power… courage to change.* That's what they'd said in that prayer, the courage to change. *What kind of fucking wimp was he? Feeling oh so sorry for himself….*

He turned into the parking lot at Lakeside, stopped, and turned on the overhead light.

Was there one this late on a Friday night? He felt around in some papers on the passenger seat, found the A.A. booklet. *A candlelight meeting. Damn!*

Better go. Try it one more time.

Candlelight sounded…kinda nice. Might even be some hot A.A. gals there.

He pointed the phallic *(phallic! Jeez Brit!)* snout of his red car toward Kenner and began chanting, "God, grant me the courage to change, the courage to change…" wishing he knew the whole damn thing.

He got to the meeting.

Brit drank brandy in her deserted living room, the fire chunks of charred wood. Wil and godd had wandered away. Despite Saunders' presence–TV sounds came from his room–she felt empty. The alcohol tasted metallic on her tongue and after the third sip, the one that usually gave a comforting glow, she got instead a burning in her stomach. She set the drink down. In a minute she'd have heartburn. *Better add milk.*

T W E L V E

Next morning she was surprised when Saunders joined her in the kitchen. Over pancakes, she talked.

"Here's what I expect, Saunders. No dope, and no drinking." He looked at her with wide startled eyes. *Good,* she thought, *that shocks him.*

"You have to help around the place. Ever since Anastasia went to LSU, it takes a hunk out of the monthly trust income. I can't afford a maid any more so we have to pick up after ourselves. I thought about Annie, but she doesn't need to be my maid."

"Maybe Rita could come out. You know, with just Dad at the condo, she won't have much to do."

"That's an idea. This is a big house and there'll be lots of laundry now. And I really have to produce some art. I'm supposed to be having a show in November in New York. Who'll pay her?"

"Supe–Dad."

"'Soup?'" She smiled and he cast his eyes down then peered up at her winningly through eyelashes. It was just this type of gesture that would make Lee want to throw up. But she knew better. Saunders truly was shy.

"C'mon. What were you going to say?"

"Just what I call Dad when he gets really obnoxious. Super Dome."

Britannia slapped her hands on the table and hooted, "Very clever!

Saunders sniggered with her.

"With that awful toupee off, it fits. Now. On to business." She drank some coffee. "Saunders. I expect you to help in the house, and with the chores. This place is loosely designated a farm and we do have one horse, assorted fowl, and a garden. I'll need your help, now that Jimmy's gone. Almost time for spring planting and I have a bumper crop of garlic and onions to get in."

Saunders face stayed blank. She felt a little nervous but she carried on. "How about I do the morning feeding, you do the evening when you get home from school? And I'll leave a note for you on the refrigerator about what needs doing in the garden that day. Because hopefully, I'll be in my studio creating great art."

Oh. She was going to close The Door on him.

She saw his blank look turn inward and she leaned forward and put her hand on his. "Hon, it's going to be okay. We'll have breakfast together every morning and supper at eight. If I find I have to work longer, I'll leave something out for you, you can do homework while I work and," she took a necessary breath, "as soon as you get into school you can invite friends over."

His expression remained blank. She shook his hand.

"Saunders. Is something wrong?"

His eyes refocused on her. "No. I was just thinking—"

"What, Honey?"

"Could I learn to drive your Jag?"

She laughed in relief.

"Of course you can. We'll have Lesson One today. But did I say anything to disturb you just now? Please tell me. Saunders," she squeezed his hand, "you can tell me anything, no matter how gross or silly you might think it sounds. I'm pretty much unshockable. That goes with being a child of the Sixties. And the Seventies."

Oh yeah? How'd you like me to tell you about banging Jane Stachs at the Lakeshore Motel? How unshockable are you really, Maw? Smiling sweetly he shook his head at her.

"Okay. I'm trusting you, Saunders."

*If she only knew...*he fought to control laughter.

"Another thing, now that we've got that settled, I want to go into the city today to the big bookstore in the French Quarter. Want to come?"

French Quarter—yes. Books—no way. He'd be bored.

"Uh, thanks Maw, but I thought I'd call around. See if I can find some of the guys I used to hang with when I lived here before."

"That's wonderful! You do that. Let's make this weekend fun and relaxing. Invite them over if you wish! Is there anything in the city you need?"

"Clothes from the condo."

"Of course."

The phone rang and she went into the living room to take it.

"Good morning." It was Grant. "You sound happy."

"Hi, Grant." She heard traffic and clippity clop sounds. "Where are you?"

"Decatur." *Oh no, he'd spent the night in the Quarter, got drunk and he was still there this morning, so much for the miracle of A.A..*

"How's your head?" She was half laughing.

"Fine. Went to a 7:00 a.m. meeting here."

"Oh." Well. Maybe it had some miraculous properties.

"Just wondered how it's going with the wayward son and can I arrange to visit out there tomorrow?"

"Sure. We had a long talk this morning–at least I talked and Saunders listened–"

"But is he listening?"

They laughed and Brit said, "He wants to drive my car so he heard something. Look, I have to get dressed, I'm coming into the city."

"You are? May I ask what for?"

"Yes. I'm going to the big bookstore on Decatur."

"I'm there right now." There was sudden noise, like a giant's sneeze.

"What the hell is that?"

"I can't believe it. A mule just sneezed right beside me!"

"You're on your car phone?"

"Yeah, the window's down and I'm stopped at a red light next to this horse-drawn carriage, only it's a big orange mule and he sneezed, and omigod–I've got snot on my sleeve–" Brit laughed.

"Quit that laughing. I know you think mule snot is like holy water or some-thing, but–Jeez I need a Kleenex–" a pause. "There. Got it. I'm driving real slow, gonna give this critter lots of space…" She heard clop, clop, clop. "Okay. He's gone. So, where were we?"

"You tell me." She thought of his ageist remark the past evening. "Any sweet young thangs walkin' down the street, gushing over the phallusmobile?"

"Aw, Brit, please don't. I'm sorry. Sometimes, not drinking, I don't know what

I'm saying."

"Ah. But you said that when you were drinking: 'Sometimes when I'm drunk I don't mean what I say.'"

"Yeah, rub it in. But it's weird, Brit, really weird. I haven't had a drink in three days. Haven't gone that long in ten years."

"That is truly commendable."

"Look, can we rewind to before the mule sneeze?"

"Okay."

"I have an idea. Since you're not ready and I'm in my car filled with Saunders' stuff, why don't I run out there, drop off his stuff and take you into the city? We could have lunch, maybe."

"I don't think so, Grant."

"We really need to talk more, Brit. We have to arrange how I'll finance him out there."

She remembered Saunders' comment about Rita. Help would be great. "You have a point. But I won't lunch for money. I'm not that kind of girl–oops, old woman."

"Brit. Please. Forgive. I'd get down on my knees right now but there's not room in this car. Can you let it go? Believe me, I've got the point. I was an asshole, okay?"

"Okay, I guess. Come on out. We'll play it by ear."

They rang off and Brit called out to Saunders that Super Dome was coming with his stuff.

THIRTEEN

"What's this fan thing beneath the virgin?" Her voice, then Lee's. "Aha! That is not a fan. That is a book. The pages are 'fanned' out, goose. '...leaves of a book as yet unread blow in the breeze.'"

This feels pretty good, thought Brit. Grant's phallus-mobile was emptied of Saunders' things and now, parked in a hotel garage, held the books she'd bought. They sat at a table at Mr. B's on Royal Street in the French Quarter. Long time since she'd lunched glamorously. They were waiting for their appetizer in the dim coolness of the marble-floored, mahogany-paneled restaurant.

Grant had followed her around Bookstar as she mused over *Women Who Run with the Wolves,* and bought it, *Ageless Body, Timeless Mind,* and bought it.

Soon Grant was carrying a load of books with more wacko titles by some

wacky sounding authors, like, *Creative Visualization*, Shakti Gawain? Hippie sur-
vivor from the sixties?

Hugh Prather's *Notes On How To Live In The World…And Still Be Happy*. For
Brit, Grant thought, *bookstores needed to supply shopping carts*.

Then, *The Celestine Prophecy*, *Getting the Love You Need*, *The Artist's Way*, *Circle
of Stones*, *Creating Money*–by who? The book sat on top of the stack in his arms,
Grant craned his neck to read the author's name. Sanaya Roman. Another old
hippie. *How could an old hippie know anything about money? Was Brit seriously
having money problems…he could help out…and, maybe…?*

Two books on self-esteem, then *The Mind of God* by Paul Davies, *The Descent
of Woman* by Elaine Morgan, *Codependant No More* and *The Language of Letting
Go*–what does she want to let go of? Then, *Of Course You're Angry*, *Women Who
Love Too Much*, *The Mystic Path to Cosmic Power*–goofy title, but he dare not say
one word. Laughing, she added, *Cats that Paint*, for godd, she said. She slapped
her hands together in satisfaction and looked around. Oh! One more. *The Blue
Dog*, a sixty buck thing by someone named Rodrigue. It weighed a ton. She
caught his raised eyebrows. "For Wilton. He'll be crazy-jealous if I get godd one
and not him." *She had to be kidding.* "Besides, Rodrigue is a famous Cajun artist
and this book is a first edition. I'm making an investment." She grinned up at
him like a girl. There were even tiny freckles across her nose. If she wasn't kidding, she was playing the game to the hilt.

"I'm done. You want to feed me now?"

He'd smiled down at her. And felt thoroughly pleased to be in a bookstore at
11:45 on a Saturday morning with this old-young woman-girl, who bought far-
out books for herself and her animals. Carrying her books he felt like an excited
high school kid.

"I will be delighted to feed you, Ms. Rhodes."

"Cool, Mr. Griffin." And she took his arm. It was nice, when one was five-ten,
to wear heels and still have the guy taller.

Now they nibbled on a shrimp stuffed artichoke splayed before them like a
raped anemone and gazed around at the other diners. Grant told her about the
Spiffy Wiffins case, not even omitting Spiffy had been naked under her sable, and
Brit howled.

She tossed her head back and Grant saw the clean line of her neck which led
to that little hollow of her throat which seemed, like an arrowhead, to point
down to her breasts jiggling now under the silk of her dress. *No bra? Pretty feisty*

for fifty!

In this light, he glanced around the room, *no one would guess she was…fifty years old*–he didn't think. It'd be embarrassing if they did and worse if they actually thought he was on a date with–an older woman. Yet he found he was staring at her breasts. Wondering. He shifted his gaze, but it lighted on her Manhattan and he thought how incredibly selfish she was to order a damn drink when he was so newly, nervously sober. *He was still shaking, for God's sake, couldn't she see?* He tipped his empty iced tea glass up and viciously crunched an ice cube.

He looked away as she slugged back cocktail.

Brit felt a twinge of guilt that she could drink and he apparently couldn't–he seemed to be taking this A.A. stuff seriously. Of course, she had cut back. Then she remembered that sometimes people nurtured feelings of guilt so they wouldn't have to do the hard work of changing things about themselves…she pushed the Manhattan away. *It didn't taste that great, anyway.*

She caught him up on Anastasia, how good her grades were, how shy and introverted she was still, she'd yet to have her first date. But she seemed happy. Their entrée arrived and she noticed her Manhattan had disappeared, and then there was another. Sucking the stemmed cherry from the drink she felt that warm cozy glow that three stiff drinks gave. Grant, she suddenly noticed, looked quite handsome in this light. She felt herself become more vivacious. Remembering her belly she abruptly set her fork down, stopped eating even though it was delicious…a couple–well, three– Manhattans were better than any diet pill she'd ever tried.

Some guy came to their table and was chatting with Grant…she felt them staring at her. She smiled very brightly at both men. "M'sieu's?" *God, was that too coy?*

Grant smiled, "Henry, this is my friend Britannia Rhodes–Brit, Henry Soulé." Henry walked around the table, took her outstretched hand, and kissed the back of it.

Brit wondered, *my friend? Not ex-wife?*

"Well, how are you, Henri?" saying "On-ree" the French way. Grant rolled his eyes. On-ree had silver hair, tanned sailboater face, crystal blue eyes.

Grant made sounds. "Ha ha. Good seeing you, Henry." Henry released her hand. She felt her eyes start to bat at him. Grant continued, voice overloud, "Call me at my office–you have my number?"

Bowing slightly, eyes semaphoring signals, Henry backed off.

Brit thought, *now Grant's jealous?*

Later, in Grant's car, Brit developed a swoozy feeling, the third Manhattan apparently well-mingled with her bloodstream so when Grant asked if she'd like to come up and see his bromeliads she said sure. She giggled about "his etchings," and he laughed with her, the preposterousness that they might…and a nasty little voice inside her also said, *Yeah, and fuck you, Scottie!* After all, they were a formerly married couple and they needed to get more comfortable with one another because of the Saunders' situation, and she needed a cup of coffee.

As they surged up St. Charles Grant took her hand and she felt a small wave action begin in her belly. Things blurred when they got inside his condo—she only glimpsed the waxy pink, orange, and crimson bromeliads because Grant was all over her and because he was so incredibly tall and big and she felt small in a sexy helpless-primitive way. They kissed frantically in the living room by the bromeliads and her nostrils filled with his musky man-smell and then…*he picked her up…*

She went limp as a dying orchid. Of all the creative erotic stunts she and Scottie'd tried, he'd never picked her up. *Perhaps he'd been afraid she was too big? Perhaps she was afraid she was too big?* Grant, she decided, could have his way with her whenever he wanted if only he picked her up first. It was wonderful to feel completely helpless, then lifted up and carried, her body and its care no longer her problem.

They reached his bedroom—a room she'd never seen—all brown like the fur-lined den of some…cave Homo…Erectus. His sheets had spots like leopard skins. Her dress slithered off and she pulled down his fly zipper while he pushed her slip up. She had a moment of panic—did he see her jelly-belly, is he overcome with repugnance? Instantly, she felt a rush of hot shameful naked rejection—but he didn't notice. Her slip flew over her head, she pushed his pants down as he pulled her panties off—he paused and stared down, and she felt a wail begin inside her: *oh no, now he's going to say you disgusting old woman*—she held her breath…instead he cried out "Oh, Britannia!" and his head dived and buried itself in her *mons veneris*, graying pubic hair and all. His only comments were moans that she took as primitive pleasure signals and soon she made moans herself. He knew exactly what to do and shortly, she felt the blossoming of an orgasm like…his blooming bromeliads, tangerine, flamingo pink, splaying out from a coiled-tight core…then he kicked his pants off his ankles, pushed his jockey shorts down and his great pink granite cock sprung free…she had just enough sense to gasp:

"Condom?"

He had a drawer-full in primary colors and he grabbed one–yellow–and she watched it unpeel down his penis making it mutate into a big lemon tuber–a big banana? She half-giggled–and then it was inside her and their bodies ground together, each body seeming to remember the other body. Little grateful "hi's" and "hello's" susurrated up and down their touching skins and they groaned in unison....

For the next four hours they wound and rewound their bodies, limbs gliding over skins as softly as tentacles of octopi. When she thought he couldn't possibly get another erection and she'd long given up hiding her belly, she went naked into the shower but soon his big arms went around her from behind, she felt a poking against her buttocks...

FOURTEEN

On Sunday morning Britannia lay under her covers in an agony of remorse. *She'd slept with Grant! Was she crazy? How could just three Manhattans hit so hard she lost her mind and fell into bed with him?*

FIFTEEN

Grant came to a dull consciousness. As he inhaled, an intoxicating smell of *Magie Noire* perfume and the musk of her, a familiar woman, filled his nostrils. He groaned to himself, he'd done it–he'd banged a fifty-year-old woman–*was he really so desperate?* He couldn't understand his behavior. They'd gone wild. He hadn't had sex like that since...since–admit it, the divorce. *God. Hitting the big Five-O hadn't dulled her erotic acrobatics. Seemed she could still bend any way he wanted...ankles around his neck–jeez!* And if he said so himself, his hand strayed down, gently massaged his dick, to come four times, repeat, FOUR times for a forty-six year old guy, not too shabby, and he was hard as granite, right now, all over again....

SIXTEEN

Saunders lay in his rumpled bed. Most of his old buds on the Northshore were gone, except Terry, and he was supposed to meet him at the arcade in the Slidell Mall. Maw'd drive him. Score some weed, maybe pills, see how hip Terry was, otherwise he'd have to call Super Dome. No, too soon for that, The Dome might want to keep him in the city since it looked like Dome and Maw hadn't hit it off so hot yesterday. One thing he'd have to get straight with Maw today: he was NOT going to any school. Therapy, maybe, no telling how much he could con a therapist. That could be fun–get her to really lay a guilt trip on The Dome and The Maw.

In the meantime he supposed he could get up and impress her by feeding the horse and the birds.

SEVENTEEN

Had it been the Manhattans? Maybe she was a candidate for A.A.. Like Grant. Saunders might already have guessed she and his dad–although they'd been pretty glum when he'd brought her home, glum, stunned, not like overjoyed lovers.

Shame, like an unending hot flash, filled her body.

Tomorrow she was supposed to stop smoking, instead she'd do it today, as punishment. She'd quit before. Agony. Fine. She'd quit. Her bedside clock said 7:53. Tough it out today then tomorrow call Stella for patches. She picked up the phone, fearfully touched "one" on the key pad automatically dialing Lee's number. Lee would give her hell, which was what she deserved.

"You've really quit smoking."

"Yep."

"For how long?"

Brit twisted her head to read the bedside clock. "Thirty-seven seconds."

Lee snorted.

"Yes. Ridicule me, Robinet, laugh your lungs out. But don't ask Rhodes to push your wheelchair ten years from now. After your lungectomy."

A chortle.

"Go on, get it off your chest, Robinet–I won't wheel your oxygen tank around either."

She heard the click of a lighter. "Aha. I hear sounds of you partaking of the devil weed."

"Brit, quit! I know, I know I know. There's just too much stress right now–money problems, breaking up with Dick, shit at work...am I whining?"

"That's okay. Whine away. I'm your best friend. A willing receptor of all your troubles–except those induced by ingestion of the noxious nicotine plant. However I too have stress. The Birthday. The Boy. The Father of The Boy and the Bed of the Father of the Boy."

"The Bed?"

"I have now been a non-smoker for one minute, twenty-nine seconds."

"Congratulations and quit evading. Back to The Bed, Brit."

"What bed?"

"Cut the coy. The Bed of the Father of the…"

"Ah yes. And I am sodden with shame, dear friend."

"You fucked Grant."

"It was, ah, mutual, I believe."

"So now you feel…all fucked up?"

"Rather. If that means like a total fool. It started at lunch. I drank only three Manhattans. Lee, usually I can handle that many."

"Did you eat?"

"Guess not enough."

"You can't ever drink on an empty stomach. Brit–remember two years ago for my birthday, you drank about three bottles of champagne by yourself?"

"And I threw up all over your car?"

"Thank God you had an empty stomach."

"Yes."

"So how was it?"

"It was rather terrific. Age hath not dimmed the Granite Man's abilities. But. He's so freaked that I'm suddenly 'an older woman'–which never mattered when we got married or I'd never have married the son of a bitch–but there's something about the number fifty that sounds very old to him, he's probably checking his body with a magnifying mirror to see if cellulite and gray hair are catchy."

"Did he actually comment on these aspects of your body?"

"No, but–"

"So maybe he thought your body was just fine."

"No. He was just super-horny, he hasn't been very successful getting women, I gather. But maybe the water from the shower obscured the cellulite on my ass."

"Cellulite? Cell-u-leet? What's that? A cell-rejuvenating tonic one sees advertised? 'Cell-U-Leet'–in convenient tablets or as a soothing tea, makes you fit and fleet? One of those ads that mimic story material in a magazine but in tiny print in parentheses, it always says 'Advertisement'? Who invented cellulite? Rubens and Titan painted it as alluring dimples on the ass and thighs of their beloved nudes, women you just know they fucked soundly between painting takes…I want to know what closet-faggot female-hating man perpetrated the cellulite nightmare upon women? He needs to be taken out–and shot–no, that would be too kind–maybe skin of 'cellulite' flesh grafted onto his buttocks to horrify his boyfriend, next time he scores. Grafted without anesthetic…"

"Sure wound up about cellulite, aren't you?"

"You betcha. If I hear you say that word about yourself ever again I will loufah your mouth."

"What do I say?"

"Well, if you must bother to comment on such a natural feminine condition call it 'dimples.'"

"Dimples. Sounds sweet."

"Betcher butt it does and it is. See, I have a theory, Rhodes, and it answers the question: Why do only women have cellulite, and not men?"

"Oh well, by now we all know men are superior beings."

"Aside from that disputable fact, why?"

"I dunno, but I bet you do."

"Right. This is The Robinet Theory of Primary Sex Triggers in Female Homo Sapiens, breasts being a secondary sex trigger."

"Breasts are secondary to…dimples?"

"Yup. Men also have minimal breasts and breasts have a primary use as infant feeders. Dimples, however, are found only on women and they do not nurture a child. Cave men used rear entry most often, especially since they were pagans and thus ignorant of the missionary position. So if a guy sees a bare butt in the distance, say in a berry patch, women out there gathering, and that butt is super smooth and small, it's a boy-butt. But if it is of a generous voluptuous size, nice and cushiony for his belly and thighs to bounce against and it has all those sexy dimples, instantly he knows he is safe to get a hardon. Charge! Those dimples beckon like twinkle lights on a tree."

"Lee, you're all wet. Young women have smooth butts."

"That is a fiction, foisted upon us by *Playboy* and armies of airbrush artists. They blast away every dimple on the naked young women that only inhabit that mythical land: Centerfold. Rhodes, I've seen dimples on the legs and butts of slender, fit, sixteen-year-olds. I have dimples. Perfectly natural, and if one thinks about it correctly, real cute and sexy."

"I'm beginning to like this theory."

"There's more. Even though I am a naturally undernourished-looking type,

the thinnest of thin, in approximately thirty years this culture has gone from trying to pour weight-gain tonics down the throats of people like me, so my mother would have Marilyn Monroe/Elizabeth Taylor curves, to saying my build,
breasts added–courtesy of male surgeons–is the feminine ideal. You've seen me
naked."

"Yes. From the back you look like a teenage boy. No offense."

"I know, and since my breasts are teeny, also from the front. Now if I went out
and had some doctor shove silicone up under my skin I'd really be desirable.
Maybe a nosejob, too. Maybe not. Anyhoo. Women with my build just can't
grow breasts but now, watch Elsa Clench on Sunday morning, all the runway
models are stick persons with half-melons like surprises on their chests. They're
all gonna have to have Cesareans, if they ever decide to reproduce, cause they ain't
got no hips. If they grow a baby with any brains at all it'll never get out. And with
silicone boobs they can't nurse. My poor mother. I remember her trying all those
bust-developer potions and exercisers. She drank gook by the gallon to try to
'turn those angles into curves,' like the ads said back then. I watched her go
through hell for twenty years, my dad, the professor of English, calling her
breasts 'fried eggs.' And first thing she did after the divorce–he left her, you know,
for a skinny siliconed chick–was get silly-cones stuck in her body, just so her nipples would stick out at the top of skin-covered hills. Now his wife, who is two
years younger than me, has leakage of her silly-cones and all kinds of health problems. She moves, looks, and acts ten years older than my dad. If he thought he
was gonna have some young thang to care for him in his dotage…Ha! He's the
nurse, big-time, for her. Of course, why should I be surprised? It's the Law of
Karma working beautifully." She took a deep breath. "Mom's implants are holding just fine, I cross my fingers and say daily prayers."

"Lee, this is great stuff. Have you considered writing an article about it? Call
it *And Man Made Woman* or something? Begin with Hugh Hefner interviewing
his first airbrush artist."

"You think?"

"Absolutely. God…I want a cigarette."

"Why don't you wait till tomorrow, go see Stella and do this like a healthy
non-masochist?"

"Nope. Got to do it now."

"Okay. You got me off the track. I want to know about sex with the ex."

"Oh–sure–wait–someone's clicking–hang on?"

"Yep."

Brit clicked the reset button and said hello.

"Brit. Please. I need to talk with you."

"Scottie. Oh God." She sighed. "Okay. Just for a minute. Lee's on the line. Hang on, I'll get back to you."

"Thanks, Babe." His voice was thick with gratitude.

"Lee? It's Scottie."

"Oh shit. I'm outta here."

E I G H T E E N

Maybe he could get used to the idea of sex with an older woman. His dick didn't seem to know the difference. Here it was filling his hand and he wasn't thinking about some perfect twenty-year-old, but a fifty-year-old. When you got right down to it, she didn't look all that bad, even totally naked–nothing a little liposuction, a few tucks here and there, the tummy could flatten, the ass and the boobs could go higher–hey, while she was under they may as well slip her some silicone, make 'em bigger–he could go for that. Then she'd look–outstanding. She'd always been an incredible looking woman, and after all that no one would ever guess she was an "Older Woman." She'd look mature, of course, but so sexy that's all the average, thinking-with-his-dick type guy would notice. And his associates and clients would be impressed, not just with her looks but that she was an artist…one of her main attractions when he married her…model-tall, a beautiful artist with shows in New Orleans and New York. He wondered what would be the best way to approach her about making these changes? If money was a problem, if this affair kept on, he could help her out. A horrible thought struck him: her days of looking good, even with surgery, were numbered. There are limits to what even the best surgeons can do…he'd like to get a real close-up look at Elizabeth Taylor in the flesh, he couldn't tell anything from those perfume commercials of hers shot through layers of gauze, Vaseline on the lens, major lighting tricks….

He was going crazy. He needed a meeting.

His head snapped up. Hartwell was speaking.

"Hello, I'm Hartwell and I'm an alcoholic." Grant had been to other meetings but Hartwell had not been at any of them. Seeing him again was a shock and then when he spoke Grant felt his blood drain out the soles of his feet. *God! Hartwell really was an alcoholic!* Bloodless and now re-filled with a humming anxiety, he listened, not noticing his right knee jerking spasmodically. Furtively, he wet his dry lips. Hartwell leaned forward smiling at the moderator, the person responsible for introducing a topic for discussion, which was "How I came to find a God of my understanding."

Grant was at a different church this time and the chairs were arranged in rows facing a table that sat the chairperson, the leader of the meeting, and the moderator. Before them was the blue "big book," the bible of Alcoholics Anonymous and a sign, *Who you see here, What you hear here, When you leave here, Let it stay here.*

"I'm glad you brought that topic up, Irwin. I guess, besides just the toughness of finally admitting I am an alcoholic—" Grant started again...*Hartwell said that so comfortably!* "—that the God thing was the next toughest thing to swallow." The head of Whitfield, Whitfield, Galliano & Griffin gazed around the room, his eyes crinkling benevolently behind his fashionable lightweight frames. Hartwell turned his head and looked right at Grant. "So, I suppose," he continued, and he looked away from Grant, "that Step Three, 'Made a decision to turn our will and our lives over to the care of God <u>as we understood him</u>,' was very difficult for me. As most of you know, I'm an attorney, and I like to think I'm in charge." Hartwell took a deep breath.

"But what finally penetrated my dense skull was that part of Step Three that says: '<u>as we understood him</u>.' I took that to mean I didn't have to accept the stern, judgmental Great-Man-in-the-Sky-God of my childhood, the Big Guy who wanted an eye for an eye, and of course wanted Hartwell's skinny ass, just so He could toss it down to the Devil if I was bad." Someone laughed out loud. Hartwell grinned, continued. "As an alcoholic—I was very, very bad." There were chuckles. Bewildered, Grant glanced around the room.

"No doubt about it—my future held only hellfire. Here on Earth—God wasn't going to wait till I died. He was burning my behind, and the main instrument of His Will was the person of my wife." The room came alive with even more laughter.

"But then I got sober and began to seek through prayer and meditation to improve my conscious contact with God, as instructed by Step Eleven, it didn't work. Kind of like a lame 'knock-knock' joke: I'm praying and meditating, saying 'knock-knock' at heaven's door, but no 'God' was behind the door, not even for long enough to go along with the joke...I began to feel there was no god for Hartwell. Despite my worldly success, the house on Audubon Park, the Mercedes and the Cadillac, the sailboat, the beautiful wife and two beautiful children, plenty of money to put them through college, travel to Europe, spend part of January in the Virgin Islands, a few dollars stashed in the Caymans–I was an empty shell, and to paraphrase from something I must have read in college, 'I had the map, but not the territory.' And so I drank breakfast, lunch, and dinner. Then–in A.A., I didn't drink. But was I spiritually sober? Not at all." He shifted in his seat. One man got up and refilled his Styrofoam coffee cup. Grant swallowed. Except for the uncontrollable jiggling of his knee, he was scared to move.

"I really like the expression 'Higher Power.' For me the word 'God' is too laden with fear and guilt. 'Higher Power' is much more comforting...and I always wanted 'power.'" He paused while the group laughed again.

"One morning I was taking my usual jog in the park. For days, weeks, months I'd tried to pray and to meditate. It wasn't working. I'd given up knocking. I'd dial God and get a busy signal. Not even His answering machine. I didn't know the trouble was on my line, not His. I had so much guilt–from things like sex with women other than my wife, grandiose sprees on out-of-town trips, like the time I set out for a conference in L.A., had to change planes in Atlanta, and woke up a week later in bed with a hippie girl in Greenwich Village in New York City." More laughter.

Grant couldn't believe this was Hartwell. If it wasn't the revered leader of his law firm speaking he'd think, in some ways, this was better than a sitcom. He didn't notice his knee had quit jiggling and he'd begun, tentatively, to smile when the others laughed.

Hartwell looked down at his hands clasped loosely in his lap and when he looked up Grant saw wetness in his eyes.

"...so this one particular day, alcohol-free about eighteen months, jogging, I realized with a jolt like electricity that if it weren't for A.A., I wouldn't be jogging. I wouldn't be in the park, hearing birdsong, watching the early morning sun slanting through those magnificent mossy oaks–no, instead, I'd be at home, pouring six ounces of Absolut vodka into a teaspoon of orange juice, hoping Celia wouldn't notice..."

Ironic chuckles. Grant thought, *these people can laugh about six ounces of vodka in the morning? I don't drink like that! Maybe I'm not really an alcoholic.*

"I was jogging in place waiting for a platoon of ducks to cross the path and...I saw them, their incredible purity. The whiteness of their feathers, the brilliant yellow-gold of their bills and big webbed feet, their cocky, waddling self-assurance–their whimsical beauty! I was stunned. If a duck–a duck!–can have such confidence–why can't I?"

Hartwell paused and leaned back. His metal chair creaked. The room was quiet.

"Doesn't an understanding God want a man, however flawed, to feel as at home in his skin as a duck in his feathers?" Silence. Hartwell leaned forward and clasped his hands once more. Grant felt himself leaning forward.

"And then it was though an optometrist had changed my lenses. I had a clearer, fresher way of seeing–I'd never even looked at a duck before–unless, of course, it was à l'orange on a plate at the Pontchartrain Hotel–" More laughter. "So even though I'm a crusty old man, a man who has been incredibly arrogant and foolish and cruel–what I put Celia and the children through!–yet, I started from that moment to look for some shreds of beauty within myself. And I've found them. They are tattered shreds. But they're something." Hartwell sat back, a smile on his thin lips, color on his aristocratic cheekbones. "That's how I found my Higher Power. Through a duck!" Laughter filled the room. Hartwell raised his voice, "And I've never eaten duck à l'orange again!" People howled. Hartwell subsided with, "Thank you for letting me share." Grant found he was grinning as he joined the chorus calling, "Thanks for sharing, Hartwell."

NINETEEN

Britannia sighed hugely. She'd taken a minute to fortify herself with more coffee and the protection of clothing. Inside a green velvet caftan she sat like a queen accepting an audience from the ambassador of a lesser kingdom, with two exceptions. Under the covers her legs were crossed like a yogi and a phone was clenched between her ear and shoulder. She felt quite comfortable listening to Scottie's phone ring. She'd gotten to hug Saunders in the kitchen. He'd just come in from feeding the animals and was eating leftover pizza for his breakfast like a perfectly normal teen.

Where the hell is Scottie? Had his mood swung again, now he was chickening out?

A breathless "Hello."

"It's me," said Brit.

"I'm sorry, Baby. Watchtower Witnesses at my door–someone left the courtyard gate open again–" He lived in the Vieux Carré in renovated slave quarters, a two-story building of apartments forming a L around a brick-walled courtyard lined with windmill palms, banana trees, and palmettos. Potted herbs and hibiscus sat around an amoeba-shaped pool. She and Scott had baptized their sexuality in the pool at 4 a.m. two years before, the moon a smudgy quarter-slice laying soft light upon their nude bodies, above them hung iridescent jessamine blossoms, its leafless vine invisible in the dark. The flowers floated like gold stars in the night air, radiating an intoxicating fragrance. Britannia had wanted to paint them.

The pool water was chilly as snow-melt...they laughed and felt powerful at handling the coldness, two Northerners arrogant in ice-water, no soft Southerner could do such a thing...but when they embraced the water seemed to come to a boil around them.

"No problem, Scottie. What do you want."

"You. I want you. Only you. Hey, it's freaky fucking a woman with more muscles than me. Brit, I promise I will do anything, anything. Crawl miles through mosquito-breeding swamps...anything, baby. Do I deserve this coldness?"

"Yes. Fucking another woman isn't part of our relationship. I can't believe I'm even talking to you. I should hang up."

"No no, please, Brit. Look. Please let me come out and talk to you. I don't want her. I was just some kind of fitness routine for her. I know this sounds very weak, but I was drunk, loaded on coke–which she gave me, I went to Biloxi clean–but now as I recall she did very little of it and pretty soon she had her clothes and my clothes off–"

"You were in her room?"

"That's where she had the stash–"

"You poor, helpless man. Tsk tsk. You were seduced. Aw. You're breaking my heart." She heard her sarcasm and then her words, and pain, like shards of jagged crystal, stabbed up through her solar plexus, into her heart and lungs and, even though she took quick breaths, it seemed she wasn't getting air.

Scott heard puffing noises.

"Brit? Brit, are you there? Are you all right?"

She couldn't answer.

"What is it, Brit, you're scaring me, Brit my love–"

"Okay." The crystals melted to a rapier-thinness and if she breathed very shallowly– "I'm okay now."

"I'm coming out there. You need taking care of."

"I do not. Don't you dare, Scott Webster."

"Brit, please babe, we've got too much going for us. I will swim naked through snake infested bayous–I will quit using, I will–"

"–Quit calling me 'babe'. That's the name of a pig in a movie." She felt a smile beginning. Scottie heard it.

"An Academy Award-winning pig."

"Are you insinuating I'm an actor? Moi?"

"The best. The most talented, on-screen and off."

Unbidden, her most recent on-screen performance dressed in leather vest, black suede chaps, cowboy boots, black Resistol western hat and nothing else, came in her mind. Scott had brought his big fancy news-video camera. What? Ten months ago? They were drunk and she'd sashayed into the bedroom cracking a whip. Scott naked in an upright kneel on the bed, huge camera hefted on his shoulder, was shooting her and he was saying, "Oh yeah, Babe, oh yeah," his cock rising. Then he'd mounted the camera on a tripod, aimed it at the bed and she'd proceeded to "break" this here wild, ornery stud horse…Looking at the immediate playback they'd laughed and laughed and got horny all over again. She hadn't noticed anything especially ugly about her naked body at that time…Where the hell was that tape anyway? She needed to examine it frame by frame to chart her decay.

"I'm on my way."

"Better not. I'm in a white rage, Webster."

"Brit. I promise, never ever again, not ever, it was so stupid of me. I am such a fuckup, all that coke –"

"Back up."

"What?"

"Back up. Earlier you said you'd quit using. Whyn't y'all just do that little ol' thang, Scottie-boy? Quit." Regally she sat up straighter. "I've quit smoking." Wilton cocked his head as her hand went theatrically to her brow. "It is hell, dear boy, but it's worth it. I'm worth it, as Stewart says on *Saturday Night Live*. I may also quit drinking."

"You want me to quit using."

"Well, I'm hearing 'the coke made me do it,' so it sounds like Demon Coke's running Scottie's life, not Scott Albert Webster. Or is it an excuse so you can fuck around whenever you want?"

"Girl, I swear I have never, ever fucked around on you, never, not even once before. And I never desired to. I did not desire to the other night. It was a huge, enormous, mistake. And now I'm scared those ten minutes will ruin the rest of my life–"

"Ten minutes? I don't believe Scott A. Webster lasted only ten minutes–"

"Believe it. That chick had muscles in her cunt–excuse me, Britannia, I know you prefer yoni–but they squeezed so hard I thought she was chopping my dick off. Brit, I will crawl over broken glass…"

"I don't want to hear these pitiful sexual details. I don't want you crawling over broken glass. You already did that, on my birthday. You stomped in it, the actual day before you went and," her voice rose, "fucked Ms. Nautilus. And that's another thing. I'm too fucking old for you, Scott."

"WHAT!"

He was yelling also, so Brit moved the receiver to godd's ear who lay purring on a pillow. The cat flinched but didn't move, yet Brit heard every word.

"–That's pure D. bullshit!" Scott saw spittle splatter from his mouth, so he held the receiver a little away. "YOU WEREN'T TOO FUCKING OLD THE NIGHT BEFORE YOUR BIRTHDAY. Goddammit! I know what this is! Brit–*forget that fucking birthday*. It doesn't mean shit. So just lose it!" He breathed deeply and lowered his voice as he moved the receiver closer. "So. You want me to quit coke."

Brit put hers back to her ear. "This has nothing to do with my birthday. I could care less if you quit coke. But I'm trying to take back some control of myself, my life, and my new agenda says I don't screw around with…with–dope fiends. If any man should want to see me, they would eschew illegal drugs."

"Brit, I will do anything, and I mean anything you say, babe. Britannia. Anything."

"Get detoxed. You stay clean for three months–let's see," she counted on her fingers, "that would take you to the end of May. Do that, then call me. If I am not otherwise occupied, we'll maybe do coffee."

"Except for 'otherwise occupied' fine. Goddammit, I'll check myself in tomorrow. But I've got one request. I'd like to see you just one time…if I'm going into some detoxification institute."

Brit felt tears in her eyes. *Oh my dear, sweet, kind, generous, beautiful Scottie, your beauty only slightly blurred from your years of drinking and using, I did love you. You made me feel new.* She sighed.

"Okay. Set it up and I'll come see you, maybe we'll lunch somewhere, just lunch, and, well…set it up. But. Only if you want to for yourself, not for me. I make no promises, Scott. As far as I'm concerned our fling is over. I have to go now."

"Brit. I love you. I'll call tomorrow."

She clicked off the phone and lay back on her pillows. A hot want for a cigarette had gathered like smog in the back of her throat. Her body throbbed in craving.

Should she also quit drinking?

TWENTY

By Monday morning Brit was shaking with desire for a cigarette. She was glad she had so much to do because only when she was focused on an activity did her craving subside. She was dressed in Viola's suit, it was perfect for taking Saunders to school and getting him enrolled, then going on to Jimmy's funeral. She even had gloves in her purse and was carrying the flighty hat.

On Sunday afternoon she'd suited up like a serious equestrienne and schooled Mokhtar as though they were planning to show. It took him a while to warm up, but once he got the kinks out he performed so well she left a message on Sugarplum's machine asking when the next dressage show was. Maybe she'd give it a whirl. Then she gave Saunders a driving lesson in the Jag–the kid was thrilled–and now she stood on the steps waiting for him to bring the car around from the garage.

He stopped the car and when she opened the driver's side he said, "Aw."

"Move it chum, you don't have a license yet." He slid away and she got in and drove toward town. He'd refused to attend St. Paul's so their destination was Covington High. Grant was faxing the necessary records so Saunders should be able to start today. Her conversation Sunday night with Grant had been all business. She felt so confused that every time he tried to personalize their exchange, she'd changed the subject.

She didn't know if she wanted to have an affair with Grant or Scottie, even if he had fucked another woman. Maybe she didn't want an affair at all. She didn't know what she wanted, except to get young again.

Later she stood at the graveside in back of the huge crowd that had turned out to say farewell to Jimmy. It was a brisk sunny day with a determined little breeze that kept women snatching at their hats. In a crowd of students, other teachers, family, she smelled new clothes, fresh earth, gardenias. Annie was surrounded, but in the moment she'd had to condole, Annie said, "Jimmy sure would love that hat, Brit." And they'd smiled.

She pulled the veil down to her chin because staring at the flower-laden coffin, the deep hole beneath it evoked more crying. First crying for Jimmy, then for Brit. Poor old Brit who'd just quit smoking…and maybe drinking. It was torture, even with a nicotine patch stuck on her left breast. *Why was she bothering? Shouldn't she just indulge herself, enjoy what little was left to her?*

The purple-robed reverend was tossing dirt on the coffin now and saying those sad, sad words, "Ashes to ashes…Dust to dust…" his voice high-pitched, making her wonder if he sang like Little Richard. Then she almost began hysterical laughter, but his voice pierced through this and she became aware of rawness inside, as if her innards had been jerked out by a mechanical plucker at a Miss Goldy plant, making her an emptied woman beneath the saucy hat, the Chanel suit, prepared to be eaten by others. Now she cried. Her crying became loud sobs but it didn't matter, everyone else was sobbing. Even the men. Black funerals, she decided, were much more comfortable to be at than white funerals–where crying was a lapse of manners.

There was such a crowd she decided not to go over to Annie's again. Quitting smoking made her feel like sandpaper was relentlessly abrading her skin. She wanted to scratch and claw at people.

At home the message light was blinking, so on her way to the bar she hit the play button. Her hand clutched the neck of the brandy bottle. Wildly, she decided it was time to quit that, too. She banged the bottle down, headed for the kitchen for Diet Coke.

Grant's voice followed her, sounding happy. "Hope the fax got there okay. Sorry I couldn't be there to help with Saunders or go with you to Jimmy's funeral. Court today. Will you be in the city this week? Could we do lunch real soon?"

"Could we fuck real soon?" she answered sarcastically.

Then Scottie. "Brit, I'm checking into Bowling Green Treatment Center on your side of the lake, you know where it is? Mandeville? Tomorrow, early. Could we meet at La Provence for dinner tonight? Please call me. I'm home today."

Very nice place to have dinner. *But was dinner a setup to have sex?* She must call him and be firm.

Lee. "Rhodes. I know you're in pain. Just sending my love. Hang in there, gal."

Then, to her joy, Asia. "Hi, Mom. Okay if I come home next weekend?" Brit thought, *she'll be even more anxious to come when she finds out Saunders is here.*

Then there was a rasping sound, like someone clearing their throat, loud coughs, a harsh voice. "Brit. Nadia foaled. UP all NIGHT. Eggs-hausted. Got a god-damn-colt. Hope that stud a yours isn't SIRING only COLTS this year. You know I ONLY want FILLIES. Oh yeah. There's a dressage meet third weekend in June. Call me. Gotta FIGURE what to do with this god-damn-COLT." Cough, cough.

For the first time in thirty-some hours Brit was grateful she'd quit smoking.

Sipping icy decaffeinated Diet Coke she called everyone back and left messages on their machines. Grant: "Maybe lunch on Thursday?" Scottie: "Okay. What time at La Provence?" Asia: "Of course come home for the weekend, Honey, I can't wait. And, big surprise, Saunders is staying here! Tell you all the details when you arrive. I know Saunders will be thrilled to see you." Before calling Sugarplum she hesitated. Somehow Sugar would make it her fault that Mokhtar sired a boy and not a girl. She took a deep breath then punched in the numbers.

"'LO?" Sugarplum screamed hoarsely into the receiver.

"Hi," cried Brit with false joy. "Congratulations on the new foal."

"SAVE 'em. Don't want a COLT. The little BOUGER wasted ELEVEN MONTHS of my precious Nadia's LIFE."

"I'm real sorry, Sugarplum. Is there anything I can do to help?"

"Well, SINCE YOU ASK, you could SEND MOKHTAR BACK and I'll REBREED and HOPE this time he'll SIRE a FILLY."

"I guess. But not for too long now. I'm riding him again." So Sugarplum wanted to breed again for free. But Brit didn't mind, much. Besides, he came home from Sugarplum's acting like a two-year-old. That slightly pissed-off energy gave him terrific impulsion at the trot.

"You want to SHOW him?"

"Sure. Gave me a good work yesterday."

"Isn't he kinda OLD?"

"He doesn't think so. He went great."

"How'd YOU hold up."

"Fine. Why?"

"Well, I DON'T want to TALK out of TURN but you did just have A BIG BIRTHDAY and all."

"I'm just fine. In fact I rode on my birthday as well." *And I'll never tell you what I wore*–Brit stifled a laugh, for she suddenly realized what she'd worn was…her birthday suit.

"I just don't like to TAKE CHANCES RIDING any more, Brit. NOT WITH MY BACK. You KNOW our bones AREN'T MADE OF RUBBER like they used to be."

"I'm not so sure I buy into that."

"Sure. BONES GET BRITTLE. When we fall AT OUR AGE, we BREAK, we DON'T BOUNCE like we used to."

"I think that's mythic bullshit, Shug. I refuse to buy into any of that aging bullshit anymore. I don't feel brittle and I don't plan on falling." She heard a little grunt, then a noise that sounded like a...fart?...followed by a trickling sound.

"Well. When can you GET HIM OVER HERE?" A toilet flushed. *God.* Sugarplum had used the toilet while she was on the phone. Brit didn't know whether to laugh or hang up in disgust. She wondered how one would state this in a letter to Miss Manners. *Dear Miss Manners, It has been my recent experience that people with portable telephones continue their conversations while apparently seated upon a certain type of 'throne' (pardon the euphemism but I do realize your column is printed in thousands of family newspapers) and... voiding themselves. By the time the hapless listener realizes what must be going on (there can be no mistaking a certain 'flush' sound) one is overcome by an unavoidable embarrassment. How do you suggest I express my discomfiture about this behavior to my friend?* There was no changing Sugarplum, so she laughed, "Well, since I gather you've gotten a perfectly healthy colt and I'm doing all this as a favor you'd better come and get Mokh yourself. Besides, I've got my hands full. My stepson has moved back in with me."

"Oh YEAH?"

"Yes."

"How BIG'S he? Could he COME OVER, help me HITCH UP MY TRAILER? My BACK'S REAL BAD after SLEEPING in the BARN all WEEK–for a GOD-DAMN-COLT."

Brit sighed. It would be more efficient to haul Mokh over herself. "You win. I'll bring him over, and I want to see this colt you hate so much."

"Wanna buy him?"

"Whoa. You're getting free breedings and you want to sell me this son of my stallion?"

"I've got almost a year's worth of feed and vet bill's in his mama."

"So? I've sixteen years in his daddy."

"Let's don't argue. When can Mokh come over? I want to breed on the foal heat, about a week from now."

"How 'bout the weekend? Asia's coming home. Hey. What's that god-damn-colt look like?"

"I dunno. He's OKAY I guess. GOT A REAL LONG NECK."

"Oh?" One of Mokh's few flaws was a slight dearth of neck.

"I'm EGGS-aw-STEAD."

"Okay, Sugarplum, go to bed."

"Bye, Brit. See YAH on the WEEKEND."

TWENTY-ONE

Saunders felt like he'd survived an endless weekend only to find himself in a hick school no different from the city one. With only slight alterations he felt like Bill Murray in *Groundhog Day*. It was all so far beyond boredom he could find no word for it. Viciously he punched a pillow. godd hopped up on top of the sofa, so he punched her. She made a soft little plop sound as she hit the floor.

And if The Maw thought driving her precious XJS back and forth over her rocks in second fucking gear was a big thrill for him, well…he shifted on the sofa. *Why the fuck did people live in the country anyway?* After you looked at the chickens, the ducks, the horse, which took all of thirty seconds, IF you took your time, that was it. The country was experienced. He'd gotten stoned before feeding the critters Sunday morning, (The Maw babbling on the phone all fucking morning. Guess the big thrill of sonny-boy's return had worn off for her. That was quick.) and had zoned out on the idiotic chickens, pecking, squawking, squabbling. The rooster had a life alright. Him and six women. Horny old thing spent all his time fucking. He half laughed and tossed a scarlet pillow in the air. *Did The Maw realize she had feathered porn nonstop in her yard?* He'd heard her talking to that punitive witch so inaptly named Sugarplum and now she was about to send her horse off so he could get laid.

Only critters got to screw out here. There was some gash worth trying on at the school, but that meant he'd have to hang around there. Maybe even attend more classes. He was not up for that shit.

godd jumped up on the sofa back and peered down at him. Saunders stared at the cat, she stared down unblinking. Saunders didn't blink, either.

"Hey, watcha lookin' at cat? She shoulda named you 'goddamn' instead of 'godd-win' like that no-brainer Sugarplum and her 'god-damn-colt.'" He punched the cat again. "Now get off the god-damn-sofa or I'll wring your neck and throw you so far in those woods she'll never find you."

godd landed on her feet and walked from the room.

He had tried to light a fire when he came in, he liked the fireplace. It was cool to get stoned and watch flames flicker. But it wouldn't stay lit. Now it was an ugly tableau of half-burned newspapers, charred kindling. He decided to try Terry, see if he knew of any action, as his stash was gone. He needed to score. In more ways than one.

T W E N T Y - T W O

The maître d', a solid, middle-aged woman in a print dress, threaded her way past a lit fireplace to a table in a dark corner. A few minutes past six and La Provence, famous for its hearty French provincial cuisine, was dim and empty, except for the yeasty smell of baking bread. Brit followed her, the turquoise silk caftan sent by Elizabeth billowing. She wore silk slippers in a colorful paisley, an ankle chain and Halima's woodsy jewelry. Her hair, clean, long and full, billowed like the caftan. It was particularly soft tonight, curlier than usual, and all she'd done was change shampoos. She still felt abraded by her nicotine craving and shaky over wanting a drink. This intensified when a gaunt, shadow-faced man rose up from the table.

In mild horror she said, "Scott?"

"Brit. Thank God you came. Please. Sit down." He gestured at the opposite seat and knocked over a water glass.

Brit and the maître d' exchanged alarmed looks, but she moved in smoothly, "I'll have that taken care of sir, don't you worry about a thing." Scott slumped down in his seat and ran a quivering hand over hair which looked dried out, thinned.

Seated, Brit accepted a menu. A bus boy arrived to mop up the water and set a new goblet before Scott. He filled it with tinkling icy water and lit the candle between them. Brit saw Scott's right hand wrapped around a drink. The busboy left, and a waiter hovered until she waved him away.

She wanted a cigarette, dammit!

"Scottie. What's wrong?"

Scott took a hasty drink, shot a paranoid glance around the deserted restaurant, and leaned toward her. Even before he spoke she smelled his foul breath.

"Had a Lost Weekend." His voice was low, his cheeks sunken, eyes flat, their brilliant turquoise filmed over. His neck looked thin in the collar of his dress shirt, his tie was crooked.

"Lost Weekend? Like the old Ray Milland movie?"

"Yeah." His voice was a breathy, deathy rasp.

"My God. Did you ever, Scott. You don't look like the same person. What could you possibly do that would wreck you so quickly? Scottie–you've lost fifteen pounds!"

"Crack." His voice was exactly like Clint Eastwood's after his stint in the desert in *The Good, The Bad and The Ugly*. A burned, raw, hush of a voice.

She reached, took his hand, held it firmly to abate its shaking, but instead it made her hand shake too. His hand was hot. He gulped the rest of his drink, then managed to set the glass on the table.

"Wanna drink, Brit? What'll you have?"

"Um." She desperately wanted a Manhattan. In fact, on the way over she'd convinced herself that quitting smoking was enough, it was just too much to try and quit drinking at the same time. By the time she reached the restaurant she was salivating for a double Manhattan, straight up. Now looking at her former lover, how wasted he was–he'd disentangled his hand from hers and was laboriously shaking a cigarette out of a package–she wondered if the Manhattan was a good idea. Avidly she watched him struggle to light a Marlboro. She licked her lips.

"Perrier and a twist of lime."

"What?"

"I quit smoking and drinking."

"Jesus Christ, Brit. I can't believe it. How come you're not coming apart?"

"I am."

"It doesn't show. In fact, you look beautiful. Gorgeous." Still the Clint Eastwood whisper.

"Thanks." But no thanks, she thought. Scottie–a crackhead! How could that be? Only low-class slime smoked crack, not successful creative people like her Scottie. Her heart felt rent. *Was there a cure? Wasn't crack the most addictive drug in history?* The love and passion she'd felt for him roiled around inside her like a weather picture of a hurricane, that round serrated-edge shape like a saw blade. Inside the little round hole, the eye, she saw a tiny Britannia Rhodes, arms upraised, imploring indifferent gods for help. Ignoring his smell, she leaned forward and saw where he'd cut himself shaving, twice, on either side of his throat. In the eye, she knew the second half of the hurricane was still to come...and it could be worse than the first half.

"Since when do you smoke crack, Scottie?"

His eyes shifted away. "Since Friday. And I want some right now so bad you can't begin to imagine." He held up his empty glass to a passing waiter. A few people had arrived and light conversation drifted around them. Brit saw no one was rushing to wait on them. She was surprised they'd seated him. "The booze and you is all that's keeping me from running out of here and buying another rock. Except I'd have to put it on a credit card. I spent three grand this weekend."

Brit gasped. "Three–"

"Yep. This crack stuff is a real killer, Brit, no kidding. One hit–*one hit*–and I had to have more. Expensive, too."

The waiter set a Perrier before Brit and another of what smelled like scotch before Scottie. Nervously Brit took a swallow thinking *I get no kick from champagne...Because now I drink Perrier.* She looked around at the other patrons. Fifty-ish, they looked, dressed, and acted their age. Rebels like she and Scottie couldn't stay in this nice, homey, five-star restaurant that was written up in *Gourmet* and *Bon Apetit.* Scottie's appearance did not inspire appetite, bon or otherwise. And on top of his bummy appearance, he smelled of vomit.

"Scottie, let's get the hell out of here. I think I'd better take you to Bowling Green tonight, not wait till tomorrow morning."

His eyes filled with tears. "No, no, Brit, I want to spend this evening with you, have a nice talk and a nice dinner like we used to..."

"Scottie. You're in no shape for anything like that." She opened a beaded bag and, fishing out a twenty, tossed it on the table. She stood, took Scottie by the arm. Like a child he was crying now and whimpering "No, no, please, Brit, I want to stay with you please..."

She set her lips, willed herself not to cry with him. A brawny waiter hustled up, "May I be of assistance, Ma'am?"

"No. Thank you. My friend is just a little tired. We'll be fine." Scottie leaned on her and she put an arm firmly around his waist. Once he bumped into a table, the silverware clashed, a goblet fell soundlessly to the carpeted floor. She didn't look back but was aware of a rush to pick it up, a hovering of people in their wake. As they left the dining room she heard a collective exhalation, as if everyone had held their breath during their entire slouching exit. A tall black-haired woman regal in susserating turquoise silk, a disheveled blond man in rumpled clothes listing heavily against her, feet dragging, knocking things over...upsetting the status quo....

Outside it was dark. Their feet scraped over gravel. She packed him in her car then went around and slid behind the wheel.

"I think I better get you over to Bowling Green right now, Scottie."

"No, please, Brit, don't dump me like that, please, please I want to spend one last night with you before I go through this. No sex. I won't even try. Please, could you stay with me?" His voice, still a hoarse whisper, came out muffled because he'd hunched forward, his head in his hands. He began crying so hard she saw tears dripping through his fingers. His shoulders spasmed under his tweed jacket.

He lifted his head. "I've got a room at that place on Old Military Road. Please. I won't try anything. I just want to lie next to you one more time before I enter the gates of hell."

"The Gates of Hell?"

"Well, you know." He gave a half-grin. She smiled slightly as she stared at his reflection in the windshield.

Headlights washed over them as Brit waited for traffic on Highway 190. The only sound now was the low purr of the Jaguar. She saw an opening and eased it into the flow. They were headed toward Bowling Green, or Old Military Road. Her stomach growled, her hands tightened on the steering wheel.

"Goddammit, Scottie! I am really pissed off at you! Why are you in my car? I don't believe this!" Briefly she threw both hands off the wheel, then grabbed it again. She was yelling at his reflection.

"Why have I allowed a man–with whom I've had a two-year affair, from whom I've learned sport-fucked another woman–in my car?" She pounded the wheel with her fist, "Was it just plain old cocaine, Scott, or crack that made you do it? Why are you in my car? In my life?" Scott's hands were back over his face.

Her hand wanted to straighten his disheveled blond hair.

"Because I love you, Brit," he cried out from his hands. "And I think you love me, even if you won't admit it."

They reached Bowling Green, her turn signal was blinking. His hand shot out and took her arm. "Please, Brit. One night. I need something to give me the strength to do this." She looked at him and his hand loosened on her arm. She stared at his haggard face, backlit by the headlights of a car behind them. *My God*, she thought, *he looks old. He looks fifty.* She got scared. Scottie was very ill. If he didn't get help, she saw he could die from this addiction, and quickly. It had eaten him up in just three days. The car behind honked. Scott held her eyes, his so full of want, or need. *Was there a difference?*

"What the hell." She accelerated and drove down the road. Maybe she'd leveled the playing field when she'd had sex with Grant. But no need to trouble Scott with that information.

"Here I come. Gates of Hell."

TWENTY-THREE

Grant spent all day Sunday going to A.A. meetings. Monday, he sandwiched in more meetings before court, and at lunch. He felt more confident in the courtroom than he had in years. At each A.A. meeting he earnestly "shared," talking about his apprehensions. It really made a difference. He had a feeling of release after he talked and he strolled into the courtroom rather than stiffly strutted.

He won the case, got a huge settlement and custody for his client, and he celebrated by going to another meeting. Afterward, he drove home, noticing only a few bars. It was almost easy to drive right past them and he concentrated on his miffed feeling at Britannia's behavior. *Why was she avoiding him? Hadn't the sex been great for her too?* He wanted to see her again. *Couldn't they "date" or something?* Things were happening and he wasn't being given proper explanations by her. His Alcoholics Anonymous sponsor, the man he was supposed to call anytime he thought he might take a drink, Irwin, had said no relationships for a year, but that was bullshit. They couldn't expect a man to give up booze and sex at the same time. *But maybe his Higher Power*–yes, he was beginning to pay attention to the spiritual side of the program–*really wanted him to have a much younger woman than Brit. That must be it.* Feeling smug he parked behind the condo. Just the same he'd call and talk with Saunders. See how his boy was making out.

Inside, the condo was quiet. Rita was gone. There was so little for her to do now, but he hated to let her go in case Saunders came back. He snapped his fingers–yes! Why shouldn't Rita go out to the country for a few days a week, help Brit? He would make this offer. Saunders, he knew, could make more mess than ten kids. Britannia would be grateful of his offer of Rita.

He called Rita's.

She was thrilled. She wondered if there was a place for her to live-in...? Did Miz Brit have a garden? Rita loved gardening. At this effusive response, he wondered if Rita was planning to abandon her own family for a chance to live in the country. Grant felt slightly put out. As he hung up he wondered if his entire nuclear group–Rita wasn't quite "family," but she felt like it–would move out to Brit's. He felt stranded.

But, gamely, he called Brit's to see if Rita, a few days a week, would be welcome.

Saunders answered. "Yeah?" Sounds like the clashing of garbage can lids played behind his voice like a soundtrack. *Metal music,* thought Grant, feeling knowing.

"Saunders."

"Oh hi, Dad. How they hanging?" Clash, bang.

"Saunders. Are you okay?"

"Sure Dome–Dad, sure. I feel really cool."

"You sound really drunk. Are you drinking?"

"Whash makes you think that?" Screech, bang.

"The way you're talking. Put Brit on."

"Ain't here."

"Where is she?"

"Spending the night at her girlfriend's. Lee. You know Lee?"

"I know of Lee. Give me Lee's number."

"Don't have it, Dad."

Grant expelled an exasperated breath. "Son. Are you drinking?"

"'Li'l bit. Ol' Brit don't want it no more. Shame to see it go to waste." Saunders giggled. It had been so long since his son had sounded anything like a child, that even though alcohol had evoked it, the sound gave Grant a lighter feeling. So there was some lightness, some mirth within Saunders.

"Maybe you better slow down, son, you're not planning to go anywhere are you?"

Terry was due in fifteen minutes. Booze was okay, but weed, better yet, Xstacy would be the bitchin' thing to do.

"Nope. Jus' hangin' at the ol' homestead." Music behind. Wildcats screeching in agony. Shouts, yelling.

"Good. Glad to hear it. I do have some good news. Rita has said she'd love to come out there a few days a week if she can have a room of her own. She doesn't want to commute. You think Brit would–"

"Bitchin'! I even talked about that to Maw myself. I know she'd love it. Me too. Cool, Dad."

"Well, that's just great. I guess I'll have to wait till tomorrow to talk with her.

Are you all right?"

"Sure. I'm fine."

"Don't drink any more."

"Nope. Feel tired. Think I'll have a nap." And as Saunders yawned loudly into the phone the cacophony behind him stopped, CD ended. Grant took a deep relieved breath before he spoke.

"Good idea. You know since I've started A.A. I'm coming to realize that alcohol is pure poison for some people and I'm one of them. Your Mother wasn't attracted to it—thank God—but there is a genetic component, son. Your dad, well, it's the truth, son, your dad is an alcoholic." He heard Saunders beginning to yawn again, so he raised his voice. "So, son, that means there's a fifty-fifty chance you could be an alcoholic, too."

"I hear you. Dad, I feel really, really tired."

He sounded like a nine-year-old. "Okay. Hit the sack. Stay out of that booze now, hear?"

"Sure, Dad." Tires crunched up the drive. "Bye." He clicked off the phone, put it to rest on the coffee table.

Grant frowned as he put his receiver back. Brit needed to supervise Saunders more closely. *Why would she want to spend the night with Lee—didn't Lee live in some cramped little trailer? Should he take a ride out there to check on Saunders?* He felt restless. Worried.

He'd ride out there. Check on Saunders.

Part Three

UNPOPULAR NAMES

...Middle Age
Home of lost causes and forsaken beliefs and
Unpopular names...
– *Matthew Arnold*

 O N E

Brit was spooned around Scottie's back at the Green Pines Motel. He'd removed
everything but his black jockey shorts and had fallen onto the bed. She'd kicked
off her paisley ballerinas and, fully caftan'd, lay down with him. Now she stroked
his shaking back and resisted kissing the nape of his neck. Feelings as complex as
the paisley of her shoes moved in her. A tiny voice was saying, *Doesn't he feel wonderful? See how he turned to you? He needs you. You need him.*

   *But I don't want to need anyone. I feel exhausted from quitting smoking and
drinking. I feel too needed by Scottie, too needed by Saunders–and Grant.* Suddenly
she saw Grant as a giant throbbing penis needing her vagina, nothing more. She
squirmed away from Scottie.

   He reacted, his voice in the pillow. "Where you going?" His hand groped back
for her, clamped on her thigh.

   If she wasn't afraid he'd get more crack–*did drug dealers deliver? Did they really
accept credit cards? They had beepers, why not?*–she'd leave. She curled back around
him. His hand stayed on her thigh.

   "Good, good, oh, Babe, I need you." Crying again. She felt anger, fear, frus-
tration.

T W O

Terry arrived with another guy, two girls, and Roofies. Brit was gone for the night
so–what the hey–this was the place to party. Terry pulled Saunders into the

kitchen, whispering his buddy had just come from Florida where he'd scored this new wonder drug. If you gave it to a girl she'd get drunk instantly and get horny. You could do anything you wanted with her, all night long–the drug lasted about eight hours–and when it wore off she had total amnesia. Couldn't remember a thing. They were called Roofies.

"Nah," said Saunders, "too good to be true."

"S'true alright. Let me slip some to these chicks, mix it in their drinks, and in ten minutes man, we can fuck our brains out. You'll see. You'll see how drunk they get."

"Okay."

Saunders strolled back to the living room and put on another CD. Terry went to the walnut cabinet and began filling drink orders.

Grant soared across a deserted Causeway. The lake lapped black around him. He was listening to oldies but goodies, the Village People singing *Macho, macho man...I'm gonna be a macho man...*thrumming his hands on the wheel, he sang along. At the end of the bridge, he kept heading north on 190. He'd be at Brit's in thirty minutes.

Slouched on the sofa, the giggling girls took teensy sips of their bourbon cokes. The guys sat on the hearth's raised stone ledge. Watching, Saunders felt like walking over, tipping their stupid heads back, grabbing them by their noses, and pouring the shit down their throats. But they might remember that part. So he sat, knee jiggling. Every now and then he met Terry's eyes, and they grinned. Meanwhile they smoked some good weed, also scored in Orlando.

Grant drove past Bennett Bridge Road then remembered Folsom was a speed trap. Decorously, he drove through the village, then floored it. Soon he'd make the turn at Tarver Tractor Sales onto 450. Then he'd be ten minutes away.

Saunders sat down beside the brunette one. She had the biggest boobs. He didn't care about the pimples on her face–he was only interested in what was under her clothes. If these chicks got real zonked he could go for some anal action, one thing he'd never tried. *Was she starting to feel the Roofies?* He put his arm around her shoulders and let his fingers walk down to her tit. He glanced up–Terry was watching avidly. He slid his hand under her tank top then dipped right into her bra. Her nipple stiffened the instant he touched it. She moaned. With his free hand he gave Terry a thumbs up. This chick was bad ready. Let the games begin.

Burn Baby Burn played as Grant's blinker flashed red on the deserted blacktop behind him. He turned into Brit's driveway.

"Should I take her up to my room or do her right here?" Saunders was asking Terry's bud. Terry was wrapped around the fat blonde, not interested in consultation.

"Well, if we're gonna go all night, you sure your aunt ain't coming back tonight?"

"Stepmother, not aunt. Nope. She's gone for the night."

"Well, let's drag her upstairs. Leave Terry and that one down here. Be better on a bed. Don't forget, I go first, those were my roofies." Terry's fat blonde had begun to moan, nonstop. Saunders saw she was naked from the waist up. Not bad honkers. He might try some of that later.

"Okay, okay. I'll grab her top, you get her legs."

The Bud grabbed her ankles, pulled her from the sofa. With a grunt Saunders hefted the girl, hands in her armpits. Her arms flopped, and she giggled wildly, whispering,"Tickle, tickle."

"Shit. She's ticklish under the arms. Wait. Let's see. Dead weight ain't she?" Saunders put her shoulders on the sofa, the Bud stood holding her ankles up, and the girl slid to the floor like a melting campfire marshmallow. She waved up at them. They stared.

"I got it," cried Saunders. He took one of her flaccid arms, bent it, and pulled her over his back into a fireman's lift.

There was knock at the door. Wil raced into the room barking shrilly. Saunders groaned as the brunette slid from his back to the floor. The Bud and Saunders stared at one another. Terry was bucking wildly on top of the blonde. The knocking grew louder, then a deep voice. "Saunders."

"Shit. It's my Dad." He jerked his head at Terry. "Get him off her." As he pulled the brunette up onto the couch, working frantically to straighten her clothes, he yelled over Wil's barks, "Dad! Coming."

The pounding continued. The Bud got a red-faced Terry off the girl and both of them fussily rearranged her, thinking it was actually comical how she kept sliding to the floor like a rubber woman. Terry whined as he buttoned his fly, "I thought you were gonna be alone all night."

Saunders flashed a look at him. "Can you control your parents, asshole?" He started toward the foyer, but met Grant coming in. Double shit. He'd forgotten to lock the door.

Grant stopped, planted his fists on his hips, and stared hard at Saunders.

"What the hell's going on here?"

Terry, the Bud, scuttled around him and slammed out the front door, leaving the girls on the sofa.

"The guys brought these chicks over."

Grant stared down at the slumbering girls. "What's wrong with them."

"I think they're drunk." The brunette coughed, moaned, and began to snore.

"They're just kids!" Grant looked around the room, Wilton danced at his feet. For once Saunders hung his head. Contrition? A feeling of pleasure came over Grant. He dropped his arms. *Brit had really screwed up.* Seldom was he so clear-cut right. He breathed deeply. It felt so good.

Damn! She needed to get home, now.

He looked at Saunders. "Son, this is intolerable. I can't believe Brit left you alone. I call and you're drinking. I come out, you, two guys, and these girls are drunk. If she's going to take on the responsibility of a teenager she can't gallivant off to her girlfriend's. What's Lee's number?"

Saunders pointed to a slip of paper stuck under the phone. Grant picked up the coffee table phone and punched out the number. He stared at his son, the girls, as the phone rang in his ear.

"'Lo?"

"Lee. Grant Griffin. Sorry to disturb you so late, but can you put Britannia on? We have a situation here."

Saunders watched his dad nod into the phone.

"No. I'm across the lake." Head shaking. "No. I'm here. At Brit's house."

Nod. "This is serious. Wake her up." Nod. "I'll await her call. Thank you, Lee." He thumbed the phone off.

"Now son. Who are these girls?"

T H R E E

Brit sat on the sagging edge of the motel bed listening to Lee. Behind her Scottie snored. She had called Lee to ask her to check on Saunders, but she never expected anything like this.

Damn that kid.

"And your ex sounds gloatingly angry."

"I believe you."

"Watcha gonna do, Girl?"

"I don't know."

"I'm not happy in the middle, Hon."

"I am sorry, Lee. Well, no matter what, I have to get home. Pronto."

She hung up, then slowly pressed out her home phone number. It was picked up mid-ring.

"Yes."

"Grant."

"Brit." He sounded lofty in just one syllable. She tensed.

"There are two very young girls here–passed out, drunk, on your sofa."

"Oh my God, I'm so sorry–"

"–Saunders is sobering up as we speak. How could you leave him unsupervised?"

Inside Grant a tiny voice squeaked, *Hey, you left him alone every night!* He spoke louder to smother it.

"So, I think you better come right away. These girls need to get home before their parents come looking. Drunk as they are, this could be grounds for statutory rape."

"Rape? Doesn't the rapist have to be over eighteen?"

Grant made rumbling noises, a thunderhead testing resonance and volume.

"We do not have the ages of the two other young men who were here and undoubtedly took advantage of Saunders."

Brit emitted a flattened "Okay." Then firmed her voice. "Grant. I'm so sorry. So very, very sorry. And you've had to drive all the way across the lake, this time of night."

Damn straight. Grant breathed deeply, soothed.

Scottie snorted. Brit clamped a hand over his mouth.

"What's that?"

"Lee's dog."

Scottie's arm thrashed over the bed like an elephant's trunk, seeking her. She made her voice very nice. "Grant. Can you make some coffee? I've got fresh-ground Chocolate Macadamia and French Vanilla in the refrigerator–" She pressed hard on Scottie's mouth, her hand getting wet.

"–I'll find it."

"Thank you, Grant." Scottie flailed, making "mumph, mumph" sounds. Brit continued calmly. "See if the girls will drink some of it. I'll get there ASAP. Okay, Grant?"

"Okay."

They clicked off.

She took her hand off Scottie's mouth. His eyes were wide open and briefly she was caught by their turquoise. Then she saw the red veins, the yellowed whites, and smelt his whisky-mouthed breath. Ugly, smelly reality.

"Scottie. I've got to go home."

He moaned, rubbing his face in the pillow. Her hand went to his hair and she wanted to pull it, she was suddenly so fucking angry–but she spoke softly.

"Stop it. Stop it right now."

He stopped, but kept his face in the pillow.

"My stepson has had some sort of wild party at my house. His father is there. It's a mess." Her hand moved away and he turned his head, watching her with one eye. She looked at the stippled ceiling, dun with ancient cigarette smoke. "It's a real mess. You're here, not safe to leave–they're there, I'm here. Damn!"

She saw a tear come from the one eye and run down his whiskered cheek. Even though he was only thirty-seven, Brit saw some of the grizzle was gray. Her hand moved back to his hair, stroking. He cried while she thought.

If she left him at the motel, would he take himself to the detox clinic? Or go out and possibly charge cocaine? Drug dealers, she'd heard, were high-tech. *Why wouldn't they take Visa, American Express, the Discover card?*

Discover Crack.

Scottie was stroking her thigh saying, "Please, please, Brit, don't leave me."

"Scottie. Do drug dealers take charge cards?"

"One I found does, he's got one of those little plate things–put the card in slide that thing across–then you sign at the bottom."

"Okay." She fisted her hand in his hair and shook. "Here's the plan. You are going to Bowling Green right now."

"No–no, Brit–"

"Yes, yes, Scottie. Jesus. You fuck around on me, you get addicted to crack, and you want me to babysit you when I've got a fifteen-year-old child in a crisis at my own home? Never mind my self-righteous ex-husband is over there wring-ing his hands and God knows what else."

He moaned and tried to pull the sheet over himself. Brit grabbed it and held.

"Get up, Scottie."

He groaned, but he rolled to a sitting position.

She got him on his feet, dressed, out the door, and in the car.

Scottie woke up when they got to Bowling Green. He began to cry again. Brit saw him plant his feet on the car floor, bracing himself like a kid. She walked around the car and opened the passenger door. Scottie's arms were wrapped tight around his body, chin pressed hard into his chest, eyes clenched like little fists.

She stood for a moment staring at him, and the moment was too long. It gave her guilt time to flare again. Grant at her house, Saunders drinking, girls at her house. She leaned in and put her arm around Scottie's neck. She had half a mind to break it.

"Scottie. Darling. Time to go."

He turned, sobbing. Her arms went around him. Her cheek got wet.

"C'mon now," she said into his hot neck.

"Baby, baby, don't leave me. Don't leave me."

Her back was starting to hurt from leaning over and mosquitoes were stabbing her rear.

"Scottie. You've got to come now. I'm not leaving you, I'm just going home."

He allowed her to coax him from the car and, with her arm around his waist, they slouched toward the entrance. He was still crying and she resisted the temptation to snap, "Shape up." She was horrified at how quickly he'd deteriorated. At the edge of the outdoor lights Scottie slid to his knees and his arms came up around her body like a big chimp's. He shoved his face into her belly so hard she felt two sharp pains, as though she was gored in her ovaries. Scottie moaned wetly against her. But the clinic was aroused and two white-clad men, living clichés, hustled to them. She almost laughed. They took Scottie's arms and hauled him to his feet. *Would they stuff him into a straightjacket?* She swallowed a giddy smile.

But they spoke gently. "Mr. Webster, let's go now." He let them lift him, but at the door shouldered them off. Wobbling, he turned.

"Stay cool, Britannia. Thanks for the lift." She was startled at the change and a satisfied little voice said, *He'll make it.* Then, a shocking white flash from his mouth, a smile, and she saw her old lover. She choked, waving, calling, "Good luck, Scott."

Like a sigh from the chest of a mechanical mother the automatic doors closed. Brit watched him turn a corner, disappear.

Shit, Scottie, shit, she said to herself, throat tight like plastic wrap. Cursing under her breath, she stomped to the car.

She opened her front door, smelled Chocolate Macadamia coffee, and walked into Grant. She wanted to elbow him aside, saying, "Look here, Lurk, what the fuck are you doing in my house?" But–

He blocked her, whispering as though to a judge on the bench.

"Brit, it's a damn good thing you're finally here. I don't know what to do about these girls."

The foyer had dim light. There were deep black lines in his brown face, but his bald head was pink. A desire to giggle came. She saw a baby's head grafted on a man's face. Like supermarket sleaze: *BABY-DOMED MAN FOUND IN BRAZILIAN JUNGLE.*

Saunders was right: Super Dome. *No giggling,* she told herself, *no hysterics.*

She took his arm, "C'mon, Grant, let's deal with this," and marched him into the living room.

The girls appeared to be in a deep voluptuous sleep on her sofa, *so flagrantly erotic,* she thought, *cover them, don't let Grant see.*

Their young flesh, overlooking the pimples on their faces, had to be more attractive than hers. God, she was sick, worried about Grant's reaction before helping these children! But she checked Grant's face, and saw only worry. Still, before she spoke, she turned him away from the abandoned girls.

"Where's Saunders?"

"I sent him to bed."

"Thank you."

She felt she was a great clot of guilt, yet giggling still threatened. She touched his bicep with her fingertips.

"Grant. I'm so sorry this happened."

"Me too, Britannia. Maybe after we get these girls taken care of, I should take Saunders home."

Panic. "No, no, please, Grant. I had no idea this could happen. He's never done this before?"

"Never." He breathed in calmness, breathed out righteousness.

She wanted a cigarette. She wanted a drink. She turned and headed for the kitchen. Have a coffee instead.

She got the girls sitting up, drinking coffee. They stayed peculiarly woozy, but she got phone numbers from them. While Grant paced, she called their parents, got them coming. Grant stood back, solemn as a funeral, as she, frenetic with apology, bobbed and bowed to parents toting out girls. As soon as the door closed she strode, coffee cup in hand, to the liquor cabinet. Jerking open the walnut door she dolloped brandy into her coffee then extended the bottle to Grant. He backed off, waving his arms as if she'd offered to make him a vampire. That made her pause. If Grant could resist a drink in a crisis, then dammit, so could she. She carried the Brandy Chocolate Macadamia coffee to the kitchen and poured it, steaming, down the sink.

Grant came behind. Turning she saw–approval? His bald head didn't look so funny now, and she began to cry. Grabbing a paper towel she mopped her face and looked at Grant again. His head was tilted, chin ducked, like a kid's. Want emanated from him, and fear, both shot with electric impatience.

So when he said, "May I spend the night?" she couldn't say no. Tears were still there, pressing like hot salt on her retinas.

If she hadn't run off to be with Scottie, this never would have happened to his son.

Sex might help.

And she couldn't give everything up.

They fell into her black-sheeted bed.

Now Grant slept and Brit decided this had to be right up there as one of the worst nights of her life. And despite the long body in her bed, even though she'd been filled with a big warm cock, she felt empty. A tiny, empty universe.

F O U R

Britannia woke before dawn. God. *He was here, wasn't he? Taking up most of her bed.* She was surrounded: Alcoholics, drug addicts, sex addicts, and she must be co-dependent. Now, also, she was old. The names of shame.

She huddled on the edge of the bed, trying not to rouse the sleeping giant, trying to organize her emotions. With Saunders, she decided she felt guilty for leaving him alone, and angry at his behavior. With Grant, conned.

Why else was she in bed with him?

She crept from bed down to her studio, dragged out a gesso'd canvas, clamped it on an easel and squirted color onto a palette like a kid with a toothpaste tube. With a hog-bristle brush she began painting paisley snakes.

She was engrossed in a cobra reared in the strike position and didn't hear anyone enter.

"I love it." Lee's voice was behind her.

Not turning, Brit said, "You think?" She picked up a finer brush and dabbed yellow onto the snake's forked tongue.

"I hear hissing."

Brit smiled and turned to Lee.

She was illuminated by the north light of the studio windows. It bleached her skin and made her eyes look black as an Arab princess. But the royal image was shattered by dozens of tatty little picaninny braids that stuck up all over her head. Brit knew better than to ask "what happened to your hair." In a few days, it would change.

Lee held out coffee. Brit took it, smelled French Vanilla, and sipped.

Lee gestured at the painting. "Clever. Cobras as paisley. Paisley as cobras."

They sat on stools. Brit's studio was an extension of the living room and, like it, two stories high. The north wall was all window, with skylights overhead. The rest of the room was white sheetrock, except the log wall separating studio from living room. The dark-stained plank floor was spattered with old acrylic, oil paint, and dried clay.

Furniture was scattered haphazardly about. Old natural wicker chairs, a curvy, worn, red velvet sofa, a hutch on the south wall with a half-refrigerator next to it.

The view was of a low stone wall that bordered the herb and vegetable garden. Beyond that were the tops of palms and banana trees, the tropical garden Brit had planted beside her pool.

The studio was untidy with little islands in the chaos: an easel next to a wheeled cart stuffed with paints and brushes, a lace-draped table with branches, flowers, and grasses stuck in bottles and vases. A plastic skeleton. A cream and black striped divan on a foot-high riser. A pedestal with a lazy susan holding a deformed clay bust. There were secret things, stained cloths over humps, walls stacked with reversed canvases, sketches tacked up, some facing the wall.

Every time Viola visited she looked around the studio and offered to clean it up, till Brit snapped, "No thanks, Mother! This is a creative place. It's supposed to be a mess. Have you ever seen a baby born? Blood, slimy stinking fluids, a slippery placenta like misplaced guts? A mess. But it's creative. So. My living room is not a mess. It is, however, the result of a mess. This place was a mess while it was being built–" Viola had tiptoed out.

Brit stopped admiring her friend and said, "I think I'd better change my name to Rue."

"As in 'Rue Britannia?'"

Brit laughed. "Uh-huh. Lot's of guilt with remorse on top," She paused, tapping her chin with the paintbrush, "and make that a double."

"Scottie and Saunders?"

"Better make it a triple–Grant, too."

"You slept with him–again?"

"Yeah." Guilt was such a sick feeling.

"Saw that long, red, snaky car out there. Figured he didn't spend the night on the sofa."

"It's insane, Lee. I must be insane. I'm consoling my young ex-lover before he has to check into a drug clinic, then I get home and find my teenage stepson has two girls here in a terrible state of intoxication and–coup de grace–I hop right into bed with my ex-husband–because I feel guilty, not because I want to. Shit! When am I going to start acting my age!"

"Never, I hope. I've been listening to Deepak Chopra tapes."

"Yes? And?"

"I can only say this once."

Brit leaned forward.

"Premature–Cognitive–Commitment."

Brit thought, then, "Oh oh. I have an idea of what fifty is supposed to be. I have a premature commitment to–fiftyness."

Lee nodded, smiling.

Brit continued, unaware she was framed by the writhing, flamboyant snakes, unaware of a dab of red paint on her chin.

"So I made up my mind a long time ago that a fifty-year-old woman would–" She flapped a hand around as if trying to whisk ideas from the air, "–well, seldom have sex. If she did, it would be with a properly anointed husband and it would be boring. She'd also be thick in the middle, wear sensible shoes, print dresses, short genderless hair."

"Pretty dull person, huh?"

"God, yes. It's the image I've fought all my life."

"So how come now, just because a page was torn off a man-made calendar, you think you have to become this boring woman?"

Brit grinned. "Premature–Cognitive–Commitment." She finished her coffee. "It's exactly what I've been afraid of since my birthday. Now it's got a name. Thanks, Lee."

Behind her, Lee saw a tall bald man wandering in the garden. Occasionally he bent, pulled a weed, gave earth-clotted roots an officious shake, then laid the plant aside. Her eyes went back to Brit, then out the window.

"You got some big ol' hunk-a-man pulling your weeds, gal."

Brit darted a look out the window. "Oh shit. Grant's up."

"He's doing fine. I want to finish this thing we're on. I want to say: Please throw all the premature cognitive fifty commitments out with the trash, girl. Lots of women twenty years younger than you'd be thrilled down to their pinkies—and if they happen to be African American, down to their brownies—" Brit laughed, "—to have two major men panting after them. Granted, no pun intended, each of them has a few little problems, but they're working on them. One is in A.A., the other a rehab clinic. But you don't need them. I hope you know that. I bring them up only to try and shatter your ridiculous image of what Fifty is—but you're not alone, girl. Most of the world don't know what Fifty is. Did you see Farrah Fawcett on the cover of *The Enquirer*? All posed like a pin-up girl? She's what Fifty looks like now."

Brit held up a hand. "I got it. Thanks Lee." She stood. "Now I feel like forty. Maybe even thirty. So that's what fifty feels like for now. But I'm hungry. Stay for breakfast and meet the man?"

In answer, Lee headed toward the kitchen, tatty braids flapping.

On the threshold between her studio and her living room, Brit felt light-headed. She grabbed the jamb. She was breathless, dizzy. There was no path before her—just air. It was as though she'd stepped off a cliff and hovered in sky. Part of her was screaming "Go back, you fool, or you'll plummet to your death." Another deeper, calmer part was saying, "Hold steady now. Don't make any sudden moves. Notice that even though you're standing in air, you aren't falling. Relax. Wait. And when it's time, your next move will be obvious."

Lee stopped, turned back. "You all right?"

Brit, staring at her, gave a slight nod and let go the jamb. She still had a feeling of airiness all around her—even though she could plainly see her feet solidly on the wood floor. Her bare toes were pink, the fourth toe curled and tucked under the third as if her mother had fleetingly considered binding her feet, but had only managed to get one toe curled back on itself. Her conscious mind ran inward asking: *"Am I ill?"* It scurried through her body checking heart, lungs, liver, spleen, ovaries, uterus, and came back up behind her brow saying, *all is well.*

Oddly, she believed the report. This disorientation wasn't from physical illness, but from something else, something new. *Was there a sense of timelessness?* The right and proper thing for earth-bound humans is a sense of time. This place she found herself in—place? it was more like a sensation. It felt like the right place, the right sensation. Everything else she'd believed, thought, felt, was a false place.

She gave herself up to it and lightness filled her body. With Lee staring at her, even Saunders clomping down the stairs, Wil dancing at her feet, she was in it.

Lee was saying, "Are you okay? Brit, you okay?"

At first she couldn't speak, couldn't even nod, she was dispersed—co-mingled?—in and with light and air. It was as if suddenly her molecules let her know of their existence—she was no longer bone, tendon, muscle, blood, flesh, a separate palpable thing, but a wondrous dance of molecules and within each of those billions of molecules was yet another exquisite floating, a belonging dance of atoms.

She wanted to stay in this place—this awareness—forever.

Was this what death was?

It was suddenly hilarious that she'd ever worried about pouty belly flesh-wattles under her chin, graying pubic hairs—if people only knew, if they could only see, they'd know they could put their hands right through her. Like a ghost. Of course she could walk through walls—solid was an illusion. Everything was a dance of molecules, atoms, infinitesimal quanta. The Void teemed.

She was spirit made form on Earth. Suddenly she thought of a cold, red seedless grape in her mouth. Cool ovid sliding over her tongue. Teeth pressing on taut skin. Grape exploding in her mouth. The intense physical pleasure of the taste, the feel of grape.

Could Spirit envy Human?

Their fabulous ability to taste and touch, feel. Weeping, she saw, was as glorious as laughing. It took the tools of a body: eyes, tear ducts, mouth, lips, teeth, and events to evoke weeping and laughing.

Was pain as good as joy?

Only flesh could have these sensations.

Suddenly she knew everything "bad" was good. Alive was good. Dead was good. No—not even "good." "Good" was a moral judgment, a human thing—she felt a gentle laugh of encouragement from unseen spirits. IS. Everything just IS.

She heard herself breathe. She became more aware of Lee, of Saunders on the stairway, of Grant just in through the west French door, staring.

No, no, she thought, *I don't want to lose this feeling—knowledge*...but it was fading. She felt all her molecules rush inward, a gentle imploding, recreating her in tangible form. She breathed deeply and raised her arms and marveled at how solid they appeared.

As she came back, she remembered part of Lee's tarot reading: "forced by circumstances to see things from a different angle."

So much. So many changes in only a few days. *Ah. Make no plans. They, and you, are subject to change.*

Lee's voice in her head: "You've got an Egyptian mummy here, it stands for death and transformation."

Had she just had a transformation?

Suddenly she was completely herself. Briskly she said, "Hey, guys, I'm fine." Stepping through the threshold like any good hostess she introduced Lee to Grant. She watched Grant's reaction to Lee. He straightened, his paunch disappeared, his lips shot open like an erection. An intense smile. She felt a very human spurt of jealousy but shoved it away as she nudged them into her kitchen offering to make Eggs Sardou.

F I V E

There was almost a feeling of family, Brit decided, as she looked around at her guests. Lee had just stacked plates in the sink, everyone was drinking last cups of coffee.

Maybe this was what she was supposed to do. Get back with her ex-husband, be a mother to Saunders, reestablish the family. Anastasia would love it.

Grant stood. He flashed a big grin at Brit, and she leaned toward him smiling, but he turned toward Lee and his plastic grin got tender.

He said, "It's been a real pleasure meeting you, Lee." *Oh Christ. Was he going to melt all over her best friend?*

Coming to Brit, he pecked her cheek saying, "Thanks for the wonderful breakfast, Brit, but I gotta go."

"I'll walk you to the door." *Asshole.*

In the foyer Grant looked down. "Could I come out tonight?"

She almost said, "Sure you want to? Lee won't be here," but instead she smiled and replied, "Perhaps we need to think this whole thing through, Grant. And I do need time to have a serious talk with Saunders."

His smile shut down. "Oh. Yes. Of course."

How could he leer at her friend then suggest coming back to her bed? The son of a bitch.

"If I didn't have an important appointment this afternoon I'd stay and talk with him too." His hand came up, fingertips on her upper arm. "Sure you don't want me to come out tonight?"

Her fickle body hummed, but she said, "Positive." Firmly, she put her hand on his elbow and turned him to the door. He let himself be guided. She reached in front of him and opened it. Still hesitating he asked, "You mad about something?"

"No." She was furious. But she couldn't admit she was jealous of his attitude toward her beautiful, younger friend. It was too humiliating.

Grant drove toward the city wondering why, after getting laid and a wonderful breakfast, he felt uneasy. Perhaps because he hadn't told Saunders, in no uncertain terms, his behavior was unacceptable? He'd taken him aside while Brit was cooking and suggested he not repeat last night's performance. And the kid had been fine at breakfast, a little somber, but that was appropriate.

He arrived at the toll booth and handed over a twenty. The attendant, a rather attractive thirtyish brunette smiled, handed back eighteen-fifty change. He gave her a big smile, sorry he was without his hairpiece.

He dropped the money on the empty seat next to him as the 'Vette surged onto the Causeway. He had a fantasy of a quick one in the toll booth, but that faded and again, he felt uneasy.

A meeting. He'd find an A.A. meeting. It'd jolt him out of this emotional queasiness.

Halfway over the bridge he got an idea. He'd invite Brit to a meeting. A.A. might help her a lot.

S I X

Lee left shortly after Grant. Brit waited until Saunders finished his chores and disappeared into his room. Then she walked to the stable and saw Mokhtar's head sticking out over his half-door. He whinnied at her. She put a hand on his soft muzzle and looked into his stall.

The water bucket was empty, the ration of hay thrown on the floor, and she smelled urine. Hungry chickens squawked at her feet.

Damn! You'd think after last night's stunt remorse would fuel him to do his chores properly. And she'd even let him off school today. She power-walked to the house.

"Saunders!" she yelled upstairs, "get down here!"

From his room she heard a roar, like an army of angry Southern locusts.

"Saunders?" The locust sound continued. Brit started up the stairs.

As she neared his room she realized it was some sort of rock band. She knocked on his door, hard.

"Saunders!"

The door opened just enough to show a half-slice of his face. She stared into one gray eye.

She flashed on Scott at the motel, and wondered why she was so often seeing half of people.

"Saunders. We have to talk. Either you answer me when I call you or I will invade your room."

An additional sound like a human trying, but failing, to imitate the cry of a distressed cougar emerged at the fore of the locust army. Arrgh, Arrgh, Arrgh, she heard, while staring into the eye.

Arrgh, Arrgh, Arrgh.

She wondered who'd written the lyric. *Did they get a credit on the label?*

"I'll come down."

"When?"

"Five minutes." Argh, soft roaring.

"Not good enough."

"Two minutes."

"I will time you."

His door closed.

Argh–the sound stopped–*maybe she could get used it, come to like it?*–then Saunders sauntered downstairs. She motioned him to sit next to her on the sofa.

"Saunders. You have to shape up."

"Or ship out?"

"No! What I mean is–do your chores properly."

"I do." Affronted.

"You don't. I just came from the barn and Mokhtar doesn't have a drop of water–"

"–Musta drunk it."

"No way. There'd be some left. The bucket was bone dry."

He looked away.

"His stall is dirty."

A cry. "I cleaned it!"

"Not well enough. If you pick it properly we have fewer flies and use less shavings. Besides, it only takes ten minutes. C'mon now. Ten minutes! Is that too much to ask?"

Yeah, he thought, but answered, "Guess not."

They looked at each other. As usual his eyes had become limpid, unblinking. *Was his chin trembling?*

She leaned forward, put a hand on his knee, afraid he might cry. He twitched ever so slightly and she saw a change behind his eyes, a flicker so deep, so brief she wondered if she'd seen anything.

She withdrew her hand wondering, *is he angry?* She'd always thought his unblinking stare meant hurt, that she was seeing a manifestation of the frightened little boy whose mama locked him in a closet while she mutilated herself. Grant had told her stories.

She folded her hands, looked at them—their whiteness, the knuckles and finger joints slightly enlarged from hard use.

"Would you rather take on different chores? Firewood, weeding, laundry–?"

"No. I'll feed." He twisted his body away and looked up at the giant painting of disquieted horses. "How come Rita's not out here?"

"You think Rita's going to feed a horse?"

His eyes shot back to hers. *Rita feeding a horse?* They laughed. She felt grateful for this rare connection. Wanted more.

"Bet she'd feed chickens though, Saw."

They laughed again. He liked that she'd called him a kiddie name, "Saw." *See Saw, Margie Daw.*

"Well. She's coming out."

"Oh."

Brit gave his knee a light slap. "Up and at 'em, Saw, that old horse is thirsty."

He stood, she shook her finger at him mock mad. "And see he gets a nice clean stall. I'll inspect."

Saunders slouched off to the barn. He'd avoided a chewing-out, a grounding, or some other ridiculous punishment.

Leaning over the stall door, a running hose in the hanging water bucket, he eyed Mokhtar.

"You're a stupid, fucking, useless animal, horse. I don't know why she bothers keeping you around."

The horse's head was raised, ears pricked. He was accustomed to affectionate words from his caretakers. The scornful, angry sounds from the boy who was also providing him with food and water confused him. Front feet planted, wary, he stretched his neck, scenting. Just as his nostrils came within an inch of the boy's jacket, Saunders shouted, "You stupid fucker."

The horse snorted so loudly Saunders jumped and the hose came out of the bucket. Furious at being frightened, Saunders aimed it at the horse. Cold water hit Mokhtar's chest and he reared.

"Stupid fucker," screamed Saunders, stabbing spray at the stallion. The horse was up against the back wall, literally trying to climb it, jumping, swiveling, rearing, utterly silent, trying to flee the ice-water. His shod front hooves scraped, slid against the log wall, taking out divots of wood. His eyes rolled, white showed.

"Saunders!"

He froze, the hose aimed at the horse's head.

He heard faint creaking sounds, and turned his head. His stepmother was bent, cranking the valve to turn off the water.

The spray fell backwards as though sucked into the hose.

White-faced, Brit walked to the stall. She'd changed into riding boots, breeches and a turtleneck. All black, and her black hair with the silver streaks at the temples seemed to fly out from her face. With eyes almost purple, she looked menacing.

"What's going on here?"

She looked from the boy to the horse, who was criss-crossed with stripes of water like whip welts.

"I was just playing with him."

It came out whiny. Saunders wished he could take it back, make it sound more cool. But he couldn't, so he stood and let his eyes grow big. This enraged Brit.

"Don't pull that blank stare shit on me, Saunders. You're a wounded little boy, we all know that, but this is The Here and Now. Mokhtar had nothing to do with your childhood." She took a deep breath. "You were zapping him with the hose, right? That cold water?"

He stared at her. She wanted to rap smartly against his temple—*Knock, knock, anybody there?* Had he, in some arcane way, taken his consciousness elsewhere? Did this lizard-like stare come from his ancient reptile brain, his frontal lobes ceasing to function?

She was definitely dealing with a chameleon. Hands on her hips, she said, "Not acceptable, Saunders. You've put panic in Mokhtar, an awful thing to feel." Her voice gentled, and the horse at the back of the stall ceased trembling. "I'm sure you've felt more than your share of panic, Saw, so why do you want to trigger it in other creatures?"

Not a blink.

"Why?"

Stare.

"Saunders. Answer me."

Nothing.

"Okay. If that's the way you want it." She turned and pointed toward the house. "Inside. You're grounded for a month." Mokhtar snorted. "Your new chores are laundry and dishes."

He didn't move.

"Saunders. In the house! " She forced her voice back to normal. "Saunders. Go in now. There's laundry. You may begin it."

"Rita."

It took a minute. "Rita? Never mind her. She won't be here till tomorrow. This is today. Go."

He dropped his eyes, then his head and shoulders, and hunched past her. His feet went crunch...crunch...crunch...over the rock path. *How slowly can one teenager go and still have some forward motion,* she wondered? She leaned on the stall door and looked down at her trembling hands. Mokhtar eased over and placed his muzzle in them.

When Grant called a few days later inviting her to hear a lecture, she thought, *oh, why not?*

S E V E N

"What's the speech about?" Brit asked as she and Grant drove the Causeway.

"Not sure. Something about alcoholism."

He flashed a grin at her, and evaluated her appearance. After all, a lot of guys he now knew would be at this A.A. meeting.

She wore a black silk pants outfit with jewelry made of wood and bits of pottery. Her hair was full and vibrant. She looked good. No one would guess she was older than him.

"Alcoholism! Why that?"

"Because I'm an alcoholic and I've been advised to attend an A.A. meeting every day for ninety days." He enunciated carefully, to contain irritability.

Brit folded her arms and stared out the window at the darkening sky. The sunset, purple slashes across apricot clouds, fanned out above the lavender-dappled lake. She said, "Does this mean you consider me an alcoholic?"

He felt better, and reached over to pat her thigh–knee–any leg part he could lay a hand on–her leg seemed to be moving away from him.

"What's the matter?" He tried to sound cheery.

"Nothing." She stared at waves, now like pink and gold porcelain.

He put his hand back on the wheel. He ground his teeth, just one little grind. "Don't say that. You're all tense. Are you worried about Saunders?"

"Nope. Rita's there."

"I know that. So what is it?"

She sighed. "I don't know." The waves moved as though pushed from beneath by a malevolent behemoth.

"Work today?"

"Tried to." The water went heave, ho.

"Ah. Maybe you're blocked."

"Maybe."

They exited the Causeway Bridge and he continued to 1-10 East into New Orleans. They didn't speak until he threaded the car into the light traffic heading into town. To their left the westbound lane was bumper to bumper with commuters draining from the Central Business District.

As they passed Xavier University, Grant said, "Hungry?"

"Could be." Then she heard herself, the petulance.

"Well, before the meeting they're having a potluck dinner. Whatever that means."

"Potluck? That means everyone brings a pot of food. Did you bring a pot?"

They were passing the Super Dome and her tone was lighter. She smiled and looked at his toupee. He felt the tension ease and grinned.

"Gosh, no."

"Shame on you." She felt a tiny strobe of sexual energy begin and she knew Grant felt it too. His giant hand tentatively reached toward her and this time she didn't move her knee.

"You look nice tonight. Dramatic."

"Why thank you, Grant Griffin." She folded her arms, looked at him. "You look good too, but I think I like you better *au naturel.*"

His hand flew from her knee to his hairpiece.

"Yeah," she said, "*sans* rug."

He'd had a difficult time deciding what to do tonight. A.A. people were used to his baldness, but since this constituted somewhat of a date, he'd finally decided to wear the hair. Now she says she doesn't like it. Decisively he ripped it off, threw it in the back seat.

"Better. I've always found bald men attractive."

"Really?"

"Yes. Something about that skintight nude-ness that's very sexy. Aggressive, too. As if they might bull on through anyone, anything."

"Oh."

"Also, I read that baldness is caused by higher-than-average testosterone levels."

"Oh?"

"Yes. Supposedly bald or balding men are more sexually active."

He rubbed the top of his head. *Was that so.*

They peeled off onto the Carrollton exit, following the street up to the bend in the Mississippi River, and turned onto St. Charles Avenue.

Grant parked near a church then turned and smiled at her. "Ready?"

She was looking down and he thought, *oh no, not another mood,* when she said in the voice she must have had when she was four years old, "Do you think I'm an alcoholic, Grant?"

"What?! Good God! I wouldn't presume!" He struck his fist on the steering wheel. "Is that what's been wrong?"

She nodded.

"Hey, hey, Britannia!" He put an arm around her. "Hey–it's just that this is an open meeting, meaning anyone can attend. Drunks or otherwise. A lot of the guys and gals bring their Significant Others. I wanted you to be with me. That's all."

He waited until her chin lifted, and he ducked his to peer at her face. "Okay?"

She smiled and gave him a light punch on the arm. "Okay, Stud."

They went into a side door of the church into a room of unfolded metal chairs. To their left long tables held pots, pans, casseroles, Tupperware, Visions vessels of jambalaya, red beans and rice, fried chicken, lasagna, pasta and potato salads, french breads, crawfish étoufée, barbecue shrimp.

The noise level was high, people were laughing, chair legs scraping on tile. Grant introduced her as "My friend, Britannia." No last name.

When they'd finished eating, a woman went to a podium and gaveled for quiet.

"Hi," she called out, "I'm Evelyn, and I'm an alcoholic."

How could she just say that? Brit started a fine sweat. She knotted her hands in her lap. *Was she going to have a hot flash?* There was praying, talking around her, but her mind raced. *Was she an alcoholic?*

She'd quit drinking without any "detoxing." That woman–no–there was a man up there now, a thirtyish man with sandy hair. He had close-set faded denim eyes, a beaky nose, thin lips, and a bobbing Adam's apple where a chin should have been. It was an inbred, deprived-looking face. Ever since *Deliverance* Brit had been afraid of faces like that.

"...and my address was a Charmin box."

The crowd laughed. He was smiling.

"You'd think I'd find myself a box for something besides toilet paper–but, it was appropriate. I'd really hit bottom." He paused while the crowd laughed again. "I was as low as anyone could go. I'd steal from you and you and you," He pointed into the audience. Brit marvelled at the man's calm. And his tidiness–he wore a starched, striped blue shirt, navy tie, navy dress pants. She knew that if she got close to him she'd smell aftershave.

"...and my mother, my grandmother. I cleaned out three girlfriends. I'd drink anything, take any pill. I've shot heroin, cocaine, gone crazy on PCP's. I weighed a hundred fifteen pounds."

He was absolutely shameless. He was not arrogant. He simply was.

IS. *Like she'd been the day before?*

She was as absorbed in him as when she painted. Evaluating, her detached artist's eye noticing: if the neat shirt and tie were removed, stubble to grow on the shining freckled skin–she was redesigning him like a police artist–he'd look like an inbred cracker halfwit. She shuddered. *He's a bunch of molecules and atoms just like you, Brit. Don't judge.*

Yes.

"One real cold night I was headed to Lafayette Park. Had the shakes bad. Wasn't much more than a brown bag of bones–and, Whomp! down I fell. Guy comin' along behind me tripped over me. Fell on top a' me. Big guy. I went oof! For a minute we laid on that dirty pavement on Canal Street. Eyeball to eyeball. Big brown eye. I was real scared. Then he smiled, then he laughed–he didn't cuss me out. Next thing he's up and holding out a hand to me. Helped me up. A huge guy. A former Saint–I won't say his name, got to protect his anonymity." The man shifted, hitched his pants. Brit felt his suppressed excitement that a football player had tripped over him.

"Next thing, I'm in a cab, then a kitchen, nice kitchen. An Uptown kitchen. He gave me a shot a' whisky to stop the shakes. I still remember how shiny white and yellow that kitchen was. So clean it burned my eyeballs. Then he put some kinda hot soup in front of me but my hands shook so bad I couldn't get a spoonful to my mouth. So he fed me. Next thing, I woke up in a real den. Books, TV, stereo, shag carpet, reclining chair and the white leather sofa he put me to sleep on." The speaker swallowed, his Adam's apple moving.

"I started A.A. that day." He grinned. "After I got a shower." Laughter. He took a drink of water from a glass on the podium. "I've been clean and sober ever since. Ten years, six months, and four days. All due to my Higher Power. Of all the people I coulda got to fall on me, I got not only a Saint," laughter, "but an A.A. Saint!" People roared. The man's face glistened with happiness as he looked around the crowd, his Adam's apple bobbing under another power.

"When I came into these rooms someone told me 'coincidence is just God's way of remaining anonymous.'" He threw up his hands, his Adam's apple flying up so high Brit wondered if it would pop out of his mouth. She realized she'd been staring with her mouth open. She closed it and thought, *I couldn't be an alcoholic. I've never lived in a cardboard box, nor panhandled on Canal Street, but a few big men sure have tripped and fallen on top of me.* Her eyes avoided Grant's. He was laughing and carrying on as though she wasn't there anyway. He even sat with his body turned slightly away from her.

"Two weeks of meetings, three times a day, getting a bit more food in me each day, and then on the fourteenth day I was leaving a meeting at Central Office. I got out on the street, Tulane Avenue, right in front of the Genghis Khan restaurant, when this powerful feeling came over me. I was somehow aware I was part of everything...it was like a pure white light just poured down onto me and then, into me–I couldn't move, I could barely breathe–I became–I was that light." He lowered his voice. "And I knew, absolutely–no matter what–I was taken care of; I did not need to worry about economic insecurity, that the horrible, sick things I did in the past were necessary and even forgiven...that I had a Higher Power words cannot describe. And then it went away and I was just this skinny guy in Goodwill clothes breathing hot exhaust fumes. But what stayed with me after my 'spiritual awakening' was an idea that my Higher Power, whom I chose to call 'HP' is all around and inside you and me and everything else–trees, flowers, grass, the sky, clouds, the dirty pavement on Canal, the spit on the pavement, the exhaust, the rock whore on the corner...in the hates and in the love. Especially in the love."

"But when I drink, when I dope, when I steal, when I lie–I block my Higher Power. Because I believe, in a way, I am 'magnetized,' that I am drawn powerfully to my Higher Power and so my Higher Power is drawn to me and this wonderful program of Alcoholics Anonymous, through the Twelve Steps, teaches me how to remove those blocks, the biggest block being drunkenness, so I can feel my Higher Power working inside me every day." He took a very deep breath, his Adam's apple rippling up and down as though through chord progressions. Then quietly he said, "Thank you." There was a silence, then people rose to their feet clapping, hooting, Rebel yelling, whistling.

Brit sat. This skinny guy with no chin, an Adam's apple the size of a baby's fist, the pallid freckled coloring of a hillbilly, had just described an experience very close to the one she'd had on the threshold to her living room.

Her heart thumped. *She was an alcoholic.* She'd removed the alcohol from her system for just a few days and wham! gotten The Experience, what this man had just described as a spiritual awakening.

Omigod. She felt terrified. How un-lovely. Viola would be wild. Her eldest daughter, it was bad enough she was an artist–now she was an alcoholic.

Grant sat back down, laid his hand on her clenched fists.

"Hey. You okay?"

She raised her eyes toward him. Her voice was hoarse.

"Grant. Omigod. I just realized...my God...I'm an alcoholic." He leaned closer, saw her lips moving, but he couldn't hear her. *Was she talking to herself?* She stared at him.

She was a hollow, empty woman. She felt so enervated she couldn't stand.

Grant frowned at her. *What was this?* Except for the bags under her eyes, more noticeable now than when they'd come in, she looked pretty good. Awful pale, though. As he asked, "Brit, what's wrong?" he glanced around in sudden fear. He'd been a fool to bring her to this meeting, men were looking at her. So many men in A.A., they must outnumber women ten to one. One guy was staring hard–quickly he pulled her to her feet and urged her out the door, nodding unsmiling at the few men he knew.

Britannia, hustled out, was relieved Grant's concern for her was so great he almost carried her out.

Safely in the car he turned to her. "Now. What's wrong?"

She stared ahead. White light from a bulbous Victorian street lamp bleached her face.

"Grant. I realized something in there."

"What, Brit?"

"I'm an alcoholic."

He almost laughed in relief. His arm tightened around her and she let herself be pulled into his chest.

"Is that all?"

Is that all! She pushed against him.

"Wait, wait, I'm sorry. That was insensitive. It's just that now I've gotten over the shock of admitting it, I'm finding it's not so bad to be an alcoholic. At least a non-drinking alcoholic in recovery, in A.A."

Her head moved. He eased his hold on her. She looked up at him, eyes purple, fathomless.

"Really?"

"Really." He kissed her forehead, but she turned her face down and away. Slowly she leaned back in the seat, then reached for the seat belt. He watched for a second then turned the key in the ignition. The great red snout led onto the dark street. He drove the few blocks to his condo.

Afterwards, Brit still felt hollow. Even with that big penis inside her, again, she hadn't felt filled up. She'd barely spoken to him after admitting she was an alcoholic.

Now they were back in his car, and she lay back on the seat and tried to think as they rode across the lake to her farm.

Where had the feelings, the sensations she'd felt on the day of The Experience gone? How could she get them back?

She didn't object, even, when Grant undressed and came into bed beside her. She turned away and slept. The next morning, when he acted as though he planned to return that night, Brit asked if he'd wait. Until the weekend. She wanted some time to absorb this new, frightening information...maybe find some A.A. meetings for herself.

After she spoke, Grant set his jaw. He stood in the bedroom doorway, suit coat over his shoulders, in yesterday's shirt. She was sitting up in the bed, a white sheet clutched over her breasts. This morning she looked fifty, he thought, some real serious bags under her eyes. The gray streaks at her temples appeared artificial, as if she'd painted them on.

What in God's name was he doing with this old woman?

He heard Saunders making noises in the kitchen.

"Okay, Brit. Whatever."

He was hurt and huffy, she thought, but she was too empty to help him.

"Can you drive Saunders to school? He might like that. Better than the school bus."

"Sure. Good idea. Well. Call me. Whenever."

"Sure."

Ten minutes later she heard the Corvette snarl down her rocky drive.

She lay back on the bed.

An alcoholic.

God help me.

E I G H T

That Friday afternoon Brit lingered by Mokhtar's stall after her ride. Asia's car, an '88 Ford Escort, came so quietly up the drive she didn't hear it. A "Hi, Mom," at her shoulder made her turn and gasp "Asia! How terrific!" They hugged, then Asia turned to look at Mokhtar. Brit studied her daughter. She was aware that Asia was slighter and paler than herself, and instead of dramatic lavender eyes, she had her father's soft brown ones, and dark brown, not black, hair. But she was beautiful in her subtle, gentle way.

Now she was thrilled to see Asia with her shoulders back, rather than in her former perpetual hunch: shoulders curved inward, arms criss-crossed over her chest, as if to shield her heart. Now her chest with her pretty breasts was open, as if to receive the world. College, and maybe being away from her, was helping.

The horse had come to the stall door. Asia stroked his jowl, then she tidied his silvery forelock, saying, "He's looking good."

"Isn't he? I'm riding him again."

"You are?"

"You look aghast, Asia. Is it because you think your mother's too old, or the horse?"

"Oh! Not you. I just wondered if he was up to it."

Brit laughed. "My zoo-major daughter! Sweetie! Use it or lose it applies to horses and humans. He's going great. And he's resumed his career as a breeding stallion."

"At Sugarplum's?"

"Yes. She wants to borrow him again." Brit laughed. "She called, furious. Her precious Nadia had a colt."

Smiling, Asia said, "And she wanted a filly. She's amazing, Mom. I don't know how you endure her."

"Oh, she's harmless and every now and then the Plum and I get loaded. Talk about old times." Brit hesitated, then put her hand on Asia's arm to draw her attention away from the horse.

"I guess that's in the past though, Honey. I quit drinking."

"You–?! Wow! When?"

"Awhile back. I feel a lot better." She twiddled index and middle fingers, "And, ta-dah! I quit smoking."

Asia's head went down, the way it used to when she was little and filled with emotion. Then she looked up at her mother, cheeks pink, making a little smile. "Mother. Really. You've become quite the quitter, haven't you?"

Brit laughed, pulled her in for another hug, and spoke into her daughter's hair. "I'm so glad you're here." She released her.

The horse stuck his head from the stall and began nudging first Brit, then Asia.

"See? He wants out." Brit quirked an eyebrow. "If you want to sling a leg over–"

Asia's hands flew up. "Nope."

Laughing, Brit hugged her again. Asia had always preferred to watch things happen rather than do them. Brit had frustrated herself when Anastasia was young. She'd tried to push her into an active role: dancing, riding, tennis, swimming, violin, and at each Asia failed. Finally, at seven, she'd retreated into depression. Brit caught it quickly, got therapy for Asia and herself. After two years their relationship was reformed. Brit had let go of the pushing and Anastasia, quietly, had bloomed. She spent hours in roadside ditches, the woods, alongside bayous looking for wildlife, catching moths and butterflies and categorizing wildflowers. At home she preferred spending her time with the horse, the chickens, the ducks. Brit was thrilled. Often her daughter came back with plants she was able to use in her paintings.

Today, she'd never seen her so confident. "You look wonderful."

Asia smiled and slid an arm around her mother's waist. "So do you."

As chickens squawked and skittered around their feet, Wilton weaving around them, they strolled arm and arm to the house.

It felt empty when they entered until godd appeared. In her soft way Asia exclaimed, "godd. Come to me," and she gathered the purring cat into her arms.

Brit held a hand to her ear. "Hear that?" A sound like the electronic buzz of katydids whined from Saunders' room. She called, "Saunders, come down," and to Asia, "I can't get used to his music."

In a few moments it stopped. He stepped out onto the mezzanine, leaned over the rail. After a moment of staring down he smiled.

Asia cried, "My God, Saw, you look huge!"

He started down the steps, "Anastasia. You look grown up. A real college woman."

Asia handed the cat to her mother, ran and hugged her stepbrother. He raised his arms as if to hug her back then let them fall. Asia stepped back and gave him a little punch with her fist. Brit was surprised and pleased by Asia's animation, yet felt a small worry. She seemed oblivious to her brother's lack of warmth. Didn't Asia see, as Brit did, that Saunders response was, maybe, too cool? Saunders made a half-smile—*why couldn't he at least hug his sister? But it must feel awkward for him*, Brit thought, *seeing Asia after what, two years?*

Later Brit got Asia and Saunders to hitch the horse trailer to the truck while she fetched Mokhtar. He ran into the trailer as if he knew where he was going. Brit drove the old red pickup, Asia and Saunders crammed next to her. Within minutes she turned into Sugarplum's broad gravel drive. Yearlings behind white fences raced the truck and Mokhtar, hearing them, whinnied loudly. The trailer shook with his stallion sound, rattling the old truck, and Brit and Asia laughed. Brit felt happy. Her old horse. Her kids.

Upon arrival, the horse ran backwards out of the trailer, still neighing. Brit, holding his lead shank, gave him slack so he could prance. Mares answered from the paddocks. There was a galloping sound and three mares skidded to a stop at a fence near the barn. The old stallion's head shot up, his penis began a slow slide from its sheath. She laughed, elated with his youthful reaction. Snorting and tossing his head, he angled sideways toward the mares. Brit fed out shank, but stayed with him. They were like two sensitive dancers, moving, barely looking at one another, aware. He touched noses with one mare then he and the mare emitted an ear-splitting screech. Instinctively, Brit was well off to his side when he struck lightning-quick, high in the air with a forefoot. The mare squealed and struck back at him, her hoof brushing the wire-net fence. Brit tugged his halter.

"Easy now, Big Guy. Talk sweet to these ladies."

As if understanding, the stallion lowered his voice and made a soft "herr, herr, herr," sound.

Brit turned to Asia and Saunders who stood back from the swift-moving stallion.

"Hear him, kids? He wants 'her' and 'her' and 'her?'" She laughed. Asia thought how young and pretty her mother looked. She looked strong too, dressed in black jeans, black shirt, cowboy boots. Beside her Mokhtar, white, was plunging like clouds. Sugarplum, in lime shorts and sweat top, swaggered down a grassy sward toward them, calling, "HEY, HEY, Y'ALL."

The third mare was the day's winner. Over the fence she intently exchanged breath with the stallion. The horses, necks arched, ears pricked, nostrils flared, seemed to read each other's exhalations, eyes unfocused, concentrating as though listening within themselves. Then the mare flipped her tail over her back, squatted and urinated. Mokhtar squealed, threw his neck out still further, increasing its stretchy arch. Brit, with four foot of shank between her and the horse, saw his beauty and felt goosebumps rise all over her body. He was a show: trumpet screams, hooves pounding his great weight on the soft earth, his scythe-like curves of hard, moving muscle, the softness of his flying mane, tail, forelock, the intelligence and passion in his eyes, his nostrils. The power and the glory of an aroused stallion. Nothing to her was more beautiful. And to be a part of that power through just an inch-wide leather strap, that this great creature allowed her to be at his side.

His dangling penis became hard. Sugarplum arrived, stood at Brit's elbow.

"You WANNA help BREED her RIGHT NOW, Brit?" she hollered.

Brit resisted a startled jump. "Sure, why not?"

"GREAT. SAVE me GETTING ARNOLD over HERE. You WANNA take him in the BARN and WASH him while I catch PETRUSHKA?"

All Sugarplum's Arabian horses had Russian names because their pedigrees traced to a Russian breeding farm, Tersk. Brit had always thought they were coarse and plain-headed compared to the Egyptian-bloodlined Arabians, like her exquisite Mokhtar, but she never commented. Some of them had great motion, and most had excellent, straight legs–something that couldn't always be said about the Egyptians. For all their prettiness, many had crooked legs, a weakness in any riding horse. Mokhtar had somehow escaped this blight.

Brit led the snorting, careering Mokhtar into the barn, with Asia alongside her. In the aisle she asked, "Well Zoo-Major, how'd you like to handle the old man for this cover?"

Asia almost jumped up and down. "Ma, I'd love to."

Brit handed her the shank, fitted with a brass stud chain which Brit had attached to his halter. Now Asia unsnapped it and ran the chain through the halter, over the horse's muzzle, about three inches above his nostrils. If he didn't pull, there was no pain. But if he acted up, or tried to charge the mare Asia had only to give a quick, hard jerk to get his attention. He weighed eleven hundred pounds, she, one hundred ten. This, and her attitude, were the only controls she'd have.

Asia had watched Mokhtar breed mares before. She knew he was obedient to his handler and kind to the mare. Even so, she felt her palms grow sweaty and nervous flutters begin in her belly. During hand breeding things happened fast.

Brit directed Saunders and Sugarplum to fill two buckets with lukewarm water. Sugarplum had Saunders follow her into a stall where the mare stood tied. She could still see and smell the stallion and was in such hard heat she kept her back arched and her tail flipped up. Steadily she gazed in his direction. Sugar pulled the mare's tail down and wrapped it in a bandage. Brit didn't like the idea of even a single hair being free, able to wrap around Mokhtar's penis. Horse hair cut almost like piano wire. Saunders held a bucket of lukewarm water while Sugarplum sponged clean the mare's vulva and buttocks.

Saunders stood back, seeing something wet and pink like a blunt, thick finger rhythmically pulse, opening and closing the gray-skinned edges of the mare's vulva. He stared at it and felt his penis stir in response.

Meanwhile, Brit held the stallion who stood at impatient attention while Anastasia washed his penis with plain warm water. The stallion's personality had changed. His ears were pinned tightly back on his neck. Once he brought a hind leg up as though to brush her hands away. Brit gave the lead a hard tug, sternly saying, "Quit." She didn't want her daughter kicked in the head. Then to Asia, "Gently now, Asia, that's not a hunk of bologna, you know." Asia quirked her head back, they laughed.

She patted the penis dry with a paper towel and stood back. She looked to her mother. "Did I do that right?'

"Perfectly."

Mokhtar's ears came forward. Asia ran a hand over his shoulder. "Sorry, old man," and his head bounced up and down as if he accepted her apology, but really he was urging them to hurry: let's get going, let's go breed that mare who wants me.

"ALL DONE," screamed Sugarplum.

"Gonna twitch her?" asked Brit.

"NAH, she's so HOT I think she'd STAND for an ELEPHANT."

Sugarplum jerked her chin at Saunders, screeched, "CATCH the DOOR for me, 'KAY?" He did and she led the mare from the stall, out the barn door. Outside, the mare was reluctant to move any further from the stallion still in the barn, so after Brit handed his lead to Asia, she walked up behind the mare and gave her buttocks a push. The women shoved the mare, who was locked into a tail raised, squatting position, until she was positioned on a flat grassy area with good footing for horses and humans. Sugarplum yelled, "'KAY, ASIA, BRING HIM ON!"

Asia took a deep breath, looked Mokhtar hard in the eye. "You behave now, Mokh, don't make a fool out of me."

The stallion blinked as if he understood. *Or was it her breath on his eyeball?*

They came from the barn, coiled.

His entire body vibrating, the stallion called to the mare. Asia saw veins, like a topographical map of miniature rivers and tributaries, pop out on his neck. The mare twisted her head back from where Sugarplum held her halter and quivering, called an answer. Then she tilted her pelvis up yet again, laid her wrapped tail over her back, and squirted a golden stream of urine.

"BRING him up ASIA," yelled Sugarplum, "but DON'T let him MOUNT till SHE STOPS PEEING."

Involuntarily Brit glanced around to see if some passing stranger could have heard Sugarplum. Of course no one was nearby. Green pastures led to dense woods, like her farm. The difference was Sugarplum had a hundred acres in pasture and her living complex of house, barn and outbuildings was centered on the land. Fences like white lace followed the undulating lay.

Saunders had followed. Suddenly he blurted, "Why can't you just turn 'em loose together? Why go to all this bother?"

Sugarplum planted a tiny fist on a hipbone. "CAUSE you CAN'T! He might SAVAGE my MARE!"

Brit added dryly, "Or, she might savage my stallion."

She walked back and stood beside Saunders.

"I know it seems like a lot of fuss but a mare can kick real quick. If she does it just as he's reared up to mount, well, she could wreck him as a breeding stallion. This way the stallion handler can get him off her fast, the mare handler can pull her away too. It's just a whole lot safer than turning 'em loose, honey. Matter of fact, a lot of stallions have been killed by ignorant people turning them out with mares."

"Why?" Saunders looked scared.

"If the mares aren't in heat they will kick the hell out of a stallion if he tries to mount. They simply will not allow any sex they aren't ready for. And these over-civilized stallions go bananas when they get around mares. They don't know about waiting for her to invite them. They'll go from mare to mare trying to breed, getting themselves sliced to ribbons. Testosterone keeps them trying and trying, until they bleed to death." *Like some men I know*, she thought.

Saunders shuddered, stepped back another pace. Brit turned her attention to her daughter.

Asia had Mokhtar at the mare's side. He sniffed her neck and withers. Suddenly–Brit heard Saunders gasp behind her–he reared up and spread his front legs across the mare's back. He began pushing his penis at her vulva, missing the entrance and Brit yelled, "Help him!" Asia, who stood near the mare's shoulder where one of Mokhtar's front legs dangled, stepped to the mare's hindquarters, grabbed the moving penis and aimed it at the mare's vulva. It slid in. She let go.

The mare's eye grew huge.

Sugarplum, watching her mare's expression screamed, "He's BREEDING her!" Then her legs twisted around each other as though she needed a toilet, and she made her whiny, wheezy laugh, exhaling "OH! It just TURNS me ON, so BAD."

Brit felt distaste. It was dangerous to allow oneself to feel sexual arousal dur-ing a breeding.

Two mating horses, quicksilver bone and muscle, with a combined weight of over a ton–anybody not fully focused was in danger. But Sugarplum was so per-fectly narcissistic, her mares extensions of herself, what she imagined they felt, she felt. Probably why she didn't like colts–she couldn't comprehend the male mind.

Saunders was transfixed. He breathed in shallow gasps, a greasy sweat beaded his lard-pale skin. That horse's dick had to be a foot and a half long and about the circumference of a Genoa salami. He just fuckin' nailed that bitch. Saunders himself almost orgasmed when Asia put her pale little hand on that big, thrust-ing hunk of black and pink meat. His hips twitched when that loud-mouthed bitch crossed her legs, shook her skinny little ass.

He backed away. No one noticed. All were too occupied with the stud humping the little black mare.

Inside the barn he entered an empty stall and frantically got himself to come, seeing flash after flash of that pale hand as it grabbed that big horse dick.

He was done. He tucked himself in and hands on hips, took a deep breath. He wanted to be together when he went back outside. Suddenly, something bit the shit out of his butt.

"Yeow!" He jumped and turned, and there stood a perky black colt. Saunders laughed even though his butt still stung. "You little shit," he said. "Who the hell are you? Where's yo mama?"

Behind him he heard the clatter of hooves on concrete, the women's happy voices. They must be done.

He held out his hand, the colt eyed it, took a step, and stretched his nose toward it. Saunders jerked his hand back then laughed at his cowardice. Slowly he extended his hand again as the colt extended its nose. Fingertips and nose met. The colt sniffed, then, to Saunders surprise, he took hold of a finger and began to suck.

"So YAH FOUND that GOD-DAMN-COLT hey?" Sugarplum was behind him. He jumped higher than when the colt bit his butt.

Brit's voice. "So that's the little monster. Sugarplum, you're a crazy woman. He's beautiful. Look at that to-die-for head! Where's his mama?"

"To die for. NADIA'S DEAD. THAT little FUCKER KILLED her."

"Omigod, Shug." Now Brit was in the stall, her arm around Sugarplum. Asia walked up to the colt who'd retreated from the crowd of humans. She crouched, began pleading softly, "Come on little man, I won't hurt you, it's okay."

While Sugarplum gasped out the grotesque details of Nadia's death by colic the night before, Saunders joined Asia in coaxing the colt. He came to Saunders first. Saunders felt something break open in his chest. He had to fight hard not to start bawling out loud like that bitch Sugarplum. With the urge to cry was a feeling of pride that the colt had chosen him, not Asia. Asia, the supreme animal-lover. He used the term "animal-lover" in his mind the way someone would say "nigger-lover."

The colt was trying his fingers, abandoning them one by one when each failed to give him milk.

"So I don't KNOW what TO DO," the voice harsh as the cry of a crow, "there's not a SINGLE NURSE MARE available TO RENT and I sure don't feel up to ROUND-THE-CLOCK BOTTLE FEEDINGS, especially for a COLT." Saunders heard Sugarplum's raspy breathing, then her squawk continued, "WHY don't YOU TAKE HIM? LOOK at HIM with YOUR SON. HEY SAUNDERS, HOW'D YOU LIKE TO HAVE THAT COLT?"

Saunders head whipped around. Brit sagged under Sugarplum's incredible lack of subtlety but also saw want in his face so strong it looked as if his skin had been jerked tight over his skull.

"Mokhtar's NOT getting any YOUNGER," screamed Sugarplum. "And you KNOW I DON'T HAVE ANY USE FOR A GOD-DAMN-COLT."

He wouldn't ask, Brit suddenly knew. *He couldn't.*

Everyone seemed frozen in place. Brit, the tallest one there, looked like a skinny cowboy in her black jeans, boots, man's black shirt; Sugarplum's chartreuse body hovering on egret-thin legs; Asia standing like a rack for her long hair; then Saunders, eyes sunken in their sockets, mouth open, neither blinking nor breathing. Then his hair came alive as a shaft of sunlight strayed through a skylight. It caught fire.

What a portrait he'd make right now, thought Brit.

"Well?" rasped Sugarplum, slightly less abrasive, as if she too was caught in the powerful current of Saunders' desire.

The light rippled over Saunders' hair so it flickered like flames. *Clouds*, Brit thought, *must be swiftly passing over the face of the sun.*

The colt stepped out from behind Asia and whinnied. High, a sweet soprano, a baby sound.

"He's hungry," said Sugarplum, in her lowest voice yet.

"But we can't," cried Brit. "A baby has to be bottle fed every two hours, night and day for three months."

Saunders drew a stricken breath.

"NOPE," yelled Sugar, back up to speed. "You JUST mix up a BUCKET of Foal Lac and HANG it in his stall. TAKE AWAY the WATER BUCKET and he'll DRINK the Foal Lac, if he REALLY wants to LIVE. ONLY way to GO. Mike told me that TRICK after he told me ALL HIS NURSE MARES ARE RENTED OUT TO THOROUGHBRED FARMS."

Brit turned to her. "You sure of that, Sugarplum?"

"Betcha BOOTS I am. CHANGE THE BUCKET whenever he EMPTIES it. MIX up FIVE GALLONS at a time, you ONLY have to CHANGE IT

MORNING AND NIGHT."

Brit felt set up by Sugarplum, but she looked at Saunders. The boy hadn't moved. If she allowed this, it would be more of a responsibility than simply changing a bucket twice a day. Then he'd go off to college, leaving the horse behind. *Did she want another horse?*

"I'd DO IT," said Sugar, "but I DON'T WANNA put all that TIME AND MONEY into a COLT. Colt's are a DIME a dozen. LESS'N ONE TENTH of 'ems FIT to use for BREEDING. A FILLY is a DIFFERENT STORY. Mike says DOUBLE the Foal Lac from what it SAYS on the directions, that way HE gets enough PROTEIN and all. I put it in my CALCULATOR and its GONNA COST ABOUT A HUNDRED BUCKS a week to raise him, for the FIRST THREE MONTHS. After that he'll eat HAY AND GRAIN just like a regular HORSE."

Brit looked at Saunders. "Saunders. This colt will be a lot of work. Besides Foal Lac preparation, his stall will need cleaning, he'll need handling and grooming, and you'll have to have my help there. Babies are a handful. And, he'll cost a fortune to raise."

Saunders spoke. "Dad'll help with the money, Mom, I know he will." His voice was high, like an five-year-old's. Brit felt herself yearning toward him, wanting to do this for him.

"But the work, Saunders. I have to start producing some serious art, pronto. I do not have time to take care of another horse. Especially not an orphan baby."

The colt began tugging Saunder's jeans pocket. Automatically the boy's hand went out to pat it.

She hadn't seen Saunders unmasked like this since he was a little–even then it was seldom. The cool dude was gone. If this colt could bring out the real Saunders when nothing else could, then the colt would be worth it.

Nevertheless, her sharp horsewoman's eye scanned the colt for conformational flaws. His legs looked fine, his shoulder angulation seemed good...there was a sound of weeping. Brit looked and saw it was Sugarplum. Of course. She'd been up all night, lost a beloved mare. And there was always leftover emotion: anxiety, relief, joy after a successful mating. Brit went to her and put her arms around the small woman.

As she stroked Sugarplum's narrow shoulders she looked at Saunders.

"Okay–"

"Yippee!"

"Not so quick, Saw. Here's the deal. We'll strap on this orphan IF. IF you take
care of him six days a week before school, which means you'll have to get out of
bed an hour earlier. I'll do the seventh day–everyone needs a break. You call your
Dad, see if he'll come up with half the care costs. I'll pay the other half. You'll
also do a good job taking care of Mokhtar, to pay me for my investment of my
money and my time in your horse. To be on the safe side, for the next year we'll
co-own, so both your and my name will appear on his registration papers. Also
your grades better morph to B's. Got it?"

Saunders was grinning and nodding with each point. Behind him Asia was
smiling. Sugarplum's weeping subsided and she stepped back from Brit.

"BETTER get a LEG on. He's NOT NURSED for SEVEN hours–only
water. Don't wanna LOSE him NOW."

Quickly they loaded the foal into the trailer and drove away from Sugarplum's,
stopping only at a feed store in Folsom where they bought a sixty-pound bucket
of mare's milk replacer powder. Brit let Saunders pick out a tiny foal halter and
then they were on their way back to Brit's farm.

NINE

Brit was on the phone with Grant. She'd described Saunders reaction to the foal and
unhesitatingly he'd agreed to help. She was about to end the conversation when
he said, "Brit, what's going on?"

"Going on?"

"With us."

"Us?"

"Yes. I thought we were kinda getting back together."

"Were we?"

"Well, what happened in bed I thought was–"

"It was. I just don't know, Grant. I feel confused."

Grant, sitting at his office desk, felt his heart rate increase. Part of him wanted to yell, "Well, fuck you, Brit," and slam the phone down but instead he held
on tight to the receiver, waiting for her to continue.

There was a long silence.

He broke it.

"Lunch, maybe?"

"Okay. I could do lunch sometime."

"I'd kinda like to see this horse I'm about to start feeding, too."

"You've already started. I just spent a hundred dollars on him, so you owe me fifty."

"Well then, I'll just drop by tomorrow and pay you back and–"

"That'll be fine, but I'm not doing any cooking tomorrow, so I can't feed you. It's for the best, anyway, we're all eating frozen food. All I do now is ride Mokhtar for an hour, then I try to spend the rest of the day in the studio."

"Okay, fine, I understand."

Why was he groveling before this old-woman ex-wife? Maybe he should discuss this with his sponsor.

He kept his tone reasonable. Something he'd learned from the Big Book of Alcoholics Anonymous, which his sponsor had insisted he memorize, was that anger is "the dubious luxury of normal men, but for alcoholics…poison."

"Well, maybe I can help out. I'll come out, meet my little four-legged investment, take Saunders and Asia to brunch. That way you can concentrate on work."

"Sounds good." *Was this Grant, being helpful? Or did he expect to spend the night?* He was still talking.

"…and, Brit, I would like a firm commitment from you for lunch."

"Okay. Next Wednesday? I'll be in town to pick up art supplies and Grant, tomorrow night I–"

"I have to get back to the city, big day Monday. Court. But we're on for lunch. Wednesday. Copeland's on Vets? One?"

"Fine. Puts me close to the Causeway, so I can get home quick."

"That's what I had in mind. I'll make us a reservation."

They hung up.

Brit lingered by the phone for a moment. *Was Grant changing, some miracle of A.A.?* Then she strode out to the barn to help with the settling in of the new foal.

That night, alone, she drove into New Orleans to her first A.A. meeting.

Sunday morning she was up at six and after coffee and a toasted bagel, she went to the barn. The foal was on his feet, big eyed, muzzle wet and white. He'd accepted the bucket feedings. Hurrah! But was he drinking enough? She went into the stall, stroked his neck, feeling the baby muscle bulging the length of his delicate vertebrae. With his tiny muzzle, big eyes and high, arched neck he looked exactly like a black seahorse. *Don't fall in love.* Gently she pushed him aside to check the bucket. Almost empty. She stood and grinned down at him.

"Good for you, Colt. Looks like you intend to survive." Normally, she'd be saddling Mokhtar for their morning ride, but she'd left him at Sugarplum's to breed the remaining mares. She could go over there and ride him...probably tomorrow she would, but today she didn't feel like it.

She felt anxious that all her sketching and thinking and meditating had yielded no ideas–the paisley snakes were a stand-alone effort. Not enough there to create a series.

She squatted and looked at the colt. Immediately he moved in and tried to suckle her hands, her hair, her face. Laughing, she pushed him away and stood up.

"You're gonna need lots of attention, aren't you?"

The colt gave a little buck and romped around the stall. He needed a name. Perhaps Saunders would want to name him after a rock group...she laughed again.

He needed outside. With some difficulty she got a foal halter on. She snapped a six-foot cotton lead shank to it, then wrapped the end around the colt's buttocks. Her left hand held the rope snapped to his halter, her right hand, on his fuzzy mid-back, held the loop wrapped around his buttocks. She pushed forward with her left hand, which was under his chin and pulled his hindquarters along with her right. He wanted to back up, escape the pressure of the rope, or bolt forward. *Good thing he was so little, only about a hundred and fifty pounds,* she thought. Once, typically, he reared straight up, forefeet climbing over her head. She was happy she had the skill, experience and strength to keep herself safe, letting him go, then taking back control. Breathing hard from the exertion, yet calm, she stayed with him, talking softly all the time, making this first experience of human restraint as gentle as possible. Often they moved sideways, and she began laughing. He'd even buck in place, tiny, baby bucks, and she'd whisper, "Quite the pistol, aren't you, Colt?" They struggled out to the paddock. There were moments when their bodies, close, seemed to link up, then he'd hurl himself forward, back, or rise up but she stayed right with him. It felt good.

Past the gate, she unsnapped the lead. He hesitated for a second, having begun to bond with her voice, her closeness. She stepped back, he followed. Then she raised her arms, spoke softly, "Shoo," and off he went bucking, running, twisting, leaping, rearing, making baby stud snorts, tiny high-pitched whinnies. She laughed, then collapsed against the fence.

He really was something.

Then it hit.

Women and Horse.

Young woman, old horse.

Young horse, old woman.

Naked horse, naked woman.

Sculpture. Ultra real.

Bronze?

Big. Almost life-size. Life-size? Could she work that big? She shook with excitement.

Not bronze. Papier maché? Fiberglass. She'd seen some works–fiberglass looking so real, so fleshy. Maybe parts in bronze. Part bronze, part fiberglass? She turned and ran to the house for her camera.

TEN

Saunders woke. He felt a puzzled excitement, then remembered. He had a colt. His very own horse. He felt so happy he was embarrassed. Nevertheless, he flung the covers off, then jumped from bed. Stopped. *What if the colt didn't drink his milk? What if he'd died?* His mind flashed on the small black body, long legs flailed out, eyes glazed, dead on the straw. Flies buzzing.

No!

He jerked on a sweatshirt, hopped into yesterday's jeans, thrust his feet into sneakers.

He raced down the stairs and outside–then stopped again.

The colt was out, running around the paddock. He laughed. Alive! He kept smiling, walking again, watching the long front legs flying out, hind legs scooting under. He was delighted at how well he used them. He seemed to float above the ground. *But how did he get out of his stall?*

Brit, leaning on the fence, a camera dangling from her shoulder, was laughing.

Stolen. She'd stolen his horse.

Couldn't they ever leave his stuff alone?

God damn them.

He stopped. Rage like flames seemed to crackle up from the soles of his feet, curling and twisting up his legs, coiling like a snake in his groin, rearing up through his belly, flaming through his chest, scorching his heart. His arms, in flames, shot up, and running he screamed, "What the fuck are you doing?"

He saw Brit jerk her head around.

He raced down the swale, past the pond, quacking ducks scattering, up the other side, then stepped on a shoe lace and fell. Sobbing, he scrabbled up from the harsh grass, clawed his way, on hands, knees, and toes, up the rise, so angry he wanted to tear up the grass with his teeth, roar. *Bring her down!*

She had stolen his horse. *His horse!*

On his feet now at the top, he felt paralyzed by his fury. Had to run, but forced himself to jog up to her. He couldn't breathe. He saw Colt from the corner of his eye, settling down now, ambling closer, walking.

Brit had come toward him, the gate open behind her. Her face was white with wrinkles all over it–fucking old woman–fucking horse thief. He stopped five feet from her, his hands fisted at his sides. He wanted to rip her head off, see blood spout, gush like a red fountain, throw her pasty-faced head down, let cockroaches eat it.

His chest went up and down and he had trouble using the air that came inside him, like there was some impenetrable barrier against receiving life. He couldn't speak. His eyes went from Brit to Colt.

Colt might escape–wander out the pasture–trot down the drive, gallop through the woods, out to the highway–an eighteen-wheeler–roaring around the curve–

Close the gate! he screamed. No words came out.

One flurried look and she turned, ran, and shut the gate just as Colt was about to walk through. She came back toward him.

He was still breathing in great gasps, some air getting through. His head pounded, he had to bend over, try to force oxygen through suddenly impervious membranes into his bloodstream, into his heart. He saw blackness rush toward him, up from the ground. *Would he faint? Here and now, in front of this thieving bitch?*

"Saunders? Saw–?"

"Shut–up."

"Okay." Her voice, so tiny, so far away.

His back moved up and down. In the old days, they hung horse thieves. He understood why now. *Horses were like a part of you.*

"Saunders, honey, what's wrong."

Still bent, he waved a hand, she stopped. He could see her feet, in those fucking arrogant English riding boots. Drops of wet dew, sticking on them. One drop ran down the leather ankle, rejoined the earth.

His head began to clear–air was getting through now. Slowly he stood. *Where was his rage?* It was all gone. Now he felt completely empty. Nothing inside him. He was nothing. He looked past Brit's furrowed face to see Colt at the gate. Saw the little black muzzle, baby whiskers spouting soft from it, watched the muzzle twist, the tiny lips part, saw pink baby gums, heard the tinkle of a baby whinny. Colt bobbed his head at him. *At him.* Something warm started, right above his groin, not fire, not hot flames of rage, but warmth. He wanted to cry. So he walked straight past Brit to Colt. His hand touched the muzzle, slid down the soft jowl, down the soft curved neck. He slumped against the gate as his other hand came up. He couldn't stop the tears now, both hands stroking the colt's neck, Colt's nostrils blowing warm air onto his face, as though helping him breath. Colt sniffing his ear, Colt mouthing the ends of his hair. The warmth filled his belly, his chest, his arms, his head.

He heard a faint scrunching, the creak of the leather boots, and knew Brit was sneaking away.

She did her damage, now she was sneaking away. *Couldn't face him.* The warmth, so good, was becoming anger again. He stood, regarded Colt. He was cute, yeah. Sure. But now there was something polluted about him.

He was still sort of glad the colt was here but it wasn't the same any more.

Colt bobbed his head at him.

How the hell was he supposed to get it back to the barn?

E L E V E N

She was busy sketching in her studio and had only a vague awareness of Grant arriving to take the children out for lunch. When she emerged to go to Sugarplum's she found a five hundred dollar check on her coffee table from Grant.

That afternoon she photographed Mokhtar over at Sugarplum's–his puffing, snorting, stallion routine. He even reared a few times, her leaping around in front of him yelling, egging him on. Him breathtakingly close, yet judiciously he kept his hooves from her. Even apart, on the ground, they were bonded. *What joy in this horse!* She clicked her last shot–Mokh coiled, neck arched, front feet curled under, a perfect levade–then he pranced off to the mare herd's fence line. He flicked one glance back at her, she caught it and smiled. Leaving for home, she was happy, the peculiar incident with Saunders on the plateau erased from her mind.

That night she knocked on Anastasia's bedroom door. She asked her, *would she pose, in the nude?* She'd be the model for Young Woman in the sculptures Brit saw growing in her mind.

Brit was amazed when her shy daughter grinned and said, "Okay, Mom."

On Monday morning as Saunders cleaned Colt's stall—still hadn't named him—he thought how he almost couldn't stand it. *To be away from his horse.* Not yet, it was too soon. Besides, he'd missed a whole three hours away from him going on the stupid brunch with Super Dome and the Chink–Asia. Yet–he paused in his raking–yet, there was still that knot of anger at Brit. Then he laughed even as the tang of fresh manure hit his nostrils, seeing Colt splay-legged, muzzle in his bucket of milk, hearing the soft sucking sounds of his drinking, the squirrel-like tail twitching happily across rounding buttocks. And there'd been no problem getting him back into the barn. All he did was open the gate and Colt followed him, right into the stall.

Brit would be busy all day behind The Door. He needed to stay with his horse, his horse needed him. He'd have to get on the school bus, but maybe he could fake throwing up or something so the bus driver would let him off. Then he could walk back, sneak through the woods, into the barn and, if he heard anyone coming, just hop up the ladder into the loft. He could spend the whole day playing with Colt. *Colt. Sounded like a gun. Maybe he could name him Magnum or something. Uzi.* Brit had said his pedigree was half Russian bloodlines and half Egyptian...*how about "Terrorist?"* He laughed out loud. Colt was still snozzling up the milk he'd just made for him, but he lifted a dripping muzzle at the sound and gazed, eyes black and innocent, right into Saunders' milk-light eyes. Saunders smiled, flapped his hand at him.

"Go on now. Drink your milk all up. Like a good boy."

The head disappeared into the bucket. The snozzling began again, a good sound.

At the bus's second stop Saunders staggered up the aisle and stood before Mrs. Boudreaux. He was blocking Angie Cruz when she came up the bus steps. He'd held his breath for a long time, so his face was red and sweaty.

Speaking in a fading monotone he said, "Mrs. Boudreaux, I feel kinda sick to my stomach."

Mrs. Boudreaux was a big tanned Cajun who drove the school bus to supplement her trapper husband's income.

She saw how flushed Saunders looked, standing there in his two hundred dollar black leather jacket. She smelled the leather. He had a rich papa. She remembered her first impression of him. A wolverine: beautiful outside, dangerous inside.

She said, "Step aside. Let Angie in. Then I drive you back home."

Saunders wiped his brow then stood back so Angie could squeeze past. Immediately he put a foot on the vacated step.

"I can walk."

"If you be sick, cher–"

"Miz Boudreaux. You don't want to make all the kids late for school on account of me." He took another step down. She stared at him. *Très étrange.* A little fear came in her. She nodded.

"Thanks, Miz Boudreaux." He stepped from the bus.

Still staring, she pulled the handle, the bus door clanked closed.

In the rearview she watched him as she drove off. He didn't look all that sick. He stood for a long time looking back at her, then he turned and slouched toward his home.

There was a convenience store on his way. He bought two Mars Bars, a large bag of Cool Ranch Doritos, a big Classic Coke and a copy of *Forum*, which was behind the counter. He'd have a real good time in the barn today.

Saunders could not believe what he was seeing.

He'd settled in the loft by pushing bales of hay around to screen him from someone coming up the ladder, broken one bale open, and stomped around on it to make a soft bed to lie on. He set out his food, drinks, two marijuana cigarettes.

While he was doing this he heard Asia's voice right below.

"I'm not really sure about this now, Ma."

Creaking sound–a stall door opening?

"I promise you, there's not a soul around. And the forest screens us completely. If anyone drives in I can hear my rocks crunch long before they get to the clearing."

A sigh. "I want to. I'm just scared."

"Honey, if you're scared, we won't do it. I can find another model. But on my birthday I rode around that pasture naked as a jay."

Saunders' heart picked up speed.

He heard their lilting voices, the foal's unshod hooves plonking over concrete..."Over there."

Where, he wondered? There were no windows in the loft but at each end there were double doors that swung out, tall enough for a man to stand up in and receive bales of hay thrown up from a trailer bed.

He belly-crawled–unnecessarily, he realized later–to the northwest doors and cracked one open. To see anything, like the pasture or the pond beyond the driveway, he had to open the door about a foot, and lying on his side, stick his head and neck out.

They walked right into his field of vision. Brit in jeans, a turtleneck, carrying a Polaroid camera and a big sketch book, and Asia, wearing one of those goofy caftans of the Maw's. It was shocking pink. Then they turned, disappeared past the side of the barn.

"Damn!" He crawled rapidly, making more noise now, to the south doors.

He stood and opened a door very cautiously, but not before glancing down. *Must be about a fifteen-foot drop*, he thought. *You might break your fuckin' leg. Don't look down.* He looked straight ahead and they came trooping past the wood-shingled eave, Brit leading Colt, Asia naked.

He couldn't breathe. He wished he was closer. Or had binoculars.

They were in the pasture now. Turned loose, Colt galloped past.

Asia began walking backwards, she raised her arms, then Brit came past the eave, camera held close to her belly like she was about to take a picture. She held a hand up, and Asia froze, one leg in the air, arms up.

The camera whined, then spit out a white rectangle. Both women huddled around it, Asia's hair so long it covered her ass. *Maybe a breeze would come along and lift the hair?* He scanned the cloudless blue sky.

The Maw and the Chink tossed their heads, and he heard faint laughter. The Maw waved her right hand around again. The Chink flopped onto the ground and–Saunders licked his lips–he could actually see her snatch. Mainly black hair, but a sliver of redness...?

Her breasts were perfectly round with red tips. In clothes they didn't look nearly so big. In clothes, Anastasia, his beloved stepsister, didn't look nearly so good.

He took a very deep breath, lowered his butt to the floor. He sat cross-legged–one knee jutting into space to prop the door open. By leaning far to his right he could watch the picture show fine. A hand slid down to his zipper.

If only they'd keep the show going on this side of the paddock. For just a few minutes.

Just as he finished, Chink jumped up and both women disappeared. There were shrieks of laughter. Tucking himself in he scrambled to his feet and ran to the opposite door, combat boots thudding hollowly on the raftered floor.

He pushed the door open, then almost slammed it shut. His stepmother was naked and his stepsister, back in her robe, was taking pictures.

He looked away, overwhelmed by feelings he didn't understand. A bit of fear, for sure embarrassment...he almost let go of the door when it was pushed by a breeze. It could whap against the barn—they'd catch him. Using both hands, eyes averted, carefully he closed the door.

He didn't want a hard-on from looking at the naked body of his stepmother.

He tiptoed back to his nest of hay, lowered himself, lit up a number.

Artists were crazy.

The women, dressed, sat on the red velvet divan in Brit's studio drinking hot Emperor's Choice tea. A low table was scattered with the Polaroids.

Speaking through steam from her mug Asia said, "Those six are my favorites... you think you'll use any of them for the sculpture? And Mom, I sure wouldn't want anyone but us to see them."

For an answer Brit scooped up all the other pictures of her daughter and began tearing them up. "I'll only work from those, okay? And they'll be under lock and key."

Asia smiled. "And nobody will ever know I was your model?"

"Nobody. They'll never drag it out of me. I'll crunch the cyanide capsule first."

"No kidding around, Mom..."

Brit leaned to her. "Never. I'll change your face, make your boobs smaller, et cetera."

"Okay. Thanks, Mom. You know," she picked up a picture of herself and studied it, "I'm glad you coerced me into doing this."

"Coerced? Who coerced?"

"Well, you practically dragged me out there."

"Me?"

"Yeah, you, Mom. But if you hadn't, I'd have missed something."

Brit got quiet, her back straight, tea in her lap.

Asia was staring at a picture of herself reclining on her side, hand propping her head, arm forming a white triangle. The woods beyond looked black.

"I look okay, don't I?"

"Darling, you look beautiful."

"I never thought of myself as beautiful–you, sure. You've always been my beautiful mother...I used to yearn to look like you..."

"Oh, Sweetheart!"

"It's okay. I guess no kid's ever satisfied with their looks."

"I went years as the tallest, gawkiest kid in the class."

"And I went years trying to be invisible."

"Yep. I know. Sometimes I was scared you'd transmute into a pollywog right before my eyes. Or a deer."

"Oh, the critter thing."

"Hey, I love the critter thing. Sweetie, you're using it. I'm proud you're study-ing zoology. You were born a zoologist–"

Asia waved a hand. "I've got to say this." She held up a picture. "Thanks for proving to me that I look okay. Maybe now I won't be quite so scared to...date someone."

Brit watched her, and a movement deep in her belly felt like a part of her was being nudged aside, as a seedling nudges aside and opens up earth, to grow.

"You're saying you're a virgin."

Asia blushed, but held her mother's eyes. "Yes."

"Good, that's good. But are you also saying that what held you back is the notion that you're not beautiful?"

"Well–yes–partly. Also partly–I'm scared to death. And partly, never met the right guy."

Considering this, Brit leaned over her knees, holding them tightly, her eyes idling over the photo, stopping at the one Asia had held earlier. Slowly she picked it up.

"My God. Wait here, Asia."

She jumped up, sprinted from the room. *Where was it? Yes.* She rummaged through the shallow bottom drawer in the liquor cabinet and found the Tarot cards Lee had given her on her birthday. She opened the deck and sorted through the cards until she found The Virgin. She held the Polaroid of her daughter next to the card. Same dark ring of trees, same white bodied, side-reclining maiden–it was as if Anastasia had posed for the artist who'd designed the card.

The nudging feeling she'd felt earlier suddenly yawed into a great canyon and cold shame came swooshing up like an Arctic breeze. Her fingertips holding the card were icy.

It hadn't been her at all—regaining some pseudo-virginity. It had been her daughter. The true maiden, the true virgin, and what was she but an old, hard-used, infertile female teetering on the lip of Hagdom?

She felt as humiliated as if she'd been simpering and flirting with a man who said, "Not you. Your daughter."

Then a new part of herself asserted itself. Hey, it's your daughter's time to know these mysteries of flesh and your time to stand back. Don't you want her to learn about the glory in the finest possible way?

Viola had never given up being the beautiful flirt—and suddenly Brit understood how she'd been betrayed. That her mother couldn't or wouldn't pause even for a moment to welcome her daughter onto the stage where the heady fertility dance was performed. Viola'd said, I'm in this dancing as hard as I can dissembling, acting, looking so young—if you want to dance, kiddo—don't do it around me, because I can outflirt, outdance, outman you anytime.

Brit remembered her boyfriends. How reluctant she'd been for them to come to her house. Because there was Viola. Beautiful, provocatively dressed, fawning over them. Afterward, sitting numb in the boy's car, driving to a movie, braced for the remark that made her grind her teeth.

"Wow. Your mother's really something."

And I'm not.

Or she'd come home from school, hear murmuring. Viola on the phone. Then the terrifying exaggerated peal of her mother's laughter. Then Brit felt the shame she was feeling now looking at the Tarot card, the Polaroid picture. Her mother wasn't just on the phone, her mother was talking to Brit's boyfriend.

Odd, thought Britannia, *she believed she had to feel shame for what her mother did.* Nevertheless, she'd broken up with Brad because he talked about her mother so much and, they'd gone steady for a year. She'd cried privately for months after that. Now she didn't want to play Viola to her daughter. She shuddered. She'd been terrifyingly close to kidnapping her daughter's transformation to womanhood.

Remembrances of sexual wildness with Scottie flashed. She'd been extremely careful never to have sex with him while Asia was home. Still, there'd been a noticeable sexual energy field around them. *Had he been attracted to Asia?* She scrolled through scenes, a wounded and wanting-to-feel wounded part of her seeking hurt, the tongue in the sore tooth.

Did Scottie's eyes sometimes linger too long on Asia? The times Scottie'd run to the store, Asia with him?

No. Her experience with Viola had made her hyper-sensitive. There'd been no hint of that.

She did some mental arithmetic. She was thirteen years older than Scottie, Scottie eighteen years older than Asia. Would a Scottie-Asia pairing have been more appropriate? Asia or someone her age could give Scottie children. But he'd always acted indifferent to reproducing. In fact, she remembered him patting his Nikon with his beachy-lifeguard grin saying, "I make all the kids I want with this and none of 'em need their didees changed." She'd write him today.

She was back to the Great Divide within her, seeing herself as a tiny confused figure on one side of the chasm, which inched ever wider. Her fertile daughter stood on the opposite side, back turned, beginning to move away. Suddenly her shame and sorrow released, flew away as if a bird had plucked it from her.

She felt now she could unequivocally applaud her daughter's new beginning. Slowly she walked back to the studio.

But was she back to that frightening place of unmapped territory she'd discovered on her fiftieth birthday?

Her daughter's path was a broad paved highway, with clearly marked road-signs, bright cheerful billboards. Go to College. Have a Career. Get Married. Have Children.

Hers? All she saw was a potholed road, pavement patched and repatched, holding sudden dips that could tear the bottom off a car–like many streets in New Orleans. The few road signs were hidden with overgrown vines, or if visible, their faces splotched with graffiti or rusted indecipherable. The road grew narrower, derelict houses listing on either side, until it became one-way.

Maybe she needed to go to another A.A. meeting.

She sat on the couch and handed the card and photo to Asia.

"Oh wow! Mom. Neat."

Brit jumped up again. "Let me get the book so you can read what the card means."

As Asia read the book, Brit put her arm around her daughter, reading silently over her shoulder. "The full face of womanhood is revealed but unseen by the young girl…I am shame and I am boldness/I am shameless and I am ashamed."

Warmth crept from Anastasia into Britannia. Brit allowed herself to smile. Asia'd never given her the opportunity to flirt with any of her boyfriends–she'd never had any!

Now shame was gone, replaced by a light, happy expectation of experiencing her daughter's next phase of life.

She wouldn't go down that potholed road. There had to be another way.

T W E L V E

Grant and Irwin sat at a corner table at La Madeleine on the corner where St. Charles' Avenue elbows around and becomes Carrollton Avenue, the high grassed levee shadowing the wrenching ninety-degree bend of the Mississippi River beyond the street.

Irwin was a wide-shouldered man with a chest so broad it looked like he was throwing it out. Under his black sweatshirt were the pectoral muscles of the long-term ex-con. Irwin had spent ten years in Angola and, not long ago, had celebrated his tenth birthday as a member of Alcoholics Anonymous. His brown eyes were limpid and compassionate behind gold-rimmed bi-focals. His skin was so healthy and smooth he was almost baby-faced. He had a short thatch of black-gray hair above his forehead, an isolated island of hair whose coastline was eroding like Louisiana's. On the back of his head his hair grew vigorously and was pulled back, rubber-banded, into a foot-long ponytail.

Grant eyed Irwin's island of hair and wondered if the encroaching baldness was what had drawn him to him.

Around them was the lunchtime babble, clink of spoon on saucer, smell of fresh-brewed coffee, tang of vinaigrette, chickens roasting, bread baking.

Irwin looked out as he listened to Grant. A streetcar clanged around the riverbend from St. Charles onto Carrollton. Right outside the window a woman in a red Mercedes convertible braked suddenly. She'd almost rear-ended a heavily-chromed white Lincoln. The silver-haired towncar driver casually raised a hand, middle finger raised. Irwin smiled.

Irwin's sympathies were with Grant. An interesting new sponsee. Big handsome guy, real twitchy though—blinked a lot, scratched his head a lot. *Maybe he'd done some drugs he hadn't yet admitted to. Was he wearing a hairpiece?*

Grant had had three cups of coffee to Irwin's one. His tie was loosened, his suit jacket off. He heard nothing but his own voice, saw nothing but Irwin's face.

"So I don't know where she's at. Like I said, we had sex—three, four times, I thought it was pretty good. Now it's 'don't call me, I'll call you' and well, damn, Irwin."

"She's an alcoholic?"

"So she says."

"I tend to respect a statement like that, Grant. She's been a drinker?"

"Oh yeah. Bloody Marys by the gallon for brunch, Martinis for lunch, she's always liked to party. Hearty. But not every day."

"Sounds like she has a desire to stop drinking."

Grant felt irritated. He'd awakened thinking that somehow Brit had diminished his declaration of alcoholism when she made hers. Now Irwin was backing her up. Irwin was supposed to be his sponsor. Grant wrinkled his forehead, his hair moved oddly. Irwin saw it. *Yep. Grant's wearing a rug.*

"So what are you telling me, Grant?"

Grant flexed his big hands and a teaspoon went skittering across the table. Irwin ignored it. Grant wanted to scream in rage or weep in confusion or just tell this superior guy to shove it. Instead, voice miserable, he said, "I don't know."

Irwin waited.

"Why doesn't she want to have sex with me? We could move in together, kinda, you know, especially with Saunders living out there, me not drinking. It could be okay."

"Maybe 'okay' isn't what she wants."

"Well, it was better than okay."

"Are you talking about sex?"

"Well, yeah. What else?" He sneaked a look at Irwin, seeing if the guy–really only an ex-con, so what if he was going for a Ph.D. in sociology?–was acting smug. Nope. He just sat there, waiting for Grant's next utterance.

"I can't help feeling, well, the truth is–Britannia's older than me." He checked Irwin's face again, expecting him to sigh and commiserate, a guy like Grant stuck with an older woman. But he saw only bland empathy.

"The age thing was meaningless ten years ago. She always looked young for her age. But hell," he hunched closer to Irwin, "she just turned fifty. I mean,"–he shot a look around the restaurant–"I should be with younger women." Irwin didn't jump in. Didn't even nod. Grant gestured, narrowly missing his coffee cup and a salt shaker. "I mean, I read where we, men that is, are genetically programmed to seek out younger women. Much younger women. I figure that's where I'm at." He took a deep breath, leaned back in his chair. A long pause. Then Irwin leaned forward.

"A couple of things, Grant. You admit you're powerless over alcohol?"

Grant nodded emphatically.

"You've been reading your Big Book and you've learned alcoholism is a disease?"

Nod. Nod.

"And if I recall, some time back, you shared with me that you'd had a father-son talk and let your son know there was a fifty-fifty chance he could be an alcoholic too?"

Such an eager look in that grown-man's eyes.

"Because it has also been pretty much scientifically proven that one cause of alcoholism is genetic?"

"Yes, Irwin."

"You believe with the help of the A.A. program you have a shot at remaining sober?"

"Of course!"

"So, Grant. I'm baffled. How can that be, since it is a genetic disease? You mean you are able to go against your genetic program?"

Grant stared. He got it. He swallowed, throat dry.

"You want more kids, Grant?"

"Oh, hell, no. Can't handle the one I've got."

"So why do you need a younger woman? Younger women've got biological clocks, going tick-tock, tick-tock. Real loud, Grant."

Grant was nodding earnestly. "I see what you mean, Irwin. But still–fifty–"

"I saw her, Grant. If she's fifty I'll eat my underwear. She's fifty?–so what. I'll eat her underwear." Irwin laughed, and Grant went heh, heh. Irwin let him twitch for a few beats, then leaned forward.

"As your sponsor I can only make suggestions. I suggest you not involve yourself with any woman of any age for the first year of your sobriety. Listen to people with more recovery than yourself. Share in meetings. Relationships really mess us alcoholics up and, in our first and most fragile year, can trigger a relapse." Irwin paused, sipped coffee, eyes never leaving Grant. "Focus on Grant. Work on that fourth step–"

Grant groaned.

"I know it's tough. It's a lot easier to worry about a woman than to write about all the people you have harmed, all the resentments you have–but if you really want to stay sober, you'll start writing, not jerking off."

"But–"

"No buts. My sponsor used to say to me, 'You got one problem boy, just one.

You want to see your problem? Just look in a mirror 'cause your problem is you."

Grant couldn't meet Irwin's eyes.

"If I was a fifty-year-old woman with any sense at all I wouldn't want some guy who's tongue's hanging out over every young chick that sashays by. Pull that tongue in, boy, zip that dick, or you're gonna trip big time." Grant felt faintly hostile. "I know I'm pissing you off, Grant, but sometimes I gotta jerk the bandage off in order for you to get well. A trip for us alcoholics can mean a slip, a slip into drinking means we eventually end up in one of three places: jail, an institution, or the morgue. You're a high-bottom drunk. I know, you kept your job, you never, by the ever-lovin' grace of God, went to jail on a DWI, you kept your condo. So maybe that arrogant alcoholic in you's saying right now: 'I don't have to listen to this shit. Who does this ex-con think he is?' Okay, I understand, but remember this: your first wife's in an insane asylum, you just lost your only son to your ex-wife, *your ex-wife*, who you're pissed at because she won't sleep with you, who you also think is too old for you. Enough insanity for you, Grant? You were picking up hookers before you got sober, scared shitless of AIDS, now you're mad at your ex-wife? You got no business banging any woman, Grant."

Irwin softened his tone. "There's one relationship that's more important than anything else. It's with your Higher Power, whoever, whatever that may be for you, Grant. Maybe Grant can't quite accept there is a power greater than himself?"

Grant shook his head.

"Good. What worked for me when I got horny during that first year was first, do-it-yourself sex, then pray and pray like hell. Then go to a meeting. Lots and lots of meetings. As much meeting time as you spent in bars. And then to do what you're doing right now. Talk to your sponsor." Irwin threw a dollar bill on the table, stood up, "C'mon, Grant, we've got time to hit the two-thirty meeting at Central Office."

With a sigh Grant stood and followed him from the restaurant.

On the sidewalk smelly, noisome lunch traffic–vehicular and pedestrian–was all around. Even the great oaks, their branches usually sheltering, now seemed to zigzag over the turmoil like friezes of black lightning.

"How do you feel?"

Someone jostled Grant. "Confused."

"Good. No one can learn anything when they've got all the answers."

Irwin stuck his hands in his jeans pockets. He smiled up at Grant. Grant felt his kindness, his compassion, like the moist warmth of the New Orleans air.

THIRTEEN

Brit sat on a battered sofa. She'd found an A.A. meeting in Covington. Actually it was an A.A. club, a place where meetings went on all day long. The meeting room was furnished with mismatched sofas, battered tables. She held a Styrofoam cup of black coffee she'd gotten from the kitchen in the back.

It was a six p.m. meeting. Up front a woman, in a sofa beside a man in half-glasses was talking. Except for her voice the room was quiet. About twenty other people, sat around.

"...so when I read that line in the Big Book of Alcoholics Anonymous, page 449, 'Nothing, absolutely nothing happens in God's world by mistake,' I felt such relief. Because, even though I had harmed many people: husband, children, non-alcoholic friends, even my mother and father–suddenly the things I did were not mistakes! I still do not fully understand why those things had to happen. But they were necessary events. When I went off on a business lunch and got too drunk to return to work, leaving my co-workers to handle a presentation, when I spent a sunny Saturday in bed nursing what I referred to as 'the flu' but what was really a hangover, when I was drunk and screaming at my husband," she paused to blink back tears, "even though all those things were awful, terrible, and now, even after two fourth and fifth steps I still feel guilt, even so, they weren't mistakes and that means I wasn't a mistake. From earliest childhood, I felt like a mistake. My parents wanted a boy–" she laughed, sat up straighter, and Brit saw how attractive the woman was, blonde, a bit heavy, "–my name, 'Georgie,' is from Georgina–after my father, George."

"I tried hard to make up for my first mistake in this life, being born a girl. I set for myself"–Brit thought, she set for herself, didn't her parents set it for her?–"the impossible task of trying to be a boy when I was truly a girl. Big, strong, but a girl. I never got good at throwing a ball. My dad hated that. However, I can change my oil and dance a real Hawaiian hula." Laughter.

"When I came into this room five years ago," Georgie paused and looked fondly around at the old Herculon-plaid sofas, black leather-look loveseats discarded from a doctor's waiting room, tattered formal damasks, tile floor that needed waxing, men and women ranged around, most smoking, some in business suits, others in T-shirts and jeans, all of them intent, clean and sober, "I took a look at the decor," people laughed out loud and Brit smiled, "and almost staggered back out."

"But my husband was going to leave me and take my three children, my boss had fired me, I had a DUI, and I had a disease. The disease of alcoholism. I thought I was one Great Big Mistake, but I wasn't. My father was an untreated alcoholic and I attended his funeral two years ago. He died of cirrhosis of the liver caused by his alcoholism."

"I think of my alcoholism as an allergy. Here in South Louisiana we're surrounded by the finest seafood in the world. I have a dear friend who's allergic to seafood—one bite and she has to be rushed to Emergency, she is instantly dying. So she can't enjoy the wonderful oysters, shrimp, crabs that I can. But she can drink, one, two, even three beers at the Lacombe Crab Festival. She feels jolly. I can't do that. Because 'one's too many and a thousand's not enough.' Unchecked, I will drink myself to death. I am allergic to alcohol. Is this a mistake? Nope. Not according to our Big Book. It's the way it is. Here in these rooms I am learning acceptance. Acceptance first of my disease, then acceptance that all those awful things I did weren't mistakes—each disaster just brought me closer and closer to membership in A.A. and membership in A.A. not only helped me get sober, it gave me the Twelve Steps, a plan for living I'm extremely grateful for. Now I'm grateful I'm an alcoholic, because without this disease I'd never have found these rooms, this wonderful plan for living that many, many people out there," she gestured toward the door, "do not have and have little hope of finding—since they are not fortunate enough to be alcoholics."

She paused, sipped a Diet Coke. "They're just regular people. I meet so many who are miserable in their lives. A church doesn't offer this plan for living. And even though I have also been in therapy, and was grateful for that help, it doesn't replace what I learned in Alcoholics Anonymous."

"What a relief to discover I am not a mistake. 'You shall not regret the past nor wish to shut the door on it' says one of our promises. That promise has come true for me." She paused, took a deep breath, and smiling slightly, looked around the room.

"Thank you for letting me share."

"Thanks for sharing," the people in the room called to her.

"Anybody want to share?"

A man in a pin-stripe suit put his hand up. He took it down and began.

"Hi, I'm Sam and I'm an alcoholic."

Brit was mesmerized. What a dynamic, courageous woman. What guts to sit in front of all these people and admit she'd been a bad employee, mother, wife, daughter. She trembled, felt guilt shake her. She couldn't concentrate on Sam. She swallowed hard and suddenly, desperately, wanted a cigarette. The Styrofoam cup shook in her hand.

"Thanks for sharing, Sam," the group said and Brit looked up to meet the brown eyes of Georgie saying to her, "How about the lady in the corner?"

Brit pointed a finger at her chest, raised her eyebrows. Smiling, Georgie said, "Yes, you, would you care to share?" People turned their heads to look back at her and Brit blushed.

"I," she cleared her throat. "I'm Brit, and I–guess–I'm an alcoholic." She half-laughed. No one joined her.

"I've never said that before in a meeting. This is just my–third meeting." She began to choke again, feeling angry, embarrassed, she didn't want to bawl in front of these people. She swallowed and heard someone speak.

"It's okay. Let it out, Brit."

Hearing that and her name she couldn't stop the crying that came. Silence while she cried. No one shifted or coughed. Her crying subsided, she reached for her purse on the floor, found a tissue. After dabbing her eyes and blowing her nose, she raised her head and said, "Sorry." Georgie's eyes were fixed on her unwaveringly, she gave an encouraging nod. Brit began again.

"I'm Brit and I'm an alcoholic." There was a small cheer from someone and a light patter of applause. A voice cried out, "You're in the right place!"

"I stopped drinking about two weeks ago because I had a big birthday–" she stopped, aghast. *Would she have to tell her age? Not yet,* said an inner voice.

"I didn't like the way I looked or felt. I'm an artist. I haven't had a decent idea in two years and that hurts my pocketbook because I'm a single mother with a daughter in college. Also, unexpectedly, my teenage stepson has decided he wants to live with me..." She shook her head. "I went to my first A.A. meeting with my ex-husband, then a couple by myself–and today I felt so scared and confused–well, here I am. I'm actually glad to be here."

People called out, "Keep coming back," then, "Thanks for sharing." Georgie gave her a big smile. "Welcome, Brit. I'd like to suggest you look for a sponsor."

The meeting continued. Sometimes Brit was able to hear what people said, other times her mind tumbled like wet clothes in a dryer.

Finally the man in the half-glasses thanked Georgie for moderating then said, "I'm Roger and I'm still an alcoholic." Picking up a plastic tray he said, "Here at the Piney Woods A.A. Club, we have the chip system where different lengths of sobriety are recognized by different chips."

He held up a green plastic disc about the size of a quarter, "Anyone here got twenty-four hours sober or a desire to stop drinking?" No one responded. He pointed the chip toward Brit. "Your first meeting with us. Come on up here and get yourself a chip."

Brit looked uncertainly around, a guy near her leaned back, whispered, "Just go on up and get you a chip. We all do."

Brit stood and the room filled with clapping. She threaded her way up to Roger who rose, put the chip in her hand then hugged her. The clapping went on the whole time and as she made her way back people reached up to shake her hand saying, "Welcome! Keep coming back!" One man stopped her and whispered, "You ever feel like takin' a drink just put that chip on your tongue. When it dissolves, why, go have you a drink." Brit looked at the green plastic disc, 24 HOURS on one side, ONE DAY AT A TIME on the other, and smiled.

She'd barely got to her seat when everyone stood up. They formed a ragged circle, took each others' hands, and everyone began to say the Lord's prayer.

When it was over someone put a green booklet in her hands, a meeting book, with space at the back for phone numbers. Several women came up to her, offering their numbers. Numb, she took them down. Then taking a deep breath, she went over to the head sofa where Roger was counting the dollars in the collection basket. Georgie was talking to a young man. The minute she saw Brit she reached across the coffee table and took one of her hands. She said goodbye to the man and turned to Brit, smiling.

"Would you be my sponsor?" Brit blurted.

Georgie's smile grew wider, "Thanks for asking–I'd be delighted. Got time to go for coffee?"

Brit nodded.

Georgie stood, took up her jacket and purse, and called goodbye to several people. She ushered Brit from the room.

Grant balanced a shiny narrow cup on a square saucer, both the color of an eggplant. He was precariously perched on the edge of a chair shaped like a hand. He couldn't bring himself to sit back even though the hand was generously upholstered. The thought of that great big hand grabbing his butt....

"Thank you for coming by, Grant," said Spiffy Wiffins. She sat primly upright in a ladder-back chair painted all over with eyes. Hundreds of them. Pucci slept at her feet.

Her mansion's interior wasn't what he'd expected. Eye chairs, hand chairs, huge canvasses with splashes of color like the one on the opposite wall. A streak of red raced up a pure white canvas mounted on the white wall, making the wall look like slashed, bloody flesh.

Here and there, in the gigantic front room in which he'd expected the obligatory Southern Antebellum Decor: oriental carpets, crystal chandeliers, antiques, oils of flowers, were clusters of weird furniture.

"I want to retain you to secure my divorce and property settlement from Alphonso."

"I gather," he said gravely, "the reconciliation at The Texas Motel didn't take." He set the odd cup and saucer down on a kidney-shaped, hammered metal table. He thought he'd been given peach herbal tea. Not bad, but the tiny cup handle was awkward for his big fingers.

"No."

He allowed his eyes to slide casually over her. Had she trimmed down? Her fifty-six year-old arms looked firm and he saw all of them since she wore a white tank top over black stretch capri-length tights, legs bare and brown from the knee down. Her small feet had pink toes with pearly nail polish. Her hair was longer, looser. Gone was the helmet of the caper. He felt a bit of smugness, knowing she was a natural blonde.

Ringed with mascara'd lashes, her amber eyes gazed warmly at him.

"You were so helpful that day, Grant. I appreciate it so much."

"Thank you, Spiffy. What exactly, why exactly–"

"Why do I want a divorce this time? Well, he's gone all the time. I am abandoned, married–but abandoned."

"You didn't catch him with–?"

"No."

Their eyes met. Knowingly. Grant said, "Too bad."

"Yes."

"It'd mean a bigger settlement."

"Yes."

Each gazed ruefully around.

Grant sighed, shaking his head. "But we've go to do what we've got to do–it takes what it takes..."

"Yes." She was nodding as she gazed unseeing at a painting of a watch that seemed to be melting. Grant was no connoisseur, *but could it be a Salvador Dali?*

"The art," he gestured around the room, "yours?"

"Some of it. But all of it was purchased at my instigation. I'm the collector, not Alf."

"The art definitely goes to you."

"I think it should."

"Yes."

Their eyes met. *There was something quite sexy about this woman,* thought Grant, *even though, by rights and her age, she was just about a little old lady.* His mind flashed a picture of her round pink belly, the blonde pubic hair. Quickly he glanced at her belly. It had decreased in size. *Was she working out? Dieting? Liposuction? Whatever. She looked pretty damn good.* If he had to guess her age...

"So," she was saying, "can you draw up the paperwork?"

...Forty-seven? Forty-five? She could pass, he decided, for his age. She raised an arm, ran it through her hair. Smooth muscle all the way up to her armpit. *Less than his age?*

"Of course. The old property settlement is still on file, like the house, the art, the Mercedes and the Cadillac," the dog opened one eye and Grant hastily added, "the dog, Pucci, of course, various stocks, shares, bonds, two properties, the rental unit on St. Charles Avenue, the other rental unit on the lake...anything new to add?"

"I want a cash settlement of five million, all my clothes, jewelry, furnishings, silver..."

"Yes, yes, I have all that."

"The only new thing is I bought a health club."

"You did?"

She grinned. "Yep. I wanted a good place to work out, but not alone, so I bought a club, fixed it up, it's open twenty-four hours a day. Jacuzzis, saunas, a pool, massage, juice and health food bar, trainers. If you'd like to try it out I'll give them a call to expect you. Anytime. I usually go around eleven at night, have a workout, a sauna, dip in the plunge pool, then home to bed. It's—" she raised her arms ecstatically, "just sensational." Her arms came down and she hugged herself. "Oh, Grant, it makes me feel so good!"

He dared get personal. "You're looking good."

"Thank you," she said matter-of-factly, but *did she suck in her tummy?*

"I also went into therapy to figure out why I thought I had to stay with that skinny little sleaze-ball Alf. I learned a lot, Grant. I've begun to care about Spiffy. I don't really need a man to complete me anymore. I feel quite whole without one. Although, in time, a relationship with a sensitive, caring, sensual man...well, if that happens, I keep myself open to possibilities."

A little motor switched on inside Grant. "Spiffy. I, too, have been involved in a sort of group therapy. Quite intensely, actually."

"You look better. Healthier. I like you *au naturel.* Those glasses give you a sensitive, intellectual..."

"–They do?" He adjusted his horn-rims, and resisted running his hand over his bald head. The hair touching the back of his collar...when it got longer, he'd put it in a ponytail. *What the hell.*

"Yes. So which therapist do you go to?"

He felt panic. He couldn't tell her he was an alcoholic, so he blurted out his sponsor's name.

"Irwin."

"Dr. Irwin. Don't know him. It is a 'him?'"

"Yes. And yours?"

"To be honest, it isn't a real therapist. I've become a member of O.A."

"Pardon?"

"O.A." She blushed slightly, "Overeaters Anonymous." She breathed deeply, sat up straighter, showing more of her new, improved figure. "It's just wonderful, Grant. I have a sponsor who's become my best friend in the world..."

He was incredulous. "Spiffy, I'll get rigorously honest here–Irwin isn't my therapist, he's my sponsor. I'm in A.A."

"You are?" Her arms flew up again and he thought she might jump down and embrace him. But her hands fell back to her lap. "Grant. How wonderful. I just love Twelve-Step programs. I never knew how to live life before. Actually it's my twelve-step program that's giving me the courage to get a divorce from Alf. The real me wasn't in love with that skinny shank of a man, my true self didn't even exist. I was just flattened. I thought I had to love a very critical, slightly evil man. Like Daddy. Now I know better. Even if I lost all this–"

Grant's stomach flip-flopped as he held up cautioning hand.

"It's not necessary to give up all this, Spiffy. That would be going too far the other way. I'll protect your interests–"

"Thank you, Grant," she said in a soft, little-girl voice. Then she jumped up, Pucci jumped up. She headed for the front door. "I must run. I meet my trainer at my club in half an hour."

Grant felt a jealous twinge. He envisioned some oiled, muscle-bound jock training this wealthy, petite lady.

He removed his butt from the great hand, strode behind her to the door.

"This has been illuminating, Spiffy." And although he groaned inwardly–he hated to work out–he said, "I'd be delighted to try your club."

"Well," she smiled up at him. Her arms went wide. "Since we're both Twelve-steppers." She meant to hug him.

So he bent down gingerly and quickly hugged her, getting only a fleeting impression of a solid little body next to his.

F O U R T E E N

Brit came home to an empty house. Anastasia had returned to Baton Rouge and Saunders was in the barn playing with Colt.

After making a strong pot of decaffeinated Hazelnut coffee, she took a cup to the living room. It was a raw March day and the house had a damp chill. She decided to light a fire, maybe the last of the season. Soon she was curled into an elbow of the sofa, afghan over her knees, Wil at her side, godd purring in her lap. The fire crackled, smelling of pecan-scented wood smoke. She pressed out Lee's phone number.

"Hi," she said when Lee answered.

"Well. Long time."

"Lots going on."

"I figured. So catch me up, gal. I've got two hours before I go sling drinks at Ruby's."

Brit coughed, wanting a cigarette. "Funny, I just spent an hour with a woman about how-not-to-drink, and my best friend's pandering the stuff."

"Whoa now. Your best friend's a writer merely bartending–"

"I know, I know."

"Besides, I don't drink that shit."

"You are a very light drinker, Lee. And I'm not. So. I went to my third meeting of Alcoholics Anonymous."

Silence.

Brit half-expected–hoped?–Lee'd say, "Gee, Brit, you're not an alcoholic." But she didn't. Finally she spoke. "Wow. How was it?"

"Amazing."

"Really."

"I need to talk to you about it."

"Shoot."

"After the meeting, I spent an hour with a woman named Georgie. We had coffee. She's been in A.A. five years. That seems to be considered great success." She half-laughed. "Of course, they think one day without a drink is also quite a success...there's a lot of talk about 'one day at a time.'"

"Ah. Staying in The Now."

"The what?"

"Now. Staying completely in the present moment..."

Brit felt a frisson ripple through her as if her cells understood something she herself did not. *Herself, whatever that was. Was there more to her-self than her constantly racing conscious mind?* Lee continued. "...almost the same as staying in 'one day at a time,' only doing it in smaller increments. Teeny-weeny increments."

"Ah. I shall think on that—"

"No, don't think on it. Clear your mind of all silly thoughts. Meditate on it."

"I don't quite understand you."

"You will. One of these days. What else?"

"Well, now this lady is my sponsor, or she was forty minutes ago," Brit felt Lee smile, "and I'm supposed to call her if I think about having a drink. So she can talk me out of it. Plus she will help me work something called The Twelve Steps."

"Sounds arcane to me. Sure you ain't stumbled into some kinda cult, girl?"

Brit laughed. "It does, doesn't it? But churches all over America talk about The Ten Commandments and no one thinks Methodists and Catholics are cults—"

"Oh yeah?" They laughed.

"I know you jest, Robinet. If you saw the people at these meetings, Lee, they're ordinary. Ordinary men and women. Not freaks or bums or weirdos. Just plain folks. I'm probably the freakiest one there!"

"Oh, you're probably the freakiest one anywhere." They laughed, then Lee said, "Like it?"

"Hum. Never considered that. Let's just say I feel drawn to it. Georgie is a hoot. I bet she was something when she was drinking. Maybe all of them were. And they're funny—they can laugh...oh shit, Lee, I've been so confused lately—"

"Lately?"

"Quit harassing me, punk, I'm an artist, I'm supposed to be out there..."

"Of course, Hon. Don't you pay me no nevah mind. I value your eccentricities. I'm getting all these new ideas reading all those books you bought. I'm learning how to meditate. I am getting in touch with the universe."

"Well, maybe I am too." A sudden remembrance of her experience as she stood on the threshold between studio and living room came to her, but she felt reticent to describe it to Lee. "I guess the universe is a power greater than myself."

"I think so. I'm trying to live in the field of all possibilities, as suggested by Dr. Deepak Chopra."

"The Field of All Possibilities..." She felt something open inside, lightly, like a door slanted ajar. "I just may be discovering the God of my Understanding."

"The God...?"

"A.A. jargon. The way I grasp it is they believe no human power can stop the disease of alcoholism–which is an addicted type of drinking. Only a greater power can do that and the Twelve Steps are a recipe to open yourself to allow spiritual experiences in, via a 'God of One's own Understanding.' This keeps it wide, wide open–Catholics, Jews, Muslims, Methodists, Atheists, Agnostics can all sit in the same room, not kill each other, and talk about their common problem: booze. Georgie was very careful to emphasize to me that it's not a religious program but a spiritual one and you know, until she said that, I never considered that there was a difference."

"So what or who is the God of your understanding?"

"Golly. Don't know yet. I know he–she–it–isn't that Episcopalian one I knew as a kid. Wanting one of my eyes, demanding the slaughter of children, animals as sacrifices," the cat stirred, "and it's not the cat in my lap–although I do think she and you and everyone and everything is infused with some godliness..." She paused. Both were silent. A log fell, Brit smelled wood smoke. "Step Two says: 'Came to believe a Power greater than myself could restore me to sanity.'" Unexpectedly Brit felt her face break up, felt lines and lumps emerge like William Hurt's arm in *Altered States*. Then a scald of tears in her eyes.

"Ever–ever–" she cried for a few moments, the lumps and lines subsided. She wiped her eyes, continued in a quavery voice. "Ever since my damned fiftieth birthday everything has been insane. Somehow I create the insanity that just–just–"

"Writhes around inside you like those paisley snakes you painted?"

"Just like a writer, she puts it into words for me. Maybe I better do another painting: 'The Field of All Possibilities.' When I understand it better."

Lee heard the titling of the phrase. "It'll have to be a big picture."

"Yeah. Haven't done anything big since the horse picture. Did that as an art student. So hurry up reading my books. I need to read them."

"Of course. Meanwhile you can dwell in 'the wisdom of uncertainty,'" and Lee laughed.

"Is that a fancy New Age way of saying I'm confused?"

"Close. 'Confused' sounds a little fearful. No?"

"Yeah. I get it. Wisdom. No fear."

"Right. It's making a choice, from many, many choices. I think choosing uncertainty says the chooser is past fear."

"I'm not there yet. I'm still afraid."

"You and the rest of the world. Have you noticed all those T-shirts and decals on trucks saying 'Have No Fear' or just plain 'No Fear?'"

"Yes."

"Says people are working on it. Getting out of fear."

Brit could hear Lee smoking and it filled her with a yearning, not for a cigarette or a drink, not for something that easily attainable. She breathed deeply.

"Speaking of work," Brit said, "I'm working like crazy. Doing something that's a total departure from my watercolor series."

"Really? Can you tell me about it?"

"Damien will go nuts. Tough. I may starve. Tough. It's what I really want to do. It's a woman-horse thing. It's an old-young thing. It's life-size sculpture."

"Wow. That is a departure from your watercolors. Can you tell me more?"

"I think my body thought of it. The morning of my fiftieth. When I rode Mokhtar in the altogether. The Altogether–isn't that interesting–that an archaic expression for nakedness should be 'In the Altogether.' As if naked, hence vulnerable, we are 'together.'

"Maybe I've got the name for my series. Anyway, an interesting thing about humans and horses is that older people do best with young horses, and younger people do best with older horses. It's a disaster to buy a child a foal, dangerous too. Yes, I know I've ostensibly let Saunders have that colt, but it's this old woman who's doing the serious handling. But a child and a sensible, well-trained older horse is a magical combination. The child has fun but is safe, and an adult who is experienced with horses does well with foals, bringing them along, getting them sensible. And the woman-horse thing, just go to any horse show and it's ninety percent females in the show ring. A few men, very few teenage boys. Boys would like horses better if they had motors."

Lee laughed, Brit continued. "So I'm sculpting an older woman in the altogether with a foal–just happen to have two models real handy–"

"What? You?"

"Yep. Asia took some Polaroids of me yesterday. And I took some of her. She's my young model–I'll pose her with Mokhtar."

"Life size?"

"Life size."

"Bronze?"

"Maybe. Maybe fiberglass. That way I can make them more real and I can paint in real colors, add real hair and manes and tails–but I'll have to be careful my horses don't end up looking like giant Breyer horses, or something for a Mardi Gras float. I'm still at the sketching stage, doing some trial models in clay, small. Of course Mokhtar will be the horse model for whatever I do of Young Woman-Old Stallion. My God. I guess Old Men could have a field day with that–which is their problem. Really. It is their problem, isn't it?"

"Yep. So what's the other part–Old Woman with Young Stallion?

"Ouch. Maybe I need to work on my titles."

"What, find euphemisms for works of art? I hear hypocrisy."

"Right. Art is Truth and the Truth Hurts. This is, I suppose, the Pain of Being an Artist." They laughed.

"Yes. You're right at the core of it, Brit."

"So the series, I guess, is *In The Altogether*. Individual pieces will be called just that–'Old Woman, Young Horse.'"

"Well, if the model is you, that's not strictly true. 'Old Woman' suggests really, really old: shrivelled, shrunken, bent."

"In that condition a person only looks at horses."

"Maybe. Jeez, Brit, I've got to get to work."

"Go. Thanks for listening."

"Anytime. Love you."

"Ditto. Bye."

Brit placed the receiver on the coffee table and stood so suddenly a startled godd rolled from her lap, but landed on her feet. Wil jumped up. Brit ignored them and strode to her studio.

It was three a.m. before she noticed how cramped she was. Her right hand was numb from working clay. The studio walls were push-pinned full of giant char-coal sketches of naked women and horses. In only a few studies were the women actually riding the horses. More often they were running, standing, sitting, reclining, while horses grazed or galloped near them. It was as if the proximity of the horse gave the woman or girl confidence, and symbiotically, the human gave it back to the horse. She thought: *Love can set you free. But whose love?*

Love of true self. Not ego.

Okay.

She brushed hair from her face and saw the tremendous productivity around her.

She'd also roughed out some clay models where the woman's shape flowed into the horse's. In one entirely fanciful study a horse galloped—neck high, tail flagged, naked woman on its back one hand holding mane, the other hand stretched out and holding a hank of tail. Her head was thrown back and her hair flew out like a mane.

She still wasn't sure which of these studies would evolve into life-size sculp-tures. She hadn't quite hit it yet.

On her way to bed she paused in the kitchen and left a note for Saunders. He could toast frozen blueberry waffles for breakfast—she might need to sleep late.

F I F T E E N

Looking after Colt was nothing like he expected.

The little son of a bitch kicked him. Those pointy hind hooves zapped right into his thigh and when he lowered his pants, right now in his bedroom, he saw two bruises—one a half-hoof crescent shape, the other a full blue hoof on his per-fectly white, golden-haired thigh. He stared at the marks. Like tattoos. *The little prick. He'd teach him. Beat the shit out of him.* He jerked up his pants, stomped from his room. He'd show this to Brit. Then she'd want to beat the shit out of that little prick-horse, herself.

She wasn't in the kitchen making supper where he expected her to be. He knew she wasn't up in her bedroom. Her car was here. He stomped back to the living room and saw the dead fire in the fireplace. Dread came over him. Against his will his eyes went to The Door. *No. God, no.* He felt eight years old. Absolutely alone with his bu-bu's...Mother either locked him in or locked him out. Sighing raggedly, reluctant, he crept to The Door. Pressing an ear against it he heard Mozart. She always played Mozart when she worked. He stepped back.

What he should do is just bang on the fucking door, make her open it, he wasn't eight anymore, for Chrissakes. But he couldn't. It was like his right arm was paralyzed. It would not come up and knock on the door.

It wasn't like Brit had spanked him for knocking at The Door. She'd just jerked it open, so suddenly it scared him and yelled, "Saunders. Don't ever bother me while I'm working, unless it's life or death. Are you dying?"

"No." His voice had come out squeaky.

"Well, then, we'll talk later. Juice and milk's in the refrigerator, cookies on the kitchen table." Then she'd yelled again, "So, git!"

He'd got. But so many times he'd wanted to knock on The Door–to show her a black and gold caterpillar undulating over his hand, or ask if he could go fishing in the pond. Once he had. While trying to cast he'd hooked one of her ducks in the eye. Then he'd had to knock. She'd been furious. But they'd gotten to spend the afternoon together, taking the duck to the vet. After that they talked and laughed. That duck had become special and they called it "One-Eyed Jack" until it laid thirteen eggs in a bucket in the barn. Then they called it "One-Eyed Jackie."

"Shit," he said, softly moving away from The Door.

He went back to the kitchen, saw a note he'd missed earlier.

"Plate in fridge, microwave 3 minutes."

God. Just like Rita. And Dad boozing it up every night.

He wanted a Whopper. He was sick of all this healthy food. Maybe Terry was home. He stomped off. By the time he ever got to show her the bruises Colt had made on his leg they'd be fuckin' gone.

His anger flared into rage and turning to the sofa he grabbed a big, black pillow, Colt's present color, which The Maw said would turn white later on. Cursing under his breath, he began punching.

BAM. Right in that little fucker's kisser. In his left hand he held an imaginary lead shank, with his right he smashed his fist into the colt's face, he saw the soft nose flesh flatten, blood spurt, Colt squealing, pulling back, in his mind's eye, he was right with him, crowding him up into a corner–POW. Another to the nose, then a whole series, pow! pow! pow! pow! Blood gushing. *Good.* He stared into the colt's rolling eye. He smashed away at it until it was a swollen, bloody pulp, Colt's squeals turned now to frenzied, pained whinnies–screaming in his mind–she can't hear you now you little shit, she won't help you now, she's working behind–pow! pow! pow!–The Door.

As he pummeled the pillow, muttering, imagining beating the colt, he became aware he was doing this in full view of The Door...and his penis hardened. A seam split on the pillow and rubbery worms of foam flew out. Sobbing he jerked open his jeans and, grabbing his penis, rapidly pulled on it, over and over, let the bitch come out The Door now and, just as he was about to come, he grabbed the pillow, pressed it to his loins, thrusting, thrusting and biting back a moan he ejaculated.

His hips bucked. Then bucked again, like they were jerked by some giant being.

Of course, she didn't come out The Door. He could murder out here, she wouldn't come out The Door.

He fastened his jeans, tidied the room, then sloped out to the barn to mix another bucket of milk replacer.

Imagine. Him. Wet nurse to a fuckin' horse.

SIXTEEN

Brit slept until noon, then woke feeling like a teenager. For the first time she didn't think about having a cigarette. Her mind roamed her studio, the sketches, the clay works. Most exciting was the armature she was building with two by fours, two by twos, the base for a life-size equestrian sculpture. She'd have to invite Damien down soon. If he objected to her doing horses she'd find another agent. This felt right. She hoped Saunders had gotten himself off to school okay, and that made her pause. *This was no good.* She couldn't continue to go on these mad creative sprees. She didn't even like sleeping in. She wanted to be up in the morning, and she wanted nothing to deflect her from her weight workouts and her rides on Mokhtar, who should be coming home any day. While he was gone, she'd filled that hour with walking through her forest.

Well. The big concept was all roughed out. She'd go to work in her studio like any nine to fiver. Get up early, ride, feed her stepson, then to work....

She reached for her phone and dialed Grant's office. Opal put her through.

"Hi, Big Guy," she said, when he answered.

"Brit?"

"Yep."

"You sound happy."

"As I recall, you invited me to lunch."

"Of course."

"I need to come in and stock up on art supplies. Tomorrow."

"*Copelands* on Vets still okay?"

"Fine." *Copelands* was a Yuppie chain of restaurants with Cajun food. The wait staff was young and beautiful.

Hanging up, Brit wondered why she'd agreed to that.

They sat in a cushioned semicircle of plush wine velvet, in a raised area at the restaurant. The place seemed filled with twenty-year-old girls greeting, hostessing, waiting tables, bartending. Brit felt unease. Thoughts like *Christ, you're an old hag,* and, *what man could resist these leggy beauties?* and, *they look so young!* piled up like cumulus clouds in her mind.

Her interior blackboard was a mass of scribbles. Georgie had told her a good way to let go of a negative thought was to imagine writing it on a blackboard, then erasing it. As fast as she erased she had to scribble more. Times like this, a drink would be great, erase everything, including responsibility for her horrible thoughts. She heard Georgie's voice, saw her standing, hands folded like a teacher in front of the blackboard, "Now follow the results of what happens when you have a drink." *Yeah, yeah, yeah.* She gulped ice-water, forced herself to listen to Grant.

"–So I feel pretty good about this case. The guy's got more money than God but he's trying to hide every dime. Imagine, trying to renege on his children. I see these guys all the time. Real deadbeats. I love to nail 'em, find those hidden bank accounts, the flaws in the bookkeeping."

Brit became more relaxed. They were eating an assortment of appetizers, broccoli and cheese balls, stuffed shrimp, crabmeat fritters, fried mushrooms. She nibbled, forgot about a drink, became acutely aware of Grant's hard leg close to hers under the banquette. She was considering slipping off her shoe to do one of those barefoot meanders up under his cuff, when suddenly he stopped talking, grabbed her forearm so tightly it hurt.

"Look at that! You see that?"

Brit followed the line of his eye. Across the room sat a paunchy gray-haired man with a fresh-faced girl, not particularly pretty, but very, very young. She was laughing, eyes adoring. The man looked pleased. Brit thought it must be a daughter or granddaughter, but Grant's hand twitched on her arm.

"Look at that old son of a bitch. What does he have that I don't?" His voice had the density of granite. Brit felt a shiver of fear.

"How does he rate? Why not me?" He took his hand from her arm, unconscious it had been there. His eyes never left the old man, the girl.

Oh, he thinks that old man is dating that young girl. I'm not sure he's right–

Tableware jumped as Grant's fist slammed on the table. "Goddammit! I want to bang young chicks!" Spittle leaped from his mouth.

Brit got still. She gathered her purse, slid her shoe back on, and quietly spoke.

"Do you like having sex with me, Grant?"

Wary. Still staring at the old man and the girl. "Yeah, it's great–"

She pushed the table away.

"Then you have the brain of a dinosaur."

She moved along the plush seat, stood. She held up a hand, thumb and index finger forming a circle.

"Their brains are the size of a–pecan," illustrating the size of their brains. Tall and strong, she was a controlled column of anger.

"They have such tiny brains, Grant, and they got so big, they required an additional one in their tails–like you. You are a dinosaur. You think with your dick."

She turned and strode away. Soft rock lilted around her as she went down four steps past a splashing fountain of copper egrets. Three young hostesses at the entrance jumped back as she whirled into the revolving door.

Grant sat. Brit, wind plastering her purple silk caftan to her body, handed money to a valet. The wind picked up her hair, and it stood high and fanning like a black war helmet. Grant saw her black Jaguar slide up. She was helped into the car by the muscled young valet.

He leaped up, throwing money on the table. The table tipped, he shoved it aside–food, water glasses crashed, but he didn't stop. He vaulted past the old man and the young girl, not seeing them, down the steps, past the gurgling fountain, the hostesses clutching menu's like shields, and shoved open a door yelling–"Brit, Brit, wait, wait"–but now she was in the Jag, it growling to the intersection.

His car? The valet held out a hand.

"Ticket, sir?"

He saw her stopping for a red light at Shoney's. He shoved the claim ticket and twenty bucks at the kid, yelling "Hurry."

The young man darted away, the light changed, the Jag roared away. He turned and charged after the valet. They ran half a block to the parking lot. The valet tried to give back the twenty, but Grant screamed, "Keep it, you fool!"

Jackknifing into the car he banged his funny bone and his knee cap. Eyes stinging in pain, he tore from the lot, slammed on his brakes with a screech–he'd almost sideswiped an oncoming car. Horns. He wrenched the 'Vette onto Vets, cutting in front of a taxi, its driver yelling "Mothafuckah Cocksuckah," jabbing The Finger out his open window at him. The light was green. He fishtailed up Vets toward Causeway Approach Road, darting around other cars, grateful for the first time ever for the 'Vette's great handling. He made the light at Causeway and, signaling, turned left toward the lake. Then he had to stop for a red light. His fingers drummed on the steering wheel. Four cars up he saw her. Two lights up, at the head of the pack. If he could just get to her before she hit the toll booths at the bridge–maybe he could talk to her–the light changed–she squealed off. He lurched forward to the next light. Red. He was in the middle lane, two cars in front, bumper to bumper on both sides. She'd be at the toll in seconds. He watched her reach it, her arm stick out to pay the toll, then she was entering the Causeway. Damn. He wasn't going to pursue her for twenty-four miles across all that water. The light changed. He drove slowly on until the turn at West Esplanade. He'd have to catch I-10 back to St. Charles, to his office on Lee Circle.

Shit.

Better call his sponsor.

S E V E N T E E N
Brit cursed and raged all the across the Causeway.

She slammed into her house and punched out Georgie's number. The machine answered. *Shit!* Then Georgie broke in. There was a high-pitched electronic wail from the machine, silence, and Georgie's husky voice, "Hi."

Brit flung herself onto her sofa and told the whole painful story.

When she finished Georgie said, "Did you have a drink?"

"Nope."

"Then you are a raving success today. So congratulations."

"Thanks. But Georgie–I feel horrible!"

"I'm sure you do. What an insensitive son of a bitch this guy must be. If he was thinking such a thing, to sit there, knowing you just went through some serious heebie-jeebies about your fiftieth birthday–to say such a sick thing–out loud. You don't need to be around such sickness, baby."

Brit felt her system clamor, heartbeat up, pulse elevated. *God knows what her blood pressure would read.*

"You know, the more I play the scene the more I'm convinced that old guy wasn't on a date. He was with his daughter. Or more probably his grand-daughter."

"Probably. That only illustrates how sick your ex is. But we are the creators of our own realities. Your ex sounds very, very middle-age crazy and he tortures himself looking at such odd couples and imagining the worst. This has nothing to do with you, baby, nothing. It's all his shit. Nevertheless you bought into the potential for this."

"You mean I created Grant saying that?"

"Not exactly. But you put yourself in proximity to a man whom you know has problems in this area. You caught the predictable fallout."

"Ouch. Double ouch."

"I only say this to you because I know you're strong. Most women couldn't handle hearing the truth. But you want to get un-sick yourself, and quickly, isn't that what you told me?"

"Yes." Brit sighed. *Why was all this stuff so damned hard?*

"We create situations for ourselves to learn what we need to learn. I notice you went to *Copelands*, not *Galatoire's*, where all the waiters are older men."

"Ouch. So you're saying that unconsciously I wanted Grant to be surrounded by all those young chicks that work at *Copelands*?"

"Are you saying that?"

"Um…"

"Further, my dear Britannia, you have great fear about growing older. When you agreed to go to *Copelands*, only a cut above *Hooter's* in its exploitation of young femininity if you ask me, you put yourself into a situation where you might have the opportunity to learn a life lesson."

"What. That Grant truly is an asshole?"

Georgie laughed. "That too. But you want to learn to handle this getting older stuff. You know, when you sort it all out, go through all the pain—willingly, not resistingly—you'll break through. There is another side to this. You will break though and on the other side you'll find you feel just fine about you, your true self. Your true self is ageless, eternal. It is the divine spark within us, that place nothing can hurt."

Brit began to cry.

"I know. I know it's hard. But you can do it. You want to be healthy and whole and connected to your Higher Power. I know you do. That's why it's so exciting for me to have you as a sponsee." She lowered her voice. "And you know, when you make the breakthrough–"

Brit spoke. "Georgie. I already made it once. Just before I got sober. I was walking through the doorway of my studio when wham! I got this feeling that–well, that I was part of everything–"

"How did it feel?"

"Wonderful. Glorious. I want to feel that way all the time."

"And you can. That's why you're doing this work. Your ego, the false self in you, is angry. It wants–it demands–Grant stop looking at younger women and appreciate you. It tells you if you just change him, stop him from looking at 'young chicks,' then all will be well. But that's his sickness, his issue. Your sickness is your reaction to his action, the pain, the hurt, the rejection you feel. You can't change him, but you can change you–your reaction. You can see what your reaction means. Does it spiral down into 'I'm too old, I'm afraid, no man will ever love me again?' Is that what this is really all about?"

"Shit. Yeah. Dammit!" She wanted a cigarette.

Georgie, softly, "Good girl. Great courage. Now that you've found out what's really going on, now you can change how you perceive this young-old thing. Then, no matter what he does, no matter how many women he ogles, it won't matter to you. You just won't care."

A wail. "But that's so hard! I feel so angry!"

"Sure you do. But try and get past that. Beyond is peace, great peace, and love and joy and harmony. You'll be free, because you've done your job. You will appreciate you. And that's all that matters. It doesn't matter what anyone else thinks of you. You are God's child and deep down you are perfect and ageless. That's it."

"But I feel awful."

"Hey. The old ego, which has served you for many years, is in its death throes. No wonder you feel so awful. Part of you is dying."

"What do I do?"

"Hang on. Don't drink. Stay with these feelings. Let them happen to you. Resisting them only makes them hurt more. Just observe yourself having these feelings, let them pass on through. Waft away. They won't kill you."

Brit groaned. "Sez you."

"I know it feels like they might. I've been where you are, Brit. I promise they will not kill you. And then, soon, they will exhaust themselves and you will know, and understand yourself, like you never have before."

Brit was crying again.

"The truth is, Brit, you don't ever have to feel alone again. You are connected to the God of your understanding. Remember, that part of you is ageless. All these feelings now are necessary. Without alcohol and nicotine to block them, here they are. They've been inside you all the time, but booze kept you numbed and stuck. It kept you from releasing, from getting free. But they'll diminish, and then you will discover how connected you are. How perfect you are."

"Thank you, Georgie."

"Don't thank me. Thank yourself. I'm proud of you. Most people would swallow the humiliation dished out by this sick man, pretend nothing was wrong, and feel such resentment they'd end up with cancer or something. It takes courage to face these things. And you've got it."

"Thanks again, Georgie."

"You okay?'

She wiped her wet face with a hand. "I guess. Yes. I'm okay. Hey. I sure am glad I picked a far-out metaphysical-therapist for my A.A. sponsor."

"Aha. She's coming alive. I hear sarcasm. Nobody sarcastic ever committed suicide. Darn. I have an appointment. See you at the meeting tonight?"

"Yes. Thank you, Georgie. You're wonderful."

"Piffle."

They hung up. Brit dragged herself from the sofa, heart still hammering in her chest. Her face was hot, but not from a hot flash. Her head felt drilled by metal bits. Lee's voice came in her mind, the tarot. Moving rapidly she found the cards and opened the book to the page about the Shaman.

"I am alone in the universe; no one else can share this experience.

For a brief moment, I can see everything clearly and my life is changed."

She just had to sit down, and cry some more.

EIGHTEEN

Late June, but with heat like August, Brit dismounted and led a sweating Mokhtar into the barn, where she stripped off his saddle and bridle. Every time Grant entered her mind she wrote his name on a blackboard and erased it. She heard Georgie's voice: "You don't erase Grant, you erase your reaction to younger women." She'd been doing this over and over. Her heart still pounded in her chest, she hadn't been sleeping well, but she knew she had to stick to her routine. So she rode.

While Mokhtar panted beside her, again she wrote "younger women," and again erased. Then she backed the horse into the grooming bay. Sick-making thoughts momentarily gone, she gently hosed him down. She turned him out on the plateau with Colt and made for the house.

A new nervous feeling began. Damien would arrive this evening for his first look at her series, *In the Altogether*. She sat in the striped divan, oblivious to the plastic skeleton behind her shoulder, and sipped iced coffee.

She'd refused to tell him what she was working on.

She was going to A.A. meetings regularly, often toting Saunders along so he could attend Ala-Teen. Asia had landed a summer work-study course at the San Diego Zoo but she was coming home for the Fourth. Saunders was the difficulty. He seemed more sullen. Allowing him to have Colt–he needed a proper name but Saunders didn't seem interested–hadn't worked. She wondered if he was depressed, clinically, but when she suggested he resume his therapy, he snarled at her. He wanted to spend a few days in the city with his dad. She let him go.

She hadn't spoken with Grant since the bang young chicks incident, but she'd gotten a letter from Scottie, dated six weeks after he'd checked into Bowling Green. It lay on the table before her. She picked it up, read it again.

Dear Brit,

I write hoping you are well and happy. I'm doing well. I've 'graduated' from Bowling Green, am back in my apartment but find I need to attend either a Narcotics or Cocaine Anonymous meeting every day. If I can't find one of those, I go to A.A.

Brit, I was insane to do anything to jeopardize our relationship. Part of me still wants to whine–'the drugs made me do it,' because that's true–but I made the decision to take the drugs.

I've taken a leave of absence from work and plan to do some traveling. Just me and my Nikon. National Geographic says they'll consider my stuff.

I've also taken a vow of celibacy. I think it's the only way I can get clear. Really clear.

If you don't object, I'd like to send postcards occasionally.

Perhaps this is not appropriate, but I care for you. Very much.

Love,

Scott.

She hadn't responded, but had received a postcard from Tierra del Fuego, then another from Ecuador. A vow of celibacy? She hadn't taken one, but she hadn't had sex since the night Saunders got those girls drunk. Sometimes she missed it, but not enough to apologize for being older or risk taking up with another alco-holic-drug addict.

If Lee was right, since more than six weeks had passed, she'd reverted to vir-gin status, or, as Georgie put it, "You're a re-born virgin!"

NINETEEN
The first thing Damien said when he walked through front door was, "Darling! You've lost weight!"

They hugged, then he held her away from him, eyeing her. She was dressed in black leggings and a scarlet silk blouse.

"You're skin looks tight and fresh, your eye baggage is gone. If I didn't know you've been working non-stop, I'd swear you had a little surgical assistance." He stepped back further and, holding one of her hands, slowly rotated her. "You are thinner. Such flat abs...such buns of steel..." He wolf-whistled. "Tell me your secrets."

She laughed. "Get a horse!"

"Ah. Riding Mokhtar again, are we?"

"Six days a week, and I've gained ten pounds, not lost them. I take a ton of vitamins, eat like a weight-lifting rabbit, and I've given up booze, cigarettes, caf-feine, and sex."

She leaned toward him, wanting his approval.

"Good grief. Haven't you gone too far?"

"Only the booze, nicotine and caffeine were conscious choices. I'd still be plotzing my ex if he weren't so middle-aged crazy. So maybe his insanity is my shield against a nowhere relationship."

"But what about that lovely blond man...the photographer? Eyes to swim in?"

"Scott." She walked to the kitchen, Damien behind, and made a tray with tall glasses of ice and Perrier. He moved to take it from her but she shrugged him away, smiling. "I'm strong. Besides riding, I also work out with weights. Day, I love it. Also, I learned to meditate."

"Oh me too darling. Everyone in the city is. Plus they're all popping pine bark, grape seed...fighting those free radicals."

"So I'm in, even though I live so far out." They smiled.

She sat and drank the sparkling water. Glass in hand, Damien roamed her living room, and she looked him over, her agent and friend for twenty years, he was forty-five. Tonight he was dressed in a gray silk suit over a collarless, navy cotton shirt. He had a male model's sculpted face, and looking at it, Brit could sense a thumb pressing into clay just there to form eye sockets, then pressing both thumbs upwards to make the high, smooth forehead, then all the fingers molding the nose that in profile had a hint of the shape of a seagull's wing. He had full, articulated lips, and a chin that jutted then merged with a deep, planed jaw. His silver hair had grayed-out when he was thirty and now curled to his shoulders. Damien was beautiful.

His dark brown eyes returned to her.

"So. When may I penetrate The Door?"

"Whenever you're ready." He placed his empty glass on the coffee table with a clink. Then he took one of her hands, pulled her to her feet, brought her close to him. His hand felt wonderful on the silk of her shirt against her newly-firm back. She tilted her head up and lightly he kissed her lips.

"Britannia, my darling, you look good, you feel good..."

"Flatter me now, Damien, but when you see what I've wrought..."

"Not rot, I'm certain darling. I'm excited. I love surprises."

Brit threw open The Door, they stepped inside the studio. Damien gasped.

Rising above his head were the hooves of a life-size silver-white stallion. He walked around it. A naked woman was astride the horse, head thrown back, a distant look on her face. She, the horse, looked absolutely real. But looking at it gave him a chill. The woman was silvered and dappled, exactly like the horse.

Damien continued to move around the sculpture.

Woman?–no, more a girl–high-set small breasts, boyish buttocks, thin thighs sloping around the horse's back, girlish feet dangling. Even her white face was the color of the horse, her lips slate-gray like his lips and muzzle. The horse had black legs, mane, and tail. The girl's black hair hung down her back. Real hair, like the mane and tail of the horse. The girl's eyes had no whites, matching the eyes of the horse. Both had almond-shaped, brown-black eyes. Her eyebrows were gray, eyelashes black.

He shuddered. It was eerie.

He stopped before a sketch of a grazing horse with a naked young woman stretched out casually on the horse's back. Her head rested on the horse's croup, her long hair fell, mingling with the horse's tail. One bare foot pressed to the base of the horse's neck, the other up, crossed over her bent knee. One slender hand dangled, the other held a grass stem which she delicately chewed. Her back curved down into the slightly swayed back of the old stallion.

For a long time he stood gazing at the sketch, the insouciance of the girl and the horse seeming to relax his tensed shoulders. Brit watched them flex, then lower.

He widened his circle, to take in clay and wax models of horses and women. The walls were papered with charcoal sketches. He wandered, never looking back at Britannia.

Then on to her other life-size work.

She barely breathed, her blood felt halted in her arteries.

He looked at another rearing horse carrying a naked woman, but this woman's breasts had a slight sag, perceptible wattling under her chin, her belly pooched, wrinkles above her knees. He was walking around the piece now. Brit knew he was seeing the dimpled ass above the broad smooth buttocks of the young stallion.

She was flesh-colored, with long full auburn hair, magnificent, as was the horse, whose flesh matched hers. He was human-skinned like his rider, his mane and tail were full and auburn, matching hers. Her golden brown eyes mirrored his, even to the whites of his eyes. His mouth was open, lips curled back as he emitted a silent, stallion scream. Hers too, as if in laughter. The two seemed alive, their flesh looked warm, their energy real.

"Oh my God," breathed Damien, staring, mesmerized.

Brit felt a trickle, blood daring to flow. But was he seeing it as Breyer horses and Barbie Dolls—or Art?

Damien stepped to the front of the sculpture. Slowly he turned, looked over the great statue before him and, clasping his hands, raised his arms high over his head. His smile flashed white and wide. "Hurrah!" His arms flew wider as he rushed at her crying, "Madam, you surpass yourself."

Brit's blood hesitated, then flowed free. Thrillingly, goosebumps coursed over her body. Damien reached her, swept her high, twirled her around. Grinning, hands on his shoulders, she looked down at him.

"You like it."

He laughed, whirling her around and around. "Baby, it's crazy. It's wild. It's camp. It's surreal. It will sell like hotcakes. This stuff is—unbelievable! I want to schedule a show for November."

"Oh no, Damien. I've only got two pieces finished."

He set her down and gestured at the rearing horse figures, "Those are not for sale. They will be the centerpieces. What will be for sale are your sketches, your models—you'll have time to fire the clay, bronze the waxes..."

She folded her arms. "Gosh. I don't know. I don't like showing just anyone my scribblings and fumblings."

"That's exactly it. Darling, one penetrates the core of the artistic experience. We don't have to wait till you're dead to market your sketches! Besides, your 'scribblings' are beautiful studies that flow, that are alive..." He turned to the sketch of girl lying on the horse's back, "The trust between girl and horse is awesome, the balls they each have, yet they're so saucy, so impertinent. So together. So 'Altogether.'"

He laughed and did a little soft shoe. "Love your title. *In the Altogether*. Naked, revealed, a woman or girl and their horses, so together. Love it. Maybe it never needs to go beyond this state, this magnificent sketch. Framed of course, very casually. Perhaps matted with that feed sack material—"

"Burlap?"

"Yes! Yes! Perhaps even a suggestion of the red and blue ink, faded of course, of such and such feed company..."

"Feed comes in paper sacks nowadays, Damien."

He waved a hand. "No matter...perhaps for the show we strew the gallery with hay—straw—oats—little brown horse apples..."

Brit cut in, "You're a frustrated set designer, Day."

"That's true. Also a frustrated artist." He sighed. "Those that can't—sell." She smiled.

He went on. "Could you sculpt some? Bronze, of course."

"Horseshit, Day!" They laughed. Damien's face grew serious.

"You know, maybe, that's not a bad idea..."

"No way."

"Okay. Okay. We don't want to degenerate into some drugstore cowgirl thing..."

"You don't think it's Breyer horse/Barbie doll—Mardi Gras?"

He swished a hand. "Mardi Gras? You're too close to it. Most of the world's never even seen it. And your other fears? Absolutely not. Darling, never say these words again."

Brit suddenly sat down on the red velvet couch. "Well, thank God. I was so nervous you wouldn't like it. An equine thing and all. If I was a smoker I'd have one right now."

"Darling, it's original. Vulnerable, naked women with naked horses are not in the realm of the usual horse pictures, horse bronzes. Especially when so melded with their horses, so at one with them–they become of the horse, the horse is of them." He paused by a clay model. "This woman is real, those rolls on her belly, the breasts, the sad, wistful sag, the slight wrinkling at the elbow, the knee, how I love her, how powerful she is, sitting there on her turf, loving this baby stallion. We might even hang your youthful folly somewhere. I'd also like some photos of you riding that old stallion of yours–"

"God no, Day, that's ridiculous."

"Darling, not really. There is great interest in how the creative process operates–not that pictures of the artist really reveal anything, but people think so. They think they're getting the inside spiffy."

"Well, if I did it, I'd wear clothes."

"Really? Well, I suppose I'll have to settle for that." He smiled. "You mean you'll do it?"

She shrugged. "You should see the numbers in my bank account." She frowned. "Too much intrusion of the Self, Day. It would be marketing me instead of what I create."

"Balderdash. You are what you create. Think of it as the same as the author's photo on the back of the book." He pursed sculpted lips. "Now that's something I hadn't thought of. The photos of you and your horse could also be for sale..."

"No. Stop. Scratch that."

"Britannia, darling. Let's adjust the perspective here. Okay, I promise those photos won't be for sale. I'll mount them in a little section: *The Artist Explores her Subject.* Something like that. Just a few–dramatically, beautifully shot. I'll need one anyway for the catalog."

"Okay."

"Let's call up that lovely young man of yours–the photographer–what's his name?"

"Scott. Last I heard he's in Peru."

"Drat. Well. I'll find someone. Maybe for the show we can have you ride up, escorted by New York's finest mounties, you in some sort of black riding ensemble in those sexy black boots–a cape..." Damien's eyes danced–he'd taken off his jacket, his arms and hands moved as he sculpted in air his growing plans for her opening.

"New York will love it. Oh, some critics will rant, call it camp, some asshole will say Mardi Gras Floats to New York, but that'll only get more people out. They'll come, they'll gape, they'll love it. They will buy! I'll get TV coverage of course. CNN, I hope."

He stopped beside the rearing horse, laid a hand on the dappled rump. "No. Definitely not. This piece is not for sale. But next year it will be, when you complete more spectacular pieces–" he cocked his noble brow at her, nostrils flaring–really an impossible face she thought, "you'll want to continue this series?"

"Oh yes, Day! I love it. I've wanted to draw and sculpt horses ever since I was three years old. And women, young and beautiful, old and beautiful. I want to change society's perception of how an older woman really looks naked. At least try to. We are still beautiful. At least parts of us are beautiful." She sighed happily. She had the feeling back, the feeling of The Experience. She floated. "I could continue this forever...." She hesitated. "At least that's how I feel right now. If it changes, it changes. I can change it anytime I want to, as many times as I want to. No guilt!"

"*Oui*, cherie." Damien came close, slid his arm around her again. He spoke into her hair, "You are beautiful." They stood under the pawing hooves. Damien shivered and hugged her closer. "What *cajones* you hung on that beast!"

P _a_ _r_ _t_ $\mathcal{F}$ _o_ _u_ _r_

IMPOSSIBLE LOYALTIES

...Middle Age
Home of lost causes and forsaken beliefs and
Unpopular names and impossible loyalties!
— *Matthew Arnold*

O N E

"You said you've gained ten pounds?"

It was early the next morning. Britannia and Damien sat out on her covered verandah. A crape myrtle tree with mauve flowers grew near a pillar behind them. Honey bees glided in, out, of the blooms. They drank rich, black chicory coffee which Britannia had seasoned with brown sugar and cinnamon. Damien picked at a silver basket of Pontchatoula strawberries. Brit swallowed a mouthful of Rita's cheese grits.

"Yep."

"But, Brit. You look thinner."

"Glad you think so."

"What did you do?"

She set her fork down. "I ride six days a week. I work out with weights. I eat raw fruits and vegetables every day. I'm almost a vegetarian. I take vitamins and herbs. I also read a lot of books and got a new slant on this age thing. Day! No one has to get old. We stop doing things and seize up like rusty old engines. If I keep doing things, I won't rust. Deepak Chopra says nothing beats resistance training, studies show, et cetera. So. Muscle weighs more than fat. So I gained weight."

"Looks excellent, dear."

"I feel better. Still miss smoking. Don't miss booze. I'm even handling no sex. I was probably as addicted to it as I was to nicotine and alcohol."

"You don't miss that blond photographer?"

"Hardly think about him. Why bother? He's roaming the world becoming a famous photographer–sober and clean–hopefully. With women flinging themselves at him. I'm the old crone at home." She pushed a strand of hair from her face, grimaced. "But I do miss Grant–I have dreams about him…I just wish that stupid son of a bitch would grow up, so he and I could be together. It would be so good for Saunders and Anastasia. We could be a family, you know?" She felt like crying.

"And nice and comfortable for Brit, too, no? Great big hunk of man at your side." Damien's voice was kind. He touched her hand. "And no more of these put-downs, hear? I love you. And when you say horrible lies about yourself it hurts me. It hurts me inside." She saw his strain not to cry. Something inside her thrashed around, then staggered upright, like a newborn foal struggling to its feet.

"Really, Day?" That someone should feel pain over her derogatory comments about herself! She smiled at him. "Thanks, Damien." Then she gazed toward the plateau.

"I need to say more about Grant. I think I'm yearning for his potential, not who's really there. Who's really there is a man who wants to bang young chicks." She set her fork down with a little bang. Their eyes met; each gave a rueful laugh. She continued, "Georgie's taught me there's only one person I can change and that's me. So with Grant, I guess I'm having the hots for an illusion. Silly as hell, isn't it?" The urge to cry was gone, leaving a bittersweet residue.

"Sweetie. He may come around."

They sat in the warming air listening to the fecund hum of insects. Brit watched a chameleon on a crape myrtle cluster attempting to turn purple. Once one had gotten into her kitchen sink and tried to turn the color of stainless steel. Any change was difficult, she mused, even for chameleons.

In the distance Mokhtar and Colt grazed side by side, tails idly swishing. From the verandah they looked white and black.

"He may. Meanwhile I have to grow out of this lapse into yearning."

"You'll get there because you are a magnificent, beautiful, sensitive, intelligent woman. Got that, Darling?"

"Got it!" They leaned across the strawberries, and kissed cheeks. Brit sat back.

"I have something I'd like to run past you." She patted under her chin. "I can't decide whether to age naturally–part of me thinks an artist should, like Georgia

O'Keefe. Or have a little surgery, you know? I think now of Goldie Hawn. On me, just the chin, the eyes? I hate the idea of being a wrinkled, gray-haired crone. I can't believe Germaine Greer–such a beautiful woman–made that choice. Gray and wrinkled looks angry. Don't you think?"

"That's your answer, then."

"But it doesn't seem honorable..."

"Maori tattoo themselves–hell, everyone's getting tattoos now, and piercing every body part they've got. Noses, tongues, belly buttons, labia, penises–"

"Penises?"

"Darling, I heard about some young man, in a rock band I think, had a ring in his penis. Got loaded on God-knows-what designer drug, tied a chair to the ring, tried to pick it up. With his dick!" They shrieked in horrified laughter. "Darling. Blood all over. Flashing lights, ambulance, the whole scene."

"So what happened–did he jerk it off?"

Day giggled. "Pun intended? Oh no, Sweetie. He stopped as soon as he felt the first little rip." Smiling, shuddering, they sipped coffee. "And you're worried about a few nips and tucks? One's body and face are an art form. Think of your body as your personal sculpting project. After all, you've reshaped it with all this exercise, good food. You wouldn't hesitate to use a knife where it was needed on one of your clay sculptures. So there. Think of your body as yet another canvas, or fresh lump of clay. You love beauty. Keeping and making yourself beautiful can only make those who see you feel a little happiness. Your outer beauty reflects your inner beauty. It doesn't have to become obsessive, darling. There can be acceptance of it. I think they do a lot with lasers now. And keep taking your herbal antioxidants, all that stuff, and, down here in the tropics, a good sun block. Like a good girl."

Brit was nodding her head. "In other words, I owe it to myself and society to stay as fit, healthy and–" She stopped, toyed with a strawberry. Thought. Raised her head. "I've gone as far as I can in fixing myself with diet, exercise, vitamins, all that...yet still I have this chin wattle," she pulled at a tag of skin under her chin, "some extra skin on my belly–having Asia created space I no longer need... so maybe just minimalist nips, tucks...?"

"No guilt there, Darling."

"You sure?"

"I am. But are you? I've read all those wonderful books, too, dear. I meditate every day now."

"Guess I have some doubt. Some guilt. I'm working very hard to change me, inside, too. And it fucking hurts, Day. I am chiseling away at some great marble block labeled, 'Britannia to Be,' hammering away ego, excessive neediness, all my addictive behaviors. And it's like that damn block of marble is alive and with every chisel stroke, every hammer blow, there is serious pain."

"What a glorious metaphor."

"I read it somewhere."

"Nevertheless, it's good. Try this. It's not as though you're not taking care of this temple, your body. You've worked miracles. But our concept of 'age' is ridiculous. We both know that. But, Darling," he leaned toward her, took her worried face in his hands, eyes like brown agates holding hers, "the rest of society doesn't know this! The truth is, all any of us has is 'NOW.' The past, the future, they're all illusion. Gone or not here–what did I hear once? 'memory is just an active imagination?'" Brit grinned, and he let his hands slide from her face, but he took hold of her hands, long, beautiful, but with slightly oversized knuckles. His thumbs rubbed the knuckles as though they were made of soft gold. "And, of course, the future never comes. Did you ever wake up 'tomorrow?' No. You always wake up 'today.'"

"You're sounding like my A.A. sponsor Georgie."

"I'd like to meet her."

"You will."

"I have more, Brit. This 'Now' thing. All we've really got is the present moment. Right now. We're only really alive right now. That's all anyone's got. We're all the same age! Sixteen or sixty we've all only got 'Now.'" He sat back abruptly. His face twisted, *some inner pain*, thought Brit? Suddenly he slammed his fist onto the table. Silverware clattered. A bumblebee zoomed away as he laughed ironically. He clasped his hands behind his head, fixed his glittering brown eyes on her again. "The sad thing is, few grasp this. So. For the zillions who don't, it behooves you to look your very best–"

"Now you sound like Viola."

He grinned. "I like Viola. Quit changing the subject. I feel that those of us who are in the midst of grasping these eternal truths have a responsibility, which is: Pass it along, so other people can get out of the mire of their thinking and get happy. Sometimes the power of physical beauty attracts people. Then if that physical beauty is illuminated by great spiritual truth, then after you've attracted them, you may get the glorious opportunity to share this truth with them." He leaned forward, elbows on knees. Brit caught the tang of his cologne. "Like this bee to the strawberries, to recycle an old cliché."

"You are your own self-portrait. How much you love yourself is displayed to the world–the ignorant miserable world–by your face, your body. Now if you were presenting yourself to be sliced and diced without all this inner work, then you'd be in error, and you'd end up with one of those mask-like faces, expressionless, dead, the face of someone seeking happiness by making changes on the outside. That always backfires. After the last operation, what are they left with? The emptiness of themselves and it shows in their vacant faces. The new car smell always wears off." He stared off unseeing at the pond, the willow weeping over it, some ancient hurt faint in the grooves of his face, like an old mask dissolving. "So they either chase the next fix, or, maybe they start to search within, where the real joy lies. You're not doing that. You're working from the inside out."

Eyes down, she twiddled the strawberry, fingertips reddening. Suddenly a gush, a redness like a menstrual period but rising, not leaving, swelled through her, pushing out guilt, fear, out, out, out. White, clean light followed, filled her, her eyes teared. She looked up at Damien, not knowing her face glowed.

"I'll do it."

He smiled. "Only if you're completely comfortable."

"Comfortable? I'm thrilled. I–I feel–Day. Gosh. Suddenly I love myself. And you. And that tree and…the pond…everything…"

"Brit. You've changed so much."

"Really?"

"Really."

"You see a difference?"

"Enormous."

"Thank you. I'm also working on giving up the need for approval, as suggested by Dr. Deepak. Obviously, I'm not there yet."

"You're doing great."

She pushed cold grits away. Listened to birdsong. A mockingbird in the magenta buds of another crape myrtle gave a credible imitation of a robin. She'd loved robins when she was little in Ohio. The Deep South was a mere pit stop during their migrations, yet apparently long enough for mockingbirds to learn their song.

She ate a fat strawberry and heard Georgie's voice…"all your needs supplied…" She even had mockingbirds to sing robins' songs to her.

She pulled herself out of reverie.

"Damien, you are probably the most physically perfect human being I've ever seen, yet you haven't a shred of vanity. How come?"

She waved another bee away from the strawberries.

Damien crossed his legs, looked past her to the pillar, the purple crape myrtle.

"Because my mother loved me. She thought I was perfect. She never criticized me. She wasn't even horrified I was gay, would never make her a grandmother." He pointed a strawberry at her. "Your mother criticized you. Too tall, too bohemian, too artistic. So your life journey, you should pardon an over-worked expression, is all about learning to love yourself, never mind what mama said."

"And my men?"

"Well, you're real attracted to alcoholics, Darling. I understand your vanished papa was an alcoholic."

"Yes. So simple from the outside, isn't it? Yet when all this stuff is churning around inside me...it's hell to sort out...One other thing, Dr. Damien."

He was pouring coffee. "Yes?"

"I feel scared. About sex. I read all this stuff about post-menopausal women 'drying up,' 'walls thinning...'"

He cocked his brow at her. "Have you dried up, Prunella?"

She swatted at him. "No! Of course, the only sex I've had in about four months is me, myself, and I."

"So. Are you dried up?"

"No."

"So there."

"But—"

"Sweetie. Don't worry about something that may never happen. You know you can't believe everything you read. And sometimes things happen because we read them. Besides, why did God invent K-Y Jelly? I could even comment on 'thin walls' in another part of humanity's anatomy, but I shall leave it up to your artist's imagination."

Oh, she thought. *Thin walls. Rectum.* Gay men didn't feel "less" because a lubricant had to be used for sex.

He stared out at the pasture, pointed a finger. "Tell me this—why do you think that black colt is going to turn white?"

"Because he has white hairs above his eye. It's gradual. First he'll turn steel gray, then his body will lighten, his legs, mane, and tail will stay black–very dramatic. He'll have gray-black dapples over his rump and shoulders–"

"Like your sculpture."

"Yes. Then he'll lighten, going through several shades of gray, then he'll be white."

Suddenly the colt's head flew up, he galloped away. Mokhtar raised his head, looked around for a threat, then returned to grazing.

Damien smiled at the colt's antic. "There's a metaphor there, black-white, shades of gray, but damned if I get it."

"Yes. But practically, these are desert horses. We all know it's better to wear white in the desert so, somehow, brown, black, and red horses taught their genes to lighten their coat color. It's a survival thing."

"Ah. So those who experience shades of gray are best at survival?"

The doorbell rang.

Saying, "I suppose so," Brit got up, walked around to the front of the house. A small trim woman in heels and a black suit was ringing her doorbell. Brit stared for a moment, then realized it was her mother. Colt had spooked at her arrival.

"Mother?"

Viola gasped, jumped back from the door, hand over heart.

"Britannia. Such a fright." Even though she'd lived in Ohio all her life she'd acquired a slight British accent. Then she swooped toward her daughter, they embraced, then stood apart.

"Darling. I'm sorry to barge in like this but–" She began to weep.

"Mom. What is it?" Viola groped in a black handbag and brought forth a lace hanky. Britannia expected it to have a black edge, but it was white. Viola dabbed at her carefully made-up eyes. Behind her rested a set of beige Vuitton luggage.

"Mom. What's wrong? Elizabeth?" Inarticulate with tears, Viola shook her head. "Victoria?" More head shaking. Dabbing.

"Nunan?"

Viola wailed and threw herself into her daughter's arms.

"Mom. What's wrong with Nunan?" She looked around the porch, the empty drive. Where was Nunan? She stood her mother up. "Is he sick?" More head shaking.

"Is he here?"

Dab. "No."

"No. Not here," said Brit. "In a hospital?"

Mute, a torrent down Viola's face.

"Mom. Please. Tell me. Is he alive?"

Sobbing, but she spoke. "Yes." Inhaling in stages: huh huh huh. Sniff. "But he's furious with me." A great heave of a breath. "Our marriage could end."

"Why, Mom? Nunan adores you."

Fresh sobs. "I know. He did, didn't he? And I had to go and ruin everything."

"Ruin? How?"

"I–I–I–had an affair with Samuel Peterson and–his wife caught us in bed." Sob.

Brit's eyes widened. "Say that again, please."

Viola pulled down her natty jacket and gently pressed tissue under her bagless eyes. Her makeup, Brit saw, was still perfect. Must be waterproof mascara: Viola always planned ahead.

With a settling sniff, Viola repeated, "I had an affair with Sam Peterson and his wife caught us." Matter-of-fact.

Brit had to fight hard not to laugh. She knew Sam–he'd been involved in real estate deals with Nunan. Her seventy-four-year old mother was having an affair–HAVING SEX!–with Sam Peterson, a man ten years younger? And here she was fifty, worrying about the female equivalent of getting it up?

Viola was crying again. "Bird is such a biddie. She'll tell everyone and I won't be able to appear at The Club anymore. Ever." Sob. "Ever again." Her voice rose. "I'll miss my tennis and my golf and my...SWIMMING." "Swimming" was a soprano shriek.

Brit heard footsteps. Then Damien had his arms around both women.

Viola's eyes widened, "Damien, you're here?"

"Vi-darling. It's perfectly okay. I heard all. All is safe with me."

"I know, but–"

"No buts. Come have some delicious coffee and some luscious berries. Tell us the whole story." He and Brit turned Viola and began walking her around the verandah to the table. Their eyes met over her head and Damien smiled; Brit smile-grimaced back, then she sniggered, stifling it, but her ribcage shook.

Viola, "Britannia! Are you laughing at me?"

"No, Mother."

"It's not funny." They seated her, poured her a coffee. "Nunan may divorce me, and then where will I be?" She sipped. "And The Club..." Her wide blue eyes, etched with surgical eyeliner, teared again.

"But, Mother. How does Nunan know?"

"Oh, that old bitch Bird will tell him."

"But you don't know she has."

"I had to get away from there. I couldn't bear the ridicule, the rejection..."

"But Mom, how can he be furious–if he doesn't know?"

Again, Viola was inarticulate with tears, or, Brit thought, *easing into her usual denial. Got to mean she's getting over this.*

Brit moved her chair around and put an arm around her mother's shoulders. Every now and then her eyes met Damien's and they fought laughter, Brit thinking, *my almost seventy-five-year-old mother is upset over her affair with a man a decade younger, and all I want to ask is: "Did you have to use K-Y Jelly, Mom?"*

"Maybe Nunan doesn't know, Mother. Maybe Bird won't tell him."

"She was furious–there we were, quite starkers, quite involved–she was in the doorway of the bedroom–" Brit saw her mother's tilted reality was back in action. If Viola thought something, or imputed feelings and actions to others, it was inconceivable they weren't real.

"–whose bedroom?"

"Hers–Sam's."

"Mom. Sam is a rich man. Why weren't you at a hotel?"

"I don't know. I dropped by to tell Sam it was over, I couldn't keep carrying on–" She looked straight into her daughter's eyes. "He's only a so-so lover–no comparison to Nunan before he drank so much–" Brit thought, *that's the first time she's ever spoken to me as if I were an adult.* "But supposedly Birdie had gone to her sister's in Minneapolis, so the house was empty, one thing led to another...and there we were in Birdie's king-size bed with that awful chintzy cabbage-rose canopy..." Her head was shaking, "That woman uses way too much potpourri." She inhaled in little, shaky, feminine uh, uh, uh's.

"So there was Birdie, screaming from the doorway. Oh! I felt so humiliated! It was awful. I am so stupid. So fucking stupid." First time Brit ever heard her mother say "fuck." Viola shot her a look. "I know all those words. I just choose not to use them." She took a breath. Normally.

"So fucking stupid...there is a pun there and it is intended."

Brit thinking: *Well so much for worrying about my sexual viability, next?* The inner voice piped up, *so why worry at all?*

Shut up, she answered.

Viola looked good, Brit saw, eyeing her in a newly critical way. Her cosmetic surgeries were subtle. Her heart-shaped face with its large blue eyes had lines, but no sags. Her hair, once as dark as Britannia's, had grayed out and was now a peachy blonde. A youthening effect. Her figure was also yclept, bosom high and firm-looking, waist nipped in attractively under the fitted black suit. Viola crossed her legs, and Brit saw smooth, firm calves.

"You look good, Mother. No wonder Sam made a run at you."

"Good! You look fantastic, Viola." Damien enthusiastically interjected.

Coyly, Viola looked at them. "He's been making a run at me for fifteen years. I can't imagine why I succumbed." She fisted her smooth, un-liver-spotted hands and diamonds flashed. "Oh! Oh! Oh! This ruins our trip to England this fall!" She sighed. "Christmas in London. Imagine...the English invented Christmas as we know it."

"I hadn't thought–but I suppose they did."

"Harrods...the theatre...and I never tire of seeing the jewels in The Tower."

"Drink some coffee, Mother."

As Viola lifted the cup to her lips the phone began to ring. She paused, "If that's Nunan tell him I'm not here yet."

Brit had risen. "He knows you came here?"

"Of course. I left a note on the fridge." Damien caught Brit's eye behind Viola's head and they grinned. Brit threw her arms up in mock despair then ran for the phone, arriving in time to interrupt her voice on the answering machine. She shouted "Hello? Hello?" over herself and heard Nunan in the background yelling, "Britannia?"

He sounded sober. The recorded message ended, and Britannia engaged him in careful conversation. Quickly she learned he didn't know about Viola's affair. *Bird would never tell–it would be too shameful for her,* Britannia thought. He was afraid he'd offended Viola. Brit invited him for the Fourth of July weekend in just a few days. Nunan said he'd be there that evening, and if having him was awkward, please make reservations...Brit cut him off. Of course he'd stay at her place. With Viola.

T W O

Brit's radio came on at 6 a.m. She was instantly awake. She shut it off then took several deep breaths. Pushing herself up to a sitting position she found her *24 Hours A Day* book and turned to the A.A. Thought for the Day, July 4th. One line jumped out at her: "All that we hope for is sobriety and regeneration..." All?

She had sobriety. Fervently she wished for regeneration. No longer did she desire to become young again. Instead, she realized with a start, she wanted regeneration of her spirit, she wanted to live in acceptance of everyone and everything, to live knowing without question the only person she could change was herself. She took a few more deep breaths, splayed her fingers over her belly and asked the universe to guide her through this day, judging no one, even herself. Just being, and accepting. And wasn't accepting a form of love?

Asia had arrived last night, Viola and Nunan were reconciled and acting like honeymooners. She didn't know what her mother told Nunan, and with her new outlook, she wasn't curious. Lee was coming. Also Sugarplum and her husband, Booth, both drinkers. They could keep Nunan company over the drinks cart. Her heart speeded up–even Grant was coming.

She looked back down at the book "...so that we can live normal, respectable lives..." She prayed that she'd want a normal, respectable life.

That maybe Grant might too.

Today, she wanted to find out.

She flung off the covers and, after using the bathroom, picked up her pink ten-pound dumbbells and began her workout.

In the kitchen Rita was making biscuits and a salad of melons and strawberries when Brit came down. They grinned at each another–without any discussion Brit knew Rita knew Grant was invited for more than a barbecue. After she got things set up, Rita was taking the truck into the city for a family picnic in Audubon Park.

Brit, in white Spandex breeches, black boots and navy tank top, drank a cup of decaf chicory coffee before heading to the barn.

"So, Rita, you think we're about ready?"

"Absolutely. You okay about sloppin that dressin on the potato salad?"

"Yep."

"Them pork and beans Miss Viola fixed are in the refrigerator. Reckon she can warm em up?"

"Yep."

"An the Doctor says he's fine about barbecuin the chicken breasts and the corn."

"And I've got a tossed salad to make and you made those luscious strawberry pies. Rita...You like working out here?"

"I love it. I even enjoy communicatin across that lake."

Brit smiled. Rita "communicated" a couple of times a week. She lived on the farm in a bed-sitting room on the east side of the house. Brit watched the thin strong form unload the last dishes from the dishwasher. When she'd first come out and seen Brit's art she'd said, "My son, now, he can really draw good. He done a self-poetry, you know, lookin in the mirror? Uh uh, look professional. Look so real." Brit had offered to look at his work, but so far none had been presented to her.

"Seems like everythins under control to me," said Rita, checking biscuits in the oven. She stood and asked, "So, how come you so jittery?"

Brit sucked in her belly, smoothed her hands over her abdomen.

"You're lookin fine, Miz Brit."

"Yes. Thank you, Rita. I feel fine."

"What happens is what's meant to happen."

Brit was agreeing when Asia came into the kitchen, hair tousled, legs bare under a yellow over-sized T-shirt. A pink and gray sleeping kitten decorated the front.

"Hi," said Brit and went over to hug her. "Rita's got a lovely breakfast going, enough even for Saunders and Grant whenever they arrive. So eat hearty, kitten, I'm off to ride."

As she circled Mokhtar at a counter-canter she saw Rita trundle up the drive in the old truck. Then, as if they'd passed on the road, Grant's Corvette appeared. She halted Mokhtar and waved. Asia came out onto the front, shading her eyes, dressed now in cut-offs and a halter top. Trotting Mokh toward the gate Brit felt excitement: All these people coming together at her house for Independence Day.

She eased the horse into a long-strided cool-down walk and rode from the plateau down the swale and up to the front of the house. She dismounted as Grant and Saunders got out of the car. Asia took the reins as Brit hugged Saunders, who actually smiled, saying, "Hi, Maw, Asia. My horse get any bigger?"

Brit laughed. "Oh, Saw, probably he's a giant now; it's a whole three days!" Then she hugged Grant. It was brief, self-contained. Brit leaned back and looked up, "Hope your grilling arm's in shape, Grant."

He laughed and took his arm from her shoulder, bent it and showed his muscle. "You bet. I've been working out."

"Well. I see that. Good for you," and she gave him a flirty bump with her hip before taking the reins from Asia.

Her daughter had an arm around Saunders' shoulders and he had an arm around her waist. Asia looked small in Saunders' embrace. Asia was earnestly saying, "...and later on come out to the stable with me and I'll help you start training Colt for halter classes. Then you can show him..." Saunders was smiling down at Asia. Brit felt a warm glow begin inside her.

It was just past 10:00 a.m., so Brit asked, "Y'all hungry? Rita left a stack of biscuits..." Saunders nodded so Brit waved them off to the part of the verandah where she and Damien had breakfasted a few days before.

"Asia, can you take coffee and food out? I'll put Mokh up, then come back and shower."

In the barn she unsaddled the sweating stallion. She hosed him with lukewarm water, scraped off the excess water, sprayed him with citron-smelling fly repellent, her mind jumping from appreciation of the new muscle groups on his silvery body to domestic-bliss images of her and Grant together as a couple: their children, good friends, Christmases, perhaps weddings, grandchildren coming to the farm, maybe she teaching them to ride, to draw pictures...Grant showing them how to garden. Mokh turned his head around and fixed her with his big black eye, as if asking, "You buy all that stuff?" Or maybe he really meant, "You finished with that spray so I can go roll now?"

The spray bottle dangled from her right hand, her left idly twirled a piece of mane on his wither. She was enjoying the great clean body of the horse by her, so strong, patient, dependable. Good old Mokh. He was rejuvenated. He rode like a young horse, only better, because his movements were disciplined. And he was safer, no longer jumping shadows or shying at woodsy noises. *Colt,* she thought, *was going to be a wild thing under saddle, the first year or two. Lots of silliness to work out...*Besides feeling safe on Mokhtar, she loved how her old black dressage saddle had softened and shaped to his back and her rear; how her legs from crotch to ankle curved into the horse's side. She hoped to convey this perfect-fit feeling in her sculptures. She took a deep, pleasurable breath as she undid the crossties. It felt so good to use her body and mind again. Mokh snorted, as if he agreed.

After turning the horse out with his capering son she jogged to the house. First, she took her vitamins and minerals, swallowing them down with her home-made smoothie. One banana, yogurt, scoop of Brewer's Yeast, two sweeteners, and ice cubes. She was heading upstairs to take a quick shower, when a robed Viola stopped her.

"Britannia darling, could I possibly have a plunge in that great whirly tub of yours?"

"Of course, Mother," and she put her arm around her mother's shoulders and they went upstairs.

She turned on the water and flipped the switch to get the Jacuzzi going. Then quickly she stripped and stepped into her shower cabinet. As she soaped herself she saw her mother drop the robe and what she saw through frosted glass was a shock: through this lens her mother appeared lithe, slender, young.

Brit realized she'd never seen her mother naked.

She rinsed herself then stepped out. Her mother's head and shoulders floated on an ocean of burbling foam. The room smelled of violets.

Brit wrapped herself in a towel, then shyly said, "Mom. This is a crazy thing to ask, I know—but, well, I've been worried lately about getting older, and here you are just fresh from an affair. You looked absolutely beautiful just a minute ago stepping into the tub—and—"

Without a word, Viola slowly rose from the bubble bath like Aphrodite from the foam, the round black tub her seashell. Water, suds streamed from her body. "Did you want to see what seventy-four looks like, Britannia?" She held her arms out and, knee-deep in the water, slowly rotated. As she turned she raised her arms above her head.

Avid, Brit stared. Her flesh was firm, smooth, not wrinkled and sagging like she'd imagined. *Premature-Cognitive-Commitment.* Lee's voice in her mind.

Under her buttocks, where her thighs merged, there were a few wrinkles but the buttocks were smooth and rounded with a few appealing dimples. As Viola turned, Brit saw a wrinkle below her belly, but the belly was smooth all the way up to her breasts, firm semi-circles with light brown, high-set nipples. Her mother would look good in a bikini. Three wrinkles above her kneecap, a few spidery blue veins on her thighs. But her thighs were as muscular, smooth, as a teenager's. And Brit had seen the fine veins on much younger women. She felt a jolt: without cosmetic surgery, her mother's body was beautiful! As if telepathically hooked into Brit's mind, Viola said, "I'm going to have these veins lasered out, and I'm sure if I'd gotten on colloidal minerals twenty years ago, I'd never have gotten them."

"Minerals?"

"Colloidal. Darling, they are amazing. Minerals in suspension so the body can truly absorb them. The veggies we eat nowadays are all grown in ground that's had all the trace minerals leached out. I'll give you an address—you can order some if you wish."

"Oh, I wish. Mom. You look fabulous. You have the body of a—"

"A fifty-year-old?"

"Well, in places like your back, your belly, your breasts, even your legs—thirty."

"I had my breasts done, dear. Fifteen years ago. Reduced. I wouldn't let them put any of that awful silicone stuff in them."

"Ah."

"And one of these days I'm going to have this droop here picked up." She bent and pulled up the skin of her thigh slightly and her leg looked even younger.

Viola flung her arm out. Brit inspected it for the dreaded upper arm droop. There was a small wattle effect, nothing seriously ugly. "Weights," said Viola. I have a personal trainer, dear, he started me on them when I was sixty-five. Weights are great."

"I'm doing weights now."

"Good. If you have to give everything up and choose only one exercise, Mickey, my trainer, says 'Do weights!' Now, I hope you've seen enough of your old mother." Gently Viola subsided back into the churning tub, Aphrodite into the waves.

Before Britannia dressed she took a close look at her body. Arms raised, she rotated before her cheval mirror, and she saw how good it looked. And, had it changed so much from the morning of her fiftieth birthday? With a jolt she saw it hadn't. All she'd seen that day were the signs of aging, completely missing her smooth, lovely arms, back, thighs and calves, even her breasts and buttocks. She'd have to change the *Old Woman on Young Horse* sculpture; she'd made *Woman* too old looking. With a flash she realized her focus had been on the negative. She'd been influenced by the societal lie. She'd been trying to show that a few sags and wrinkles weren't so bad. Well, they weren't, but the truth was, there weren't that many of them! If she made *Old Woman's* body look exactly like hers did now, everyone would assume she'd sculpted someone thirty or forty—not fifty.

Now she wanted to sculpt seventy. Hell—seventy-five! She'd change her titles. *Young Woman, Old Horse* to *Nineteen and Nineteen.* The human-skinned piece, *Fifty and Three.* Would she have time to do *Seventy-Five and Five?*

No one would believe it. Tough. Maybe what she needed to do was get more into photography—she heard her mother getting out of the tub. Quickly she pulled on her new silver lamé swimsuit and a black and silver cover-up. She brushed her hair, then went out on the verandah to nibble at fruit salad.

The Fourth of July could begin.

A little later Sugarplum and Booth arrived, and Booth and Nunan immediately bonded as the heavy drinkers. In the midst of chatter and laughing, pool-splashes, shrieks, and smells of barbecue, Lee came strolling up doin' her cheetah walk. Behind her was Old Jimmy's handsome son, Leroy.

T H R E E

Brit stared, then squealed. "Lee Robinet! You've been holding out on me, girl!" She hugged Lee, her eyes over Lee's shoulder meeting Leroy's. He was laughing. Then she let go Lee and embraced Leroy. Stepping back, but keeping hold of his hand, she asked, "How's your Mama?"

Leroy, taller than Old Jimmy, and much darker, but with Annie's fine features, nodded, his mouth held tight. "She's doing okay, Brit. How're you making out?"

"Without your daddy here, Leroy, things just aren't the same."

"Yeah."

"So, what you up to?" She let go his hand.

He sighed. "I sold out. I'm teaching like Daddy." He laughed. "Just couldn't stand Corporate America."

"That's the best kind of sell-out. The schools need people like you. So where'd you find this wild woman?" Lee was giggling like a kid. Leroy flashed a grin at her then put his arm around her, half-lifting her in a hug.

"Surrounded by honky's in a trashy bar."

"Oh. So you're going to save her from her sinful bartending life?"

He smiled down at Lee. "If she'll let me."

"Well. Maybe she needs some saving. She's a great writer, Leroy."

"I know it."

Brit looked at both of them. "This is just the best surprise. You two together."

Later she got Lee aside. "Damn Lee, why didn't you tell me about Leroy?"

"Just wanted to make sure it might go somewhere."

"And is it?"

"Think so."

"What made you go out with him?"

"Besides he's drop-dead gorgeous? And kind and generous and funny? Some old urge to explore my other roots, girl."

"Uh-huh. And...?"

"Great root."

Laughing, they rejoined the crowd around the pool.

Dusk. Everyone sprawled by the pool. Asia and Viola had cleared leftover chicken, salads, and pies, and Brit had served homemade lemonade to all but Nunan, who sipped Wild Turkey. Sugarplum and Booth had theirs with vodka.

She sat next to Grant, relaxed. She was still marveling over the wonder of her mother's body, that a woman could have a sexy body in her seventies. She'd long had a nightmare image of two wrinkled, sagging, chicken-armed-legged people groping under the sheets. It came every time she read a column about old people having active sex lives. But then she'd think, maybe it isn't so bad if both bodies are pruned up, maybe that brings acceptance. Maybe they do it in the dark. But now she knew those bodies weren't all that changed.

Whew.

She turned her attention to Grant.

He'd enjoyed taking over the cooking when Nunan flipped a chicken breast into the pool. Sugarplum had commented, "HEY BRIT, YOUR FATHER'S FLIPPED," and everyone howled, even Nunan. Wil retrieved it and ate it to even louder laughter.

Over the black trees the sky was a crimson wash suffused with lavender and blue. Now the sated people felt the cool descent of darkness. The banana trees became tropical silhouettes, leaves like black scimitars curved over them. Above the more distant treeline Venus popped on like God had flipped a switch.

Asia and Saunders had taken their glasses of lemonade to the barn to play with Colt.

Viola was complacently satisfied, her marriage to Nunan, a man emotionally absent via alcohol, renewed, her sexual indiscretion wiped from her mind. It had almost never happened. In a few weeks, Brit knew, if she brought it up she'd get a blank stare from her mother. Earlier, Brit had suggested she and Grant take Nunan to an A.A. meeting–she was surprised her mother answered, "He won't like it! You'll be wasting your time!" Brit pulled back. Did her mother want a drunken husband? Her inner voice said: *She doesn't want anything to change.*

Really?

Really. If Nunan changes, she might have to change.

But he's killing himself.

Yep.

Even so, she'd taken Nunan for a walk one morning before he got drunk for the day and told him about A.A. Throughout, he nodded politely, thanked her, and said, "I'm happy this is working so well for you, Britannia. Your mother and I are proud of you." She'd stared. He really thought he had no problem. Perfect denial. Had she been that separated from reality? She decided, as she'd been taught in A.A., to just love him. Poor, sick alcoholic.

A thought of Scottie. His last postcard was from Brazil. She thought of him: on the beach, surrounded by all those tanned, topless, thonged bodies. Bad thought. The postcard had the same message as the others: "Hi! Life, clean, is good. Wish you were here. Luv yah, XXX OOO–The Web." A slightly scary play on his last name "Webster." *Real cute, Scott.* She didn't want to get caught in his web.

She had bantered with Grant all day. When she'd come out in her silver swim-suit–low-cut front and back–he'd ogled. She'd blushed–not a hot flash. She thought she looked as firm as her nineteen-year-old daughter who lounged, shy, in a blue polka-dot bikini. Brit saw, toweling her hair after some laps, she had more muscle than Asia, not that she was into a sick competition with her daughter. But it was interesting to her to compare nineteen with fifty, as she'd just compared fifty with seventy-four. Asia had a firmness to her upper arms and thighs just naturally, from youth. Hadn't Deepak said that sixty-year-olds and beyond can have the strength of twenty-year-olds? In fact, he'd written that a sixty-year-old who works out can be stronger than a twenty-year-old who doesn't. Now she knew all this was true. She paused on the lip of the pool and let a warm feeling whoosh through her, her Higher Power rewarding her for caring for herself. Then Grant swatted her on the behind with the barbecue flipper and she'd shrieked, almost fell, regained her balance, then come at him, hands fisted, laughing. Wil barked, excited. Everyone poolside looked on with that half-embarrassment, half-titillation that watching sexual teasing evokes. When he came at her she jumped in and he'd followed, Izod shirt and all. Chest deep he reached under-water, caught her legs and laughing, shrieking, she'd thrashed clear.

She felt like a pilot light had been lighted and a woozy desire began in her body.

Later, she'd dropped her towel on a chair and walked up behind Grant at the grill and hugged him. His head jerked back and for a moment she saw a guard-ed look in his eyes, but it changed, became happier. He turned and gave her a hug back, but an A.A. hug, with annoying little pats on her back. It made her angry. *Were they buddies or lovers?*

As she pulled on her cover-up and lavished herself with sunblock she wanted to get his attention sexually, because part of her daydreamy *en famille* scenario included erotic acrobatics with Grant, the Granite Man.

Now she lay on a chaise, her black and silver caftan over her swimsuit, Grant beside her. Lee, Leroy, Sugarplum, and Booth were gone. Viola had herded Nunan to bed; the kids were still in the barn.

There was complete darkness. Citronella candles burned around them, one floating on the pool emitting the scent of lemons. Grant, his chair at a right angle, was at touching distance. He clasped his hands behind his head.

"I always forget how beautiful it is here."

She was silent. But thinking, *Yeah? Want to be out here on a permanent basis? Could be arranged.*

In the candlelight, half-moon rising above paper-rustling palms–and beyond, deeper rustlings of magnolias, live oaks and pines, hints of secret scurryings–she looked at him. Handsome, even without his hairpiece. Big knees jutting at her, bare below khaki shorts. He hadn't swum when he'd jumped in the pool–he'd stood and grabbed for her. She'd been surprised, pleased, when he'd come in after her. When they'd gotten out, he said the same thing he always did, earnestly. "I can't swim. I have negative gravity." *What the hell did that mean,* she'd always wondered. *Was he some kind of human Black Hole?*

She prodded his knee with her toe. "Lookin' pretty serious, Ol' Negative Gravity."

His arms came down. "Am I?"

Actually he was perplexed. Seemed he had his pick of older women. He heard Irwin's voice, "The deal is, Grant, for this program to work, we follow God's Will, not our will." *So. Was this God's Will? Brit and him?*

He'd been working out–half-heartedly, he hated physical exercise–at Spiffy's gym. They'd lunched a few times. Now here was his sexy-looking, long-legged ex-wife who'd been so enraged by his wanting to "bang young chicks" observation she hadn't spoken to him, except about Saunders, in months. *Was she coming on to him?* He sighed. Both women had become more attractive to him, either because of all those reality-check talks with Irwin, or was he finally growing out of his middle-age craziness? Maybe he was just horny and they were…available.

Brit's reactions threw him. Sometimes she seemed to want him, the next minute, even after really great sex, she'd reject him. *How could someone reject someone after really great sex?* It made no sense.

Why did he keep coming back?

Really Great Sex.

Okay, okay, he thought, *I might have a tiny problem.* Fuckin' Irwin hinted he might check out S.A.–*Sex Addicts!*–meetings. "What," he countered, "and wait for someone to have a relapse?" Irwin had frowned.

So what was he, himself, becoming–Mr. Fucking Anonymous? He couldn't handle any more Twelve-Step stuff. A.A. was hard enough.

He had no idea what he really felt. He stared at the blurry moon, a child's chalk-swipe in the sky. More stars here than in the city. Confusion. His throat acted like it wanted to close. He hated it. He didn't know how to find out what he felt, except, he knew he wanted Brit's toe to walk up the inside of his thigh...*But wait–was sexual turn-on a feeling? Like happy? Sad? Mad? Or was it a physical reaction, a sensation? Sensation, emotion...was there a difference?*

There's the Big Dipper.

Of course, Saunders adored her, so did Rita, dammit. Spiffy was richer. But Brit had shown him the stuff for her next show, and though he definitely was not an art critic, nor interested in horses–although he'd admit to a serious interest in naked women–he got a good gut feeling looking at this art. She'd make money with this stuff. It was so eerie. So real.

There was one sketch he wanted to buy, right now, it was so erotic to him. Six "Horsewomen"–horse's bodies and women's bare-breasted tops, like centaurs. One woman faced out, defiant, hands on her human-swelling-to-horse hips, big round breasts thrust straight at him. The others in a gossipy, womany cluster laughing, whispering in each other's ears. Were they Centaur-essas? Brit said she wanted to sculpt them, bas-relief. Parody a Grecian frieze of Centaurs.

He had a fantasy of riding one of these half-women, half-horses, hands on her breasts, her-it galloping.

And he didn't like riding.

Her toe moved back to her chaise. He wished it hadn't.

He leaned forward, took her bare foot in his hand, then pressed its sole into his crotch. A moment later he heard the silk caftan slither over her head, fall. He watched it puddle black, silver on the bricks.

Trees rustled. Candlelight, moonlight, some bird singing high opera.

FOUR

Saunders and Asia were in the loft of the barn. He'd put a Roofie in her lemonade.
Sure was taking its time. They'd admired Mokhtar and Colt and rather than actually train the colt they'd talked about it. He'd told Asia he couldn't wait to ride
Colt, a lie, but it thrilled her. She didn't like riding herself, but she did want
everyone around her involved with animals in some way.

He'd gotten her talking about school, her working vacation at the San Diego
Zoo. He watched as her cheeks grew flushed, her eyes bright. Then he suggested
they sit up in the loft, open a door. Talk, watch the moon rise. Babbling about
the birth of a giraffe, up the ladder she went, her ass bobbling under her cut-offs.
He thought how it had looked in her bikini today. And before. White melon
halves, for the camera, in the pasture.

He had two of those Polaroids, snitched before going to The Dome's. His
townie buds had really gotten off on them. Of course, he'd said he'd taken them
and that he was banging his stepsister. They were impressed.

Now they sprawled on a horse blanket spread over hay. The moon, obliging,
rose. It sent cool blue-white light through the open loft door. Zephyrs moved the
door crick-creak, crick-creak. Not a bad sound. Tree frogs began. In the distance
a bird sang. He turned to Asia. She was silent, eyes closed, she even gave a little
snore. Her body was splayed all over the red blanket.

His penis, semi-erect for an hour, became stone hard. He listened. No sounds
anywhere, except for wild critters, and the horses softly eating below. The adults
must be asleep. His hips made involuntary twitching movements, pressing his
erection against the zipper teeth on his cut-offs. While he savored the intermit-
tent pressure, another part told him–*Slow down. You've got all-night-long.* The
only hitch would be fireman's lifting her down the loft ladder, and into the house
without waking anyone.

For this to work she had to wake up in her own bed in one of those giant kitten T-shirts she always slept in. *Well. You'll have to get her naked first, won't you?*

FIVE

After Grant pressed Brit's foot against himself he'd leaned over, scritching his chaise
closer, so they could kiss. The chair-back suddenly flopped back, jerking them
apart. Eyes on hold, they laughed as he sat up. She watched him looking at her
and saw The Change come over him. It happened every time they made love. Just
knowing–he seemed to know this telepathically–she was willing to have sex with

him, he became an assured being she never saw in daily life. It struck her—of course he was always checking every woman out, of course he "really looked for that one good part"—because with "one good part" he could make this transformation with any woman—old, young, fat, thin, deformed, plain, downright ugly, because that one good part, be it a breast, throat, ear, butt, calf, arm, lip, toe, maybe a flighty eyebrow—that visual trigger was the stimulus he needed to get to himself. Then the whole of that woman, when he was in his change, became beautiful to him. Because she could give him the gift of Himself. Or what he construed as himself.

She felt a rush of sadness for him, that he couldn't see he had to give the gift of himself, to himself, by himself.

She was trying to give herself the gift of herself. No outside help. Only a growing connection with...something...

Could he ever break away from this?

Meanwhile back at the ranch, she thought, feeling her wryness mix with giddy anticipation—where would Himself lead them tonight? She would follow. Her ovaries tingled. Because he was never mundane in lovemaking, and she wanted to be made love to. She gritted her teeth.

Smiling, this changeling took her hand, stood gracefully, and invited her to her feet. In the silver swimsuit, she rose, shining like a chrysalis.

He brushed a hand over her black hair, trailed his thumb over her white, white face. Candleflare caught her lavender pupils, and his eyes mirrored the flare. He bent and touched his soft lips to her lids, mauve shadows, then the shadow under her cheekbone, the cleft of her chin, the hollow of her throat.

His big thumbs inched her swimsuit straps over her shoulders, down her arms. Her woozy desire started a pulse. Her breasts popped free. He gasped—thrilled to see them—this sending a zing of triumph through Brit—*they're still beautiful!*—then bent his mouth and suckled, like a man, not a babe. Confidently lithe he knelt, eased her suit down, buried his face in her pubis.

She gasped. Yet a tiny worry, *would those few gray hairs show? Turn him off?* Apparently not.

His arms insinuated around her buttocks then—abrupt, his intensity taking her breath—he lifted her up. Her toes dangled, her legs parted, pushing against the Spandex—even the push was erotic. She clamped her hands on his shoulders—took a sharp breath.

He browsed his way in, found her clitoris with his tongue. When her groin rolled in pleasure, he set her down, reached behind, jerked the padded cushion on the chaise, and it slithered to the bricks. She folded herself down, down into his arms, feeling the skin of that soft place under his biceps silk along her arms. Cradling her, he bestowed her on the cushion.

Banana fronds dipped over her head. Beyond, the darker silhouette of the forest, the card, the tarot card, she now the virgin in the moonlight. The bird sang. His clothes came off. Standing above her. Naked, a giant. Grinning now, plotting his sensuous takeover.

Her ovaries, her uterus came alive, tingling hot, making irresistible twitchings. She smiled. The famous cock was rising. She started to wriggle out of her suit but he whispered, "Don't." He came down over her, knelt on one leg, slithered his other leg down her side, leg hairs sliding along her body making her skin jump, cells clamoring for touch. His articulate fingers searched through her labia. Then he whispered, hoarse, "Oooo–so wet!"

Brit's arms flew up in exaltation. The moon shone on her. *I'm sooo wet,* she whispered in her mind. Tree frogs sang. Trees rustled. Creatures scurried. Night life. She only wished the moon was full. She inhaled his leathery musk smell. He peeled her suit lower, now it was a silver slash across the top of her thighs, cutting her in half, accentuating her pubic hair. He brushed his cock back and forth across her belly, which quivered, then slid it up and down between her breasts, now licking, taking great wet mouthfuls of her breasts, making them slidey-wet, then bringing his extended leg forward, sliding it up along her shuddering body. She felt his hard knee brush her hips. Kneeling over her he pressed her breasts around his penis. Thumbs rubbing her nipples, he slid back and forth. Her palms moved over his thighs, moved behind him, to the furred softness between his legs. She hefted the imperious weight of his testicles. She wanted to put her mouth around them. Feel his balls on her tongue, on her palate. He was whispering in a ragged, sucked-in way, "So beautiful, Brit, so beautiful,"

God. It feels so good to hear those words!

She was just lifting her head to try and suck his cock when he slid away from her. He moved his penis back and forth across her acceptable pubic hair. He was still whispering, "Beautiful, beautiful." Then, moving farther down, he slipped his penis under the Spandex, and rolled it back and forth across himself. Eyes intense, he watched himself on her. She felt his teeth-gritted core-tight heat. Her fingertips walked across his chest, feeling the rubbery soft-hardness of it, nails rippling through the hairs, pausing, fingers gently pulling, then tugging harder on his nipples. Abruptly she sat and sucked first his right then his left nipple.

He threw his head back. "Oh, yes!"

But he pushed her down and this was right, he was the leader–he pulled his cock free and peeled her suit down to her toes. He pressed her sole into his scrotum. She undulated her foot against him. Hot, warm, his hairs clinging to her sole.

He put the heels of his hands within her thighs, just above her knees, and kneeling between them licked and sucked her soft thigh-skin to the edge of her plum-like pussy. Then to her other leg, loud sounds of his sucking, teething of her skin, sucking, sucking, till she felt his nose brush at her hairs, a little growl, his teeth taking hairs–tug! tug!–the tiny plum of her clitoris feeling the pull, the pull–her belly convulsed–she sucked air in through her teeth–then tiny wiggling movements along her innermost lips–tongue into her vagina–gasp–now soft, seeking, seeking–her plum throbbing, pulsating, the first touch, the very tip of his tongue on her–and he lipped and sucked and nibbled and lapped at the juices of her. Blind knowing fingers came up to squeeze, roil her nipples.

She sank into a place…

Oh-sweet-god-in-heaven-thank-you-for-making-me-a-human-woman-who-can-FEEL-every-part-myself-soar-up-and-down-and-in-and-around-and-BE-WITH-this-soft-flesh-of-Other…God! Could he shake these feelings from her! Her plum tree.

A while…then, "God! I–You–!" Her ovaries flung out billions of sparkling ova, sapphire emerald diamond ruby, each scintilla an orgasm itself, orgasms within orgasms–they plumed out and out, arching, curving, spiraling into a deep black, now illumined from her center, the pluminess of her–this endless orgasm a microcosm of the making of the universe.

She, dried-up, infertile? Hell, no! Her inner voice, checking in, bringing her Down to Earth: *Yeah! Baby! How's that for ovulation?* Then an all-knowing peal, laughter, sardonic, amused, cynical, from-the-belly, innocent–real. Hers. All hers. From herself.

Then, rough. That big hunk of bologna shoved up into her, in so slick, his torn whisper, "God–how you move!" He got still, to feel her moving around him. Gem-like scintilla rushing back into her, to her filled center.

He began. Drawing himself slowly all the way out…she gasped, her fingers flying through the air, nails scritching at his back, *don't leave me!*

Then again and again. Again. Each time a thrilled terror of losing him. His knowing laugh, low and evil and sexy, and she twisted herself up and pressed her

belly–joy! her firm belly–to his softer, rounder one, but just right–give to it, rubbing her belly on his, making the outer flesh move–she slung her legs over his
back, her hard calves on his hard muscles, and she locked her ankles. She let her
head fall back, caught his eye and he laughed, that demon edge. Now his hands,
sliding under her sweating back, separating her from the plastic cushion, peeling
it away like the rind of a ripe mango, then holding her up while he thrust, intent,
and steady. He stopped, her vagina clutched his cock like a wet hand, he saying,
"Oh!" Then sliding himself out, the little hand that was her vagina gripping,
gripping trying to hold him in–but–out. Then easing her over, she scrabbling to
comply, she stuck her bottom up to him and, his tongue lapping, his lips sucking, his teeth taking great mouthfuls of her round white up-tilted bottom, then
a teasing, probing cock circling and figure-eighting around both her openings,
she knew his hand was on his cock, guiding it, leading it around and around.
Like a ripe mango, juice dripped from her. She heard his intake of breath, a
pause, then the great hot girth pushing, sliding in, inflating her again. He began
thrusting, groin slapping her buttocks. Sweat and suction formed between them.
Soft thwacks behind, his balls hitting her clitoris, pleasure in each hit. A sandpaper sound–the plastic cushion jerking over bricks. Then harder, harder, terrifical-
ly hard, so hard, she yelled, "Oh!"

   The cushion halted at the lip of pool.

   "Oh! Oh–yes! Brit–Brit–"

   Thrilling–hearing her name.

   Then. Breathing in the night. Bliss. Water lapping. Lone candle floating.

   He rolled her over, sniffing her breasts, grizzly chin nuzzling her wet tummy,
growly-voiced, a playful mock-European accent, "You smell–terrific–you
taste–von-der-ful!" And her body sliding up like a mermaid's, slick nipples,
breasts crushing up along his chest, arms going around each other, tight, squeezing, trying to push each other into each other's body, softly-open lips coming
together and she tasted herself, wet, sweet, in his mouth.

   They kissed for a long time.

   Coming down. Coming down.

   In a while he sat back on his heels, entirely at ease. The moon shone on his
bald head. His cock dangled, still wet from her. She reached, stroked it, then up
to his head, fingerpads touching the tight, bone-hard baldness.

   Head cocked, grinning, in his animal voice, "Voman! Me, Man, now really
hungry." Then normal, light, grinning, "Let's take this show to bed, huh, girl?"

SIX

Up close, her body was better than the Polaroids. Breasts sticking straight up. Little virgin pinky-brown nipples hardening as he ran his finger, tongue, penis over them.

Running his chore-roughened hand from breast to pubic hair–thick, black–he found a mole where her belly flattened before sloping to her pussy. On the left. He'd remember this secret about her body.

Standing to strip his cut-offs, pull his T-shirt over his head he gloated–his virgin-victim-sister. So white, so black, her various hairs, how red her lips.

Well, Snow White, here I come–Ha. Ha.

He lay on her grunting, thrusting, seeking her hole, her eyes flying open, looking right into his. He froze. He wasn't even in her yet. He remembered: *Total amnesia–total, Dude.* He grinned, resumed his probings, harder, her eyes wide open, staring into his. He wanted to hurt her while she looked at him. He moved a hand, took hold of her breast roughly, she whimpered, moved against him–hands and arms pushing–trying to foist him off. *Bitch!* Of course, she couldn't. Then he shoved hard–aah–his penis broke through, and she made a high wheedling sound. He felt it down his spine. So. She really had been a virgin, and he'd just busted it. She subsided.

His eyes glazed over, like hers.

He began to fuck in earnest.

SEVEN

In bed, Britannia was stretched to her utmost, even then her toes couldn't find Grant's feet. They'd made love again, this time she spending time, her mouth, his cock.

He was so long.

Now he breathed through the hair covering her ear, "I want to be with you as long as you'll let me."

Yes. Yes.

She was full of warmth and gratitude and just a smidgen of smugness. Georgie would grill her for the smugness–but what the hell, some are sicker than others, right?

Her smugness was from thinking: *No other woman could possibly respond like she had tonight–this kind of lovemaking had to be so rare–that they alone could experience it. Tonight's hard-soft sex would bind him to her and her to him, vanquish stray yearnings for Scottie and, no other woman, not even one twenty–hell, thirty–years younger, could give him what she just had.*

Right?

Grant stared straight up through a skylight over Brit's bed, watching a rectangle of the universe. She on her side, temple in the hollow above his armpit, cheek on his chest. Now and then her eyes turned up and she'd also see the black cutout of the universe. She saw the belt of Orion, the hunter. She had a sense almost of the earth's rotation, every time she looked up the stars had moved. It felt as if her bed was tilted, her head lower than her feet. An uncomfortable feeling, like sliding backwards. But she didn't want to move–it would disturb Grant.

"Be good for Saunders, us together, we stand firm with him," Grant was saying, also feeling his head lower than his feet, but he didn't want to grab for a pillow, disturb Brit, she seemed so comfortable. She felt so good stretched out along him.

Brit thought of the children in their beds, after the long wet sunny day. She sighed in near perfect satisfaction. *En famille.*

He'd move back out…they'd keep his condo for weekends and for the times he worked big cases.

He chuckled, "Good thing Rita likes it out here."

"Yeah. She loves 'communicatin.'" They laughed, loving Rita.

"She'll be real pleased about us," he said as his mind spooled on.

He'd never get to try on that sexy little Spiffy. *What the hell. This must mean he was maturing.* He couldn't wait to talk to Irwin.

He turned toward his woman, sliding an arm under her and pulled her to him. He began again to evoke in himself the sensation he loved most.

E I G H T

Saunders lay back, chewing a stalk of hay. He stared out the loft door at the stars, brighter now that the moon had sailed away but darker in the loft. Below, the horses shifted in their stalls. His stepsister moaned. Her body, in this lesser light, was purple. He stared at her enfolding curves, the lasciviousness of her nude sprawl.

His penis began to rise again. He spat out the hay, whispered, "Break's over, L'il Bitch." He moved over to her on all fours, knees not touching the floor, like some giant insect holding its body aloft. At her side he looked at her pubic hair and said out loud, "Boring." Then he put his hands on her flesh and flopped her over.

N I N E

Brit and Grant were making love again. This time he'd entered her, then holding her hips, turned on his back so she sat above him. She moved slowly, finding a rhythm. He groped beside him and came up with his leather belt–wicked grin, she grinning back. She grabbed it from him and slipped it around her waist, end through the buckle, pulled it tight, tight, and he took the long free end and gave it hard little jerks to encourage her movement. Sweat started and her thighs slid now with each gallop movement, and he flashed on his fantasy of riding the Centauressa. He bucked his hips up to stop her, put the end of the belt in his mouth, then hands on her hips lifted and rotated her. Now her back was to him, buttocks mounded on his belly...he slid higher in the bed, stuffing pillows behind him, shortened the belt in his teeth so it pulled even tighter around her waist, making her hips bulge out white and full and globulous–he kneaded the irresistible soft flesh, then his hands came forward, took her breasts–her nipples slipped between his index and middle finger, up into the inner part, which felt soft to Brit, like the insides of thighs. She slung her hips hard, back and forth like the good horsewoman she was...*better*, thought Grant, *than any horse*...They rocked and Brit felt frissons of molten pleasure flow out from his cock inside her...Grant felt rippling spear-flames of sensation fanning out from his cock....

Then her body was filled with sensation, bursting and bursting and falling and falling like mortars over jungle–is this my first vaginal orgasm? And while she was soaring he grabbed her and turned her again, sitting right up and pressing her bottom down hard into him, his other hand pressing down hard on her white-butter thigh, he pushed–and pushed–up–up–his lips torn back from set teeth, unh–unh–unh–and the flames exploded from a hot ball at the base of his cock, sent spears up through his spleen, liver, lungs, and heart, turning each organ red and molten. Flame shot from the tops of his shoulders, the top of his head. He fell back on the steamy sheets, Britannia slid in their sweat down on top of him.

They breathed, feeling the wonder fade, a golden glow which slithered through each of them.

Then, still on Grant's chest, him still in her, she smiled.

Saunders had wanted fireworks, but she'd said, no, too much danger of setting fire to the buildings.

Grant could only stare into her eyes. Never...went through his mind...never before...such sensation–such–feeling? He felt bound to her now.

Did he love her?

She felt bound to him. She laid her head on his hard-breathing chest as his penis gently slid from inside her. He moved his chin in her hair, pressing against her scalp. His arms went around her damp back, gently holding her to him. He stared wonderingly at the stars above his head…could some young chick give him what he'd just felt? It was the first time he'd ever asked this question of himself…He stared at the stars. A feeling of great tenderness spread through him…tears came in his eyes…a picture came in his mind. Standing in the kitchen, six years old, his thin harried mother turning toward him, her face knotted in anger…then her seeing. He held out a floppy bouquet of pink wine cups, the first wildflowers of the spring. He'd picked white clover too, and the sweet clover smell overwhelmed the bacon-grease odor of the kitchen. Her face unknotted like a rope jerked straight. She bent to him, smiling, her light gray eyes, so like Saunders', glowing. She took the flowers, kissed his forehead, then in slow motion folded him into her hard thin body. He didn't mind the smell of homemade dandelion wine on her breath. Suddenly her body felt soft—it was the first and only time she ever hugged him. He had the same tender feeling then as he had now. *Imagine. Wait thirty-eight years to have this feeling again—it was as if he'd forgotten he was even waiting for it.*

The tender feeling came from Brit…had to…but as it continued, in waves, and he stared at the stars…he knew the feeling really came from some secret place inside himself. A place so secret he'd forgotten it existed.

The True Self Irwin talked about? That Self that is a piece of God?

The stars stared down at him. They sparkled, twinkled, like they were grinning, happy little kids of stars. He smiled up at them, they blurred, more wet in his eyes, trickling down his crow-foot ridge's, down into his temple, a wet track that seeped, it seemed, directly into his brain.

Somehow, being with Brit had triggered all this.

His hand touched her thigh. "Brit. I love you."

Flesh, Brit was thinking, *is billions of microscopic cells, each one impregnated with spirit.* Her billions sang. *Had she ever felt so happy to be alive, to be flesh which could be touched?* All these wondrous things she felt had nothing to do with the shape, the age of her body. It was from completely letting go, from completely giving up her inner self to this man, to the potential to feel within her, and that, she now knew came from the universe…from God. She felt her thigh fitted to Grant's, she slid an arm across his chest, her cells singing louder, a great chorus and, she heard words, they were singing, *I'm young…forever and ever…we are all always young....*

She felt his hand on her thigh, heard his words, and she whispered, "Oh, Grant. I love you too."

T E N

Asia over his back, Saunders struggled down the loft ladder. Since the ladder was nailed to the wall he couldn't get enough foot into the rung–his toe hit the log wall–so he was carrying all her weight on the balls of his feet. His hands ached from holding on–but Christ–he couldn't drop her now. She couldn't have any unexplained bruises, say, like on her head.

He was a grotesque humpbacked shape moving down the wall.

The old stallion made a low sound. To Saunders it sounded like the horse was saying "Her, her, her," and he hissed through the concrete darkness, "Shut the fuck up, horse."

His foot touched cement. *Thank God.* He stood on the floor, felt his way down the aisle, once touching a horse's nose, the warmth and aliveness so startling he got a squeamish feeling. He found the door, shoved it open. Creak! He froze, but they couldn't hear, not all the way up to the house. He left it open in case it made more sounds.

Humid air moved like caterpillar feet over his skin. Pausing to shift the weight on his shoulder, approaching stealthily, he moved toward the house.

When he got to the French doors on the northeast side, his back ached and he still had to get through the house, up the stairs.

E L E V E N

Later. Feeling...overwhelmed... Grant closed his eyes to the universe. He was having alarming thoughts of cute blond Spiffy. How could he? He and Brit had just had knock-down, drag-out sex. The Best. He had just told her he loved her. He must be one sick mother!

He breathed deeply and tried to follow Irwin's instructions on how to let go of unwelcome thoughts, tried to put Spiffy into a big pink ball. The last big imaginary ball he'd experienced was the giant martini olive. The instructions were: Put the thought in the ball then let it float away. Had to wrestle with that, because the Spiffy he saw was pink and naked and it took some will-power to get her into the pink ball. She didn't want to go. He was beginning to get another hard-on, imagining that soft little body, like a baby's, but with a real woman's breasts, sweet little blonde pussy…Like fog, there was suddenly an aura of fear around him.

After you get the unwelcome thought into the pink ball, Irwin had said, see it drifting away, see it getting smaller and smaller…wave goodbye. The ball floated up and away, getting smaller and smaller, but the instant before it disappeared, she was pounding her cute little fists against it, crying, "Grant, Grant…" It popped, vanished. He felt sorrow. Then shame.

Reality check, Big Guy. The long firm woman beside him was real, the sex had been fantastic, and he remembered that even Irwin had the hots for her. Brit, that is.

He'd better appreciate Brit more.

They could have a wonderful life together. Suddenly he knew the thoughts of Spiffy made his fear: He wanted a backup.

Then the tender feeling for Brit came back. Relief, like sweat, popped out all over his body.

Thank God for Brit.

T W E L V E

He made it up the stairs. Grateful, he dumped her on the bed. He shut the door and clicked on her bedside lamp. There was the yellow T-shirt, kitten on it, over a chair. He pulled her up, she came half-to, moaned, and held her arms up like a little girl wanting mama to dress her.

He couldn't help sniggering.

Once she said, "No, Mama, no, please don't," and he whispered, "It's okay, Babe. Be cool." He put a finger on her breastbone, pushed, she flopped down. Out cold.

He pulled the covers over her, turned out the lamp, sidled out.

T H I R T E E N

All the bombs had landed and Brit lay by Grant like a smoking jungle. She felt—good, but in a dim corner a bit…conned…? By *whom—Grant?*

Aah. By Herself.

That needy Self.

But I don't have to need anybody. Georgie had told her this. Lee too. Did she NEED Grant? Her body was still in orgasmic aftershock. Hard to think. *But you love him,* an inner shriek.

Maybe. A bit.
I really think I want him.
I guess I do.
En famille.

P a r t   F i v e

Wandering between two worlds,
one dead, the other powerless to be born…
— *Matthew Arnold*

O N E

It was the first of November, and Brit was in New York. A bleak three-day rain had given way to sunny crisp weather.

She couldn't get out of the one-woman circus she'd let Damien talk her into. She picked up one of her new English riding boots. Black leather, supple as kid gloves. She marveled she should finally have boots this good after thirty years of riding. If only she didn't feel so embarrassed about how she was going to christen them.

Custom made, they snuggled up over her calves stopping at the crease behind her knees, curving slightly over her kneecap.

She'd refused to wear a cape, but now, as she looked at herself in a mirror of their suite at the Algonquin Hotel, she was almost sorry. Black breeches, white cashmere turtleneck, houndstooth jacket. *Trés dramatique.* Damien, of course. Her hair was longer now, down to her bra-line. She'd kept the gray that zoomed out from her temples, but the rest was a deep brown-black. She'd kept up her workouts, her body had the rubbery snapback of youth. Wear them britches, gal, second skin, ain't no pimples on your ass! Lee's reaction, when she'd watched Brit try them on.

She leaned into the mirror, and studied her eyes. Despite all the discussion with Damien–she'd even made an appointment with a cosmetic surgeon–but, at the last moment broken it. That artist thing in her, that wanting to see how she'd look if she just…let it flow…to be at one with natural forces. She was curious. She wanted to observe the changes in her face as a detached, nonjudging being. She imagined self-portraits in ten years–as she really would be. So, she'd kept her chin the way it was, even the darker under-eye softness.

To her surprise, both continued to improve with her self-care regimen.

Deepak Chopra had said that every cell in a body was replaced each year. With affirmations and care why couldn't those new cells be young, vibrant cells? Why did she have to accept she'd replace old-looking cells with pre-programmed old-looking cells? Despite misgivings, she felt this was possible. Daily she affirmed, I am strong, healthy, youthful. Grant had joined her, discarding his hairpiece, his contacts. He'd even begun to gulp vitamins, minerals. Together they attended A.A. meetings. It became their church. She thought of the wild azaleas, the young dogwoods sitting out back in nursery tubs, waiting for her and Grant to plant them throughout her forest. Their spring would be beautiful.

They weren't married, but Grant had managed somehow to get her and Asia on his company health insurance. They'd had five near-blissful months together, partly because they'd made a pact never to let their words and thoughts stray into the past.

She smiled at herself. It was hard to believe that here, in her fiftieth year, a whole new life had begun for her. And a crazier one than her other life. What she was about to do was an example.

In The Altogether: Woman and Horse opened this afternoon at Damien's gallery. She'd ride seven blocks on Mokhtar to the gallery—the press was welcome. They'd built a temporary stall for the horse in front of the gallery. Damien paid for everything, her outfit, Mokhtar trucked up in an air-ride horse van, stabled in Central Park, round-the-clock security guards for him, the suite at the Algonquin for her and Grant.

She could barely admit to herself that riding seven blocks through New York City was the realization of one of her great girlish fantasies: as a gawky teenager, passionately horse-crazy, she'd dreamt of riding high above all the kids, the adults who'd ridiculed her. To show them! She didn't know what, but...to show them ...Well, kids, turn on your TV. There'll be some kind of show on, maybe a whole minute on CNN...She was slated, rare for a studio artist, on The Today Show. Willard was going to be at the gallery, he'd interview her with her horse, next to her sculptures. Since Willard had the gig, it meant NBC was treating it as a fun thing. More serious artists, like the ones who wrote books, got interviewed by Bryant, Lee had said. She agreed. But months ago it had been Willard's hundred-year birthday wishes that had begun changing her prejudices about aging.

Well. She was excited, scared. What if Mokhtar spooked? What if people laughed at this ridiculous pageant? And Mokh had never been a parade horse. *What if...she fell off? He ran away?* Police horses in pursuit through the buttes of Manhattan

Island…in front of The Whole World on CNN?

Don't project a mental picture of yourself falling off, or you will.

I know.

Okay then. What do you project?

A hilarious, wondrously silly, ridiculously fun, lovely, elegant ride.

Right.

She checked her wristwatch, diamond, a gift from Grant after their Fourth of July reunion. They'd begun to talk re-marriage. Maybe in the spring.

Damien had argued if Anne Rice can come to book signings in a hearse, then Britannia Rhodes can come to her art opening on a horse. *What the hell. It would make for Good TV.*

Her palms were sweaty in the slightly chilly room. An hour to showtime.

She was envisioning Mokhtar in his high, slow-motion trot, the passage, moving through Manhattan streets. Felt his movement in her thighs, buttocks. She reached for the phone. Damien answered on the first ring.

"So, is it too late to get me a cape?"

He laughed. "It just so happens, darling, in the event you'd be swept away by the drama, I happen to have just such an article on hand. Be right over."

She recradled the receiver. Grant had gone to Kennedy to pick up Anastasia. Saunders was home with Rita. Rita'd be excited, in front of the TV, probably with Wil and godd…Saunders had been quiet lately, attending school, even doing homework—he might watch. She hoped he would.

Fifty minutes till showtime. She dropped onto the bed, arranged herself in a semi-lotus position, not drawing her crossed legs all the way back to her crotch because of the constriction of the knee-high boots.

Taking deep breaths she began a prayer.

"Universe, Great Creator, thank you for my sobriety today. Thank you for my new good life, my health, my vitality, my youthfulness, my creativity, my new relationship with Grant…my family, my friends, my pets, my gardens. Always please show me Your Will for me. Let my will be completely aligned with Your Will, so that I and Thou are One, in Perfect Love. And please, give me the power to carry out Your Will for the greatest, most loving good of all concerned. Let me this day live in total harmony with the universe. I give You this day my life, to do with as You wish. Let me trust You utterly. Amen." It was her transposition of prayers written in The Big Book of Alcoholics Anonymous, with help from the writings of Shakti Gawain. She took slow, deep breaths, felt all thoughts dissolve from her mind, felt a Self within her sink deep, deep, waited until a delicious calm came over her. It filled her body, then radiated from her until she felt she had a nimbus of love surrounding her, a buffer from whatever the day held.

A knock at her door. She uncrossed her legs, jumped up, answered it. It was Grant, followed by Anastasia.

She saw lank hair, a rash of pimples around Anastasia's mouth. A bony knee, like a broken bone, protruded from a hole in her jeans. Her oversized brown sweater was raveling, cowl collar separating from the sweater body, a scimitar-shaped gap across her chest showing a faded gray sweatshirt beneath. Her fingers looked red, frostbitten. Her nails were chewed to the quick.

Brit and Grant's eyes met, his hands made a helpless gesture. Alarmed, Brit stepped close, put her arms around her daughter.

With her chin in her daughter's oily hair, feeling Asia's arms creep around her like a delicate vine, she murmured, "Sweetie. You don't look so good. Have you been sick?"

She hadn't seen Asia since the Fourth...she recalled that Asia, after the big feasting day, had suddenly upped, gone back to Baton Rouge. Since then she herself had been putting in sixteen-hour days. There'd only been a few quick phone calls. Brit had assumed Asia was re-absorbed in her animal studies...

Against her chest Anastasia began to cry. Brit held her closer. Her eyes went to Grant's. He nodded, concern on his face. Frightened at the bones beneath Asia's raggedy clothes, she turned her daughter and led her into a bedroom. Shutting the door behind them she sat with her on the bed.

The light was low, the shades down. She clicked on a bedside lamp in the plain room. Silently she held her daughter. Through the door she heard the arrival of Damien.

"...Looks like we'll have NBC, CNN–hoorah!–and, get this Grant–MTV! It's almost a media circus out there! I brought this cape for our star..." His voice stopped, probably motioned to by Grant.

Asia's weeping lessened. She sat back from her mother, wiped her eyes on the bristly sweater.

Had she bought it from a homeless person?

Brit rose, got tissues from the bathroom. She sat back down, handed them to Asia. Asia blew her nose, rubbed her face.

"Now, my dear. Please tell me what's wrong."

Asia looked at her, opened her mouth, and began to cry again.

There was a light knock on the door, Damien's voice, "Everything okay in there, ladies? Thirty minutes till showtime."

"In a minute, Damien," called Brit.

Asia was speaking, "Go do your thing, Mom. I don't want to ruin your big day."

"Sweetie. With you so unhappy–who cares? Please tell me what's wrong."

"No, no. You go now."

"Anastasia. CNN can shoot traffic jams, Damien can knock his knuckles raw. I am not leaving this room until I know what's wrong."

Asia put her head down and Brit looked at the top of her uncombed head. She smelled it. When was the last time Asia had washed her hair?

In a whisper, "Something happened, Mom. To me. On the Fourth." She shredded tissue, looked up. "I'll tell you. Tonight. After your opening."

"My opening can wait. You're a wreck, Asia. I'm worried. Just tell me."

"You promise you'll have your opening and we'll talk after?" Tears oozed from her eyes. Her face was gray, like unpainted clay. Brit worried the wet would dissolve the clay…

"I promise."

"Saunders raped me."

"What?"

"Saunders raped me."

Brit stared at gray mini-blinds shuttering a window on a far wall. The light was trapped behind them, trying to break through. There were bright vertical slashes where the shades met the sash. Eyes smarting, she looked back at Asia's clay face.

"You're saying. Asia–my God. You're saying–your stepbrother–raped you?"

"Yes. I'm sorry, Mom–"

"Sorry! Christ! My God!" She felt poised at the lip of a precipice. *Black seeds lie dormant.* "That–son of a bitch–!" She stared hard at Anastasia. She felt she was descending, fast, in an elevator. "This is true, Baby?"

A knock. "Twenty minutes, Brit."

Brit ignored it, stared at her daughter. An arm could thrust right through her midsection, nothing there but a few hurtling molecules.

"Yes, Mom, it's true. I was afraid you wouldn't believe me–"

"I believe you." Brit's eyes hard now, she felt her elevator land with a thump. "I'll kill him–when–how?–Anastasia–tell me. Please, baby."

"That night, the Fourth."

She sat back. Thought. Recalled. Shame came over her. That was the night she and Grant–by the pool–oh, God, the doors sliding open–Saunders–then?

"The Fourth of July? Our big pool party? Sugarplum–Lee–Leroy–Gramma, Nunan?"

"Yes. At night. Everyone was gone."

"Where, Honey, where did this happen?"

"I think it must have happened in the loft of the barn. We were out there. Having lemonade. Something about the loft–the moonrise–I still have a lot of amnesia about it."

"Repression. Is that why you didn't tell me back then?"

"Not repression. Amnesia. I didn't know. My therapist and I are pretty sure now he gave me Roofies, Rohypnols, a European drug. They make you drunk real quick…when they wear off, you have amnesia. I felt funny the next day, the fifth, I was so sore–my vagina–my–my–rectum. Had to get back to Baton Rouge. Had to."

Brit knew her body was on the bed next to her daughter, that her face was hard with concern. But she felt dispersed, floating, like she'd alighted upon an anomalous world. She turned, half-crouched, fingers grasping Asia's bristly forearm. "There? Even there?"

Solemn, Asia nodded. "I had bleeding–there–so I went to the campus clinic. She–the doctor–checked me–checked–I had tears inside me. And–I wasn't–a virgin–anymore."

The Virgin card came in Brit's mind, white-bodied girl, blood dripping from her finger, ten black trees, full moon, unread book before her. Now the book was revealed. A horror story.

Brit wanted to scream, rail, weep…molecules hurtled, she hovered in a gray place, her consciousness had abandoned her. She felt fear.

She sensed Damien breathing at the door.

Don't let Fear in.

Okay, okay! God! Guide me! Help me! Show me Thy Will! There can be no good in this!

Everything bad is good.

No!

Yes.

Surprisingly, calm came over her. She heard Anastasia's voice as if from a void.

"Mother. Listen to me. You must go do your ride. You must." *God guiding?* Then Asia weeping. "Oh, I am so sorry I told you. I'm a terrible, selfish person."

Asia's hand on her knee squeezing. She looked into Asia's red eyes.

"Mother. Go. Please! You must ride."

God's Will? Or her selfish desire to escape?

She stood.

"Okay." She took a deep breath. "Okay, Asia. I'll do this." She stared at the backlit blinds. "We might need money." She touched the coarse sweater. "Can I get you anything?" She watched Asia's head move from side to side.

"No, Darling? If you need room service—use it. I'll be back as soon as possible. I won't hang around." Then almost to herself. "I'll ride. Just ride. Then get off Mokhtar. Damien will have to handle the glad-handing. I'll come right back here." She caressed Asia's shoulder. "To you."

"Mom, I've been in very intensive therapy. At school. I'm doing pretty well."

You don't look it, Brit wanted to say, instead, "I'm proud you're taking care of yourself." Her mind began feeding her bits of information. Saunders had to go—Grant—

Asia started to cry. "That day was so nice, so sunny, the pool, Wil jumping in after the chicken breast—we were like a real family again, even Gramma and Grandpa were there..." She stopped.

God, thought Brit, *she looks anorexic.*

"I guess now we can never be a family again. Can we, Mom."

Brit knelt on the floor. Reaching up, she took her arms. "Honey. You and I, together, were always the real family. There's all kinds of families. There'll always be you and I." Brit's throat was sealing over; she cleared it hard to avoid crying.

"You better go, Mom. I'll watch you on TV."

"I can't believe this...But. Yes. I must go. We'll resume...all this... shortly."

"I'm fine. The Gone-Key's got good room service."

She smiled at Asia's use of her baby name for the Algonquin. The Gone-Key. They'd stayed here for all Brit's openings.

"Well, Baby. I'm Gone-Key also. You stay put."

"I will. I love you, Mom."

"I love you, Anastasia. With all my heart and soul."

T W O

Up on Mokhtar. White velvet cape, black satin edges **flaring down from her shoulders** fanning over his rump. Dully, Brit wondered: *Do I look like a medieval lady on her palfrey?* But medieval ladies didn't ride stallions, or astride. Men wouldn't let them. The men had to perform the first rape, they couldn't let a horse do it. Her mind was flying around, feeding her useless information. Her hands shook on the reins. Mokhtar was wound up, hyper-tense. Veins like rivelets lifted the tissue-fine skin of his neck. She could see his eyes, black and glistening, bulging from their sockets. His mane shimmered against the sheen of sweat on his arched neck.

He'd nickered loudly at the four escort police horses–probably more of a check for mares rather than for equine company–Brit almost smiled as he moved under her. She shifted her buttocks, took a deep breath, settled into the saddle as deep as it allowed. Except for mouthing his bit he stopped fussing. She listened to his champing, the jangling of the double bits and the loose curb chain under his chin, knew he was working up a frothy saliva. His wet mouth was good, it meant acceptance of the bit–acceptance of her–as his Higher Power? The jangling pinged within her. He whinnied, trying she knew, to assure himself flesh and blood creatures existed in this place of echoing pavement, concrete buildings, mirror-like windows. A police horse swung its neck around, stared at the active stallion, didn't answer.

Typical New Yorker, thought Brit.

Then Mokhtar saw his reflection in a window. Brit felt his muscles pump, he let go a stallion scream, a challenge to the white stud he saw mirrored. His cry echoed like a hawk's, bouncing around the buildings. The police geldings' heads jerked up.

That got their complacent attention, thought Brit. *Did they now expect a mugging?*

Mokhtar pawed, shod hoof sparking on pavement. Brit legged him hard away from his reflection, he swiveled, the mirrored stallion vanished. He settled. Except for champ, champ, jangle, jangle.

If only, so easily, she could make what happened to Asia disappear.

Embarrassed now, she shrugged at the nearest mounted policeman. "He thought he saw another stallion in that window challenging him," she tried to explain.

The cop grinned, sitting easy on his lax gelding, "Sure gets your attention, don't he?"

She found she could smile back. "Yep."

Now, thought Brit, *all we've got, Mokh, is screeching metal vehicles, honking, noxious smells. Maybe some glinting one-eyed cameras. Maybe crowds.*

He was still bunched up tight and to the novice eye looked beautifully collected–neck arched so extremely his chin almost touched his chest, hindquarter muscles curved and tucked hard under him–but Brit knew his mind was disconnected, like hers. They moved forward in his high springy trot, so slow there was a pause, two diagonal legs suspended in the air before lighting on the pavement, the next diagonal set rising. He passaged down the street, silver-white, mane and tail swinging, making small, alert snorts. The flat-walking police horses at each corner emphasized the fantastic appearance of Mokhtar. Damien led in a silver antique Rolls Royce, a convertible. A graphic design on a satin sash was draped around the car, *Britannia Rhodes, In The Altogether: Woman and Horse,* and in smaller print, *Damien Galleries.*

From somewhere began the low, ominous-hopeful sounds of Rimsky-Korsakov's *Isle of the Dead.*

She felt a great thrill run through her, through her horse. *This was it.* But part of her was still at the Algonquin Hotel, next to her weeping wreck of a daughter. *You must put Asia away for now.* She touched Mokhtar's neck to connect with him but his mind, too, was out, in the buildings, the traffic, the four horsemen before, behind him.

Just stay on. Wrench your lips apart. Imitate a smile. Leave it on your face.

The music lifted. Mokhtar responded when she laid her right leg on him. He eased obliquely to the left, half-passing diagonally across hollow-sounding pavement. When he came up beside a police horse she squeezed both legs, made her bottom rock-still, and he halted. The music had entered them. She pushed with her left leg, gave a hitch with her pelvis and he began a high collected canter. *Good boy!* Easily, she moved him diagonally to the right. As she came up to a cop, the guy slanted his eyes at her and breathed, "Wow. Some horse." All those years, training, the two of them, working on the plateau so now they could segue into automatic pilot, and perform intricately, effortlessly...in a dream state. *Thank God for the music.*

Part of her flew up above everything...and looked down on the tiny black-haired woman on the white horse...she saw, heard? the woman's mind screaming *"Trust is dead! Trust no one! Sons rape daughters..."* That woman teetered at the brink of the void, then peered in, and she saw not a void but a dank pit teeming with slavering monsters, cackling hideously in slime, crying out to her grotesque ideas: "You are us. We are you." Chanting.

French horns.

Had she created this sinister reality visited upon her innocent, virgin daughter? *Had Asia?*

How could she not have seen how sick Saunders was. Is.

Lee had seen. She hadn't listened to Lee.

Grant had to remove him from her house instantly. Terror. She would lose Grant.

If she ever saw Saunders again she'd kill him—claw his face, tear into his solar plexus, rip off his penis and testicles. With her strong bare hands. Her rage foamed like the scarves of silvery saliva swinging from Mokhtar's lips. It fed the monsters of the void.

The woman and horse bodies continued an exquisite, Grand Prix dressage dance down the streets of New York. She had faint peripheral awareness, a few jaded New Yorkers seeing this exotic procession, working not to react. But one little kid cried out.

"Mommie look, horsee."

Three girls, one boy followed jogging along the sidewalk. Others, in storefronts, stared.

Damien stood up and waved at non-existent crowds, turned, hissed back at her, "Wave!"

To whom? There were hardly any people, and most were ignoring this miniature parade. Then she saw the bulbous eye of a news camera. Putting all four reins in her left hand, mechanically she waved her right. Then laughed. Here was this pitiful parade—to see a parade they should go to New Orleans! Back home people would be cheering, crying out, "Throw me something!"

Throw me something!

Her eyes slid past the cyclopean camera recording her passage. A deformed electronic monster, hungry, predatory, eyeing her, her horse—suddenly she recognized the human passers-by were not the parade goers. The real parade-watchers were behind the camera's single-eyed brain...a brain feeding the world...Planet Earth a blue-green brain-swirl. Neuro-transmitter cameras feeding the synapses of billions of television sets all over the great Mother-Brain. Again, part of her consciousness detached from her body, lifted on high. From above, she watched the tiny glittering black-white, woman-horse dance balletically over blue-black pavement.

Kettledrums. She slowed to piaffe–high slow trot–no forward movement…
Trumpets. Her pelvis moved deep, once. Mokhtar thrust forward, hard, a gallop,
hooves ringing past the lead horses to the bannered bumper of the Rolls, its silk
lifting slightly, Damien's face aghast–was she going to jump the horse into the
car? His hands flying up–

She used her right knee hard, Mokhtar wheeled a half-circle, a hard gallop
back, his mane whipping her face. At the center of the outriders, the imaginary
X of the dressage arena, she sat down, legs stiff on his bellowsing sides. His rump
dropped, he made a brief Western-horse slide, then…his rump rose under her.

Cymbals clashed. It was a perfect halt. A thin cheer rose up. Then silence. She
knew without looking his legs were square beneath him. She felt the power of the
earth rise up through old soil, through cobblestones, through layered blacktop,
spiraling up through Mokhtar's strong horse legs up through his vibrating body
and into her solar plexus…She was grounded.

The last two police mounts passed.

She faced away from the cavalcade, alone on the black street.

Death proceeds life. This was a Death.

*So in the great cosmic dance of life and death and life…how significant is the rape
of your daughter?*

Not significant at all.

The most significant event of all.…

Feeling was returning. She was coming back in. Coming back in meant pain.

Clip clop, clip clop, clip clop, clip clop. The four horses moved away from her.
Their sound was beautiful.

A light mist, not quite rain, lowered like gauze. Now she saw pavement,
police, parked cars, pedestrians. Storefronts glittered with a sheen like birthsweat.
There was suddenly a sharp tang, a freshness.

My life is changed, Brit cried inside.

Yes.

I've been expecting people to make me happy.

Yes.

Only my self with Thy Self can do that.

Yes.

This new warm feeling, this is Love?

Yes.

This Love is available to everyone? God–why does it take so much pain to find this love?

Ego. Gets in the way.

Everyone, everywhere can feel and know this Love anytime, anywhere. It's sitting there waiting. Inside. Just waiting for us to find it.

Yep.

I can't help Anastasia.

Nope.

All I can do is feel this love, let it flow to her.

Yep.

And...and...Saunders?

With a click, she was fully inside herself, on the horse. She felt Mokh greet her with just the tiniest shift of his consciousness, glad she was back. He snorted plumes of air. His bits jingled, her good saddle seemed to wrap her legs around the warm horse torso. Slowly she turned him, a rotation on his hindquarters, front hooves clattering on pavement.

Suddenly she was able to feel pity for the sick, sick fifteen-year-old boy/man. What monsters he must have inside him. Bigger, uglier than hers. Grant would have to put him away...he needed help...would he rape again? Women and girls must be protected...God...was he a sociopath? A psychopath?

Briefly, shame came, but she remembered the words on the Virgin Card: "I am shame and I am boldness." She straightened her shoulders. She saw the ten trees in the card and knew they were only an illusion of protection, her forest-ringed farm was not protection. The Devil had penetrated her fastness, stolen the innocence of her child, and her innocence. She also had been a virgin, naive....

There was "collapse and disintegration."

She'd never seen Anastasia look so terrible.

Remember, all this leads to a completely new beginning.

There'd been another card...something about...

Gullibility.

In a collected canter she rode back into the parade. Smiling, waving–more noise now, nearing the gallery–she let shame pour over her like a hot flash.

Also remember: It's self-indulgent to wallow in a state of shame.

Maybe that's all my hot flashes were anyway, shame at losing my nubility.

Good insight, Brit.

Being gullible allowed me to pretend I was a semi-helpless girl creature who need-ed help from big strong men. Stay a child.

Didn't work, did it?

Nope. I got fucked, metaphorically, and the Devil I trusted assaulted my daughter.

That's her problem.

Oh! No! That is so hard.

The truth is hard. Don't want to rob her of the chance to learn about gullibility, do you? Look how long it took you to learn.

Yes. Too long. But—I can be there for her...?

Yes. You just can't be for her.

There was an actual crowd around the gallery entrance, waving, making cheering sounds. She saw Willard's face, beaming. Some sanity. The Reading. There had been victory and celebration there too.

Now a cluster of television cameras sucked in her image. On his own, Mokh stopped. He snorted and with a plunging motion moved sideways. His consciousness was outward now, gone from her, checking for danger, watching for challenges.

She gasped, almost laughed. The crowd moved back, afraid of Mokhtar, and she saw her silver horse/woman sculpture. Damien had moved it outside!

Then a police horse banged into her, and she smiled as the young policeman grinned, legging his horse away.

"My horse thinks that statue's real," he said. "You make that?"

She nodded, legs firm on Mokhtar, who had a straight-up neck, erect ears. She knew his eyes were showing white, his nostrils distending. He was evaluating flight or fight with this strange horse, holding the challenge of a rear for so long.

"Pretty damn good, if I do say so, ma'am."

Tuned to Mokh, aware of the cameras, she answered from the side of her mouth, "Thanks, but drop the 'ma'am!'"

Damien was in front, hands on hips, puzzled by Mokhtar's adversarial dance. Brit called down, "He thinks it's real."

Damien's hands flew up, he turned to the crowd. "Britannia Rhodes' stallion thinks her sculpted stallion is real..."

The crowd aahed, jostled to get a clearer look at Mokhtar.

Brit saw four TV cameras, maybe six still photographers snapping away, her thirty seconds of fame, maybe five minutes on a Sunday journal program—Andy Warhol had been wrong. No one got fifteen minutes—they got a sound bite.

She tightened the reins slightly—he felt light enough—would he remember...? She clamped her legs hard on him, pushed her seat deep. Her fingers twiddled the reins, whoosh! Mokhtar rose up, paused, then tucked in his front legs, in a classic levade, a frozen rear, then at her urging, glaring at his indefatigable rival, took her up further until his front hooves pawed the air inches from the sculpture.

And then he did it!

Cut loose that great stallion scream, everyone gasping, surging back, it ringing out so unearthly loud–the crowd's aaah, an enchanted sigh of awe, the releasing satisfaction of seeing myth come to life.

His front feet plonked down, Brit triumphant, *I love you, Mokhtar!* Her head swinging around, thinking, we could leap tall buildings in a single bound! Laughing now. *Betcha you never heard the likes of no horse like that, y'all folks here in Noo York City!* The reins loosened now, letting him prance, leaning over him, stroking his great curved neck, babbling, praising him, "You really laid it on good, Big Guy!" And, "Who loves this horse, who loves this horse!"

Then her mind saw her daughter huddled in rags, red-eyed, weeping, watching her crazy mother cavort idiotically in front of the world. She heard cheers, clapping, Damien shouting "Bravo, Bravo..." saw a grinning Grant in the crowd, brandishing his fist, victorious for her.

She dismounted, handed the reins to a waiting groom, whispered a few words to Damien, then climbed into the Rolls. As she told the driver to take her to the Algonquin, Grant jumped in beside her.

"What's up, Baby," he whispered, as both gave cheery waves to the onlookers. She squeezed his hand.

"At the hotel."

In silence they rode back, Brit holding Grant's hand, hard.

THREE

Immediately she went to Asia's room and when her knock wasn't answered, looked in. Asia was asleep, her head at the foot of the bed, one arm dangling. Brit closed the door. Her mind suggested a drink, then a cigarette. She let each desire pass.

Grant stood watching her.

"Brit, what's wrong? What's going on with Anastasia?"

"Bad stuff, Grant." She flopped onto a loveseat and pointed to the one opposite.

"Better sit down."

He sat.

"Saunders raped her."

"What!?" Then, his eyes sliding away, across carpet, "No."

"Yes." She told him everything as he listened intently, eyes coming and going. He clasped, unclasped his big hands.

He felt terrified.

Inappropriately, at one point, he felt himself acquire the beginnings of an erection, and for a second hated his testosterone, his penis...then he began to cry. Brit was crying. He moved to her side, wrapped his arms around her, her head folded into his chest, his cheek pressed against her crown, his tears wetting her black hair. He smelled her herbal shampoo. Why was he crying? A mix of unidentifiable emotions eddied through him. A thought rose. *Saunders didn't do this. This must be a big mistake.* He felt relief, moved his head away.

"Brit." Felt her cheek shift on his chest against the silk, felt the wet silk stick to her cheek.

"Uh."

His chin rested on her crown, her hair shifting as he spoke. "Are you sure–?"

Her head whipped up banging his chin, he bit his tongue, tasted blood. She was yelling–

"–press charges!" he heard. She stopped. They stared at one another.

"Press charges? Brit, can't we keep this in the family–it'll be on Saunders record forever, ruin..."

"Grant. I said Asia doesn't want to press charges."

"Oh. I'm sorry. This is really, really hard. A shock–" He ran his big hand over his pate. "Hard to grasp...What then?"

"He needs help, Grant. He's a very sick boy."

Grant felt bile-like objections rise–he couldn't help thinking, even as he knew it was a clichéd reaction, *what about your daughter, how much did she lead him on...? He's fifteen–she's nineteen! Maybe she was making up all of this "Roofie" total amnesia stuff. He'd never heard of these "Roofie" drugs.*

He cleared his throat. "Brit. I know you will probably get very angry, but I have to ask. Are you sure she's telling the truth?"

Brit clenched her fists to stop herself from tearing at his throat, forcing her foaming anger down. She might ask the same if the roles were reversed. *He was right. This was hard. It was hard to grasp.* And, she felt ashamed, there was still a tiny part of her that loved Saunders. And a lot of her loved Grant.

"Yes. I am."

"These 'Roofies'...I've never heard of them."

Brit felt a chill. "Grant, that night you came out." *That night I was with Scottie.* Her hand went out, squeezed his knee. "Those two girls at my place, they acted so strange–you think...?"

His face set. She saw horror come. "He gave it to those girls...No."

"Grant. Lee told me the cops warned them to be on the lookout for guys slipping little white pills into girls' drinks. At the bar."

"Oh my God."

"Yes. Mine too."

"I need a meeting." He jumped up, paced. "You think there's a goddamn A.A. meeting anywhere in this rude, fucking town?"

"Probably hundreds." She watched him pace the room. Suites at the Gone-Key were tiny. Grant made only six strides before he had to turn.

"Before you go though, Grant, I need to know your plans for Saunders." Hollowness inside her. She wanted to cry again. *What about Grant and Brit?*

"What?"

Now anger came. "Grant. Dammit. Pay attention." Her voice rose. "This is serious. Your son–"

"–my son!"

"Yes. Your son has committed a felony. Rape. Sodomy."

He stopped. "Christ." His hands rose as though to cover his ears. He brought them back down, shoulders falling, "This is–it's–."

Brit continued to cry. "Yes. She was sore, bleeding–bleeding! So she went to the campus clinic. She had tears in her rectum, her vagina. Her hymen, of course, was gone."

"Hymen–she was a virgin?"

"Yes."

"Oh Christ. Jesus." He smacked a fist into his palm. "How could he do such a terrible thing?" He faced Brit, she saw tears come back in his eyes. "Brit, what do we do?" He looked away, then back at her, his eyes wide. "What about...us? This is unbelievable. Brit. My God. I love you."

"I love you too. But...we are history."

"That little son of a bitch, that sick, demented–"

"Yes. But now we each take care of our children, the best we can. Grant. You must go back tonight, remove Saunders from my house, so I can bring Asia home. She can't see him. I can't see him."

"I'm not sure I want to myself."

She yearned to go to him, put her arms around him, comfort him....

I guess this means we can never be a family again, Mom.

She kept her seat.

He ran his hand over his baldness. *He looked so good,* Brit thought, *black and gray sidegrowth pulled back into a ponytail. Gray silk turtleneck, black leather sport jacket. Big, beautiful, baffled hunk of man...not her man, no longer.* She felt a quick flash of rage at both children. It passed.

"Brit, I'll go tonight, there's gotta be a flight out, I'll have him out of there tonight." He gestured with empty hands. "What about us, Brit?"

Inside, a screaming, *I love you, Grant!*

"I love you, Brit," he said, taking a step toward her, his voice crunched, the sound like tires leaving her rock driveway.

Suddenly she was up, into his arms, feeling them wrap around her like a big warm bear's. She cleaved to him. He held her tight, big paw-like hands sliding up and down the columns of her back.

"We'll work something out, Brit. We just got together–it's been so good–" he stopped.

She put her hands on his chest, stepped back from him.

"Yes. This is a disaster." She looked at him with dead eyes. "There is no 'us', Grant. Not any more. I see no way–"

There were tears again, in his eyes. "Damn! Hell! How could we–? Not after this." He felt so sad. He was just getting really comfortable, so gentle-happy with her. Now that was blasted away. "Goddammit! I could smack him from here to kingdom come," he cried.

"Me too."

"The stupid, selfish, sick little son of a bitch."

"My feelings exactly."

He took a stride and embraced her again, long and hard and again she pressed herself into his body. They cried, holding tight to each other. She felt the stiff hide of his jacket under her palms, his shaking back beneath. Smelled him, lemon, leather, and his faint personal musk.

"I'm sorry–" They jumped apart. Asia had come into the room.

Brit ran to her, "Oh no, Sweetheart, no–"

"I'm sorry, Asia. I'm so damn sorry," said Grant. He extended a hand to her then let it drop.

"Thank you, Grant…it's not your fault—"

"I don't know about that, Asia. I want you to know this, though, I am on my way out of here and I'll remove him tonight. You'll never have to see him again—"

"Please get help for him, Grant. Put him away. He'll do it again." She began crying, "I'm scared he'll do it again…"

"You're right. Help. Yes. Asia, I—" He held his arms out to her, she stepped into them. At that, Brit felt a small relief. Asia sobbed in his arms, he stroked her greasy hair. Over her head he looked at Brit. She nodded and gave him a brittle smile as he said over and over, "I'm so sorry, Asia, so sorry." Then Asia pulled back, wiping her nose on the sleeve of her sweater.

"Well," said Grant. "I'll throw my things in a bag. Then I'll be gone."

Brit put her arm around Asia's shoulders as he disappeared into a bedroom.

In a few minutes Grant reappeared. He paused, put his arms around both women, then left.

F O U R

After landing at Moisant Airport from New York, Grant had driven like a blind man across the Causeway, waves seething black around him, no stars, no moon, all hidden by a heavy cloud cover. He sprayed rocks all the way up the drive and slammed through the front door. Marching in, he yelled, "Saunders. Get your shit together, you're coming home with me." He went quickly to Rita's room and said she could borrow the truck and take the next week off. One look at his expression and she didn't ask questions, she just began to pack.

Saunders appeared at the mezzanine rail, light from his room flaming his hair. Skin opalescent, he looked like a Botticelli angel standing up there. *Could this…boy…his son…really have done those terrible things?*

Haltingly, on the way back, his speed vacillating from forty to eighty and back, he tried to confront Saunders.

"Brit has told me everything, Saunders, but I want to hear it from you."

Saunders slouched indifferently in the bucket seat beside him, green light from the dashboard glowering on his marble face.

"Hear what?"

"I want to hear from your own lips what you did to Anastasia."

"Nothing."

"That's not what I hear."

"Give me an example." He shifted, and his leather jacket scritched against the leather seat.

Grant felt such fury he wanted to wrench the wheel to the right, plow them right through the concrete guardrail, plunge them into the killing black waters. He gritted his teeth, clenched his hands harder on the steering wheel.

"You want an example? I'll give you an example. Try rape! Brit says you raped your stepsister. You drugged her –"

"No way, man, she's crazy. Middle-aged crazy old woman–"

"Don't you dare, ever, call your stepmother 'old' you little shit–I could beat the hell out of you right now–"

He saw a stopover and whipped the car squealing into it, screeched to a halt, grabbed Saunders' leather jacket, felt metal studs biting into his palm, his fingers. He shook him, hard, then shoved him back. Saunders was limp, staring straight ahead.

Grant, in his fury,, leaped from his car, banging his head and his knee, pain lashing his rage. Almost catapulting over the carhood he wrenched open the passenger door, jerked Saunders out, flung him up against the concrete rail, bent him backwards over the concrete. Saw inky waves frothing around concrete pillars. They were directly under one high bridge lamp, pinioned in its yellow funnel of light.

"Ow," whined Saunders, "ouch, Dad, you're hurting me!"

"Hurting you! I'll hurt you. You hurt your sister, you little fuck."

Saunders muttering something, "…not even related, not my real sister…"

But Grant had to shake him, hard, knowing the concrete was biting into Saunders' back, not caring. "I've got half a mind just to shove you overboard, let you fall into that cold fucking water–drown you like a rat–now talk to me!" His mind caught up with his rage, he processed what Saunders had just said. It sounded like the beginnings of justification, the beginnings of confession. He jerked him upright, lifted him completely off his feet, slammed him down, Saunders sprawled, looked up, one arm came up to shield his face.

"Get up. Get up on your goddamn feet before I kill you. And start talking, now."

Cautiously Saunders rose. He limped a few feet away, began elaborately dusting himself off. Grant lunged at him. Saunders stopped, turned his large Weimaraner eyes on his father.

"It was all in fun."

"What was."

"Just a little fooling around that's all. I–I had a couple of drinks. The Fourth. Brit's big bash, remember?" Grant remembered. Brit's silver swimsuit, her white and silver body–the joy he'd felt–a chill all through him. *This had happened that same night?* It was just beginning to register.

He made his voice steady. "What exactly did this 'fooling around' comprise?"

"I think she'd had some drinks too. We just went up in the loft like we used to when we were kids. Play in the hay. We started giggling, tickling, I might have touched her boob, or something–shit–an accident–she wanted it, Dad." He gave his father a knowing look, a look that discomfited Grant. *Should a fifteen-year-old be able to give such a look?*

He wanted to believe Saunders. Desperately. Then he thought, this sick act–this alleged act–juxtaposed with the greatest night of his life, that sensual, loving night with Brit–then Brit's voice, screaming, came in his mind "...drugged, assaulted, raped, and sodomized..." Grant felt dizzy, he shook his head. *This was unbelievable.*

From the north, thunder. Big drops splatted around them. Lightning cracked over the water. A winter storm, coming fast. A wind came.

He yelled. "You did a hell of lot more than that, son, a hell of lot more–" Thunder was drowning him out, then rain like a wall of water. They hunched, ran for the car. Again, Grant banged his head, his knee, *this fucking car,* but he hardly felt it. He started it, pulled back onto the Causeway, wipers barely clearing the water. A sudden wind-gush flung the car sideways as if to carry out his earlier intent, and he leaned over the wheel tightening his grip, grateful he didn't have to look at his son.

It seemed his car was wading through the rain.

Suddenly Saunders shrieked–they were passing through a funnel of light from a bridge lamp–Grant looked, gasped, saw a water spout, now illumined by more lightning–coming at them. The Causeway was too high for waves to surmount but a cascade of spray flooded the car. He was creeping along in blinding water. *Where was the waterspout?*

Should have sat it out on the turnaround.

The spout. Could it crash through the concrete like a twister and lift the car, hurl them to oblivion? Remembered the movie *Twister,* cow flying past, helplessly bellowing. He felt like that cow, and almost laughed. Instead, he drove.

Rain poured over the car, but the waterspout never came–it must have turned away at the bridge or maybe it passed over behind them. He couldn't see a thing in his rearview. Could never turn around now. The car smelled of wet clothes, his leather jacket over his silk turtleneck felt slimy. They inched through the water. At the end of the bridge the rain evolved into a normal heavy rainstorm. He caught I-10, headed for the Carrollton exit, to the riverbend, to home.

F I V E

In the condo, they showered, then Grant demanded Saunders join him the living room, demanded the truth.

"Dad. I told you the truth." It was raining here too, persistent, beating on the glass doors of their balcony. Way below limbs of oaks thrashed in the night. Horns sounded from tugs and ships on the Mississippi. Grant imagined a runaway tanker plowing through the levee, through the park, slamming into the base of his condo, the building toppling. Not possible. The condo was too far from the river.

"I think you're leaving out a lot. Brit says that Anastasia was drugged–"

"Drugged?" Saunders began shrieking. "She's outa her mind!"

"Yes." He had to say this, had to get it all out. "That you then raped her, then you–"

He imagined a witness on the stand, him coolly breaking the criminal down. "Yes, that on the night of the fourth of July, in the loft of the victim's mother's barn you raped and sodomized her daughter."

"She's fulla shit, Dad. No way." Saunders sat in a chair opposite Grant, the black wall of the entertainment center behind him. He flipped a scarlet pillow up and over, up and over. Grant wanted to rip it from his hands, beat him over the head with it.

"You put a drug that causes amnesia into the lemonade–"*Lemonade! How innocent! How poignant!* Grant suddenly imagined a ghostly jury nodding, one old lady patting her eyes, lace hanky shaking–"lemonade that the victim was drinking." The imaginary jury gave him courage to confront Saunders, it kept things formal, and detached like this, he found he could say the things he needed to say to his son. "You then forced yourself upon her. When she woke the next morning, in considerable pain and confusion, she drove herself all the way to Baton Rouge where she resides on the campus of Louisiana State University. On arrival she checked into the clinic at her campus, and had herself examined." He paused, thought of the pain, the fear Asia must have felt. Her courage. He wanted to cry for her right now. He cleared his throat and continued.

"The attending physician found lacerations and tears of the walls of her vagina, her hymen was broken, she'd been a virgin–" he saw Saunders face twitch, Saunders mind picking up on that, and Grant felt a knowing sinking feeling and thought, *he did it.* Saunders himself remembering how hard it had been to break through, his triumph when he knew he'd busted her–Grant leaned forward, face bronzed in anger, "–and found also lacerations and bleeding in her rectum, evidence she'd been penetrated there, sodomized brutally, to cause the tearing and bleeding." Grant surged up, stalked to Saunders and bent down, eyes inches from his son's unflickering gaze.

"Admit you did this to your sister!" Spittle leapt from his mouth. His teeth were bared, feral.

Saunders stared back, and then he blinked. Grant saw the blink. *Aha. Again.* "You admit it, then," he said softly, withdrawing, unbending, his body flowing back up to a standing position.

Saunders twitched. "I admit nothing," he said in a low, venomous voice. "All that coulda happened from some date-rape on that campus of hers."

"Coulda?" *Saunders is speaking like a two year old.* "Date rape on the morning of the fifth? I think not, I think not. And we know she spent the night of the fourth in her own bed at her mother's farm."

Saunders folded his arms, hunched into himself. Rain beat on the glass. "Didn't do it."

"You better start talking. Brit could have you arrested. They've got a ton of evidence, documented by the campus doctor."

"Arrested? Shit! She's crazy–"

Grant held up a hand. "Never call your stepmother crazy, ever again, hear?"

Both thinking, *the real mother is the crazy one...*And, Grant thinking, *is my son crazy? Like his mother? What had that fucking therapist he'd been shelling out to all these years ever done for his son? Would putting him away do any good? It hadn't helped Margie.* He squeezed his temples between his palms. *Christ! A drink.* He needed a drink.

Saunders watched. Letting the fear that had come in him when his father said "arrested" fade. *No way. His dad would never let that happen.* He just had to stay cool. And lie, and lie, and lie.

He could tell his dad wanted to believe him.

Grant dropped his hands. "Enough for tonight. Get to bed. And you will not leave this house until we get to the bottom of this." Saunders stared, then surprisingly quickly got to his feet, and left the room. Grant heard his door slam. He sank to the sofa, hit the button that automatically dialed his sponsor, Irwin, listened to the ringing, then Irwin's voice: "Hello. Hello?"

He hung up. He couldn't share this. Not with Irwin, not with anyone. His stomach cramped, hard. He hobbled to the bathroom, made it just in time–a rush of diarrhea flooded from him, like his guts were coming out. He bent over, groaning.

Can't get a conviction from one twitch, one blink.

Over the next days he confronted Saunders again and again. He got nothing but twitches and blinks. He performed at work like a robot, he made a meeting every day, he didn't even notice Thanksgiving was approaching.

He missed Brit terribly.

S I X

When Brit got home with Asia the next day, they slept, then talked. Brit coaxed Asia to eat. She got her up and out. They fed ducks and chickens and walked through the woods with Wilton, got the garden in, planted broccoli, cauliflower, onions, beets, and cabbage for winter. The nursery tubs of azaleas and dogwood sat, while weeds grew around their spindly trunks. But, Brit and Asia picked pecans and spent hours shelling, talking quietly. Or, shouting.

"–and I trusted him, Mother. I trusted that little ape. Ape? No ape would do that! I loved him, like he was my real brother." Then Asia would begin to cry. This time, as always, Brit reached toward her, but Asia's shoulder gave an angry twisting movement away from her mother.

Today, when the violent crying diminished, Asia, sitting on a concrete bench with curled lion feet for legs, stared at her mother. They were in the herb gar-den–rosemary, thyme, tarragon in the air. Brit sat in a swinging bench, hanging by chains from metal posts. Late yellow roses bowered the steel frame and trem-bled each time Brit gave a push with her toe. Rose scent spurted into the air with each shove as though misted from a sprayer. Brit stared back, hands on each side of her knees, clutching the weathered wood of the swing. She watched her daughter's face warp as she said, "We had such nice times when he was little. Catching crawfish. Playing horses. Climbing trees."

She paused to cry again, she spoke through softer tears.

"Even with my stepfather, his father...Grant...some of it was nice. Thanksgiving dinner. Christmas Eve. The dumb way he read *The Cajun Night*

Before Christmas. He never could do a Cajun accent. Easter–" she laughed. "He seemed so big and so dumb, hiding our colored eggs in the garden like some giant goofy rabbit. All of us together. Like a real family."

When Brit left the rocking swing, sat and put her arms around her, Asia let her.

All over the farm, at the grassy edge of the pool under Asia's weeping willow, in Brit's forest beneath scented, sighing pines, they repeated this scene. Everywhere but the barn loft. When Asia was comforted, often she'd sleep, and Brit would find a private place for herself. She'd sit, feeling weighted down as the concrete bench among the herbs, but with pain crawling through her as though she'd been bitten by a snake, and her veins carried a slow-acting poison. She went to A.A. meetings alone, almost daily, and at night had long talks with Lee and Georgie. Twice weekly she took Asia to a therapist.

Lee never once said, "I told you so."

Georgie said, "Remember the Big Book says there are absolutely no mistakes in God's world."

She was on the phone with her sponsor. "That's harsh. In this case." She wanted a cigarette, furiously.

"Yes it is."

"I want a cigarette, dammit."

"Have one. Just don't drink."

"No." Brit was in the corner of her oyster sofa, phone to ear. "Funny thing, though, not once have I wanted a drink."

"That's great! Sounds like the compulsion to drink has been lifted. If you don't drink over this, nothing can make you."

"I really miss Grant."

"Of course you do. How's he doing?"

"Frantic one minute, a dead man the next. He's wading through stagnant pools of denial. He just does not want this to be true. Although he says he's trying to get Saunders to talk, to admit what he did."

"I think these things are even harder for a man."

"Yeah, yeah, yeah, I know. Our culture still frowns on wimps that weep. I know. But Grant can weep."

"Has he gotten Saunders any help yet?"

"Some. Not near enough." Wil came in the room, stared up at Brit, his eyebrow tufts questioning. She patted the sofa, he hopped up and curled next to her stocking feet.

She wore her "uniform" of black leggings, black sports bra, and over-sized man's white silk shirt that covered her thighs. The silk sighed sorrowfully against her arm as her fingers smoothed Wil's forehead. The fireplace was lit. Thanksgiving coming...Christmas. She shuddered.

"Well thank God for animals, Georgie. Unconditional love."

The odd thing was she'd hoped so much Colt would help Saunders–instead he was helping Asia. Although, at first, Asia wouldn't go near Colt, she'd been adamant: "I won't touch anything that belongs to him."

They had been in the barn. Colt's head barely cleared the half-door of his stall. His eyes, liquid Hershey chocolate, black schlera like a kohl-eyed pharaoh, looked inquisitively from Brit to Asia. His eyelashes were long and thick, like Asia's.

"This god-damn-colt picked that scum. He's a stupid horse!"

Never had Brit seen Asia reject any animal. In her lexicon, all animals were perfect, humans, not. *Was this a peculiar form of growth?*

"I just thought you might enjoy working with him–" Colt began bobbing his head, urgently, trying to get their focus on him.

"Look at him," cooed Brit. "This baby wants attentions! Little orphan baby...hims needs attention. Hims is just an innocent child, hims loves every-one, doesn't hims?"

Reluctantly Asia threw a quick look at Colt, whose head-bobbing stopped the instant her eyes met his. Brit saw their eyes were the same color. The foal's expression became hopeful.

"Big mean girls won't play with hims," Brit said, continuing her baby talk, careful to look only at Asia, and not the foal.

"Oh, damn!" Asia cursing? "Dammit. C'mon, brat. I'll teach you how to lead." She picked up the foal halter and entered the stall. "Put your silly head in here." The foal sniffed the halter she extended. "But you better behave, or I'll whip your little butt, hear?"

SEVEN

Two and a half weeks after Asia had begun to train Colt, Brit sat in her oyster sofa, phone to ear, on one of her daily calls to Georgie. Now, through the French doors she could see Colt's front half, back end obscured by oleander. Asia stood in front

of him. As Georgie murmured meaningless encouragement, she saw Asia carefully raise the lead shank attached to Colt's halter. Raise it to the left and Colt's
right front leg moved. To the right, his left hoof came forward. She was patiently
teaching him to pose for judging in a halter class. Her daughter was in the only
clothes she'd wear: baggy jeans, and baggy gray sweatshirt. Brit had discarded the
brown bristle sweater.

The colt got stubborn, wouldn't move his left foot. She saw Asia flip the lead
shank up and down, Colt bunch, then run backwards, Hershey eyes on Asia. Asia
followed him, then slowly led him forward, herself walking backwards. Then she
stopped, her body rigid. Colt stopped, too, imitating her body language, the language a horse understands best. *A skill humans have pretty much lost*, mused Brit.
It was as though Colt was teaching Asia about the power of her body–that it sent
potent signals that could stop even a three hundred pound animal.

"Coming to the eight o'clock meeting tonight?" Georgie was saying.

"Think so."

"Brit, I'm afraid this is something you just have to get through. You can't force
acceptance. But, I promise you, everything that seems terrible right now has
some good buried in it. The good will come to light someday–" there was a click
on the line, and Georgie said, "You've got another call. I'll hang up."

"Okay. Thanks, Georgie." Brit clicked a button, said "Hello?"

"Hi, Brit." A tender-voiced Grant. "How you doin'?"

"I'm having a really tough time with this. Really tough."

"I'm sorry. Not much fun here either. How is she?"

Grant had trouble saying Asia's name, Brit noticed.

"So. Did you find a place to put him away?" So did she, Saunders' name.

"Brit. Jesus! He's seeing his therapist twice a week!" She envisioned Grant's
face twisting in pain. "I've already got his mother 'put away.' Besides, something
like this could follow him all his life, be on his record forever."

Brit felt incoherent rage. *Why was he vacillating? How could he stand to be near
that little son of a bitch?* She screamed, "If you don't put him away, I'll hang up
and call the D.A. right now! He'll put him away! You're worried about a record?"

"Okay, okay."

"Quit dragging your feet on this, Grant. I don't understand you. Days and
days have passed. Are you planning to hide him out in that condo forever? Do
you want me to have Asia's clinic records, describing her injuries,
forwarded–no–faxed to you?"

"No, no, it's just–"

"No justs, no buts. I know you can afford to get him into the best hospital there is Grant; he's a psychopath–and, dammit, he needs help!"

"Well, now, I don't think–"

"I can't believe you're minimizing this heinous crime! He drugged, assaulted, raped, and sodomized his stepsister! Hell, the only sister he has! May ever have!" She felt crazy for a cigarette. "You're in denial. Fucking denial. Jesus. Quit acting like a damn practicing alcoholic. Do the right thing. Are you going to get that boy checked into a hospital, where he needs to be, or do I call the cops?"

Grant imagined Fitz at the door, wheezing, handcuffs jangling, "Real sorry about this, Grant, but–"

"Okay." He slumped back in the sofa. The reality was, he and the therapist were getting nowhere with Saunders. He'd yet to admit anything beyond some mild fondling. Maybe Brit was right, maybe hospitalization, the confinement, would shake Saunders, scare him, get him talking. "Okay, Brit, I'll have him somewhere tonight."

Brit exhaled. "Good, Grant. Good. You're doing the right thing. Please call me when he's checked in. They may want to interview me. I will be available."

"You will?"

"Of course I will. Dammit, Grant, I still love you, you know, even him sometimes, a little bit–but I can also hate! God. He's the only son I've got. This is so fucking horrible. This is the worst nightmare in the world!" She would not cry.

"Brit–Brit–I–love you–this's been tearing me apart. I feel like someone took a chainsaw to my chest. I'm like you. I love him, then I hate him, then I–"

"I know. I hate what he's done to Asia. I hate what he's done to us."

"Yes. Thank you for saying that. Okay." His voice rose, squeaky, childlike, a tone she'd never heard from him. "Brit–I miss you so much…" Silence on the line, then intense breathing, she felt him gasping for control…"I'll make sure it gets done. I'll call you tonight with the details."

"Good. Grant?"

"Yes?"

"I know this is hard."

"Yes."

They hung up.

E I G H T

Grant quietly replaced his high-tech receiver. Saunders was in his room. Rita, who'd returned to the city with them, unknowing, had just left for the day. The room had an innocent smell of lemon furniture oil.

His and Saunders' eyes never met. Both spent their days moving through the condo, heads down like cowled monks pacing through a monastery. Rita tiptoed around as if someone had died. Grant knew she assumed there'd been some great rift between himself and Brit. Well, let her think that. And, wasn't there? In a way, didn't Brit blame him for what Saunders had done?

He sighed deeply then began making calls. Later, he called Brit back and told her Saunders was checked into a psychiatric hospital, in the adolescent ward. Saunders' therapist had rallied, she knew Dr. Suzette Frume, the woman who was now to be his doctor at the hospital. And yes, in about two weeks, they'd want to interview her. After Thanksgiving.

N I N E

Asia was eating and sleeping normally. Her weight had picked up.

Brit missed Lee. Seemed she spent all her time with Leroy now. So she went to more A.A. meetings. Then spent more time with Asia. She rode Mokhtar. When Damien called to inform her she was several hundred thousand dollars richer she smiled, but did not feel overjoyed.

Nights, she lay awake for hours. The guilt. She stared up at cold stars through her skylight. *Her fault.* If she hadn't been so selfish, so self-absorbed in her fuck-ing fears of turning fifty, she'd have seen, seen Saunders was off–but no. He was there to redeem her. Save her. Instead, he was there to be saved. By her. And by failing him she'd brought this horror upon her daughter.

She just couldn't believe there were no mistakes in God's world. Maybe not in God's world, but plenty in Man's.

Again and again she went crying with this to Georgie, who said, "I hear you Brit, but you just aren't that important. You aren't that powerful. You gave that boy a home. You did your best. And you believed in him. It's not a bad thing to believe in someone. That's what he needed. It was just too late. Nothing, from what you've told me while he was with you, would give anyone a clue he was so angry. Not that angry, at least. I want you to go to a meeting every day. I want you to pray and meditate every day. And keep calling me every day."

After a while she got a different perspective on guilt. She began thinking, maybe, it too, was just another way to be self-absorbed. If I feel guilty enough I don't really have to change myself, do some work on myself, become more aware, pay attention to what's really going on. Just beat myself up with lots of painful guilt, then continue on as before.

Guilt was easier.

Her white eyelet comforter these nights was tumbled with books, the ones from Bookstar, with Grant following her around the store like a high school boy, that first reunion lunch at Mr. B's–that first…fuck…confused in her mind with bromeliads, booze…Grant the Granite-man…*Don't go there, don't start crying again.*

godd and Wil picked their way through the books as though stepping over stones in snow.

This night she was getting a strange comfort from reading a book by a man named Vernon Howard, *The Mystic Path to Cosmic Power.* If she ever said this title to anyone, they'd think she was as insane as Margie. What he seemed to be saying was she had a false self, a phony construct that had been formed as a defense system from early childhood and–that false self obscured her true self, a true self that was connected to God, was part of God, was actually Divine. And so–did Saunders. This false self lied to her, to everyone, under the guise of protection. It was so powerful everyone came to believe it was all they were. *Another great lie.* She knew she had another Self. She'd experienced it, time and again, on the threshold having her "experience," riding Mokh through the streets of New York when she was detached, floating high above everything, looking down on the monsters in the void–looking down on her false self?–and often during meditation, when she felt that nimbus of calm and joy emanate from within her. The trick was to live from the true self all the time. The true self embodied the perfect love she prayed for each day.

Did even an evil person like Saunders have this true self?

And how could she love, even imperfectly, Saunders? *Wasn't his crime unforgivable?*

And Grant. She and her body missed him so much. After a while it became her routine. Lie in bed, pray for guidance, clear her mind, to let the Great Creator have a chance to get a word in edgewise, then cry. Cry for an hour, missing Grant, cry for her daughter. Then start reading.

One night she read, "I must wash away confusing emotions, like depression and self-pity, which make self-clarity impossible. How can we see things clearly when our eyes are full of tears?" She stared up at brilliant stars framed by her sky-light, felt the pillows soft under her shoulders, and thought, *yes.*

Then she read, "One permanent enrichment given by universal principles is a flexibility that enables us to meet and handle any situation...If it is a family crisis, we remain in calm control." She almost laughed. *Calm control?* A candle on her bedside table flickered.

She read on. "A person living from his false self cannot do this. He reacts rigidly and mechanically to everything. He has no choice; he must obey the tyrannical dictates of the artificial self, which leads to distress and disaster." *Saunders. Had his act been "mechanical?" Had he been obeying "tyrannical dictates?"* His actions had certainly led to disaster.

"Disaster." Dis-aster. *What did the word really mean?* Something to do with stars? She fumbled for her *Funk & Wagnalls* dictionary, awakening godd. Unruffled, godd moved and settled near Brit's head, one paw up on the pillows. She began purring.

The roots of words were important, Lee had taught her that. She had to get to the root of this. She looked up "disaster." It was, "An event causing great distress or ruin; sudden and crushing misfortune. 2. Obs. The unfavorable aspect of a star..." Then in her *Merriam's,* she found "Dis–a Roman god of the Underworld; Aster–From the Latin word, 'astro' star." She looked up "aster," which was Old English, it meant "apart," which also derived from the Latin, and meant "two."

Underworld, death. *Saunders, god of the Underworld? Dis-ing them all apart?* Two apart. Her and Grant. Saunders and Anastasia. All of them...apart. She mused on this for moments, stroking godd, then picked up *Mystic Path* again.

"...So can we, by dismissing the false ideas we have collected over the years be free and flexible. One useless idea is that a mere discussion of our faults, that is, merely talking about them, does any good."

Talk, talk, talk. That's mostly what she and Asia had done, then more talk, Asia with her therapist, she with Lee and Georgie. Her A.A. meetings. Of course, there, she never could reveal the root of her pain. Only the pain. godd purred in her ear.

"Self-confession must be followed by self-insight. Talk becomes an endless procession of wrongdoing and confession, misbehaving and admitting."

Like her guilt.

"The New Testament term *metanoia,* sometimes translated as 'repentance' means 'change of mind.' That is what we gain when we see into ourselves...Another false notion to dismiss is that we are threatened by our past follies. Listen! Once we determine to find ourselves, past experiences turn to profit."

Even this...disaster?

"This includes everything unhappy, sinful, shameful...regretful...Human folly is done while in a state of non-awareness, of psychic hypnosis."

She stared off unseeing, not noticing that the triplicate mirrors of her vanity showed three slightly different images of herself.

Was Saunders in a state of "psychic hypnosis"? Thus, not really guilty?

No!

Pulling the comforter more closely around herself, she returned to her reading. godd's purring became louder.

"...This encourages us to become more awake, for we see that wakefulness is the true and only answer to human folly. Finally, we see we can become entirely free of guilt and shame stemming from past behavior. We realize that it was not done by the True Self, but by the artificial self–which is now fading out. Who needs a candle in the sunlight?"

Was she "awakening?" Was there a way to awaken Saunders? Asia?

She'd tried to read these things to Asia, but met an avalanche of anger. Asia was working hard with her therapist learning to "set boundaries," *not seeing,* thought Brit, *that they weren't really necessary, that just by holding her body a certain way, Colt–they had to get a name for him!–did whatever she wanted.* And also by paying very close attention to other people–she had a flash of Asia's first encounter with Saunders, the day she came from Baton Rouge, how his arms did not go around her when she embraced him. His half-smile, the dead way he responded to her. And she, herself, had seen this and felt some faint alarm but had not paid attention. She had chosen to stay in a state of "psychic hypnosis," too.

And Grant, when she tried to share these new concepts with him during a phone conversation, had said, "I'll just stick to A.A., the Twelve Steps. You're getting too far-out for me, Brit."

Okay, she'd thought, *this then is for me.* Because these ideas, while terrifying, had a resonance she could not turn her back on.

Did they mean Saunders did not have to "repent?" That he merely had to "change his mind?" Maybe "merely" was the wrong word. He'd have to completely turn himself around, sear through all his fears and hates and see that acting on these hates kept him as imprisoned as his victim.

Even if he was able to make this incredible change, *could she forgive him?*

Her stomach knotted, her cells screamed, *NO!*

T E N

One day Brit and Asia sat deep in her forest, Brit in a semi-lotus on a cushion of russet pine needles, Asia sprawled against a log. Suddenly Wil stood and stared, and his tail began a hesitant wagging. There was a thunderous crashing, then Asia had a slobbering Mime in her face. She'd been crying, now she began to laugh.

"Mime, down girl," she cried as she rolled around with the huge dog, releasing pine fragrance as she laughed and mock-struggled. Wil gazed adoringly at his giant passion.

"THERE you are! Whatcha HIDING for?" Sugarplum wore a scarlet sweat outfit which clashed with her orange hair. Gold bangles embroidered in an arc over her aggressive breasts glinted jarringly. A camcorder dangled from one hand.

"Bin lookin' all OVER for you." She hefted the camera. "Wanna take PICTURES of Mokhtar. And that colt of MINE you've got. Saw HIM in the pasture. Looking awful PRETTY."

Mime settled beside Asia, who said, "For a god-damn-colt?"

Brit, startled, laughed at Asia's boldness but felt a warning jangle toward Sugarplum. *Was she beginning to "awaken?"* She spoke. "We're pretty glad we were able to take him off your hands. Asia just loves him."

Frowning, Sugarplum looked around. She set the camera down, fumbled in a pocket, and got out a cigarette. The tobacco smell bothered Brit. She waved her hand to clear the air.

"What? You QUIT?"

"Yep."

"Well, I ain't READY for that yet. Booth just gets on my NERVES, so bad!" She sat and blew smoke toward Brit. Brit shook her head, *she doesn't even know what she's doing,* she thought, then laughed again. Also, she realized there was plenty of fresh air around, Sugar's few puffs of smoke wouldn't hurt her, so why make an issue of it?

"Glad YOU'RE so happy," said Sugar sourly, wriggling her skinny butt in the pine. "Look. Gotta potential BUYER for THAT COLT. I can take him OFF your hands now. It was REAL nice of you to KEEP him for me, while I GRIEV-

ED over losing Nadia. But he can come HOME now. I wanna get some VIDEO of him to send to this guy in TEXAS."

Brit saw alarm in Asia's eyes. She also realized her warning jangle had been correct. *So there was something valid about "awakening" after all. Had she been getting these signals about people all along and just ignoring them? Think of the grief that could have been spared if only she'd been "awake."*

"Sugar–I love you, but, he's not yours to sell." She marveled at how calmly she was able to speak to Sugarplum.

"What–"

"You gave him away. You didn't want that god-damn-colt–remember?"

"Brit! I was GRIEF-stricken–I didn't KNOW what I was SAYING, doing–"

Brit put her hand on the thin scarlet arm. "Sweetie. He is ours now. Part of the family. Tell that man in Texas he's just not for sale."

She'd never stood up to Sugarplum before. Something inside her tumbled around, then righted itself, like a cat dropped from a height. She braced for battle.

To her surprise, tears came in Sugar's eyes, she spoke–softly. "Oh, okay, Britannia, but this guy would pay–oh, five thousand dollars and Booth's on my back about how much the horses cost–and–I'm scared he's gonna DIVORCE me–"

Sugarplum was eternally frightened Booth would divorce her.

"I'm sorry Booth's on your back, but the baby stays here. Tell you what, though, if it'll help, I've got some nice sketches–"

Sugar's face brightened. "You DO?"

"They might appreciate. My show was a success."

"Oh. Okay."

Just like that. Brit was quietly amazed. They clambered to their feet, brushing off needles and, dogs cavorting ahead, made their way to Brit's studio.

Brit made tea while Sugarplum agonized over sketches.

Asia began helping her. Brit walked in the room carrying a tray and watched the two of them slide sketches around on the floor, talking like old friends. One was of the girl draped over a horse's back. Before Brit's eyes, the girl flipped around, her head and neck now lying across the upright shoulders of an alert mare. A black mare...no, black-bay–the little black mare Mokhtar had bred that day over at Sugarplum's. She was beautiful. Almost all-black except for gilded bronze triangles, like pyramids, on her flanks, her muzzle, under her eyes. Brit

almost gasped out loud–the woman so insouciantly lying across her back
was–Rita! Rita, thin, tough, yet oddly regal, like a Nubian–Egyptian goddess.
Would Rita? She felt joy flooding her like a hot flash. Her next work. Something
about Rita–it would be a "poetry"–told Brit she'd do it, pose for it. And, of
course, a mare! The Bedouin rode only mares, even pregnant ones into battle.
They didn't trust stallions. Rita on a war mare… *To hell with those commissions.
They could wait.*

Sugarplum had narrowed it down to three, one of them of the girl lying across
the horse's back. Asia stood back, "I don't know which is best, Sugar. What do
you think, Mom?"

Should she give the girl-sketch to Sugar since it was the jumping-off point for
her next sculpture? Why not? That one could really appreciate.

Brit set the tray down and smiled. "Take all three, Sugar. But make sure you
frame that one." She was pointing to the recumbent girl. Then she was pleased
to see Asia's face brighten as much as Sugar's. Sugar turned and flung her arms
around Brit.

"Thank you so much, Brit. And, BOY, Asia is just getting WONDERFUL!"
Then she turned and embraced Asia. "I WISH I had a DAUGHTER like YOU."
Asia returned the hug and stepped back, grinning. "Boy, she's really CHANG-
ING, Brit."

Then they sat, drank tea, nibbled on red grapes. Talked esoteric Arabian horse
bloodlines until Sugarplum had to leave to feed.

Brit raised her eyebrows at Asia, and they collapsed laughing.

Maybe things were beginning to turn around, thought Brit.

By the evening before Thanksgiving Asia looked good. She told Brit she wanted to go back to school after the holiday.

ELEVEN

Early Thanksgiving Day, Brit went out to feed and found Mokhtar lying in his stall,
groaning. He was black with sweat, even though it was a chill forty-four degrees.
She raced to the house, called the vet. Yelled to Asia, and the two of them ran
back to the barn.

He was still down but now was thrashing, pivoting his body in a circle, his
shod hooves taking divots of wood from the plank side walls, the back log wall.

Brit called, "Mokh!" and he paused. She darted in, bent over him. His rolling
eyes stilled as she tenderly slid on his halter and lead shank. His brown eyes had

become almost blue. He seemed very far away. He felt cold. She raised his lip. His gums were pale, almost white. She did a pinch test, picking up a fold of skin on his shoulder, which normally would pop right back. Instead, it stood up, a small pyramid and then, with agonizing slowness, slid back into place. Serious dehydration.

He was very sick. *Colic,* Brit thought. From the stirred-up mess of his stall it looked like it had gone on for a long part of the night. *Mokhtar!*

If he'd twisted an intestine while he was down....

She pulled on the lead shank while Asia bent and pushed on his hindquarters. Together they yelled, "Mokh, get up. C'mon now. You've got to get up." He resisted, groaning.

Had the collective pain of the humans somehow gathered, erupted in him? He'd always been so sensitive to nuance of mood. Brit shuddered. *No! No! Mokhtar–you don't have to assume our suffering.* She continued to urge him, tugging, yelling, "C'mon, big boy, up, up on your feet!"

After a hard struggle they got him on his feet. He staggered one pace, then tried to lie down again. Sweat dripped from his belly. His head hung to the ground. Moaning, he swayed against Brit.

This is really bad.

She heard the vet's truck rattle up her drive, and jerked her head toward Colt's stall.

"Asia. Get Colt out of here, okay? Outside. Better stay with him or he'll go crazy missing his daddy." She didn't want Asia going through this. Or the baby horse.

Asia stepped back from Mokhtar.

"Is he going to live, Mom?"

"I don't know, Baby. This isn't good."

"Oh, Mom..."

"Go. Please."

"Okay."

As the vet walked in, Asia led Colt in a scrambling clippity-clop past Mokhtar's stall. Brit heard her say, "Now you just settle down, Colt; you'll get turned loose in a minute."

"Harry."

"Well, Brit, what have we here?"

"Bad colic, I think."

"Uh-huh." Dr. Harry bent, put his stethoscope to the horse's heart, listened, then straightened. He was a small man, lean, with fuzzy, graying, sandy hair.

"Heart rate's through the roof. Let me just give him a shot of Banamine, help him out a bit."

Harry administered the drug in Mokhtar's neck. The horse kept trying to lie down. Brit held his head up, both hands gripping the halter. His head sagged into it. Her shoulders and arms ached from holding it up.

"Let's get a tube in him. See if we can find the obstruction." Brit's arms gave out and Mokhtar staggered, slid to the stall floor. He lay on his side, legs feebly waving, some part of him trying to run away. Brit stepped forward to exhort the stallion up, but Dr. Harry motioned her. "No. Let him rest." He rubbed his fuzzy head. "Think it's twisted intestine, Brit. I'll listen for gut sounds." He walked around the prone horse and leaning over his back, listened to the swollen belly. He raised his eyebrows at Brit. "Dead quiet. Not good."

"I know, Harry."

"Now maybe we could try to load him up and you try to haul him to LSU's veterinary surgery in Baton Rouge–but if he's necrotic in that intestinal tissue–his color's real bad, pulse faint–he's what, twenty now?"

"Harry, for Chrissake. Do something. He's dying in front of our eyes."

"Yes. Brit. Do you want to try and take–"

"No. His pain. Stop his pain."

"That Banamine–"

She yelled, "Put him down, Harry! Please, let him go!"

Their eyes joined, his a concerned faded green, hers horror-dilated purple. Harry watched a pulse jump in her white neck. A stench of urine rose from the stirred-up stall. Brit still held the lead shank in her hand. It hung limp, useless.

"Are you certain?" Her mind saw them loading a staggering Mokhtar onto the trailer, the jouncing ninety-minute ride to Baton Rouge. She remembered once accompanying Sugarplum to the veterinary school. She saw Mokhtar on his back, all four legs pulled apart, trussed up like some big game kill, the scalpel slicing through his exposed belly, miles of intestine slithering out, the earnest search for the affected part–through all those miles. Sugarplum's mare had died on the operating table.

"Please!" She couldn't bear any more pain.

"Okay. Yes. It's the right decision, Brit."

She stared down at Mokhtar. He was black, all black from his intense sweating, his skin color showing through.

His eye rolled, *was he pleading with her?* Of course.

While Harry went to get the lethal injection, Brit fell to the floor and tried to pull his head onto her lap. It was so big and heavy she could only get his muzzle across her knees. She kept her eye on his eye. It was calmer now that she was holding him, stroking his face, tidying his long forelock. He swallowed, his eye never leaving hers.

Harry stood above her, holding the needle straight up. "I need to ask this one more time. Are you sure you want to do this?"

"Yes." *Am I?*

It is the thing to do. She nodded at Harry.

Mokhtar groaned, shifted his head closer to her belly as if to cuddle up to her. Tears welled in her eyes as she stroked his mane, his neck, fingered his thin-skinned ear.

"Brit. God love you. Mokhtar's too magnificent a horse to come down pitiful slow and gradual."

He knelt. Petted the horse's neck, gently moved the long white mane aside, so startling now against his blackness, then shoved the needle into a vein.

Brit was crooning, rocking his head, one hand stroking his jowl.

"Goodbye, Big Guy. I love you, I love you–"

He thrashed so hard she was rocked onto her back. As she struggled back up, urine-soaked shavings sticking to her jacket, he gave a big sigh. Life vanished from his eye. Harry had his stethoscope to his heart.

"Britannia. He's gone."

Tears streamed down her crinkled face. She nodded at Harry, then flung herself across Mokhtar's body. She cried for him, her daughter, her human man, her lost, demented stepson, for herself.

She lay over Mokhtar for a long while.

"Brit? You going to be okay?" Dr. Harry.

She raised her head. "He always–gave. And gave."

"I know, Brit. He was a very special horse." Her head went down again on Mokhtar's shoulder. She heard Dr. Harry tip-toe out.

Mokhtar forgave everything. Late feedings, dry water buckets, forgotten in storms. He was all about giving, forgiving, loving. He always gave her his best. The diminishing heat from his body seemed to soak into her body. Gradually calm came to her. As her body grew warmer and warmer, his colder, she felt as though his soul was entering her, with his body heat.

She began to cry quietly again.

He gave her the last thing he had to give.

T W E L V E

Saunders had been in the hospital for several days. He was learning the routines. Now he sat across from Dr. Frume, thinking, *fuck this shit, they're not keeping me here.* He obediently answered the same questions from previous sessions, "No, I didn't rape my stepsister. I'm not crazy. She's lying." He kept his voice soft, believable. He was enraged at his dad. Placidly, he plucked at his loony-bin clothes.

Already, he saw easy ways to escape. The trick, too, was not to swallow the drugs they gave him the minute his dad took off.

After the nurse left, with her little tray, her small white paper cups, he sniggered as he slipped the one pill, the two capsules under his mattress. Then he stretched out on the bed, thinking, *How excellent, Dome, that your guilt's got me this private room.*

When he got out he'd fix Brit-Maw good.

Maybe Thanksgiving? Might be lots of confusion around here then.

T H I R T E E N

Feeling oddly strengthened, Brit stood over her dead stallion, hooking fallen hair behind an ear. She backed from the stall, slowly closing his door.

I'll figure a way to get Mokhtar's body out of his stall. Tomorrow.

Today she and Asia would cry and play with Colt and try to eat the Thanksgiving dinner she'd put together the night before.

Such complete dissolution. She hoped this was the end of it.

Lee and Leroy had gone to the Smokies for Thanksgiving, but Damien and Viola called. Damien said he had three more horsey-artsy clients who wanted to commission her to sculpt them naked on their favorite horses. She laughed, then she told him Mokhtar was dead.

"You're really catching it hard, aren't you darling? He was so beautiful. Let me buy a grave marker for him."

"Thank you, Damien."

"How's Asia?"

Damien, Lee, and Georgie were the only ones she'd told. About the rape.

"Doing very well, considering."

"Good. It's always darkest before the dawn. Keep hold of the knowledge that your career, at least, is doing very well."

"Yes. Goodbye, Damien."

FOURTEEN

Grant woke Thanksgiving morning without his usual morning erection. He didn't want to get out of bed, yet he was filled with a nervous jangling.

Saunders in the hospital, Rita had the day off. *Brit–don't go there.*

He was alone. *Why was he always ending up alone?*

He heaved himself up and padded past Saunders' tightly shut door into the kitchen.

Coffee awaited him, set up the evening before by Rita. He almost cried, *bless her heart.*

He poured himself a mug, sugared it, added a dollop of whole milk, carried it back to his chilly bedroom. Didn't feel like turning on the heat. The coffee should warm him.

He sat on his bed and sipped the coffee. Wondered if Brit–

Automatically his hand went out, picked up the little black book from his bedside table, titled in gold letters, *24 Hours A Day.*

Irwin had bullied him into the habit of reading from this book each morning, then trying to pray, even meditate–whatever the hell that was. He made Grant quote Step Eleven back to him: "Sought through prayer and meditation to improve our conscious contact with God as we understand him, praying only for knowledge of his will for us and the power to carry that out."

The reading for today, November 23, said: "'In the world ye shall have tribulation. But be of good cheer–'" he shut the book, set it down. No God could expect him to be of good cheer today. The only God he'd ever heard of was from the preacher in the country church on the outskirts of Tylertown, Mississippi. He'd only been exposed to this preacher a few times, when he was very young. He remembered sitting beside his thin, nervous mother, head tilted back, crick in his neck, terrified. The patch on the seat of his jeans bit into his rear. A small, skinny man in a tight black suit stood way above him. His fisted arms kept flying around like that man with the funny mustache he'd seen once in an old war movie. Hitler? Just like Hitler's this man's eyes were wild, spit flew out of his mouth as he screamed that the undernourished women and children and a few men, trembling before him in thrift-store clothing, were the "Children of Satan!"

Screeching they'd all "...perish in eee-ternal flames, be damned to everlastin' hellfire!"

A lady in front of them stood up, then crashed to the floor. Grant buried his face in his mother's cotton dress, smelling her Old Rose cologne, a clinging scent of cigarettes, the Budweiser she'd gulped before they left for church. No one moved to help the woman who'd fainted. Grant heard "–unless ye repent, ye sin-ners, reee-PENT–!" The whole church sighed. Grant peeked out as the man softly said, "Or the Devil's gonna getcha, sure's I stand here an' witness...Y'all are sinnin', boozin',"–his mother had flinched–"thievin', lyin', whorin', foooor-nicatin–'"Grant muffled his face, blocked out the words, thought about the wild baby crow at home, soft, shiny purple-black feathers, heart beating so hard in the delicate ribcage, frightened gleaming black eyes, how it settled as he crooned to it, fed it–he even thought of the "A" he'd gotten in English Composition, writ-ing about his pet crow.

Now the words, the smells, the fear of that time came in his mind as if he was seven again, sitting on the hard pew, except now he understood the words, and knew he'd fulfilled every one of the preacher's prophecies.

He'd taken this to Irwin, who said, over coffee at Rue De La Course on Magazine Street, "Not a real happy picture of a loving God, is it Grant?"

Grant nodding, stirring his cafe latte. Irwin was eating a cinnamon raisin bagel with fat free cream cheese.

"That's why I've been, well, sort of agnostic. And neither of my of parents really 'believed.'" He snorted. "Most Sundays they drank. I actually only got to that church a few times, but it sure left an impression on me."

"Haunted you all your life, sounds like."

Then Irwin gave him an assignment. "Go read the Big Book chapter '"We Agnostics.'"

He'd never read it. This morning he picked up the blue book, let it fall open, not at his assigned chapter. He saw, in the middle of a page, "...unless this per-son can experience an entire psychic change, there is very little hope for his recov-ery." So, if he didn't find some sort of "Higher Power" he could, would drink again? "Once a psychic change has occurred, the very same person who seemed doomed, who has so many problems he despaired of ever solving them, sudden-ly finds himself easily able to control his desire for alcohol, the only effort neces-sary being that required to follow a few simple rules."

"One feels that something more than human power..." *but what else was there?* He felt nothing, fear maybe. "…is needed to produce the essential psychic change."

Essential. Psychic change. Sounded crazy. Far-out. Like something Brit would latch onto. His fear grew, he was peering into a fog-shrouded world, flames beyond the fog. Peopled with–devils?

His eyes were drawn back to the page. "…we physicians must admit we have made little impression upon the problem as a whole. Many types do not respond to the ordinary psychological approach."

Thought of Margie. Not responding. Even–Saunders. There was, he had to admit, something–off–about his son. And Saunders had been exposed to "the ordinary psychological approach" for years–since he was a little kid–since–he'd found him curled up in the pool of his mother's suicidal blood. Soaked into the comforter, soaked into Saunders' little denim overalls. Maybe it was a good thing he was in that hospital.

The fog closed in, feeling hot, not cold.

Beginning to sweat, he quickly flipped to the agnostic's chapter Irwin had assigned. Counted the pages. Thirteen and a half. He breathed and began to read, occasionally running fingers over his sweating pate.

"…you may be suffering from an illness which only a spiritual experience will conquer."

Damn! He wanted to slam the book shut. He didn't want a "spiritual experience"–raging, saliva-spouting preacher screeching hellfire, he suddenly smelled cigarettes, beer, old roses. Shuddering, he read on. "…such an experience seems impossible," *damn straight!* "but to continue as he is means disaster…"

Disaster.

He took a quick gulp of lukewarm coffee. His clock radio suddenly blared and he slammed it off. He was thick in the midst of one, alone, on Thanksgiving Day. Irwin's voice "–don't give in to self-pity." *No.*

His eyes refocused, he read, "…but it isn't so difficult."

Difficult? It felt impossible! No loving God would let a son rape a sister, even a stepsister.

A tiny voice. *But God didn't do it.*

Who did then?

A sickening lurch inside. Sex drove him. The need for it. Now that the obscuring fog of alcohol was cleared from his system, he saw the devil that really drove him.

He and Brit–the sex was constant. They weren't careful–another lurch. He remembered one night–both were drunk. Hadn't made it up to the bedroom, so they did it in front of the fireplace. Saunders had been on the stairs, in pajamas, clutching a stuffed rabbit. He and Brit leaping up, grabbing clothes.

How long had Saunders been watching?

Could that–?

After that, although they were "careful," they were still loud. Brit's bed banged against the log wall–thump, thump, thump–they'd thought it was funny. Never thought the kids, way across the mezzanine, could hear. Night after night. Cries and moans. They'd even laugh and say "a night without sex is like a night without starlight, no! Moonshine!" then laugh harder, polishing off another bottle of wine, guffawing at the double entendre. His lust for Brit preceded him like a fog. They were constantly grabbing for each other, in front of the children, kissing passionately, "sneaking" up to the bedroom. Had this pervasive sexual atmosphere somehow seeped into his son to erupt, finally, in this assault on Anastasia?

He wished he could talk to Irwin about this. But the shame–he heard Irwin's voice–"Keep reading, Grant."

"Lack of power, that was our dilemma. We had to find a power by which we could live, and it had to be a Power greater than ourselves. But where and how were we to find this power?"

Exactly. He sipped his coffee, cold now. "Well, that's exactly what this book is about." He felt a sliver of–gratification, he was getting in tune with the book. "It's main object is to enable you to find a Power greater than yourself…"

"… some of us have been violently anti-religious…bothered with the thought that faith and dependence upon a Power beyond words was…weak, even cowardly."

His intestines coiled, twisting like angry snakes, like Brit's painting of paisley cobras. He tensed, prepared to bolt for the bathroom. But it settled as a dull ache.

"How could a Supreme Being have anything to do with it all?"

Yes! How could a "God" let this disaster happen?

"Yet…we found ourselves thinking, when enchanted by a starlit night…"

His mind went back, under Brit's skylight, after the cosmic lovemaking, seeing stars, fat diamonds pressed so firmly into black velvet. "Who then, made all this? There was a feeling of awe and wonder…" Yes. And love, powerful surging love for Brit, for himself, for the wondrous universe he'd found himself so alive in.

With an oily slither the snakes in his belly came alive. Remembering, on that same enchanted night, his son was tearing into the drugged body of Anastasia under those same indifferent stars. And it might be all his fault.

"…but it was fleeting and lost."

The snakes wricked, spasmed. "…as soon as we were able to lay aside prejudice and express even a willingness to believe in a Power greater than ourselves…"

Pain contorted his gut. His face made a rictus, mirroring his insides.

Willingness.

"we commenced to get results…"

His vision blurred.

"…to our relief…"

Was he crying?

"…as soon as we admitted the possible existence of a creative Intelligence, a Spirit of the Universe"–a shaking rumbled up from the soles of his feet to his hands, to the book–"underlying the totality of things…"

The book fell. Clutching his abdomen he hobbled to the toilet. Felt the seething fetid mass of snakes gush from him.

He flushed.

Another rush.

Another flush.

Sweat rimed his body. With a trembling hand he picked up a spray can, Wizard Rose Bouquet, something Rita'd bought. He sprayed and sprayed, vanquishing the stench, recalling now only the old rose fragrance of his mother, hearing now quavering voices singing…*Amazing grace…wretch like me…*smelt roses blooming in Brit's garden.

Had she planted those azaleas, dogwoods?

He went back to his bed, picked up the book, let it fall open, and read, "How dark it is before the dawn!…I was soon to be catapulted into what I like to call the fourth dimension of existence."

Grant looked out a window for the first time this day. Sunshine. Perfect, puffed clouds. A blue sky on Thanksgiving Day.

His eyes went back to the same page, which he saw was from "Bill's Story," a founder of Alcoholics Anonymous. "Near the end of that bleak November…" and he felt another shudder, the sunshine a jibe.

His eyes roved, then found "…I was to know happiness, peace, and usefulness, in a way of life that is incredibly more wonderful as time passes."

It was all a cosmic joke. He felt bleakness overwhelm him, a hot fog move in.

He found himself slithering to the floor, on his knees, head down, hands wrapped around his skull as if to ward off a grenade. He wept, whispering, "Please, please, help me. I am so ashamed. I am so confused." For a long time he didn't move.

The hot-fog was shame and fear—*he knew it!*

He let himself feel it, with no energy to resist. The fog grew, like the giant martini olive the day he'd become sober, filling him, the room, the universe, then began to dissipate, as if it weren't real at all.

Patches of fog scattering, interstices filling with…calm.

He felt a peculiar warmth, a tingling, coming right from his gut, the recent nest of those snakes. It filled him and he heard, *what?*

Answers will come.

Carpet pricked his forearms, he smelt cleaning fluid rising from the fibers, slowly he raised his head, a whiff now of old roses. Got to his feet. Thought.

Wow.

Wow. Then a gush of gratitude.

Answers will come.

The phone rang, mechanically he said, "Hello?"

Spiffy's chirpy voice. "There you are, Grant. Where have you been all these months?"

"Oh. I—hello, Spiffy. Long story. How are you?"

"Great! I'm calling a bunch of old friends, wishing them Happy Thanksgiving."

"Oh, yes, Happy Thanksgiving."

"Have you made plans for today?"

"As a matter of fact, my plans were suddenly canceled."

"So, nothing to do on Thanksgiving Day?"

"Well, I'll definitely go to a meeting."

"Of course. But after that, I have a motley crew dropping by, around three. Buffet-style eats. *La Madeleine* is catering. Artists, writers, politicians, fitness nuts. You're welcome to come."

"Three? I might do that. Thank you for thinking of me." He felt some guilt, but not much, the calm feeling too all-pervading. There really hadn't been anything between them, a few coffees, he'd worked out at her club three times, but just couldn't enjoy it. Then the Fourth of July at Brit's.

"This will be very casual."

"Very casual. Right. Thanks again, Spiffy, for thinking of me. See you soon." Slowly he hung up. *Was Spiffy an answer? Or was just being with people the answer? If it was God talking to him, He wasn't very clear.*

FIFTEEN

Good thing he was on the bottom floor. He was dressed weird, in dumb gray hospital sweats and paper slippers, but he'd fix that quick. *This was so easy.* He'd been able to hide in a broom closet after the midnight shift change.

Keeping a plastic knife he'd held back from lunch, sharpened on the mesh screen covering his window, he scooted across cut grass to bushes, and from there to the corner.

He began walking toward Fat City, Metairie's emulation of the French Quarter.

A guy came staggering out of a strip bar. Saunders was on him in an instant, the plastic edge hard against the man's neck, whispering, "You make one move, I'll cut your throat."

The man whimpered as Saunders dragged him into an alley behind a dumpster, slammed his shoulders against the metal. Then, grabbing the guy's hair he banged his forehead against the bin until the guy went limp. He let go, the man fell. For a moment Saunders was scared. *Had he killed the guy?* He leaned over him. *No. Still breathing.*

Minutes later Saunders stepped out from the alley dressed in too-long black jeans, a smelly T-shirt, and a stained beige windbreaker he'd pulled off the guy. He also had fifteen dollars, three marijuana cigarettes, and three pills. He stomped forward in the guy's too-big cowboy boots.

This outfit would get him across the lake, into the barn. He could hide in the loft all night.

SIXTEEN

The next morning Brit woke with a wild thought. Asia felt extreme discomfort in the barn now. So. They'd torch it. A pyre for Mokh. She could afford a new stable.

SEVENTEEN

Saunders slept in the loft. It had taken him hours to get out here–few people wanted to give him a lift, so when he arrived he felt like he'd walked the whole fifty miles.

He'd tip-toed through the blackout barn, up the ladder. Taking off the boots in the dark he felt broken blisters on his feet.

He smoked a jay then dropped a pill. It was dawn when he finally passed out.

At seven Brit excitedly woke Asia, told her of her plans.

First they had a big breakfast: They hadn't touched Thanksgiving dinner. Brit banged pots and pans around and came up with Eggs Benedict, á la Britannia. She made fresh biscuits, a substitute for English muffins, hot Jimmy Dean sausage patties for the Canadian bacon, poached four tiny eggs from her Banties, and whipped up Hollandaise sauce in the blender. They drank Macadamia Nut coffee sweetened with local wildflower honey.

"I think there's enough gas in the storage shed. If not, we can run to town."

Asia was carefully cutting a piece of the layered breakfast, biscuit, sausage, poached egg, hollandaise. She asked, "You sure you want to do this? That's an expensive building."

"Darling. Since *The Altogether* show I'm practically rich. I may even do some commission work." She sipped her coffee, rich and strong. "I can't bear seeing you flinch every time you walk into it. I can't bear that it's the first thing you see when you drive home. It's got to go, and it may as well go like this. Both of us get some catharsis from it."

Half an hour later they walked to the stable lugging five-gallon gasoline containers. Brit had moved blankets, bridles and saddles out, and now they were scattered around the drive.

They set the red buckets down. Brit's half-full, Asia's full.

They entered the barn and poured gasoline around, sloshing it up on the walls. The sharp gas smell rose up stinging their eyes.

Brit knew Asia couldn't go in the loft so she was going to go. But her gas can was empty. She'd spilled a lot of it on Mokhtar's body, which had cooled and returned to pure white.

She'd paused to thank the universe for giving her the experience of this wonderful horse. Then, she'd stooped, gently closed his eyes, and snipped a hank of his silvery mane. Asia came to her side, smiling brightly. She held up the red can, saying, "All gone." She sounded like a five-year-old.

They stood and looked at the dead horse. Gently Asia took Brit's arm. "Mom. I wonder. Colt has so much of Mokhtar in him–could we name him 'Mokhtar's Legacy?'"

"'Mokhtar's Legacy.' Honey. I like it." She sprinkled a last few drops on the horse like holy water.

"Farewell, Mokhtar. Thanks for your son, Legacy."

Surely they'd used enough gas. Brit took her arm, led her from the barn.

There was no breeze. It was safe for burning.

EIGHTEEN

At 6:30 a.m. Grant was awakened by a call from the hospital.

Saunders had disappeared. Was he at home?

Grant, angrily saying "No," flung off the covers, got out of bed. He hung up, staring at the phone for a moment.

Goddamn them!

Goddamn Saunders. He was beginning to think his son really was crazy.

NINETEEN

Asia was to light the fire. She stood in the front entrance striking big wooden matches, flinging them into the barn. The first five matches landed on the concrete floor without igniting. Her hands shook as she took each match from the box. Brit contained a desire to snatch the matches from her and set the damn place on fire.

Asia walked in a few paces, lit another match, tossed it at Mokhtar's stall. Whump! The shavings caught. She threw another at the loft ladder. Loose hay at its base caught and flames climbed the ladder. Backing out she threw another match into the feed room. A bale of hay flamed.

Turning, she ran to Brit.

The fire had begun. Arms around each other, they backed away from the burning sound. The phone began ringing from inside the house. They heard it faintly, but ignored it.

Grant let it ring and ring, then cursing, slammed the phone down. *What a time for her damn machine to be off! Better get out there. Just in case. Damn.* He'd planned to meet a friend at Rick's Pancake House for breakfast.

TWENTY

Flames chewed at the dry logs like kids eating corn cobs. Leaping from log to log, they licked around the windows. Great puffs of smoke began to pour from the building. Brit and Asia could see pointed flame-tongues at every ground floor opening.

TWENTY-ONE

Grant pulled on clothes and was in his new car, a champagne-colored Lexus. More comfortable than the 'Vette. He headed down Carrollton to catch I-10 to the Causeway bridge.

TWENTY-TWO

Brit and Asia felt heat. Judging from the height of the flames, the fire was at the loft floor.

TWENTY-THREE

Saunders, deep in a dream, was so warm, he began to urinate on himself. He wanted to wake up, but he was hot–stifling, *who'd turned off the air conditioning?* His eyes wouldn't open. Wet on his leg, the urine was soothing. Finish the dream.

TWENTY-FOUR

Brit felt Asia's body grow rigid with excitement as smoke poured from the loft. She began to jig in place. Brit dropped her arm. Released, Asia began to hop up and down. She was chanting under her breath, getting louder until Brit heard, "Burn. Burn. Burn. You son of a bitch, burn. You hurt me, you son of a bitch. Burn."

Eyes wide, her chanting grew cadenced.

TWENTY-FIVE

Grant was halfway across the bridge, the water dead calm. An early crabber was out, his boat laden with chicken-wire crab cages he chugged alongside the bridge. Leaving him behind, Grant picked up the phone and redialed Brit's number.

TWENTY-SIX

Saunders' eyes shot open. His throat and lungs were stinging. Smoke was everywhere. He tried to breathe, couldn't. He began coughing. Then he screamed.

TWENTY-SEVEN

Asia's chant wove with the fire's roar. There was a sickeningly good smell, steaks on the grill. Brit shuddered. Then she heard a thin, high cry. *Mokhtar couldn't be calling. He was dead. Imagination.* She turned. Colt–Legacy–was wildly galloping, back and forth, along the near fence line screaming. It had to be he was afraid of the fire. The ducks huddled on the pond under Anastasia's weeping willow, Banties hung like jewels in its drooping limbs.

Wil and godd were shut up in the house.

"Eeeeeeeee." *There.*

Asia's body arched and she leaped, screaming her rage.

"BURN, BURN, BURN, BASTARD, BURN!"

TWENTY-EIGHT
Saunders screamed. He was on fire! The whole fucking barn was on fire. His clothes–that guy's clothes–flaming, there was a wall of fire around him–he couldn't breathe–*shit, fuck, no God, please.* His hair caught on fire.

TWENTY-NINE
Grant slowed, left the bridge, and headed to Washington Parish. He stopped at the Texaco in Covington for a coffee, then continued. Still no answer at Brit's. They must be outside caring for the animals.

THIRTY
Brit held herself. She watched her daughter shriek out her anger and felt relief. Then felt her sorrow over losing Mokhtar, remembering his name in Arabic meant "The Chosen." He had chosen his legacy. Tears came in her eyes. *We chose each other....*

There. There! Thin, reedy, a scream came high over the hot roar, over the frantic neighing of Legacy. Even Asia paused, then a burning ball cannoned from the loft, and landed with a horrible plop on the crushed rocks.

Asia froze, Brit ran.

His face and body were black, but she recognized him. She grabbed a horse blanket and threw it over him, tamping and patting all over his body to stop the flames. Her back felt hot. They were too close to the burning barn.

Legacy ceased neighing.

"Asia," she yelled imperiously. "You must go inside. Call 911. Get an ambulance!"

Asia stared, and in a moment she realized that this charred being was Saunders. A wave of guilt came over her–she'd just been imagining him burning, and he had. She felt like she'd put him in that barn, that she'd burned him. Then anger flared up–this was none of her doing. *Served him right.*

She sprinted off, relieved to have a reason to get away from her stepbrother.

Gingerly Brit peeled back the blanket. The boy was making odd gurgling sounds. Still alive. She peeled the blanket back farther. Blisters big as pancakes were on his face and his arms–his shirt was burned into his chest.

She had to get them both away from the building–the roof would soon cave in, hunks of shingle, log could rain on them.

His blackened hands moved back and forth clawing the air like baby crow's feet. She lay the blanket out beside him then, praying incoherently, she moved her hands, her arms under him. She felt his flesh slide wetly against her arms. The blisters breaking.

Do it quick.

With a heave she lifted and got his shoulders onto the blanket. Her arms were wet and she had a sense of…amniotic fluids…birth waters from him, on her. She stared at his contorted face. Then quickly she stood and lifted his charred legs and placed them gently on the blanket. She dragged the blanket over the rocks away from the fire.

In the pasture, Legacy padded behind them, panting. The fire was more crackle now than roar. Asia had disappeared. She sank to her knees before Saunders, who was curled into a fetal form. She didn't know how he could survive. His face was a charcoal blister, his eyes swollen. He smelled like barbecue.

Her tears fell in huge slow drips and landed on his face.

"Saunders. I hope you can hear me. Asia is calling an ambulance."

What a price he was paying. Something inside her broke open. There came in her…Sorrow–Pity–Horror? Love?

She leaned over him.

"Saunders. I want to say that…despite everything…I love you."

He jerked. An involuntary spasm?

She felt right now, inside.

Where's that damn ambulance? she shrieked in her mind.

"Saunders, hang in, baby-boy, hang in…help's coming!"

He mewled and it became a thin scream. She sat back up, wanting to cover him with a fresh clean blanket but remembered how dangerous infection is to burn victims.

Ambulance, come on!

He couldn't sustain the screaming, even though the pain must be beginning. His eyes jerked open, startling Brit. She couldn't touch him, take his hand, nothing. He stared at her, his gray eyes almost black. His mouth moved. His eyes filled with water which slid down his face. His claw hands moved feebly, trying to reach for her.

She leaned closer. A gasp. Then, was he saying, "Sorry?"

Far in the distance she heard sirens.

She put her ear to his mouth hearing a harsh burned sound.

"Sorry…forgive…"

"Oh, Saunders, Saunders–" she wanted to touch him, desperately, but he was walled off, too blistered to touch, so she spoke, clearly.

"Yes, Son. Forgiven."

The sirens were close. *That was fast, thank God.*

THIRTY-ONE

On 450 Grant pulled over to let a fire truck and an ambulance pass. They screamed on and he resumed driving to Brit's.

His phone rang. He grabbed it.

"Oh! Spiffy! About our breakfast date this morning…"

THIRTY-TWO

Asia came out of the house but she sat on the verandah. Brit saw the rigid set to her body.

Brit felt torn in two. He might be dying. She wanted to go to her daughter, but she had to stay with this terribly damaged boy, her son.

The fire truck, then an ambulance, pulled into the yard.

Seconds later Grant arrived in his new Lexus.

Part Six

LAST ENCHANTMENTS

Whispering from her towers the
Last enchantments of the Middle Age
Home of lost causes and forsaken beliefs and
Unpopular names and impossible loyalties!
– *Matthew Arnold*

O N E

"*You went to see him?*" Asia, arriving from Baton Rouge, stumbled over Brit's unpacked suitcase in the foyer. Quickly Brit had explained she'd just returned from Houston, visiting Saunders at the Shrine Burn Hospital. They faced each other, eyes wide. godd wound and rewound herself around Brit's ankles, but Brit didn't feel it. She felt horror. *Not like this! Not for Asia to find out like this!* Wil gazed up at Asia, the energetic wagging of his tail gradually stilling. Asia's eyes didn't leave her mother's.

Then, as if a pressure hose was abruptly turned on behind Asia's eyes, tears like spittle spurted at her mother.

"Mother. Oh my God, Mother! How could you visit him? How could you!"

Brit swallowed dryly. "Oh, Honey, oh dearest–I didn't want you to learn like this…" She shook her head back and forth. "No. Not like this." She turned slightly away from Asia, smelled the French Vanilla coffee brewing in the kitchen, and felt a nausea like morning sickness. "Oh my dear, you see–he needs me," she said as she turned back to Asia, held out a hand.

Asia arms went tightly across her chest. "So what? He raped–" She glared at Brit. "You betrayed me, Mother!" Brit's hands flew up to her face, her head still shaking mute "no, no, no's." She calmed herself.

"Sweetheart. Hasn't he paid?"

"Paid!? Paid!" She was screaming. "Get this, Mother! The little son of a bitch did not choose to be in that fire! He was doped up! It's not like he leaped into some burning bush to pay for his sins! He burned because he was an asshole–true to form! He hasn't paid at all!"

Brit's hand went out again. "Sweetheart–"

Asia made an angry shrugging gesture as if Brit had touched her. "You cannot convince me that that twisted little jerk chose to burn himself up from remorse."

"No–"

"Of course he's filled with remorse now. It's the 'in' thing! That's easy! He hurts. He's got to say he's remorseful, that he's sorry–he's a psychopath–they know what to say to squirm out of tight corners!"

"I'm aware of that possibility."

"Mother! Don't be a dupe! He's conning you, and Grant, and probably everyone at that whole hospital!" She turned and paced up and down beneath the painting of the desert horses in the sandstorm. The top of her head, Brit saw, was level with the bottom edge of the picture. At her feet Wil trotted like a silent little soldier turning at each of her abrupt changes of direction. She stopped mid-picture, beneath a red stallion whose mouth was open in a silent scream. Wil sat at heel.

Brit bent, took godd in her arms. "Look. Can we calm down and discuss this? Honey, there are things you don't know–"

"And I don't want to know!" Asia stood, red-faced, defiant, beneath the oasis. Both women held their breath. Brit took a step toward her, then another, and when Asia didn't flinch, she put an arm around her waist and gently herded her into the kitchen, sat her down, and set a mug of French Vanilla decaf before her.

Asia curled one hand around the warm mug. She kept her eyes down and muttered, "And I don't want to know."

Brit stood by the stove. "And you don't have to know. That's okay." She picked up a spatula. "Want some breakfast? Got fixings for Lost Bread."

"No! I'm not hungry." Nevertheless Brit dunked oval slices of French bread into a milk and egg mixture, and dropped them into a skillet. She poked at the sizzling bread with a spatula. A cinnamon smell rose from the pan.

Asia pushed her mug away, slammed a fist onto the table. "I feel so betrayed! You sneaking around behind my back giving love and succor to that grotesque worm! That's all he is–a worm! No! He's less than a worm! Worms do good. But not him. He's mind-fucking all of you–can't you see that?"

Fucking? wondered Brit. She'd never heard Asia use this word before, but she answered, "You may be right. I've thought of that. But I'm learning whole new things about…forgiveness. That I have to forgive. For me. Not you. Not even for Saunders. Because when I hate, when I resent, I'm not at peace. I'm chained to the person I hate, not them. So I visit him for me. To free me."

Asia glared. "I think you're selling yourself a load of horse manure, Mother."

"You may be right. I admit I can get rather far out. But I want to be happy. I think the universe wants all of us to be happy. What kind of a cruel God would create us, then allow us to experience only misery? Think about it. If God is Love and I believe He is, and Love is the quantum energy that powers the universe, that powers us–'love' just a kinder word for 'energy'–what sort of Creator would deny us happiness? But we're rather smart–not as smart as we think we are, but still smart enough to make choices. And we really only have two choices. We can choose to think lovingly or fearfully. It all boils down to those two: love or fear. Most of us choose fear! We choose fear and that's choosing hell on earth." She took a breath. "I'm trying to think differently nowadays. I'm trying to choose love, which includes first loving myself. Because if I can't love me, the first human being I know, how can I possibly love anyone else?" She stared at Asia. *Was any of this getting through?* "It's impossible. And to love myself I must not keep myself shackled to anger and resentment. These are just other manifestations of fear. Anger is only an explosive form of fear. So I must forgive your stepbrother. I must. Not, as I said earlier, for him–not even for you–but for ME! Forgiveness is misinterpreted I think–the idea that we 'forgive' another is so condescending–I forgive you your sins–suggests a lofty arrogance that actually harbors fear. What is arrogance but a form of anger, hence a stepchild of fear? And Asia, I have looked into his eyes. They have changed! But I want to make this very clear, *even if his eyes hadn't changed,* I would still forgive him, do you hear me, I would still forgive him! Because I want to be free–of sick, cloying, soul-rotting emotions, the sickness of a deep grinding grudge, a seething resentment. I do not want that poisoning my system!" She felt her chest heaving to breath. She gripped the edge of the warm stove, felt herself calm. Then in a tiny voice she said, almost to herself, "I want peace."

"So you'll forgive him at my expense. That's what I'm hearing. I think you've gone crazy with this ridiculous mystical bullshit!" She waved her arms around. "I know where you're going! You're trying to convince me that in some deep, subterranean way Saunders connived to get himself burned–to pay for his sins! It was an accident, Mother! Accidents happen!"

Brit paused, spatula raised, looked at her. "You're right, it seems they do. But I believe, and my life experience has born this out, there really are no accidents." She wanted to add "in God's world," but knew that might evoke another accusation of being "mystical" from Asia. She laid the spatula down, leaned her hips against the warm range and looked pleadingly at her daughter. "Baby, I think that while Saunders, in his 'conscious' mind, didn't plan to burn himself to 'pay for his sins,' on some level, my dear, I believe now the barn fire was for that reason. I don't know how the universe works. It's truly mysterious—but I've seen some connections that don't make sense with any other interpretation. There is some sort of Divine Intelligence out there," she gestured at the window, "and, all around us. Even in us. We just don't know real well how to tap into it. I'm learning how. And it is—awesome. It's even helpful. So while maybe Saunders' small mind, his ego-mind was oblivious to the potential for his burning, his deeper Self was not. There's a part of us that's always awake, even if we're asleep. It's always ticking, checking things out, knowing. Most of us labor not to know it's there. We don't want its help. We think we can do it ourselves." She laughed ironically, then checked Asia. She was listening, mouth slightly agape. Her expression reminded Brit of when she was a little girl, listening to stories Brit wove about the horses in the sandstorm. Then Brit felt a thump seeing how beautiful Asia had become. *Please God, let me get through to her!* She folded her hands, let them dangle at rest on her belly, and continued.

"It's like we have a TV set inside us. Messages are zooming to it night and day, but we don't bother to turn on the set. We'd rather listen to the amateur radio set we've built ourselves, with its scratchy and poor, if any, reception. So we fail to receive the big messages. But some get through. We don't acknowledge where they're coming from. The radio mind doesn't want us to know, because it's afraid we'll start ignoring it, once we experience the power, the love, and the creativity that we can access through our greater mind." Asia's eyes were huge and black now. Brit smoothed her shirt over her abdomen, her hips. "So Saunders getting himself into that barn fire was unconscious—he was operating from his radio mind. But maybe, he was just as unconscious, when he raped you?" In the silence that surrounded them now, she smiled feebly at Asia. Quaking inside, straining, hoping Asia would understand. The silence continued. Asia's eyes dropped. Finally she turned and poked at the sizzling Lost Bread.

She thought about Saunders. His fire-red body, adrift on a waterbed, naked except for a diaper loin cloth, silvery plastic tubes snaking from his body as if it was maintained by an invisible being. But his eyes were conscious now. *Had the intense physical pain from the burning served as electric shock treatment? Had it brought him to himself?* That dead, monotone look he'd affected was gone.

And, he might actually live. He'd survived one surgery and was slated for more. Grant was a skin donor. But the doctors weren't sure if he'd ever walk, and in cruel poetic justice the fire had burned his groin. He'd never rape again.

Then, "Oh, I get it. I get it." Asia slammed both palms on the table. Silverware jumped. "Was Grantsie-boy there, mumsey-wumsey? Are you sure you're not doing this Mother Theresa bit because you're horny and it's a way to get Grant back again?"

Brit wanted to scream. *Hadn't Asia heard a word she'd said?* Then she shook her head. She set a plate of Lost Bread, dusted with confectioner's sugar, in front of Asia. She saw her hand trembling. "He was there all right, in a hospital bed." She sat opposite Asia.

"Oh yeah? Where, on the nut ward? Strain too much for the Granite Man?"

Brit felt a jolt. *She knew that nickname?*

Viciously Asia cut into her breakfast, sawing away like it was gristle. Her knife made a whiny grating sound on the china. Outside the window, four cardinals fluttered around a bird feeder that dangled from a bare-branched mimosa. Two females, brown as the December grounds, and two males. The males looked like animated specks of blood, the only color outside, except for the bottle-green of more distant pines. Red and green. Christmas.

She looked back at Asia. Her brown eyes shining black, her dark brown hair leaping full and strong from her white face. Her lips blooded, ruby, like the cardinals. Her whole body taut, like she'd pumped iron.

"I don't mean to go below the belt, but he was a skin donor for Saunders–"

"Don't say his name, Mother, or I will throw up all over this Lost Bread." She stabbed her knife at her mother. "I am revulsed by the thought of him. Why didn't he die? He should have."

"You've got that right." Brit sipped coffee. "But he didn't."

She leaned forward, tried to touch Asia's arm, but Asia snatched it away. Brit rested her hand in her lap. She took a calming breath before she spoke. "If he had, it would've been nice and tidy for all of us. You. Me and Grant."

"Oh. Well. I guess I'm a bit sorry about that. Too bad his evil son had to wreck your new lovey-dovey relationship."

"You don't sound sorry."

Asia concentrated on her plate. Her long hair fell forward. Brit saw gold glints in it and wondered, *had Asia highlighted her hair?* She couldn't believe this new Asia. *Loud, gorgeous, and swearing?*

Asia swallowed, picked up her mug in both hands, held it between them. "I never liked Grant. Y'all were always making out." Suddenly she slammed her mug down and stood, knocking over her chair. She didn't bother to pick it up.

"Yeah. My mother. Always fucking her brains out. I didn't want to be like you, Mother!" She larked, body sarcastic, around the kitchen. "Sex, sex, sex!" Stopped, put a hand on her hip, then thrust it out, taunting. "I know where you're heading Mother. No more spiritual gobble-de-gook with me. We rape victims don't get over it, we merely learn to live with it. My therapist says so." She stopped, flounced her hips. Brit was amazed. *Asia moving like a sexy, grown-up woman?*

"Next you'll say I led him on!"

Almost smiling, Brit opened her hands. "I'm not saying anything, except you sure look good."

"Oh, no, no sweet-talk. I know what you're up to. I see it in your eyes, sitting there, pretending to be so innocent."

"What?"

"You're going to say before this I never grew up! That I picked zoology for my major so I could keep playing with animals. Like some little kid! I know it!"

"Playing with animals? Well, sure, but what's wrong with that?"

"Yep! Getting my affection from animals instead of people."

More serene now, Brit watched her.

"Well?" Asia demanded.

"Anastasia, have you changed. I can't get over it! Perhaps something good has come out of this."

"Good! Fuck!"

"You just said fuck, again!" Brit clapped her hands. "I love it!"

"Mother." Brit saw Asia's eyes turn mean. "My asshole was shredded! You call that good?"

Very softly. "But it's healed now, isn't it, Darling? That's in the past. We don't have to drag the past along with us like an over-stuffed trash bag. We can let go. We can even be happy, now. Didn't your doctor say–" Brit shook her head. "Never mind."

She stood to move to her daughter, who held her arrogant position. Asia swatted her away.

"Don't come on all huggy to me, Mother! You're visiting that scum." Her hands flew up, her voice became nasal, sarcastic. "You've forgiven him. You probably want me to make friends with him!"

Brit turned, walked over to the Mr. Coffee and watched her still-shaking hands pour a refill. *Please God, don't let me lose my daughter!* She carried it back to the table, sat down. "Who said anything about friends? I'm happy to see you looking so strong now. I don't see a victim."

Asia's hands dropped to her sides. "You don't?" Her little girl voice. "What do you see?"

Asia was framed by the window giving Brit the illusion that a redbird was in the room fluttering around her daughter's head. She knew she'd paint this. Asia, hands down, palms open, redbirds like stigmata on her palms and feet. More bright birds hovering round her head like a living feathery crown. On her face, this serious, pleading expression.

"That little voice, Asia, now that's the voice of a victim—your old voice. But just a second ago I was seeing and hearing a strong, grown-up, very beautiful woman. And I really liked her."

"Oh. So, just because I—lower—my voice, I'm a 'victim,' am I? Mother. You really are sick. You'll say anything, won't you?"

Brit shrugged in a gentle way, but still she trembled inside, like her hands. Asia glared.

"It just so happens I have a boyfriend."

"Oh, now that's—"

"His name is Steve Turnbull." She crossed her arms, tapped a toe. "He was part of my coffee group. When I got back after Thanksgiving, he asked me out. Finally. So I went. So there!"

"Asia. This is great—I'd like to meet—"

Her fists flew to her hips. "You meet no one unless you swear by all your delusional mysticism that you'll never, ever, visit that scum again."

"Asia. I can't swear any such thing. I'm as much his mother as I am yours!"

"Mother! You're insane. You were only a stepmother!"

"Sweetheart." Brit set her mug down, leaned forward on the table. "Can't you find just a tiny part of you—a part that can go back to when you loved him? Honey, sometimes we need damage, we—we attract it. It wakes us up. And the damage seems to be directly proportional to the amount of waking up we need."

"So you think I needed a hell of a lot of 'waking up'? That's no fucking excuse for what he did."

"You're right. But he is sorry."

"So?" Asia, listening, eyes arrogant.

"Those nightmares. Remember? When you both were little? Saunders waking up screaming, his face as red as his hair, strange dreams, always something about his mother. You woke up too, you felt so sorry for him, you hugged him..." Brit looked out the window, felt wetness in her eyes. *That it should come to this...*the birds had flown off.

"This sounds like bleeding-heart psychobabble to me. Like our court system. The victim loses, the criminal gets off because of his pitiful childhood."

"Okay, my dear. I–I'm not expressing all this very well, very–clearly–"

Asia had turned away. Brit let her eyes go past Asia's tense profile, out the window, hoping to see birds and was rewarded when a bluejay landed on the feeder. She said, "I'm sorry."

"Sorry enough to swear you'll never visit him again?"

Brit breathed, shook her head. "I can't say that!" It came out like a wail. "No, Honey, he really needs me. His very life..." Asia blurred before her, tears welling.

"Then, Mother, I'm outa here. Don't call me. I won't call you." She strode from the room.

Brit hesitated, then jumped up to run after her, also knocking over a chair. She stooped, righted it, then followed Asia to the foot of the staircase.

"Anastasia, please, please, please, don't do this–" she called up.

Asia yelled down, "End of fucking discussion, Mother. Not one more word. You're sick, you know that? Sick!"

Brit backed away from the staircase. She wrapped her shaking arms around herself, let the crying take over. *Oh God! Not to lose Asia too! Could she agree...? Did she really have to visit Saunders? But he genuinely needed her, like never before*–she found herself slipping to the floor. She lay on the cool pine boards, curled up. She cried.

When godd's soft tail brushed against her cheek, she thought, *I can't let Asia see me like this.* Hearing drawers slamming upstairs, she dragged herself up, cat clutched in her arms. Asia raced down the stairs, a suitcase in each hand, her portrait by Brit under an arm. She didn't even look Brit's way. The front door slammed, then rocks spurted as Asia gunned her Escort down the drive.

Brit went across the room into her studio and sat on the striped divan, the plastic skeleton looking over her shoulder. She stroked the cat in her lap, staring dully at nothing.

T W O

Later, she went into her living room, picked up the phone, and called Lee.

Now they sat in the great oyster sofa, drinking French Vanilla decaf. The fireplace glowed. Lee had lit it.

Brit sipped coffee. "I wonder if Asia'll ever speak to me again?"

"Why wouldn't she?"

"That's why I called you. We just had a huge fight. She's furious I visited Saunders in Houston. She thinks I'm betraying her."

"I understand that."

"Me too. But I also think he's paid. Christ, Lee, has he paid! One surgery so far, countless more to come. Even so, he'll be disfigured for life. And he's castrated—a hideous poetic justice. Surely that's enough punishment."

She leaned forward, more urgent. "But more important than his horrific physical suffering, Lee, he has remorse. Genuine. Grant's had him seeing a therapist, she confirms it. His—his eyes, Lee, are different. I've never seen his eyes look—so alive! He really is experiencing terrible guilt. Terrible shame. And, in A.A. terms, he wants to make amends." She shook her head. "My God. I can't seem to win. Gain a son, lose a daughter."

"She'll come around."

"Oh, Lee, I don't know, I've never seen her so angry. She was raging—Anastasia! Can you imagine? And swearing. She said 'fuck!' Can you imagine?"

"Hum. Sounds like growth to me." Lee sipped coffee, thought. "Another of Robinet's trivial bits of info. I read somewhere that anger in humans was created for the sole purpose of helping juveniles separate from their parents—and they had to go—to eliminate the danger of incest, which weakens the tribe—oh, my God, Brit, I'm sorry."

"Don't be. It's okay. I'm sacked out, like a wild horse, you know? You scare the horse and scare the horse, flap feed sacks around her, rattle cans, deliberately freaking her out until all her adrenaline is burned up. Nothing left inside. A good trainer can move in then, stroke her all over, fill her emptiness with love—" She pushed her hair off her face. "Sorry. Getting off track. You were saying?"

"I'm saying that only anger could give the post-puberty young the courage and the energy to leave—leave the cave, strike out on their own. And in those days, what with saber-toothed tigers and all, that took a hell of a lot of courage. Maybe that's what's happened here. Asia was so connected to you, Brit. Normally this rebellion, this anger at the parent would have begun when she was much younger–thirteen, fourteen. She never had that. She was always so placid. Even while at college. Hell, she couldn't even make herself date."

"She's dating now."

"Wow! Great! You know, maybe it took something this awful–to get her to separate–to pull away from you, thrust her out of that fog of introversion and fear."

Brit raised her eyebrows. "Thank you! That's exactly what I was trying to get her to see."

"Maybe you were too soon. She's not ready to acknowledge this. Time is miraculous."

"Damn me and my big mouth! But you should have seen her this morning. Lee. Raging, tall, strong, beautiful. Even–sexy! Can you imagine Asia–sexy?"

Lee laughed. "Nope. But if you say so. That's great. High time."

"Yeah. Like, everything bad…is…eventually good."

"Yes. You've even got me believing that. Hard as it is."

They watched the fire. Brit stroked godd, pushed away thoughts of that other fire, the one she'd instigated.

"She'll come back, Brit. I promise. She may never be able to face her step-brother, which is okay. But in time she'll come back to you." Lee eyed her. "What about you and Grant?"

Brit looked her at her. "Well, we've talked. A lot. Mostly about Saunders. After he's healed from donating, literally, the hide off his back, we each plan to visit Houston on alternate weekends." She laughed ironically. "Like a weird form of custody. We've decided we better get on with our lives. Hearing Asia this morning, that cinches that. Grant and I being together can never be."

"Never say never."

"Lee! It's impossible. That would be asking for the truly impossible! Asia would have to totally forgive Saunders. Saunders is facing a long time in the hospital and whenever he gets out he'll have to live at home for ages, maybe the rest of his life. Think about it!"

"I am. I see the problem. If you and Grant are together Saunders would be living here. So Asia would feel she could never come home."

"Yes!" Brit jumped up, spilling godd from her lap. "Let's get out of here. I need to move or I'll start crying again."

They grabbed jackets, headed outside. There was a clatter of hammering, sawing, a smell of fresh-cut wood. The new barn was under construction. They
headed down the swale, past the pond, to the fence line. Immediately Legacy
stopped grazing and came to them, thrusting his muzzle into Brit's hands. She
opened them, "Sorry kiddo, no carrots!" She smiled at Lee. "Orphans! They
think they're human."

"Golly. He's really getting beautiful. What're all those silvery hairs on his face,
in his mane?"

"Starting to gray out."

"Oh. So some day he'll be the same color as Mokhtar?"

"Yes. But not for a long time." At her feet, Wil woofed, and Brit looked down
at him. "Jealous puppy. He's going to be as jealous of Legacy as he was of
Mokhtar."

"You gonna ride this colt?"

"I don't know. First I hoped Saunders would–" she paused, "but the only riding Saunders could ever do would be like those handicapped people, you know?
Two people on each side of the horse to hold him, one leading. I doubt if this
colt would be able to do that, he's a hot horse!" Her mind went off. *Could
Saunders, with help, someday ride his colt? Would the colt be sensitive enough to calm
down and accept a handicapped person...?* She scratched Legacy under the jowl,
him tilting his head to accommodate her. "Then I'd hoped Asia would want to.
But she never liked riding." The colt groaned in pleasure as she scratched.

"Maybe the new, improved, angry Asia will have the guts to ride. Someday."

"I don't know. The horse world is funny. There are many people who love
horses passionately and never get on their backs. They get their joy working with
horses on the ground. Asia seems to be one of the grounded people. She did
wonders training this guy for halter. Me? I always was a rider–from the get-go.
Hated all that groundwork."

Brit slid her hand down the underside of Legacy's jaw, petted his muzzle. "Bye
for now, Ace." She looked at Lee, "Let's walk."

They strolled along the fence toward the forest. Once under the canopy of
trees, Brit looked at Lee. "So. How about you? How's your love life?"

"About time you asked, girl." She thrust out her left hand.

Brit gasped. A tiny diamond sparkled on her third finger. "Does that mean
what I think it means?"

Lee, grinning like a well-fed cheetah, said, "You bet, girl. I have succumbed to

Leroy's pleas. And I want you for Best Woman."

Brit war-whooped in joy and hugged Lee. They hopped around holding each other, yelling. When they bumped into a tree and toppled to the ground, Brit sat up, grinned, and said, "I accept. When?"

"Sometime around Christmas."

"Wow, so soon?"

Lee grinned wickedly and clucking her tongue, said, "Tick–tock, tick–tock."

Brit stared. "You're–oh Lee! You're in foal?"

"Always the horsewoman! Yep, I'm pregnant!"

More hugs.

"Golly. I couldn't be more thrilled, Sweetie!"

"Gonna do something real simple, Justice of the Peace office, but I can't stop my folks from flying in. They're so pleased I'm not marrying some honky they're actually speaking to each other."

They laughed. Then Brit grasped Lee's arm. "Lee! Have a nice wedding. Have it here! Let it be my wedding gift to you! I could fix up the place, holly, poinsettias, mistletoe, kill and roast an ox–food, fun, people–"

"Oh no, not after all you've been through. That's too much, Brit."

"No! I need this! Lee, my dearest, you'd be doing me a favor. I've been dreading Christmas."

"But it's only two weeks away."

"Money has the power to make a trifling thing like mere time vanish. Pouf! Presto! I can put on a wedding feast just like that!" She snapped her fingers. "Lee. Please! Let me do this! It'll be so much fun. And I love Leroy's family. His daddy Jimmy was one of my best friends, ever. Maybe it will even lure Anastasia back. But if it doesn't, well then, I'll have fun anyway."

"Would you invite Grant?"

"No. That'd be like ripping off the bandage. Besides, I hear he has a friend. A lady friend." She laughed. "An Older Woman. Has he changed! Someone named Spiffy Wiffins."

"Spiffy?"

They laughed.

"I really don't know anything. It was gossip from Sugarplum. Mokhtar's new foal crop is arriving so she's calling me almost daily. She's getting fillies."

"Hum. About this older woman and Grant. You can't believe Sugarplum."

"Yes. You've mentioned that. Often." Brit smiled, nudged Lee with her foot.

"Maybe you're right. You were right about Saunders." Her eyes slid to the forest floor. "But so what? There just can't be a Brit and Grant anymore." She shivered. "It's getting cold. Let's head back to the house. I've got something to show you."

Inside, Brit picked up something from an end table, dangled it between thumb and finger.

"A postcard." She paused. "From Mexico." Then she blushed, a real blush, and felt grateful she didn't have hot flashes any more.

"What is it, girl? What you hiding from me?"

They'd sat on the sofa and Lee began bouncing, grinning.

"It's another of those postcards from Scott. He's awful close now. The Yucatan."

"You really wanna take up with that guy again? That cokehead?"

"Well. He says he's clean and sober."

"Still."

"I don't know. I don't know anything." She smiled. "Let's just plan your wedding."

THREE

Grant sat at his desk holding a Polaroid photo. He shifted. His butt was still sore where they'd removed skin for Saunders. He sat on a inflated donut cushion. Not a single person in the office cracked a single joke, not even Opal. He kind of missed that.

But he was worried about Saunders. The doctors had told him that Saunders' attitude was crucial to his recovery.

He picked up the therapist's report on this subject, skimmed past all the stuff about "borderline personality" and came to a paragraph in layman's terms: "Saunders shows deep remorse which I believe is genuine. He is sliding into a clinical depression which, if not arrested, could jeopardize his life." He'd talked with the M.D.'s about these observations. They agreed they were not too far-fetched.

So he'd taken these pictures of Saunders, without his permission, as he slept his short drugged sleep. He never slept long–the pain came back quickly. There was concern about him becoming addicted to painkillers, especially with Grant's admitted history as an alcoholic and what could be figured out about Saunders' previous drug use. But with his permission he'd also recorded Saunders talking, weeping actually, into the cassette tape sitting on top of more photos.

He lay in his hospital waterbed in a diaper, his skin scarlet. Grant winced every time he saw him. *No one could look at these pictures and not feel pity, could they?*

He wanted to show these pictures to Asia. Desperately.

He tapped the pictures on the edge of his desk, then leaned forward and pressed his intercom button. "Opal. What's on this afternoon?"

"Ah, you have a two o'clock with Mrs. Wiffins, and you're supposed to be preparing Round Two of Braggart vs. Braggart custody. Goes to court next week."

"That's it?"

"That's it." Grant realized he'd better tell his partners he was back on-line. They'd taken over most of his caseload. "I need to go to Baton Rouge this afternoon."

"Okay. Want me to rearrange Mrs. Wiffins?"

"Uh–I better do that one. Thanks, Opal."

Grant dialed Spiffy's home phone number. Her houseman Arnold answered.

"Hi, Arnold, where's the missus?"

"She's at Number Three."

The health club on Prytania. "Do you have that number?" Spiffy now owned a chain of health clubs.

"Yep." He gave Grant the number.

On hold, Grant listened to sterilized rock 'n' roll.

"Hello?" Spiffy.

"Hi, Spiff, Grant here."

"Hello, Grant." Her voice took on a low, seductive tone.

Grant felt a nervousness in his stomach. "I–need to cancel your appointment this afternoon, Spiff–got a fire to put out in Baton Rouge–" he winced again at his choice of words. *Enough of fires.*

"Oh." Did she sound slightly miffed? He'd told her, very gently, at this point in time, all he could be to her was a friend. He thought: *Miffed Spiffy*–and wanted to giggle. *Maybe he had to stop even being a friend?*

But, as always, she said, "I understand, Grant. So when can we reschedule?"

"Uh–have to put you through to Opal for that, Spiffy. She knows more about my life these days than I do."

"Oh. Well, before you go, how about lunch? You've got to eat something before you get on the road."

"Uh–thanks anyway, Spiffy, but, I'm just not hungry."

"You've got to eat, Grant, take care of yourself. How's your–bottom?"

He laughed, nervously. "Oh, it's definitely there. Weird place to get scalped."

She laughed. "Still sitting on that cute little cushion?"

"'Fraid I am. Even in the car."

"Oh, I hate to see you driving all that long way in pain."

"It's bearable. Aspirin helps."

"And your son, how's he doing?"

"Okay. We're worried he might be sliding into a depression. That's why I'm going to Baton Rouge." Grant had told her Saunders had accidentally gotten caught in the barn fire.

"Oh?"

"Yeah. I want to talk to–never mind." Grant realized he'd been about to tell Spiffy his reason. Saying he wanted to see Asia, Saunders' stepsister, would only lead to Spiffy asking more questions. His stomach tightened. The fewer who knew, the better. But he'd finally told Irwin, which had been a great relief.

"Got a ladyfriend up there, Grant?"

"Oh, God, no, nothing like that, Spiffy. You know I'm not ready for anything like that. No. No way. It's just there's someone up there–from Saunders' past–whom I think might be able to jolt him out of this depression. That's all."

"Oh. Well. I won't keep you. But call me when you get back. Maybe we can do something tonight. Maybe just talk?" Her Southern lilt lifted her words.

"Okay, Spiffy, thanks."

Could she be just friends? Grant shook his head. Didn't know. It felt like she was coming on to him, lovely as a Cherokee rose, which slowly chokes its host tree. Maybe he hadn't been entirely honest about his five month's with Brit. Maybe he had to tell her that part, anyway. He stood, picked up his whoopee cushion, left the office.

F O U R

Brit drove down St. Charles Avenue, trying not to think how near she was to Grant's place. She'd just left the florist and was headed for the Riverbend, to a shop that specialized in handmade hats. Lee wanted big, glorious hats and pencil-thin gowns. Lee would be in white, of course, and Brit would wear crimson velvet, a hat to match. All of Leroy's sisters would be bridesmaids, in Christmas-tree-green velvet. Brit had seamstresses working around the clock. At the Broadway light she glanced down to the seat beside her at her sketch for Lee's hat.

It resembled the hat Audrey Hepburn wore as Eliza Doolittle to the Ascot races. A six-inch swooping brim, lace draped to fall over her face to just below her chin as a veil, to be lifted by the groom. After the kiss, Brit would quickly step forward and using faux-pearl clips, secure it at the sides. She hoped the design would work. Velvet and lace, ostrich plumes, velvet and satin rosebuds, so lush, so rich. Hers and the bridesmaids' hats would also have the wide brims, ostrich feathers and velvet roses. An Edwardian wedding.

Grant temporarily leaving her mind, Brit blessed New Orleans, where extravagant fabrics and feathers were always available, along with cunning seamstresses accustomed to creating the royal robes of Mardi Gras Kings and Queens.

Caterers were lined up to prepare crawfish bisque, French onion soup, seafood gumbo, two suckling pigs, enormous turkeys, oyster-cornbread dressing, jambalaya, shrimp creole, barbequed shrimp, bourbon sweet potatoes, salads, smoked salmon–Brit laughed at herself. She'd gone crazy. Even Viola and Nunan were flying in. Lee had even relented and allowed her to invite Sugarplum and Booth.

The buffet would be set up in her cleaned-up studio. The sofa would be removed so the wedding could take place in front the fireplace. The staircase would be garlanded with cedar and red roses. The entry, the foyer, the whole house would be filled with pots of white and red poinsettias, and a huge basket of mistletoe was to hang right over the nuptial couple. The cake, four layers, was ordered and would have real red rosebuds embedded in the white frosting at the last moment. A hundred people were invited. She'd even ordered garland for part of the fence–have to put Legacy up in his new stable or he'd eat it. And candles. The whole house, even the bathrooms, would be lit with scented candles.

As she made the riverbend she couldn't help glancing left, seeing Grant's condo. She whipped her eyes forward.

The wedding was slated for Christmas Eve.

God, she thought, *couldn't I please invite Grant?* Asia hadn't called. Still angry. She wouldn't be there. *Couldn't she just see Grant this once?*

Better not.

F I V E

Grant drove slowly down a street in Baton Rouge. He was looking for the off-campus coffee house Brit mentioned Asia frequented. He'd try that, then if she wasn't there, he'd go search out her dorm. He saw it and found a parking spot across the street. Feeding quarters into the meter, he felt his stomach lurch. Dug out the envelope of Polaroids. Stuck it back into his blazer pocket. His palm was sweaty. He'd gone home and changed into this camel blazer, a white collarless shirt, gray pants, hoping a casual look would not be as intimidating as a suit and, maybe, help him keep to a soft approach.

He was scared. He whispered the Serenity Prayer as he crossed the street and entered the coffee house.

It was dark. He blinked, remembered his contacts, and felt grateful he'd finally given them up.

Then he heard her laughter, but more powerful than he remembered. He looked toward the sound. In a corner was Asia, beside some hulky guy, tossing her head, running her fingers through her hair. Then placing her hand on the guy's bulging forearm. Laughing.

Asia?

Hard to believe.

He straightened his shoulders, and walked toward her.

Her face turned to him, her eyes widened, and she frowned. She took her hand from the guy's arm and put both hands flat on the table. He noticed her squaring her shoulders.

Not an auspicious beginning.

"Hello, Asia."

"Hello, Grant. What brings you here?"

"I came to see you."

"What the hell for?"

He felt himself falter but, still, he patted the envelope that contained the pictures, the tape. "Uh–could we talk privately? Just for a moment?"

"I don't–" said Asia. Then the hulk stood, stuck out a hand as hammy as Big Earl's. Grant took it, felt a grip like he'd caught his hand in a car door.

"Steve Turnbull."

"Grant Griffin, Steve, nice to meetcha. Anastasia's stepfather–uh–ex-stepfather, that is."

"So. What do you want from Asia, Mr. Griffin?" Asia's hand came out, back to that forearm. "Steve. Sit down." She nodded regally at Grant. "What's up, Grant?" Slowly Steve sat, the chair creaking under his weight. *This guy must live in a health club–Spiffy'd love him.* A manic part of Grant's mind was saying, *the Bull sits, Sitting Bull...*

"Asia. I want to ask you something. Privately."

The Bull's huge extremity descended to Asia's shoulder. "Asia and I are very close. You can do your asking with me here, Mr. Griffin."

"Uh–Mr. Turnbull–this is a rather sensitive family issue, you see, and–"

Asia cut in. "Go ahead, Grant, talk. Steve knows everything."

Grant gulped, met her eyes. "Everything?"

"Everything," she nodded firmly, one hand straying back to Steve's massive arm, which was covered in red-gold hairs, coiled like copper wires. *More like she couldn't get enough of him than asking for his support,* Grant thought. It was also interesting to Grant that this guy was a redhead, but of a different type than Saunders. Steve had the blue-green eyes, blondish eyebrows and eyelashes of the typical redhead, hair the color of canned Sockeye salmon.

I have to take what I can get, thought Grant. He took hold of a chair. "May I?"

Asia nodded, moved her hand and patted Steve's mitt, and he took it from her shoulder. At his sides Grant's hands fisted, getting, he realized, a grip of nothing. Quickly he unclenched them. *Must not seem threatening to Asia or Sitting Bull*–he felt a wild desire to laugh. He swallowed. The Bull raised an arm to a passing waiter, asked Grant, "Coffee?"

"Thanks. Cafe latte, please."

Grant sat. He gazed at Asia. "Well, Asia, you are looking very well. I'm happy to see that." She looked stunning, healthy, glowing. *Must be working out with Bull.*

"Thank you." She met his look head on. This was not the shy, evasive Asia he was used to.

The coffee arrived, Grant poured in a packet of sugar, stirred. He cleared his throat.

"Here's the thing, Asia. I need your help. Saunders–" she looked away. *Not good.* "Your brother–I mean, your former stepbrother is in pretty rough shape."

"So? That's my problem?"

Grant breathed deeply, let it out slowly. "Definitely not. No. Of course not." He reached in his pocket, brought out a small tape player, set it square on the envelope.

"What's this?" Bull stirred.

"Something I hope Asia will let me share with her." Grant hitched his chair slightly forward. The floor was concrete. It made a grating sound. Asia's stare was almost as unflinching as Saunders' used to be. "You see, Anastasia, he's really sick. And now he's getting dangerously depressed. The doctors and his therapist are concerned this compromises his chances of recovery." Not one blink so far that he could see. Her eyes seemed to be getting bigger, darker. "I don't know if you know of the extent of his damage, but I need you to know that he was burned so badly that, well, he'll never be able to–" he glanced at Steve, whose look was steady, with a hint of menace, "–to–do again–what I mean is, he'll never be able to have children. He may never walk. He might not live."

Silence. Someone dropped a crockery plate behind them, and it smashed on the concrete floor. There as a pause, then laughter. Grant smelled his coffee, felt a faint nausea.

"The thing is, Anastasia, he feels terrible remorse, he is so terribly sorry. His therapist feels that if you could find it within you to just say a few words to him–" Asia glared, The Bull snorted, Grant held up a hand–"not in person, not even over the phone–that's why I have this tape recorder. It's a player, too–and, I have some pictures of how he looks now. So you can verify the extent of his physical damage." He placed a trembling hand on the cassette recorder. "And hear how genuinely sorry he is." His fingers moved, almost caressingly over the small black machine. "I've got a tape in here of–Saunders–asking–"

"I don't know about this shit–" The Bull scraped his chair back, but Asia put a hand on his arm.

"Steve, chill out." She glared at Steve, who slumped in his chair. She turned to Grant and took a deep breath. Still holding his eye she said, "I might look."

"You will?" Grant heard himself gush.

"I didn't say I would, Grant. Get that straight, hear?"

Grant dipped his head. "Sorry, Anastasia, sorry–I was presumptuous–"

"Yes. You were. Listen to me: I might look. No promises." Then she shuddered, shook her head, *beautiful hair*, Grant thought, *all that gold in it. Hadn't noticed that before.* The hair flew back, her head whipped up, her eyes hard.

"But you've got some fucking nerve, Grant! Wanting me to listen to a tape of that–that–"

His stomach sank. *She was taking it back.* Quickly, he rallied. "You're right, Asia. Of course, I shouldn't have bothered you–" He scraped his chair back, reached for the envelope, the cassette recorder. "Just one thing. Please. You're looking so good, Asia. I've never seen you look so beautiful, so strong. I hope this means you're recovering, that maybe you've even recovered from what Saunders–did–to you. He's not recovering. Not very well. He might die. Now that's not your problem, as you said at the beginning. But you have the power to–no, it's too much to ask–but, to help him to live. Not that he'll have much of a life–"

Then he saw there were tears in her eyes. Her hand came out and stayed his. "Leave it. I'll–think about it."

Grant stared, then tears just leaped from his eyes and he didn't care. They rolled fat, wet, down his cheeks. Asia's eyes flickered over them, then back up to his eyes. Her hand lifted from his. "There's more, Asia." He set a blank tape on the envelope. "If you could just record a few words to him—."

"Dammit Grant–you're pushing–"

"Sorry. Sorry. I–"

"No promises," she whispered.

S I X
Brit surveyed the work of the decorators. One middle-aged woman was carefully twining cedar down the banister, a young man followed her with red silk roses and tiny white lights. She tapped one of the light boxes on her thigh. *Would the lights be too much?* Her doorbell rang. She marched into the foyer and yanked open the door, expecting another decorator carrying another big box. Instead, it was Scottie.

"Scottie! Gosh! Come in!"

"Brit." He took one step forward then wrapped his arms around her. She felt her body tighten, resisting, then with peculiar reluctance she hugged him back. The light box dangled against his back. He let her go. She stood back, pushed hair off her forehead and smiled.

"Come in, come in. Wow. The wanderer returns." He followed her into the living room. Looking around he asked, "What's all this?"

"Lee's getting married here in three days."

"Terrific! Glad to hear it's not you. Who's the lucky guy?"

"Can you believe it? Old Jimmy's son, Leroy."

"That's wonderful." He'd stopped looking at the room and looked at her. "Britannia. You look fabulous. What have you done to yourself?"

She smiled, "Oh, a few workouts, good food, no booze–"

"Great. Well, I can attest that the sober life is the life for me. I sure hit some weird and wonderful A.A. meetings in South America. Had to brush up on my Spanish. Didn't make a dent in Portuguese, though. In Brazil."

"You look terrific." He was tanned, his turquoise eyes clear, hair sunburned almost white. "But don't let's stand here. The kitchen is almost unhectic. Come have some coffee. Catch me up." Then his familiar lewd grin came over his face, and she felt an answering tingle in her ovaries.

"I'd like to 'catch you up,' Miz Brit, in more ways than one."

He was reaching for her, but she put a hand on his forearm to stay him. And even though his arm felt hard and warm and she felt aroused, she said, "No. Let's not go there, Scottie. Lots has happened since you've been away."

"Since you've been away...sounds like a song. I think the next line is something about 'missing you...' which I've done. Mucho missing you."

That stopped her. *Had she missed him?* She scrolled through her mind looking for moments of missing him. Came up blank. *What a surprise, she hadn't missed him.*

At the kitchen table, coffee and fruit before them, he told her war stories of photographing vicuna in Patagonia, parrots on the Amazon, ocelots in Bolivia. She was able to admire him. But. Though he was good to look at, fun to listen to, he wasn't Grant. The bumbling vulnerability, the clumsy sensitivity of Grant was just not there in Scottie.

She told him she and Grant had "tried again" for five months but–she waved a hand around vaguely–now were apart. Still friends, in fact, better friends than ever, but they just couldn't live together.

Scottie could assume anything he wished to.

She spoke of the death of Mokhtar, the "accidental" burning of Saunders and said that Asia had suddenly been struck by rebellion and independence, so she didn't hear much from her. She also had her first boyfriend.

"That explains it, Brit. She's so wrapped up in her 'first love' experience she doesn't have time for you."

"Perhaps you're right."

"Speaking of boyfriends, how about you? Got any?"

Brit moved her eyes to the floor. *Why did she suddenly want to cry, dammit? Oh Grant!* "Not at the moment–"

His hand came out, took hers. He grinned. A lock of hair fell across his forehead and he looked like some generic hunk on a soap opera. "Well, then, maybe your boyfriend's back, and maybe the two of us can get in trouble?" His eyebrow quirked upward, like a soap actor. *Had he been like this before?* She couldn't remember. She'd probably been too drunk to notice. All she'd seen then was his cock, but she didn't want to see it now. Her pelvis, tingling, argued with her.

She put a hand over his. "Scottie. I've changed. A lot. I'm really different now. I like you, but I want–"

His hand slid out from between hers. "–me for a friend?" A wry look came on his face. He leaned forward, intense. "If you only knew, Brit, how you've kept me going–nights, lonely, around campfires on the pampas, Argentinean beef lowing in the distance, squatting in jungles for hours, sweat trickling down my back, waiting, waiting for some elusive critter to show itself–you were with me every moment. I wanted so badly to be able to show you I could make it. That I could clean up my act."

"Then I'm glad I was such a great help to you. I did send up prayers for you."

"And they were received. With thanks."

"But now, Scottie, I want to get clear again. My time is taken up with commission work–and flying to visit Saunders twice a month."

"Don't you miss it?"

"Miss what?"

"You know. Sex."

She laughed aloud, from the belly. "Of course I miss it! Lots. But it's no longer the main event of my life."

"Brit. I would give anything, just anything, for a welcome home–"

"Fuck?"

"How about one last making love…"

"Why? Why stir up something, and forgive me for saying this, that can't go anywhere?"

"Just because. Just because you once loved me and it's been a sustaining dream all these months."

Why not, said a little voice, *Why not just once? Did sex always have to mean heavy-duty commitment, chains that bound two resentful people together? Why couldn't she and Scottie just come together like two happy animals and have a roll in the hay?*

"You could get hurt."

"Don't presume too much, Senorita. I am a changed man. I practically wore out my A.A. Big Book around those fires. I am now a man of no expectations. I live in the now. If you can't, you can't."

Their eyes met, both gleaming. She jumped up and grabbed his hand.

"Come on. You'll be helping me out, too, I guess."

She led him outside toward the newly completed barn. It was board and bat-ten siding, stained a cypress gray. A copper rooster windvane swung back and forth on the red tin rooftop. She led Scott through the new barn, pausing only to grab some horse blankets then led him up the steps to the loft. She'd chosen steps instead of a ladder, wanting this barn to be as unlike the old one as she could make it.

The air was pungent with alfalfa and alicia-bermuda hay.

"Got a pocketknife?"

He smiled and took out a Swiss Army knife.

"Whack open a couple of bales."

Together they spread the bermuda around and flung the horse blankets down. They stood, hipbone to hipbone. "One time only Stud, as a welcome back, and to christen this barn with happy times."

"One time. I promise."

Their clothes flew off. Brit felt like she was in a movie where the couple come at each other like hungry octopi. They fell laughing onto the hay-bedded blankets. She reached for him but he grabbed her hand.

"Since it's just one time, Brit-Baby, this one is gonna last."

He kissed his way down her belly. She sighed, and felt her body grow ethereal. She felt she was floating, floating–but that was it. That was all. She couldn't go any further. This was old behavior, behavior she'd thought she'd left behind. She touched his shoulder to get him to stop, and he slid his nakedness up hers and kissed her, mouth wet with herself. But she moved her mouth away and opened her eyes. His closed eyes flew open and met hers.

"Baby. Don't tell me you can't do this."

"I can't do this. I'm terrible. But I can't, Scottie." She felt so embarrassed, like a man suddenly impotent. She began to cry. *It should be Grant up here with me! Not this man!*

He sighed. "Okay, okay. Baby, come here," and he nestled her up onto his chest and stroked her hair. "I shouldn't have pushed you."

"No–no, Scottie, I'm sorry. I'm just not ready for sex–with anyone." *Except Grant.*

Scottie kissed her forehead, her damp cheeks. "Look, Baby, it's okay. It's been wonderful holding you. I really love you, you know. And if I'm not the one you're meant to have sex with at this time, so be it."

She raised her head, not caring her face was swollen. "You did learn a lot out there on the Patagonian pampas, didn't you?"

"Argentinean pampas," he grinned. "Yeah."

She stroked his cheek. "Dear, sweet Scott. I think I'll plant some pampas grass in front of this new barn. Then I can think of you and how kind and loving you've become. Maybe this was the right way to christen this new barn."

His look was puzzled.

She touched his cheek. "Never mind. Long story. Now, dear friend, I've got to hustle, I'm throwing a big wedding in just three–no–two and a half days."

Companionably they walked toward his car, Brit asking, "Are you going to be traveling any more?"

His wry look again. "Well, I kinda wasn't for a bit, but now…" he spread his hands, smiled crookedly at her. "I've had nibbles about going to Africa…"

"That's wonderful."

"It is. I may keep sending postcards."

She leaned forward, kissed his cheek. "I'll look forward to them." He hugged her once fiercely, then quickly got into his car. Carefully he made his way down the drive, stopping once for a three ducks and a goose waddling across the road.

S E V E N

The room was scented with bayberry, jasmine, cedar, roses. Pecanwood burned in the grate, candles glowed everywhere and people were settling into folding chairs. The plateau was a parking lot. A string quartet on the mezzanine played Bach. In her bedroom, Brit fussed with Lee's hat. They heard bridesmaids' voices and laughter across the way. The girls were using Asia's and Saunders' rooms to dress. Annie stuck her head in the door, looked at Lee, and began to cry.

"Lee Robinet, you are the most beautiful bride to walk this earth!"

"Isn't she though?" cried Brit, herself sheathed in crimson velvet. Her hair was in a French twist beneath the red velvet hat. She'd carry white roses, Lee, deep wine-colored hybrid teas.

Lee's white velvet dress had a silvery sheen to it, reminding Brit of Mokhtar's coat in moonlight. It was Empire-waisted (although there was still no sign of "Lee-junior") with a tulip neckline that left just the edges of her cheetah-gold shoulders bare. Seed pearls decorated the neckline, the train, the tiny poufed sleeves in a pattern of roses. She wore opera-length satin gloves. Her wide-brimmed hat sat low on her brow emphasizing her large brown eyes, her full lips. When Brit had set it on her head crying this, Lee wailed, "And my big nose!" Brit had swatted at her saying, "Hush! Your distinctive proboscis, darling!"

In response to her future mother-in-law's "beautiful bride" compliment, Lee cried, "I am?" then blushed. Lee's mother, Caitlin, skin like gilten Savannah grasses, eyes like a springbok, also arrived and began to cry. Lee was elated her parents had agreed to get along during her wedding.

"Whoa, girls," said Brit, "save the tears till later."

Caitlin dabbed her eyes, agreeing. "Lee, dear, your groom is about to faint from nervousness. Are you ready?" She had a New England accent, very Harvard.

Lee nodded.

"Okay dear, I'll gather up the bridesmaids and your father." She smiled. "He's as nervous as your groom."

Moments later Brit heard the strings begin the wedding march, felt a tingle all over, winked at Lee and whispered, "Go get him, Girl." She paced from the room.

Downstairs, arrayed before the hearth, the bride and groom stood before Charles Ahern, gracefully silver-haired, ruddy-faced, a Thoroughbred horse breeder and local justice of the peace. When the fluttering crimson-dressed bridesmaids settled and the last cough had died from the guests, Ahern began to speak with a mellow Southern accent. Lee had authored her wedding ceremony, often quoting from her favorite poet, W.B. Yeats. After the traditional opening words Brit heard Ahern say:

> "Between extremities
> Man runs his course;
> A brand, or flaming breath,
> Comes to destroy
> All those antinomies
> Of day and night;
> The body calls it death,
> The heart remorse.
> But if these be right
> What is joy?…"

Between extremities…was the poem inappropriate for this couple, wondered Brit? They seemed so young suddenly, Lee thirty-one, Leroy only two years older. Yet she, at fifty, was "between extremities," and Grant–she steadied herself, *put Grant from your mind, woman.*

Rustling the parchment booklet that contained the wedding service, Ahern continued to read, now at the part Lee had written.

"We live our lives caught, it seems, in the middle, between the paradoxes of beauty and death, fear and bliss, so…'what is joy?'" He paused to smile at the couple before him. The great lace-draped hat on Lee's head trembled, sending Brit delicate ripples of her flowery scent. Leroy kept turning his head, darting nervous smiles at his bride while Lee's head stayed fixed, straight ahead.

"Our joy," read Ahern, "is in the present moment, so 'extremities' are never known, and as Lee and Leroy today vow to stay always in the eternal Now, then every moment shall be joy. Lee, Leroy please take each other's hands." Lee turned and handed her bouquet to Brit.

Charles Ahern looked out over the assembly. "The bridal couple request that all their guests take the hand of whomever is next to them." There was a ruffling sound, and Brit glanced quickly around, caught smiles at this unusual request, saw hands taking hands. Her hands were full, holding two bouquets, and she thought, *I place my hands in my Higher Power's.* Softly the violinist began a passage from Vivaldi's 'Summer' as Ahern intoned: "May the bridal couple…

> …walk among long dappled grass,
> And pluck till time and times are done
> The silver apples of the moon,
> The golden apples of the sun."

Brit couldn't resist the tears that came in her eyes, for that passage of Yeats was what she'd used when she and Grant had married. When she'd told Lee of this, Lee had cried, "Would you mind if I…?"

"No! Of course not. It's so beautiful–"

"But would it make you too sad, to hear it at my wedding–especially since–"

"No. It needs to be shared and passed on, and maybe you and Leroy can walk those dappled grasses, enjoying each day's golden apples, each night's silver apples." Brit laughed ruefully. "It seems Grant and I had our days and nights, our splendor in dappled grass. We plucked some glowing silver apples of the moon, beside the pool, under my skylight. So please. Use it. I'm flattered you want to. In a way, it's 'something borrowed'…"

Lee had pressed her cheek to Brit's. "Thank you, Brit."

Of course, now, it brought back her wedding to Grant, in this house, at this hearth. *It was better he wasn't here…*She also knew Lee had sent an invitation to Asia. *Of course, she wouldn't be here either.*

Lee's neck in front of her looked too slender to bear the dramatic Edwardian hat.

"Do you, Lee Valentine Caitlin, take this man…"

Brit heard the front door open, close. She frowned. What rude person dared arrive late? But she couldn't look. She focused on the gold nape of her best friend. Heard careful footsteps crossing her pine floor.

"Do you Leroy Earnest Charles, take this woman…"

The door, again.

"You may now kiss the bride" –creak, creak, more footsteps tiptoeing over her pine floor. Brit felt enraged. *Why hadn't she instructed the valets to bar entry to anyone until after the ceremony?* The bride and groom were kissing.

The violinist stood, Mendelsohn rolled through the room, Lee turned to her, crushing her in a hug, followed by Leroy. She heard cheers and applause from the guests. Brit laughing, half crying, wondering, still feeling small sizzles of anger….

Quickly she scanned the room, saw no one unusual. Then–a bald head sticking up above the crowd. The tallest man in the room. *Grant.* The anger became a peculiar fear. She took a step back, one hand going to the mantel to steady herself. The rose petals in her bouquet shook as fear dissolved into a dissociated feeling of having no form, no body, she'd again become dizzy, hurtling molecules…

Guests were milling, reaching to hug and to congratulate the bride and groom, and the quartet now played "I'll be Loving You, Always…" Brit watched Grant make his way to her. It seemed to take a very long time. She felt impatient with guests who stopped him, shook his hand, called out hearty, meaningless–stupid–words. Then suddenly, he stood before her. To see him she had to lift her chin higher than usual because of the dipping brim of her hat. She met his eyes, gray and grave. His large, teak-colored hand came toward her–she saw the veins on it, his finely sculpted long fingers, a flash of them working fertile black soil, gently setting a delicate seedling into the soft earth–his hand stopped, hovered near her shoulder. She took her hand from the mantel and clutched her bouquet hard. White petals trembled, some drifted to the floor. He was whispering to her, she could barely hear, then…more clearly, "Britannia. I have missed you…My God, Brit you're a vision…I–I couldn't stay away. Lee's invitation…"

Her throat tight, like laryngitis was starting, she whispered back, "Lee invited you?"

"Yes. You didn't know?"

"No." It was okay then. It was proper. He'd been invited, was here simply as a guest, to pay his respects, not for her, just him being Grant, doing the right thing....

What had he just said to her?

"I'm sorry I was late, but I had to meet someone about–something–impor-tant."

Brit was shaking her head, mildly surprised she had a head to shake. Had she not just been dispersed quantum matter moments before? "I–"

Grant stepped aside. Asia–standing there. Brit had a blurred impression of a burly redheaded man behind her daughter.

Was Anastasia smiling at her?

"Hi, Mom."

Grant was sliding a hand into the pocket of his dinner jacket. Brit felt confu-sion, emotions zapped through her body like indecipherable signals from far-off galaxies...he retrieved an audio cassette. He waved it before her eyes. "Brit. Anastasia called me. We met before coming here. It made us late, I'm sorry we were late, I hope we didn't disturb the ceremony too much..."

Get to the point, Grant, she wanted to yell.

"She had this gift for me...for Saunders..."

She blinked. "But what is it?"

Grant took a deep breath. "Anastasia has done something–so incredible." His hand holding the tape shook. Brit heard the bustle of guests, excited conversa-tion, a man's deep laughter, a woman nearby sobbing. Wil yipped as though someone were teasing him with hors d'oeuvres. Mozart's *Eine Kleine Nachtmusik* wafted from the mezzanine.

What the hell is it?

Suddenly she smelled jasmine, a fat candle on the mantel had flared.

Asia has forgiven Saunders, she thought.

She knew it. Then felt an implosion of emotions that cascaded down to a tiny point and glowed warm and sweet within the chalice of her pelvis.

"Asia. Anastasia," she whispered.

As if plucking the words from her mind Grant blurted: "Asia has forgiven Saunders."

Then he turned, "Asia, once again–I can't thank–"

Asia's eyes never left her mother's face. Brit watched blooded lips draw back, cheeks bunch, crinkles appear around eyes dark and rich as Legacy's, a dazzle of white teeth–Brit knew her daughter was smiling at her. The sweet point within her flared, then a melting bliss, a rapture surged through her body. She felt her mouth twitch, felt her lips part, knew involuntarily she was answering Asia's smile. Her eyes went to Grant. She saw his quirked, unsteady smile, *was Grant crying?* Asia's arms extending to her, incredulous, she watched her beautiful daughter throw back her head, heard the new Asia's mellifluous laugh. Saw Asia's elbow playfully bump Grant as she said, "Save it, Granite Man! I need to hug my mother."

She felt her daughter's arms come hard around her, her lips brushed her ear, her warm breath tingling, then a whisper.

"Mother, when you said how I woke up, how I hugged him when he had his nightmares, those awful nightmares...I couldn't get that out of my mind, Mother, I couldn't stop my feelings for that damaged little boy...he did not know what he was doing...he did not know...thank you for saying that to me."

Brit held on and murmured, "Asia..."

Then she felt a familiar hand touch hers behind Asia's back. Still holding Asia she turned her hand, opened it, and felt Grant's fingers close around hers. She gave his hand a tug, felt Grant's arms encircle them both, like a great warm bear, and heard Grant saying, "I want to love you both."

Brit felt a squirming, Asia disentangling from them. Alarmed she looked at her. Asia stood back, the large redheaded man now close behind her, one of his large arms going around Asia's waist. *Had to be the boyfriend.* Brit and Grant opened up, Grant keeping an arm around Brit's shoulders. Then Asia nodded.

"Just one thing, Mom, please. Don't think this means I'm able–or willing–to be around him...yet."

Brit reached out and took Asia's hand. "Honey, you don't ever have to see him, I promise. But you've done something...miraculous. Thank you."

Then she felt Grant's embrace pulling her into him. He reached under the big hat and tipped up her chin. As his mouth came down to hers he said, "I don't know how we'll work it, but Britannia, I want to be beside you."